**Outstanding praise for Michael Hiebert
and *Dream with Little Angels***

"Hiebert has an authentic Southern voice and his
protagonist is as engaging as Harper Lee's Scout.
A masterful coming-of-age gem."
—Deborah Crombie

"Gorgeous prose and some thoughtful
characterizations, with attention given to theme and
setting . . . Michael Hiebert's debut delivers . . . a
breathless, will-they-get-there-in-time affair, with a
heartbreaking resolution. Hiebert's skill at character
and storytelling should take him a long way."
—*Mystery Scene*

"A trip to the dark side of a town much like
Mayberry, filled with that elusive quality of
childhood and the aura of safety that often settles,
unjustifiably, over rural small towns in the South."
—Carolyn Haines

Books by Michael Hiebert

DREAM WITH LITTLE ANGELS

CLOSE TO THE BROKEN HEARTED

A THORN AMONG THE LILIES

STICKS AND STONES

Published by Kensington Publishing Corporation

DREAM
With
LITTLE ANGELS

MICHAEL HIEBERT

PINNACLE BOOKS
Kensington Publishing Corp.
www.kensingtonbooks.com

PINNACLE BOOKS are published by

Kensington Publishing Corp.
119 West 40th Street
New York, NY 10018

All Kensington titles, imprints, and distributed lines are available at special quantity discounts for bulk purchases for sales promotions, premiums, fund-raising, educational, or institutional use. Special book excerpts or customized printings can also be created to fit specific needs. For details, write or phone the office of the Kensington sales manager: Kensington Publishing Corp., 119 West 40th Street, New York, NY 10018, attn: Sales Department; phone 1-800-221-2647.

This book is a work of fiction. Names, characters, businesses, organizations, places, events, and incidents either are the product of the author's imagination or are used fictitiously. Any resemblance to actual persons, living or dead, events, or locales is entirely coincidental.

ISBN-13: 978-0-7860-3940-1
ISBN-10: 0-7860-3940-X

First mass market paperback printing: May 2016

10 9 8 7 6 5 4 3 2

Printed in the United States of America

First electronic edition: May 2016

ISBN-13: 978-0-7860-3972-2
ISBN-10: 0-7860-3972-8

ACKNOWLEDGMENTS

I'd like to thank John Pitts for his help in building the city of Alvin. I appreciate it so much that I even gave it his middle name. Also, Paul Tseng and kc dyer for being constant support systems. And I couldn't have done it without Julianna Hinckley, who read all these pages at least twice, and offered myriad suggestions—all of which I implemented and all of which made this whole thing even better.

I have to mention my children: Valentine, Sagan, and Legend, who, I suspect like the kids of most authors, gave up a portion of their father to writing. The act of putting pen to paper (or, in my case, fingers to keys) is a severe balancing act with normal, everyday life that I don't know I'll ever master completely.

Then there's my girlfriend, Shannon, whose constant love and support keep me stable and at the computer cranking out words. I think she was the last one to do a read-through of the final manuscript. I couldn't have done it without you, babe.

And finally, I'd like to thank my mentors, Dean Wesley Smith and Kristine Kathryn Rusch, who taught me more about writing over the years than anyone else ever could have.

Michael Hiebert
July 2013
British Columbia, Canada

PROLOGUE

Alvin, Alabama—1975

The grass is tall, painted gold by the setting autumn sun. Soft wind blows through the tips as it slopes up a small hill. Near the top of the hill, the blades shorten, finally breaking to dirt upon which stands a willow. Its roots, twisted with Spanish moss, split and dig into the loam like fingers. The splintery muscles of one gnarled arm bulge high above the ground, hiding the small body, naked and pink, on the other side. Fetal positioned, her back touches the knotted trunk. Her eyes are closed. Above her, the small leaves shake together as their thin branches shiver in the cold breeze. The red and silver sky gently touches her face. Her breath is gone. The backs of her arms, the tops of her feet, are blue. She's too small for this hill, too small for this tree.

She's too small to be left alone under all this sky.

CHAPTER 1

Twelve Years Later

When she was nearly fifteen, my sister Carry got her first boyfriend. At least that was my mother's theory when I asked why Carry suddenly seemed to live in a world I no longer existed in. She used to goof around with me and Dewey after school. Then, in the summer, she stopped paying much attention to us. After school started, she just ignored us altogether.

"I reckon she's shifted her interests," my mother said, washing a plate at the kitchen sink. "She's round 'bout that age now."

"Age for what?" I asked.

"For boys." She sighed. "Now we're in for it."

"In for what?"

"The hard part. My mama said my hard part started when I was thirteen, so I guess we should consider ourselves lucky."

I didn't rightly know what she was talking about, but it sounded like something bad. "How long does the hard part last?" I asked.

"With me it lasted 'til I was seventeen. Then I got pregnant with Caroline." She let out a nervous laugh. The Lord Jesus dangling from the silver chain around her neck swayed as she laughed. My mother always wore that chain. It had been a gift from my grandpa. "Let's just hope hers ends differently and not worry about what stretch of time it takes up, okay?"

I agreed I would, even though I still didn't rightly know what it was she was talking about. But I had other, more important things to worry about anyhow. A month ago, the Wiseners sold their house across the road because Mr. Wisener got work in Pascagoula, Mississippi. The house was purchased by a Mr. Wyatt Edward Farrow from Sipsey, who moved in shortly thereafter. My mother took me and Carry over two days later with a basket full of fresh-baked biscuits, Golden Delicious apples, and a jar of her homemade blueberry jam, and introduced us. The jam even had a pink ribbon tied around its lid. She made me carry the basket.

The door was answered by a tall, thin man, with dark brown hair trimmed short and flat. His most distinguishing feature was his square jaw that, from the look of it, hadn't been shaved in at least a few days. The rest of his facial features, like his forehead and eyes, were more or less pointed.

"I'm Leah Teal," my mother said, "your neighbor from across the way. An' this here's Caroline, and this is my little Abraham."

"Here," I said, holding up the basket.

"I'm Wyatt Edward Farrow," he said after a hesitation. I got the feeling he wasn't used to strangers showing up on his doorstep with baskets of biscuits, and he didn't know how to properly respond to our welcoming. When he spoke, his voice was quiet and pensive.

I don't think he trusted us.

"Pleased to meet ya," he said, but by the way he said it, I had a hunch he didn't like meeting people much. There wasn't a trace of a smile on his thin lips. I was relieved when he finally took the basket from me, though. It was getting heavy with all them apples in it.

An uncomfortable silence followed that my mother broke by asking what it was Mr. Farrow did for work.

Something flashed in his gray eyes, and I got the distinct feeling Mr. Wyatt Edward Farrow didn't like being asked questions just as much as he didn't like strangers on his doorstep. "I'm a carpenter," he said. "Work out of my home. Hope the noise don't bother ya none."

"Hasn't yet," my mother said with a warm smile.

Mr. Farrow didn't smile back. Something about him didn't sit right with me. It was like he was being sneaky or something. "Haven't been doin' nothin' yet," he said. "Still settin' up my tools in the garage."

"Well, I'm sure it will be fine," my mother said.

"Sometimes I work in the evenings," Mr. Farrow said. He narrowed his eyes and looked from me to Carry as though daring us to tell him we took exception to evening work.

"I usually do, too," my mother said, "so that should work out fine." That my mother just told this suspicious-looking stranger that me and my sister spent most nights alone in our house didn't settle so good with me at all. I was glad when she followed by telling him what she did for work. "I'm a police officer. My schedule's a bit irregular too, at times." I saw a slight twitch in one of his eyes when she relayed this information, though he hid his reaction well.

Three days later, Mr. Wyatt Edward Farrow finished setting up his tools. The sun had just dropped behind my house and me and Dewey were in the front yard trying to see who could balance a rock on the end of a branch the longest. It was an almost hypnotic exercise, especially with the quiet singing of the cicadas drifting by.

That was until a loud roar suddenly ripped through the evening.

Dewey and I both jumped, our rocks tumbling to the ground. My heart raced against my chest. Trembling, we both stared across the road. Behind Mr. Farrow's garage door, something had sprung to life.

"Sounds like a mountain lion," Dewey said, his eyes wide. Dewey was my best friend for as long as I could remember. He lived eight houses down Cottonwood Lane, on the same side of it as me, and we were almost exactly the same age. His birthday came two days before mine.

My heart was slowing back down to normal again. "Must be a saw or somethin'," I said. I told him about Mr. Farrow being a carpenter. "Least that's what he claimed. At the time, I didn't believe him."

"Why not?"

I shrugged. "He just seemed to me like he was lyin' about it."

"Why would he lie about somethin' like that?"

"I don't know. I just didn't trust him."

"Sure is loud."

With a whir, the sound stopped. Me and Dewey stood there in the dim purple light of early evening, watching the garage door expectantly. From underneath it shone a narrow strip of white light. Sure enough, a few minutes later something else started up and we both jumped again. This thing was higher pitched than the other and even louder.

"Sounds like a hawk," Dewey said.

"Lot louder than a hawk," I said.

That night, me and Dewey heard ten different animals screaming from inside that garage. For the week following, we spent most of our evenings lying in my front lawn, our chins propped up on our hands, staring across the road, listening to Mr. Farrow work and speculating on what it was he could possibly be building. Far as we could tell, he never left that garage. The windows in the rest of the house were always dark.

"Part I can't figure out," Dewey said, "is when does he go to the bathroom? We should at least see lights come on *sometime* for that, shouldn't we?"

"Maybe he just goes in the dark."

"Maybe."

A few days after that, Dewey made the observation about the roadkill.

We were coming home from school when he said it. Dewey and I had walked to school together for as long as I could remember, but that would all end after this year. Being so small, Alvin had only an elementary school. For middle school and high school, you had to go down to Satsuma. For four years, Carry spent over two hours total on the bus going to and from school and I listened to her complain about it every day. Well, until this year. Now that she was the right age for boys, she didn't talk much at all to me anymore. I wasn't looking forward to going to middle school. I enjoyed my and Dewey's walks.

Autumn was doing its best to settle in. We walked along Hunter Road, beneath the tall oak trees, sunlight filtering down on us through their almost orange and yellow leaves. Neither of us had said much since leaving school. I was hitting the ground in front of me with a piece of hickory I found a couple blocks back, and Dewey had his head down and his hands stuffed into the pockets of his jeans. By the way he walked, he seemed to me like he was thinking hard about something, and I didn't want to interrupt.

Finally he looked up and said, "Have you noticed anything different lately?"

I thwacked the trunk of an oak with my hickory. "Different like what?" I asked.

He hesitated like he was thinking whether or not to tell me. "I just . . . a week ago I started noticing there weren't no dead animals on the road anymore."

I laughed, but he was serious.

"So I have been payin' attention to it ever since. And for a week now, I ain't seen a single piece of roadkill anywhere."

"I guess the raccoons are getting smarter," I said and laughed again. I reckoned this was a strange thing to have spent so much time over.

Dewey stopped walking, so I did, too. "Abe, you don't think it's strange? For a whole week I ain't seen a single dead squirrel, chipmunk, snake, possum, nothin'. Hell, not even a skunk. Even when old Newt Parker was still alive, you still saw at least a couple skunks most weeks."

"Newt Parker never really ate roadkill," I told him. "That was all just third grade stories going around."

"He did so. Ernest Robinson said he saw so himself. Said he was riding his bike past the Parker place one afternoon and old man Parker was sitting right there on a chair out in the front lawn munching on road-killed raccoon."

"Ernest Robinson is full of crap. How did he know it was 'coon?"

"Said it looked like one," Dewey said. "What else looks like raccoon but raccoon?"

He had a point there, but I still wasn't convinced. "How did he know it was road killed?"

Dewey had problems answering that one. Eventually we started walking again and I resumed hitting the ground with my hickory stick. "I still think it's strange that I haven't seen any for a week," he said.

"You want me to go find a rabbit and throw it in front of a car for you?" I threw the hickory into the woods as we turned down our street.

"I just think it's weird, is all," he said, and that was the end of it.

Except after Dewey had brought it to my attention, I couldn't help but start looking for roadkill everywhere I went. Soon I understood Dewey's concern. After only three days of seeing none, a feeling of uneasiness began creeping into my stomach. By the time a whole 'nother week went by, we knew we had stumbled onto evidence of foul play of some sort. Only neither of us could come up with an idea of what sort of foul play could possibly result in cleaning up dead animals from every street in Alvin.

It was a mystery that wove through my brain nearly

every minute I was awake. While I ate breakfast, while I sat through school, always. Even while Dewey and I laid in the grass staring at the strip of light beneath Mr. Farrow's garage door on the side of his darkened house, and pretended to ponder what he might possibly be constructing, we were actually trying to puzzle out the roadkill phenomena. When I finally went to bed, at least an hour was spent staring up at my ceiling while my mind made one last attempt at solving the riddle before shutting down for the day. Neither me nor Dewey could come up with any sort of explanation for what we were witnessing or, I suppose, *weren't* witnessing would be more precise. Even if an entire *family* of Newt Parkers moved into Alvin, they couldn't possibly eat up all the roadkill in the whole town. Nothing about it made any sense.

Then, four days later, Mary Ann Dailey disappeared.

CHAPTER 2

The Daileys lived on the other side of town. Mr. and Mrs. Dailey had two daughters, Ella Jane and Mary Ann. Even though Ella Jane went to my school, I didn't really know her well on account of she was a year below me. But Carry knew Mary Ann, who was a grade ahead of her. They rode on the same bus to school every day.

Carry had been home a couple hours when Dewey's mother called him for dinner from up the street. A rumble in my stomach told me it was time for me to be doing the same, so I went inside to find Carry sitting on the sofa talking on the phone. I figured that's what she'd been doing since she came in. Most of her time at home these days was spent talking on the phone. She didn't speak much to anyone else, though. Especially not to me.

I didn't bother asking her about dinner. It became apparent early on in the summer that, unless I wanted to starve to death, I better learn how to fix my own food. Luckily it wasn't hard. My mother always left us something in the fridge ready to be heated up. Today it was leftover green bean casserole. I was just spooning a portion out on a plate when my mother came in the door. Right away, I knew something was wrong. She wasn't supposed to be home until eight.

She marched straight into the living room and told Carry to get off the phone. "I've been trying to call for an hour and a half!" she said.

Sitting up from where she had been strewn across the sofa, Carry told the person on the other end of the line that she had to go. "My mother is flippin' out 'bout somethin'."

I half expected my mother to blow up from the look my sister gave her. "What's so important?" she asked after hanging up.

"You get that tone out of your voice right now, Caroline Josephine!" my mother said.

Carry's gaze fell to the carpet. "Sorry," she said.

My mother's voice went quiet. "Mary Ann Dailey's gone missin'," she said.

Carry looked up, surprised. "She was just on the bus with me twenty minutes ago. I saw her get off at her spot." I almost laughed out loud when she said *twenty minutes*.

"It was closer to two hours ago," my mother said, "but, yes, I know. I've already spoken to a lot of your friends. She got off the bus, but never showed up at her home. Mrs. Dailey called the station a half hour later."

Carry flopped back down across the sofa, her blond hair bunching up against the worn armrest. "She's probably downtown or something, hangin' out with friends. It's Friday night. Even here in this stupid little town, we do have lives." That tone was still in her voice. Even *I* could hear it, and sometimes I wasn't so good with that sort of thing.

"Well, that's a possibility," my mother said. "I have Chris driving around looking for her."

Christopher Jackson was the other officer who worked with my mother at the Alvin Police Station. He started a few years back, and I still remembered how much of an uproar some folks made about it on account of him being black. There were still folks occasionally outright refusing to acknowledge his authority, and whenever that happened, Police Chief Montgomery went and paid them a little visit. After that, they generally didn't make such a fuss anymore. I like Officer Jackson. He was always very nice to me and Carry whenever he saw us.

The telephone rang and on reflex Carry sat up, her hand jerking toward it. My mother beat her to it. "I'll get it." Carry sneered at her as she answered. When my mother either didn't notice the sneer or just chose to ignore it, Carry dropped the sneer onto me. I turned away, looking up and listening to my mother's side of the phone conversation.

"Hello? Yes, Mrs. Dailey. No, not yet. We're doin' our best. I've got an officer checkin' around there right now. No, ma'am." There were lots of pauses between my mother's responses, but this one was the longest. Finally, she said, "Mrs. Dailey? Listen, I'd appreciate it if from now on you call through the station instead of my home. No, ma'am, I understand that, but there's always one of us there who can answer any of your inquiries. Well, ma'am, I appreciate that and it's nice of you to say so, but, no, that ain't the way it works. I promise to call as soon as we know anythin'. In the meantime, if you think of anyplace else she may have gone, let us know. Just try to stay calm. There's no need to worry yet. You know how girls her age are. Yes, ma'am, you certainly did tell me that already. Thank you, ma'am."

She hung up and let out an exhausted sigh. I looked up at her expectantly, realizing I was still holding the plate of cold casserole.

"Why is she calling you at home?" I asked.

She sighed. "Cuz she don't want to talk to Chris. Says only another parent could possibly understand what she's goin' through."

"But it's really cuz Officer Jackson's black, ain't it?"

My mother hesitated. "I don't know, honey. Maybe. Maybe not. She's pretty stricken with grief right now. I would be too if it were you or Caroline that went missin'." She looked to Carry. "Caroline, are you absolutely certain there ain't nowhere else you can think of where she might be? Someplace maybe her other friends wouldn't want to have told me about?" This caught my attention. Seemed like a weird thing to be asking my sister. "Like, does Mary Ann have a boyfriend, maybe?"

Carry shifted uncomfortably on the sofa cushion, looking to me like she wanted to bolt from the room. "I hardly know her, Mom," she said.

"But you ride the bus with her every day. You must hear things. You must see her at school." Squatting down, my mother had reached out and gently pushed Carry's bangs off her face. "This is important, honey.

It's not like you're tattlin' on your friends when it's somethin' like this."

A tinge of anger flashed in Carry's blue eyes, as though my mother had just offended her. I didn't quite understand why. "I know it's important," she said. "You think I'm lyin'? I don't *know* if she has a boyfriend."

"Are you absolutely *certain*?" I wondered why my mother thought my sister might be confused on such a point.

Carry got real angry now. "Yes! I'm absolutely certain! To the best of my knowledge, Mary Ann Dailey does *not* have a boyfriend! My Lord, is this how you treat all your witnesses? Or is it just *me* you don't believe?" Jumping up from the sofa, she stomped out of the room. I heard the slam of her bedroom door following shortly thereafter.

My mother looked down at me in frustration.

"This part of the hard part you tol' me 'bout?" I asked.

She nodded, frowning.

"Hope it don't last long," I said.

"Oh, we got a while to go yet." My mother's attention drifted to the living room window that looked out over the front lawn. Thick, yellow drapes hung down on either side of it. She didn't seem to be looking at anything in particular, and I got the feeling her thoughts were someplace else entirely.

My eyes were drawn to Mr. Farrow's garage door squatting across the road with its white-toothed sneer. The view was partially obscured by the cedar shrub growing between our front steps and the living room window. The shrub was in much need of trimming, just as the lawn was starting to be in serious want of mowing. My mother used to pay Luther Willard King ten dollars to ride his bike over and do all the yard work every couple weeks, but it had been a while since he came around. My mother told me Luther Willard's father had gotten very sick near the end of school last year, and Luther Willard didn't have time to come out and help her anymore. His own mother needed his help now.

Even though he wasn't working, my mother still got me to ride my bike all the way across town every two weeks to give him the ten dollars anyway. It was a long way to his house. The Kings lived down Oakdale Road, in a section of town known as Cloverdale where most of the other black people in Alvin lived.

"How come he still gets paid for doin' nothin'?" I asked the first time she sent me.

"He ain't doin' nothin'," my mother said. "He's lookin' after that family. He's got three younger sisters, a mama, and a really sick papa to tend to."

"How do they all live off ten dollars every two weeks?" The youngest two were twins and only three years old, but I thought even three-year-olds must eat more than ten dollars' worth of food every two weeks.

"They get other money, too. But not a lot. Our ten dollars means a lot more to them than it does to us."

That hadn't made much sense then. To me, ten dollars was ten dollars, no matter how you looked at it, or who was doing the looking. Then, the first time I brought it over, I figured out what she meant. The farther you went down Oakdale, the deeper you went into Cloverdale and the more rundown the homes became.

The ride to Luther Willard's took me all the way past Blackberry Creek, almost to the turnoff leading to Cornflower Lake; one of the prettiest yet poorest areas in all of Alvin.

The Kings lived in an old green shotgun house that looked just about ready to fall in on itself. Some of the wooden slats were missing from the front, and the roof drooped to one side. I left my bike lying on the edge of the road and stepped across the yard where the twins sat, their legs almost as black as their shadows being cast by the early-afternoon sun. They played there in the dirt; there was no real lawn to speak of. Neither of the girls had shirts or shoes on, and their shorts were dusty and torn. They looked up at me with interest as I passed, their eyes and teeth bright white against their smudged brown faces, a swarm of midges buzzing over their heads. I noticed a thick caking of dried mud beneath their fingernails and toenails.

I climbed the broken steps to the porch and opened the screen, nearly pulling it off its hinges. Most of the screen was busted. I knocked on the wooden door behind it and glanced back at the two girls. They no longer paid any mind to me, they were back to playing in the dirt. Leaning against the side of the house, I recognized Luther Willard's bike. Most of the white paint had flecked off since I last saw it, and it looked more rusted than I remembered it.

The other King daughter answered the door. She wasn't nearly as dirty as the two in the yard, and her clothes looked recently scrubbed, although awfully worn out for a girl who couldn't have been no older than six, and probably outgrew things at least once a year. I reckoned they were hand-me-downs from someone who probably over-wore them in the first place.

"Luther round?" I asked.

She stood quietly considering me, and for a minute I thought she wasn't going to answer. Eventually, though, she nodded and trod off inside. From one of the rooms, someone suddenly began coughing something fierce, with wheezy breaths drawn in between sounding so thin, I expected them to end the life of whoever they were coming from at any moment.

The coughing continued as Luther Willard, wearing a gray T-shirt and worn jeans, appeared in the doorway, looking at me, puzzled. He had short, curly black hair and scratched at the back of his neck as I held out the ten dollars to him. "This is from my mama," I said.

I thought he was going to cry, so much disappointment fell over his face. "Tell her I'm sorry, but I can't do her work this week," he said. "I probably won't be able to for quite some time."

"She knows," I said, still holding out the bill. "She says she's gonna pay you anyway, on account of she doesn't want to lose your services once you're ready to come back." My mother had told me to say this, explaining most folks don't like accepting anything that even slightly smells of charity. But they have no trouble taking the money so long as you can give them any reason to feel it's okay.

This one felt a bit farfetched even to me, and as Luther Willard stood there thinking it over, the summer sun beamed down hot on my neck and back. His father coughed and wheezed up a hurricane in the back room, and I thought for sure Luther Willard was just going to send me back with the money, making my entire ride out here a complete waste of time. A trickle of sweat ran from under my unkempt hair, winding its way down the side of my face until I wiped it off the edge of my chin with my arm.

Finally, Luther Willard took the bill from my hand and a great big grin spread across his thick lips. "You tell your mama I'll be round as soon as I can and that I'll make sure she's got the prettiest little yard in all of Alvin," he said.

I said I would do just that, but really I was just happy he took the money.

The twins once again watched me as I walked back to my bike, only this time I noticed different things about 'em. Somewhere in those big brown eyes was a mixture of sadness and hope that made me understand what my mother had meant. Ten dollars was not the same value no matter who was doing the looking at it, and these people saw a lot more in it than we did.

Since then, Luther Willard had accepted my ten-dollar delivery every second Saturday without question, always reminding me to tell my mother how beautiful her yard was gonna be when he finally came back to work for her. And each time he told me this, it was over top of the sounds of death wheezing out of a room somewhere behind him that grew worse each and every trip. I couldn't imagine living with those sounds every day.

Now I just lived with the silence of Carry completely ignoring me.

I looked back at my mother, still standing there, staring off into space. I guessed she was puzzling about where it was Mary Ann Dailey might have run off to. Or maybe she was weighing whether or not to believe Carry about Mary Ann not having a boyfriend. That thought brought a weird feeling, because until this summer, my sister's virtue was never called into question.

Then again, until this summer, Carry had been a completely different Carry. She had been a sister I could rely on. Now I wasn't so sure that I could. When I was sick from school last year for them five days, it was Carry who would come home and make me chicken soup.

"Chicken soup for my little chicken nugget," she had said as she brought it into my room. She was always saying stupid things like that to make me laugh. Even when I was sick, Carry had a way of making me laugh.

I didn't know if this new Carry would even care if I was sick or not. Since she now so readily ignored me on a regular basis, I had my serious doubts she'd be making me any chicken soup or calling me her "chicken nugget."

So much had changed in Carry, it made me wonder about her school grades. She was normally really good at pretty near all her subjects, getting almost all As or Bs. I wondered if that had changed. Then I wondered if my mother had considered this at all. Maybe I should bring it up with her when I had the chance.

Then I realized this was one of those things where my mother would most likely tell me to mind my business. She was always telling me to mind my business. More and more, it seemed, as I got older. Maybe this was because the older I got, the more I cared about other people's business. There had to be *some* reason.

Whatever it was, I just knew all of this came from the same thing: Carry's sudden interest in boys. I hated that thing. I wished Carry had never noticed boys. They were obviously no good for nothing.

Then my thoughts went back to Mary Ann Dailey, and a thought struck me. "Hey, Mom?" I asked.

It pulled her back from wherever her thoughts had taken her and she looked down, eyebrows raised.

"Reckon maybe this is like when Isaac Crosby ran off and got lost in the woods behind Shearer's cotton farm couple years ago?"

"I don't know yet, honey."

Isaac Crosby had run away from home, only he didn't run very far, just into the woods, where he managed to get himself completely lost. It happened in the spring, and Isaac was found at the breaking light of dawn the next day by one of the Mexican workers. The Mexican had gone into the woods to do his business when he found Isaac huddled beneath a cluster of maples, shivering, scared, and hungry.

The Mexicans came up every season to find work. Because of the acres of farmland wrapping the outskirts of Alvin, there always was lots of work available. They usually stayed on through the summer, going back home around October. Harvesting season was pretty near over now, so there weren't too many of them left. The ones that *were* still here would be leaving very soon.

This brought another possibility to my mind. "What

if maybe one of them Mexicans snatched Mary Ann Dailey on his way out?"

Concern came to my mother's face, and I knew she disapproved of my idea, but I couldn't figure out how come. "Why would you say something like that?" she asked.

"Well, because they're always comin' and goin', so it'd be easy for them to just grab her and go. And some of 'em *are* just leavin' now, right? So I was figurin' this might make a lot of sense. Besides, Dewey told me in Mexico they use kids as slaves, makin' 'em do all the chores and whippin' 'em if they refuse. Sometimes even just whippin' 'em for fun."

She crouched down, straightened my dirty blond hair, and set her hands upon my shoulders. I could tell she was collecting her thoughts on the matter.

"Abe, what you just said was a very racist remark. I don't want you sayin' things like that. Not about black people, not about Mexicans, not about anyone."

"How is it racist, if it's true?"

"Because it's not true."

"Dewey said—"

"Don't pay attention to everything Dewey says. Think about things for yourself and ask yourself if it makes sense before takin' it as the Gospel truth. If you still can't decide on your own, come and ask me 'bout it. But don't judge people by their skin or where they come from or how much money they have. Judge them by who they are individually and how they act. Okay?"

I thought about this. It made sense. Mr. Farrow wasn't black or Mexican and he was the only person in the town

I *knew* was up to no good; I just had yet to figure out what it was he was up to. "Okay," I said. Then I decided to take her up on her offer. "Can I ask you somethin' I'm not sure 'bout, then?"

"Of course."

"Ernest Robinson said before old Newt Parker died, he rode his bike past the Parker place and saw him eating road-killed raccoon. Did Newt Parker really eat roadkill, do you think?" I knew I was on tricky ground here because Newt Parker was black, but I was pretty sure it was okay because I was judging him individually, and not on his color. Only his diet.

She laughed. "Quite honestly, Abe, I don't know. But I suspect on this particular point, the rumors may actually be true."

"I see." I nodded. Then I went back to Isaac. "Do you reckon Mary Ann Dailey maybe just ran away from home?"

"Again, I'm not sure yet," she said. "Mrs. Dailey is quite adamant on the point that her daughter is a very happy, well-adjusted girl, who, as she would have me know, comes from a perfect balanced family environment full of positive support. The woman did everything but tell me she deserved the Mother of the Year award today."

I didn't understand a lot of them words, but it sounded like my mother was making fun of Mrs. Dailey. "You reckon she's lyin'?" I asked.

With a soft smile, she shook her head. "I reckon she's very upset and wants her daughter back, is all."

"Well, if Mary Ann ran off like Isaac Crosby, she's

probably just lost," I said. "And I reckon after what he went through, Isaac was taught a pretty good lesson. Reckon he never thought of runnin' off again."

"No," my mother said, "I reckon you're right on that." She looked down at my plate of cold casserole. "What you say you let me take that away and make you somethin' real to eat 'fore I head back out?"

My stomach rumbled again. I told her I thought that was a great idea.

CHAPTER 3

The next morning, when Mary Ann Dailey still hadn't turned up, Mr. Robert Lee Garner organized an all-out search for her. Mr. Garner owned the Holly Berry Cattle Ranch, and had, by far, more head of cattle than anyone in Alvin. For at least five miles, his farm stretched east from Tucker Mountain Road, following along the curve of the Anikawa River. On Mr. and Mrs. Dailey's behalf, he spent the last night's evening making phone calls, requesting that folks help out in searching for their daughter. Everyone was to meet in front of the library on Main Street at eight o'clock sharp, first thing in the morning.

Just as she was fixing to head out, my mother asked me and Carry if we wanted to come along and join in the hunt. Carry, who had been sound asleep before my mother woke her, declined. "I can't believe you'd even imagine in your wildest dreams that I'd get out of bed on a Saturday before eleven. Especially not to go traipsing through some ol' mud and creek beds." The conversation stayed barely this side of civil before my mother finally just let Carry turn over and go back to sleep.

I thought it all sounded like an adventure and so I was more than eager to come along. On my mother's advice, I pulled on my galoshes and put on my rain jacket. The day outside looked as though it had the ability to turn sour on the drop of a pin.

Just before we left, I remembered Dewey. "Can we bring him along with us?"

"If he wants to come, sure."

" 'Course he wants to come." I quickly phoned over and told him to get ready, mentioning the galoshes. We picked him up in the car on the way. He was waiting outside his house, wearing a puffy olive drab raincoat, looking ridiculous in black rubber boots at least four sizes too big for him.

"What are those?" I asked, laughing.

"I ain't got none myself," he said. "So I took my pa's. Don't worry. I stuffed socks in the toes."

"You look like a duck," I said.

Shaking her head, my mother told him to climb into the back of the car.

As soon as we turned down Main Street, Dewey and I both gaped, saying, "Wow!" at the same time. Somehow, Mr. Robert Lee Garner managed to convince pretty much all of Alvin to come out and help look for Mary Ann Dailey. I couldn't remember seeing this many people in any one place before anytime in my whole entire life. They spilled all down the street, gathering around the steps of the library. There were so many people, we had to park a half mile away in front of Igloo's Ice Cream Parlor.

"There must be a thousand folks here," I said.

"Well," my mother said, "I don't think there's near a thousand. Maybe a hundred. I don't think there's even two thousand people living in all of Alvin, Abe."

"Still a lot," Dewey said.

When Isaac Crosby ran off, I couldn't remember anybody coming together to try to find him. But then, everyone knew he'd run off on his own volition. They reported him missing to my mother, but Mrs. Crosby even said then, "I wouldn't put too much effort into findin' him. He wasn't even smart enough to pack a lunch. That boy'll be back on this doorstep in one day. Two at the latest. I don't wanna waste any taxpayer's money."

I reckon with Isaac it was more a case of just seeing how long it took before he figured out what a stupid mistake he made. I remember hearing that the first thing Mr. Crosby said when he returned was, "Guess that shows *you* now, don't it?"

Mary Ann Dailey was a different thing entirely. I was starting to realize folks were taking her disappearance very seriously. Seeing all these people standing around brought an uneasy feeling to my stomach. "How come some of 'em got rifles?" I asked as we walked through the crowd.

"They're gonna be searchin' in the woods," my mother said. "Never know what you might find in the woods."

"You mean like black bears and cougars an' all?" Dewey asked.

She nodded. "You never know what you're gonna find. Just always better to be prepared."

The day was overcast and gray, with a chill breeze on the air. One of those days where you could almost taste the rain wanting to shower down from some of the black, heavy clouds hanging overhead. Mr. Robert Lee Garner climbed the concrete steps in front of the library, carrying an apple crate. His brown leather jacket almost blended into the red brick building behind him in the dull light. Even the American flag, snapping violently in the wind above his head, seemed colorless this morning. He set the apple crate at his feet.

Mr. Garner was sixty-eight years old and was one of them men who looked like he fought for each and every one of them years, barely winning every time he did. He was a stocky man with a large square head and barely any neck. He always reminded me of one of them army sergeants you see in the movies, especially on account of Mr. Garner liking cigars so much. Only, Mr. Garner had never been in the military. The military had a definite effect on his life, though. His father was a U.S. Air Force pilot during World War II and died during the bombing of Dresden. Then he lost his son somewhere in Beirut. Killed by a suicide bomber. Despite all that bad luck with the army, Mr. Garner was probably the single most patriotic person I ever met, with nothing but pride for our country's military forces, and I never understood why—after how the military killed his papa and his son. My mother tried to explain it one day, saying that pride sometimes *is* the only way you can keep going after something like that, but it still didn't make much sense to me.

I gave up trying to understand it.

"First o' all," Mr. Garner said. He spoke with a deep, powerful voice that once again made him seem like an army commander. As soon as he started talking, everyone in the crowd went quiet. "I wanna thank y'all for showin' up so early on such a cold and miserable morning. It means a lot to me, and I know it means a lot to the Daileys. This is a terribly frightening thing for anyone to go through, as I'm sure you can all imagine. It's especially terrible when it happens to folks as nice as the Daileys. When my Martha was sick all them months before the cancer finally took her, they were there for me, and now I hope that all'a you can join me in bein' there for them. Right now, we just have a lost little girl on our hands. Nothing more than that. Let's hope that together we can change that and bring her home today."

Elbowing Dewey, I quietly pointed out the Daileys standing near the front of the group. Mr. Dailey put his arm around his wife as Mrs. Dailey burst into sobs, burying her face into her husband's chest. I did a quick scan for Mr. Wyatt Edward Farrow, but didn't see him anywhere. Not that I expected to. He didn't seem like the helping type to me.

"Now there's a lot of folks here and a lot o' potential for this to all dissolve into anarchy unless we keep things organized," Mr. Garner said. Bending, he took a stack of squares cut from construction paper out of the apple crate at his feet. He removed the thick elastic band they were bound together with. "What I've done is made up these colored cards. There's five different colors. Red, blue, yellow, green, and black. Everyone should take one and pass them on. If you're wantin' to stay in a group, just take one color per group." He handed them to Mr. Dailey, who began passing them around.

"Okay, now listen up," Mr. Garner went on, reading from a sheet of paper. "Red cards will set out and search down around Cornflower Lake. Don't forget to check the woods and the wetlands." He paused, frowning as though he was trying hard to think of a better way to add the next part: "Yes, even the lake. Try to be as thorough as possible. Blue cards, same thing only Willet Lake. Yellow cards will be going through the woods in and around Clover Creek and the Old Mill River area. Green cards will take the grounds around and including Tucker Mountain. Don't forget to check along the Anikawa and the valley running between it and Old Highway Seventeen. Finally, black cards will be searching the area on the other side of Tucker Mountain Road, following along the Anikawa, the Painted Lake area, and the swamp buttin' up against my ranch." He held up his card and I noticed him pause slightly, almost gravely. "I've got black."

Someone passed my mother a card. It was also black. "We're on Mr. Garner's team!" I said excitedly, but my mother shushed me.

"Now," Mr. Garner said. "I want to further thank Police Chief Ethan Montgomery and *everyone* at the Alvin Police Station for the loan of five of these high-powered walkie-talkies. Every group should take one. This is how we're gonna stay in contact. The minute anybody finds anythin', y'all let the rest of us know immediately. I don't wanna be wading through Skeeter Swamp any longer than I have to." I felt a tension ripple through the crowd following his last sentence that I didn't understand. I made a mental note to ask my mother about it later.

"I'll leave it up to you to organize yourselves within your own groups, but I strongly suggest assigning one person to be leader. This isn't a popularity contest, this is a manhunt to find a missing girl. So let's all put any egos we may have aside and work as diligently and efficiently as we can. Are there any questions?"

There weren't none.

"Okay, then. Everybody in the black group, gather with me and Dixie down at Hunter Road. We'll walk our way from there down to the Anikawa. Everybody else, make sure someone from your color group grabs a walkie-talkie." He stepped over the empty apple crate and came down off the stairs with his rifle strapped over his shoulder.

"Guess we know who our leader is," Dewey said.

My mother shushed him. Putting her hands on our backs, she turned us toward Hunter Street and we began walking, separating from the rest of the crowd as everyone figured out where they should be going. Mr. Garner swung his rifle into position while he whistled for his dog, Dixie, who was sitting patiently next to the library steps.

Dixie was a mottled brown coon dog. Mr. Garner had her for as long as I could remember, and even though she was getting on in years, she was still as fast and alert as ever. I'd once seen her chase down a jackrabbit from a standing start a hundred yards away.

By the time we broke apart, I realized my original estimate of a thousand folks was off considerably. Turned

out to be twenty-two in our group, so my mother's cal-
culation was probably much closer than mine. I felt like
part of a platoon of soldiers as we marched north down
Hunter Road, continuing past where it turned into a
dirt trail and then ended altogether at the grassy bank
that rolled down into the Anikawa River. We crossed
over using an old wooden footbridge made of six logs
strapped together with steel ties. The bridge was much
older than I was, but nobody doubted its safety as the
river chopped and raged in the narrows beneath us.

We stepped off right at the edge of the thick, tangled
woods that ran along this side. How deep those trees
went in the northerly direction, I didn't know. I did
know we would come to Bullfrog Creek if we kept
going maybe half a mile that way, and continuing on
that path led roughly the same direction as the Anikawa,
eventually taking us to Painted Lake.

There was a lot of dense forest to cover here. Much
more, I realized, than twenty-two people could easily
do in the course of a few hours. Then there was the
whole area up past Painted Lake: the tree line that
opened onto Mr. Garner's ranch, and the wetlands we
called Skeeter Swamp bubbling back across the river,
where gators—*big* ones—regularly were spotted. Maybe
that's what made the crowd seem to react to Mr. Garner's
mention of the swamp earlier on.

"Let's spread out and all head through the forest toward the lake," Mr. Garner said. He gestured to my
mother. "Leah, you take half the group and walk
through until the creek, then follow it up to the lake.
I'll take the other half this way along the river. We'll
cover more ground that way."

My mother nodded. "You two stay with me," she said. "I don't want you by yourselves."

"Why?" I asked.

"In case somethin' happens."

"Like what?"

"I don't know. But I have a gun."

"So does Mr. Garner," I said. "Can we go with him?"

She considered this, then called out. "Bob, do you mind if my boys tag along with you?"

"Not at all," he said. "Come on, you guys, you can walk up front with me and Dixie."

"Thanks, Mom," I said, beaming. Dewey and I raced through the woods, ducking under pine branches and dodging the thick trunks of oaks until we caught up to Mr. Garner. We fell in close behind him, stepping on a soft bed of fallen leaves and undergrowth, occasionally climbing over the odd fallen log.

Mr. Garner happened to glance at Dewey. Without even a smile, he asked, "What's with them boots, son?"

Dewey's face flushed red. "They're his pa's," I answered. "He ain't got none of his own." This seemed to satisfy Mr. Garner's curiosity, for no more was said about it.

We had now separated from everyone else and, far as I could tell, were roughly following the Anikawa that was only a few hundred yards in. I sometimes thought I could hear it splashing off to our left, but I wasn't sure. Mr. Garner seemed to know his way all right though, so I wasn't afraid of getting lost or nothing.

As we walked, he scanned the forest around us, looking like some sort of eagle. His strides were so long, Dewey and I spent more time struggling to keep up than we did looking around the woods, but I reckon Mr. Garner did a good enough job searching for all three of us. Dixie trotted ahead a few yards, stopping here and there to sniff out a tree or stare down a squirrel that got her attention.

"Go get her, girl," Mr. Garner would say, and Dixie would gallop through the woods while the squirrel scampered away or raced up the trunk of an oak.

I looked at the rifle in Mr. Garner's hand. "Hope we don't come across no bears."

"I think we're safe from bears," he said.

"Then why're ya carryin' a rifle?" I asked.

"Just in case. You never know."

I sighed, wondering why nobody could explain exactly what it was I never knew might be lurking out here, requiring the use of a rifle. I decided to let the issue drop for now. Instead I ran up, practically jogging to keep beside him, and asked, "Mr. Garner? You think Mary Ann Dailey's gonna turn up today?"

The forest began breaking around us. Through the sparse trunks, I began to make out Mr. Garner's ranch coming up on our right and the edge of Skeeter Swamp that flanked the Anikawa on our left. Mr. Garner's attention immediately went to that swamp. Farther up, the river banked toward us and a stone bridge arched across, leading to a small hill where a willow stood, its leaves shaking in the morning breeze.

Without taking his eyes off that murky green swamp water, Mr. Garner responded, "I don't rightly know. Sure hope so, Abe. Sure hope this don't turn out to be another Ruby Mae."

I searched my mind for any recollection of what he might be talking about, but I couldn't remember anyone named Ruby Mae living in Alvin. When I tossed a puzzled glance at Dewey, he just shrugged back. "Who's Ruby Mae?" I asked.

Keeping up his pace, Mr. Garner continued scouring the area, without answering me. I thought maybe he hadn't heard my question and so I was about to ask again when he spoke. "Ruby Mae Vickers," he said. "She was another little girl went missing from these parts, oh, must've been ten or twelve years ago."

No wonder I didn't remember. I was either not born or just a baby. "Was she related to the Vickers living out on Finley Circle?" The Vickers had five children, four boys and one girl. Far as I knew, none of them went to school. Most were probably too young though, I thought.

"Yup," Mr. Garner said. "Ruby Mae was their first daughter."

"And she went missin'?" I asked.

"Yup."

"Just like Mary Ann Dailey?" I asked.

"Dunno yet," Mr. Garner said.

"And nobody ever found her?" Dewey asked. He had jogged up on the other side.

Mr. Garner stopped and pulled a cigar from the front pocket of his jacket. Biting the end off, he stuck it in his mouth and lit it with a match. He blew a big puff of blue smoke into the cold morning air. Out here, surrounded by the woods, the wind wasn't blowing nearly as hard as it had been out in the town, and the smoke kind of hung there like a sour cloud until we finally walked through it. This time, Mr. Garner went considerably slower.

"Oh, she turned up, eventually," he said. We continued along the Anikawa River, just edging Skeeter Swamp that settled in on either side. "Just not in the same state she disappeared in. I found her a few months later. Her body turned up under that big willow." He pointed across the river to the tree growing atop the small hill. Fresh flowers were scattered around the bottom of the trunk. I think they were roses. Red, pink, and yellow.

Dewey's eyes went wide at this news. I couldn't believe we'd never heard this story before. It was the sort of thing that would scatter through school faster than an outbreak of cooties. I wondered if maybe he was putting us on, but his face was serious. Very serious, in fact. "What happened to her?" I asked.

Mr. Garner pulled his cigar from his mouth. "Nobody ever did find that out."

"Where did those flowers come from?" I asked.

Mr. Garner hesitated before answering. "I put them there."

"How come?" Dewey asked.

"Let's not talk any more about them flowers, okay?" Mr. Garner said.

From here we could now see most of Mr. Garner's ranch. There was a structure set off from his house in the process of being built. "Whatcha making?" I asked.

"Toolshed," he said.

"What for?" Dewey asked.

"Tools, likely," I answered sarcastically.

"Actually, I just like doing things to keep me busy," Mr. Garner said. "The devil finds work for idle hands to do. It's important to remember things like that."

I glanced back at the willow with the ring of flowers on the other side of the river as we continued.

"You reckon it was one of them cougars that got Ruby Mae?" Dewey asked.

Stopping, Mr. Garner once again inspected Dewey standing there in those giant boots. "Yeah, son," he said, "I reckon it was some kinda cougar. Just not the kind you's thinkin'. Somebody killed her and tossed her away afterward."

We continued in silence. I don't think neither me nor Dewey could think of any proper response to something like that. This was likely the reason for everyone reacting the way they did when Mr. Garner mentioned Skeeter Swamp this morning.

Once again, we entered a wooded area. We came to a rotted log in our path so big even Mr. Garner had to step up on it in order to get over it. Dewey and I struggled to climb across, the hollow wood breaking apart beneath our hands. Dewey had an especially hard time, being all clumsy in his father's galoshes, but eventually we made it, just as the first heavy drops of rain fell through the thick ceiling of leaves and branches hanging above our heads.

Dewey and I pulled up our hoods. Mr. Garner didn't seem to even notice. Something else was on his mind.

We were getting close to Painted Lake. I could hear Bullfrog Creek coming up along our right. Not only the water quietly rushing over the stones, but also the croaking of the animals that gave it its name.

Mr. Garner spoke again, but I got the feeling this time he was talking more to himself than us. "I sure as hell hope this don't turn out to be another Ruby Mae," he said.

That was all we heard of it for the rest of our wet walk through the trees and up to the lake.

CHAPTER 4

Nobody found Mary Ann Dailey even though they searched throughout that entire day and into the night. My mother brought me and Dewey home after our group finished up at Painted Lake, and made us a quick lunch before she went out again. I was glad she didn't ask if we wanted to go with her. By then the rain was coming down something fierce, and I'd really had my fill of walking through the woods.

My mother didn't end up finally getting home until long after I was in bed. I was still awake though, on account of I couldn't sleep, thinking about what Mr. Garner had told me and Dewey about Ruby Mae Vickers. About it being some kind of cougar that was responsible, just not the kind of cougar we was thinking about. He was talking about the human kind, I figured, and I couldn't imagine what sort of person would take a girl away only to kill her a few months later. I wondered if Dewey was lying in his own bed thinking something the same, and I suspected he likely was. The rain pounded on my window and I thought about poor Ruby Mae out there by herself, dead beneath that willow tree. My stomach flipped and I near enough threw up right there in my bed. So I rolled over, pulled up my covers, and decided to try to think about something else, but I couldn't. Just that poor girl out there, being "tossed away," like Mr. Garner said. The more I tried to get her out of my head, the more she insisted on staying, the thought growing more horrible every time it came back.

She finally drifted away after my mother returned home. After fixing herself something to eat, my mother came down the hall and opened my door, the way she always did to check on me when she got home.

I had my back to her, and she probably figured I was asleep, but just before she closed my door again, I turned over and said, "Mom?"

"Honey?" she asked, coming over and crouching beside me. "You're still up? It's late."

"I'm havin' troubles falling asleep tonight."

She placed her hand on my forehead. "You not feeling well, baby?"

I didn't answer right away. I didn't rightly know *how* to answer. It wasn't that I was sick or nothing like that, but I wasn't feeling good. So, instead, I asked, "Did you find Mary Ann?"

With a deep breath, she looked down at my floor. "No, honey, we didn't."

"Do you reckon someone took her?"

My question seemed to surprise her. I saw her eyes open wider just a bit, but then she answered plainly, "I don't know, baby. I sure hope not."

"I hope not, too," I said.

"Is this why you're having trouble sleepin'?"

I nodded.

Reaching over me, she pulled me to her in a tight hug, burying my face into the side of her neck. She smelled like the rain and the woods. "Don't you worry, we're gonna find her," she said. When she let go, I saw tears standing in her eyes. Sniffling, she wiped her face with the arm of her sweater. With another big breath, she swallowed and told me Uncle Henry was coming up from Mobile tomorrow to stay with us awhile. I didn't ask why, but she explained anyway. "I just don't want you kids to be alone right now, is all. You understand that, right?"

I nodded.

"Now I want you to go to sleep and not worry about Mary Ann. That's my job, remember?"

I nodded again. She kissed me on my forehead and tucked my blankets under my chin. "Good night, my little man," she said, and stood.

"Night, Mama."

She walked out, leaving my door open a few inches so the yellow light from the hall stretched into my bedroom. It had been more than a year since I slept with my door partway open and the hall light on, but tonight I certainly appreciated it.

I turned back over and pulled my blankets up even tighter.

This time Ruby Mae left me alone to sleep, but I guess I didn't sleep too well, because when I woke up in the morning, I felt just as tired as if it were time for bed all over again. I couldn't remember any dreams, but I had a feeling a few had floated through my brain and maybe it was forgetting them on purpose. Either way, it was Sunday and I had to get up for church.

My mother liked to think we went to church every

Sunday and Wednesday without fail, and in her own heart, I believe she thought it was true, too. Fact was, we missed church more often than we went, but it wasn't because my mother didn't respect the Lord. Usually it had to do with her schedule. Things just tended to get away from her most of the time.

But on those days when things didn't get in the way? It wouldn't have mattered if I'd had my leg bitten off by a gator the day before—we'd still be going to church. I think even if I had managed to not sleep for four days straight, my mother would still drag me to church and force me to keep my eyes open for the whole service before bringing me back home and putting me to bed.

And this morning we were definitely going to church, so I had to get myself out of bed and get dressed. Besides, the smell of bacon sizzling and popping in the kitchen was winding its way down the hall and through my open door. I think someone could be near on at their deathbed, barely able to get out of bed in their final throes, and still not be able to resist the smell of frying bacon and hot coffee on a wet morning. They would postpone the afterlife for one last breakfast; at least, I would. I'm surprised Jesus didn't have a last breakfast of bacon and coffee instead of that supper. Not that I drank coffee, but my mother did, and sometimes, lately, so did Carry. I didn't drink it, but I loved the smell. When accompanied by bacon, it always smelled like weekends.

"You're up!" my mother said as I came into the kitchen, still in my blue pajamas. "I was beginnin' to think I was gonna have to go in there and pull you out by your feet."

I sat at the table just as she slid a plate with bacon, two fried eggs, and two pieces of freshly toasted white bread in front of me. She went back to the stove for the skillet full of fried potatoes and dumped some beside my eggs. "Caroline!" she called out over her shoulder, pausing with one hand in an oven mitt clutching the handle of the hot skillet and the other hand grasping the spatula.

There was absolutely no response from Carry's bedroom down the hall.

"Caroline!" my mother called out again, but still my sister didn't answer. "Now, she might be in need of more than just a little feet pullin' soon," my mother said, giving me a few more potatoes before returning the pan to the stove. She disappeared down the hall toward Carry's bedroom, which was right across from mine. "Caroline!"

I didn't bother waiting. Nothing tastes worse than cold eggs, at least that's my theory, and it was good enough to allow me to dunk my toast into my yolks without feeling even a pang of guilt for not waiting for my mother and Carry to come to the table. I was on my second or third bite when I heard the back door open and someone come into the house.

It wasn't unusual for people to come visit, especially Sunday mornings before church. Because my mother was a police officer, she had good relationships with many of the townsfolk; many of them was just like family. So it also wasn't unusual for someone to show up and walk in without knocking first. I figured maybe it was Miss Crystal from next door come over to borrow some eggs or maybe a cup of milk or sugar. Miss Crystal was always coming over to borrow something. It was almost as though she never actually did any shopping for herself, she just got her groceries off people living on the street.

Turned out, though, that I was wrong. I had forgotten what my mother said the night before about Uncle Henry coming to stay awhile and so I was pleasantly surprised to see his round, pink face when he came into the kitchen.

"Looks like I made it just in time for breakfast!" he said, the lights reflecting off his glasses and the teeth of his big grin. He was wearing a gray baseball cap with the brim pushed high on his head, and a white knitted sweater. I liked Uncle Henry a lot. He lived down in Mobile. Normally, we got to see him only a few times a year—mainly at Christmas. But he retired a year and a few months back, so I guessed we'd probably be seeing more of him now. I sure hoped so.

From her room, Carry yelled that she had no intention of going to church—loud enough that Dewey might even have heard it at his house way up the street. Uncle Henry gave a look of surprise. A few minutes later, Carry came bustling down the hall, preceded by her sour mood and followed by my mother. Carry was partially dressed, wearing a baggy white school sweatshirt, but she still had her pink pajama bottoms on. Her hair was naturally curly and she generally kept it perfectly brushed (especially lately) with clips behind her bangs, but this morning it was a blond nest of tangles. With a harrumph, she thumped down into the seat across from me, her arms crossed, her blue eyes staring at the pine tabletop somewhere between me and her.

My mother sighed, then seemed to notice Uncle Henry

for the first time and her expression improved dramatically. "Hank!" she said. She walked over and hugged him, kissing his cheek. Uncle Henry *was* actually my mother's uncle, which, I suppose, made him our great-uncle, but we still called him Uncle Henry anyway. He was Uncle Henry to a lot of people we knew. Even people his birth had nothing to do with. Seemed like the only person who called him Hank was my mother.

Uncle Henry pointed to Carry. "I see my little sugarplum's not her regular sweet self this morning."

"Oh, never mind her," my mother said, picking up a towel from the counter. "She's been in a mood goin' on six months now. I think it's boys." She whispered the last part, but not near quiet enough for neither me nor Carry not to hear.

"You don't know nothin' about my life, Mother!" Carry snapped, her eyes still fixed halfway on the tabletop between us, her arms still tightly wrapped together.

My mother rolled her eyes at Uncle Henry. "Apparently I know nothin' 'bout her life. I only grew her in my womb for nine months and spent the last fifteen years puttin' bandages on her scrapes and makin' sure she stayed clothed and fed." She turned back to Carry. "Caroline, say hello to your Uncle Henry."

There was a pause, and for a moment I thought Carry was going to be unconscionably rude, even for her new self. She loved Uncle Henry as much as I did. I knew this, and so she had no business making him the victim of whatever frustrations had recently crawled inside of her. I wasn't sure she had any business taking it out on me and my mother neither, but I suppose by virtue of simply living together, you automatically assume certain responsibilities. I was just about ready to give Carry a piece of *my* mind when she came to her senses. "Hello, Uncle Henry," she said, even turning to look at him. "It's nice to see you." She didn't say it with quite the proper emotion such a sentiment required, but at least she said it.

Uncle Henry nodded and winked back. "Nice to see you too, sugarplum. Sorry you're goin' through whatever phase you're goin' through. Just try to remember that everyone who grows up pretty much grows up the same way, and every one of 'em thinks they're different than all the others who came before them, but one day you'll see that's not the case. But you can't skip over anythin', cuz it's all important and it's all part of becoming who you'll eventually be." He gave my mother a sideways smile. "So your mama here, she's just gonna have to hang on and do her best to keep the train from runnin' off the tracks. But try to remember from time to time that we're all on your side."

Now, normally these days, if someone said something like this to Carry it would result in a blowup so extreme I would have been looking for cover. This new Carry, the one I really didn't care for so much, didn't like having anything explained to her that even slightly smelled like parental advice. I think I even flinched halfway through Uncle Henry's little speech, waiting for the knife and fork in front of my sister to come flying across the room like poisoned arrows, but Carry surprised me this time. Her eyes did narrow when he finished talking, and she was obviously thinking something over, but it turned out to not have anything to do with throwing a fit. She just nodded back to him, the edges of her lips nearly even raising enough to qualify as a smile, and said, "Thanks, Uncle Henry. I'll try to remember that."

Uncle Henry gave her a wink. "Thanks, sugarplum." He went around to where she was sitting and squatted down beside her. "You got a kiss for your Uncle Henry under all that angst?"

Now she did smile and gave him a hug and kissed him on the cheek the same way my mother had.

"How about you, young soldier?" Uncle Henry asked, coming around to where I was sitting with a mouthful of potatoes while my mother set a plate full of food in front of Carry. "You got a handshake in you, or are you too busy shoveling all that grub into your mug?"

My mouth still full, I set down my fork and took his outstretched hand. This was new. Normally Uncle Henry asked me for hugs and kisses too, but I guess he thought I was getting too old for such things. I felt his grip tighten and I tightened mine back. I hoped he wouldn't tighten again, because I was pretty much putting all the strength I had into mine.

He didn't. "That's a firm grip you got there, boy," he said. "You're gettin' strong. You're turnin' into quite a young man now, ain't ya?"

Swallowing, I nodded and just beamed back. Like I said, Uncle Henry was good people. He always made *me* feel good, anyway.

My mother had her oven mitt back on and had brought the iron skillet of sizzling potatoes back to the table. "Pull up a chair, Hank. I made lots."

Uncle Henry waved the idea away. "I ate before I

came. You guys go ahead and eat. Just pretend I'm not here." He sat down anyway and added, "Of course, I'll have a cup of that coffee, if you don't mind."

My mother set down a mug on the table in front of him and filled it. "Well, I'd say it's pretty near impossible to pretend you ain't here," she said, smiling. She removed her apron and brought her own plate to the table. With one of his big arms set upon the table, Uncle Henry lifted his cup and sipped his coffee. Outside, the rain continued to fall. It wasn't near as bad as last night, but a dull gray shone in from the window. It mixed with the brown from the shade over the light hanging above the table, casting the black-and-white checkered floor in an ugly dirt color. A cold hollowness fell over me and I remembered lying awake in bed last night, waiting for my mother to return from the hunt for Mary Ann Dailey.

"Is everyone gonna go back out and look for Mary Ann again after church, Mom?" I asked.

Putting down her fork, she wiped her mouth, glancing at Uncle Henry. "I'm not sure yet, honey. I need to go to the station and meet with Ethan and Chris. You guys are gonna come back here and stay with Uncle Henry."

I nodded. Carry said nothing. She was sitting with her elbow on the table, her head propped up on one hand while she watched the other poke her food with her fork. Her knotted hair hung forward over her shoulder, practically falling into her plate. I could tell my mother was on the verge of giving her heck for not sitting properly, but she took one look at the scowl on Carry's face and decided to just ignore her instead.

"Mom?" I asked.

"Yes, honey?"

"Did you know the Vickers used to have another girl? Someone named Ruby Mae?"

Once again, my mother looked at Uncle Henry, but this time the look was different. Almost like she was scared or something. I hoped I didn't say anythin' wrong.

"Who—" She started speaking, but her voice broke. After a second she tried again. "Who told you about Ruby Mae Vickers?"

"Mr. Garner," I said. "He said somebody took her away and then they killed her and put her on the hill underneath that big willow on the other side of Skeeter Swamp. You don't reckon somebody took Mary Ann like that, do you?"

My mother very slowly swallowed, put down her knife and fork, and wiped her mouth. She looked at Uncle Henry, but he just turned his head away. I kept going back and forth between them, trying to figure out why she wasn't answering my question. Then my mother brought her elbow up and put her hand in front of her mouth while her eyes dropped to the table, as though she were thinking. I was about to ask if I said something wrong when she said, "I don't know where Mary Ann is yet, honey, but I'll find her." She got up from the table and walked past Uncle Henry into the living room.

"Aren't you gonna finish eating?" I asked. She hadn't even touched her eggs.

Uncle Henry frowned. "I don't reckon your mama's that hungry anymore right now, son," he said. Then he gave me a wink, but it wasn't his normal happy wink.

"Did I say somethin' wrong?" I asked.

With a big breath, he shook his head. "No, young

soldier, you did not. Don't give it another thought, okay?"

Hesitantly, I agreed not to.

"Good," he said, and followed after my mother.

I looked across at Carry. "Way to upset Mom, ass face," she said. Despite the fact that this was probably the first thing she'd said directly to me in over five months, I ignored it and got off my chair. Quietly, I walked over and stood in front of the fridge, trying to listen to my mother and Uncle Henry talking.

"What are you doin'?" Carry asked.

But I shushed her. Surprisingly, she shushed.

My mother was trying to talk quiet, but she was having a hard time of it. It sounded like she was crying while she spoke to Uncle Henry. "Why would he tell them about Ruby Mae?" she asked.

"Well," Uncle Henry said, "to most folk, Ruby Mae's ancient history."

"But—" She stopped to take a breath.

"But not to *you,* right?" Uncle Henry asked.

"No," my mother said. "Not to me." I definitely heard tears in her voice.

"You have to let go of things, Leah. It's been twelve years."

There was a pause and then, "I can't, Henry. I think about that little girl nearly every day of my life. I promised those folks I'd get their baby back to them. I *promised* them."

"Leah, it was pretty near your first case. You can't blame yourself for what happened."

My mother's voice rose, but stayed in a clipped whisper. "You know what I told Sally Vickers the day Ruby Mae went missing? I said, 'Don't you worry, ma'am, I got myself a little girl, too. I ain't about to let anyone hurt Ruby Mae. I'll bring her back home safe and sound, you'll see. She's probably just out lost somewhere.' " As she spoke, she became more and more anxious.

Uncle Henry cut her off. "You had no control over what happened."

"Oh, I brought that little girl home all right. Three months later. After . . . after , , ,"

"Oh, don't work yourself up, Leah. Come here."

After that I heard soft, muffled sobbing.

"It's this Dailey girl," Uncle Henry said, his voice still as calm and quiet as ever. "She's just knockin' at the door of old memories, that's all."

"But what if this *is* another Ruby Mae?" my mother asked. "What if it *is*, Hank? I . . . I don't think I can go through that again. What if—"

"What if a twister hits Alvin and wipes us off the map tomorrow?" Uncle Henry asked back. "You're gonna *what if* yourself to death. Take it one step at a time. Right now, all you know is you got yourself a missin' girl."

"But we searched everywhere yesterday. She's not in Alvin, at least not anywhere outside."

"Well, maybe you missed a spot. Or maybe she don't wanna be found. Maybe she left town. Or maybe it *is* somethin' worse, but let me tell you somethin' right now. You're not the same person you were twelve years ago. You're a *good* cop. You're a *detective,* for Christ's sake."

My mother laughed sarcastically at this. "You know damn well why I'm detective. It's got nothing to do with my detectin' skills."

"Maybe, maybe not. But it does have somethin' to do with you being good at what you do. Your daddy'd be awfully proud of you. He *was* awfully proud of you." There was a sniffle or two from my mother. "Now you need to get some control," Uncle Henry continued. "And you need to separate your emotions from your job."

"I . . . I can't. You know what I told Mrs. Dailey two days ago? I told her I'd find her daughter. I promised her I'd find her. And the minute I said it, it was like a rock fell straight into my stomach, because it all came back to me, and right then I knew I was gonna end up breakin' my promise just like I did with the Vickers. I *still* can't look Sally Vickers in the eye. When I see her at church, I . . ." She drifted off, then: "And this is gonna be just the same. Just like—"

Uncle Henry shushed her. "You need to take a step back. If you really wanna find this girl, you can't do it with Ruby Mae lyin' there in your head. You have to focus. Right now you ain't no good to nobody. You're not bein' fair to the Daileys and you sure as hell ain't bein' fair to yourself."

My mother stifled back another tear.

"Leah, I know you don't need me to tell you how to run your life. God knows you've managed to get this far on your own. But I remember how you were those first few years after the Ruby Mae case, and I don't wanna ever see you like that ever again. And, if having another girl now missing barely a day's already got you like this? Well—I don't know how you're gonna do it, but you need to put what happened twelve years ago into a box and squirrel it away somewhere for now so you can concentrate on doin' what needs doin' today," Uncle Henry said. "You think you can do that?"

I didn't hear any more crying, and a few seconds later Uncle Henry said, "Good. That's good. Now, don't you worry 'bout those kids of yours none, I'll keep a close eye on 'em. You just worry 'bout findin' that girl. And don't you dare give up on her already. You hear me? Don't you goddamn dare."

CHAPTER 5

After that Sunday, my and Dewey's walks to school came to an abrupt end. My mother drove us, picking up Dewey along the way, even though it wasn't along the way at all. It was, in fact, exactly eight houses down Cottonwood Lane the complete wrong direction, but my mother insisted on Dewey not walking even that far by himself first thing in the morning.

"It's only eight houses," I said. "What can happen in eight houses?"

Even Dewey's own mother thought he could manage eight houses and stay alive. When my mother called her and offered to drive, she thanked my mother and said she'd make sure Dewey was at our house in plenty of time so I wouldn't be late. "No, Francine," my mother said, "I think it best if I just come pick your boy up. Until this Mary Ann Dailey affair is behind us, I feel we should make a point of knowin' exactly where our kids are at all times." I didn't actually hear the call, but I heard my mother tell Uncle Henry about it afterward.

You probably think being driven to school got us there a lot faster, but it actually had the opposite effect, resulting in us being late more often than not.

Because my mother was a police officer and because all of Alvin was kind of sitting on red-alert status due to Mary Ann Dailey disappearing, my mother's cell phone was going off like Lady Fingers on the Fourth of July. And just like not letting Dewey walk eight houses, my mother refused to talk on her phone and drive at the same time. So, many mornings found us just a half block from where Hunter Road met Pine Street (which put us maybe a block away from the school) sitting on the side of the road, listening while my mother chattered away, and watching all the other kids walk past us carrying their knapsacks and their lunch pails. Their numbers would slowly thin until finally we'd hear the bell ring and still my mother would go on talking. I would look at Dewey and Dewey would look at me and we would both just shrug. It made no sense to us. Then there were the days when my mother forced us to leave early because she had "just one quick stop at the station to make" before dropping us off. Her "quick stops" were *never* quick stops. The only times I knew we would make it to class on time were those when my mother had to go into work really early and so arranged for Uncle Henry to give us a lift. My mother once told me Uncle Henry was as reliable as the Union Pacific.

This not-being-allowed-to-walk-anywhere-on-our-own-thing was fine with me and Dewey. Heck, other than going to school, we never really went anywhere anyway. Before this, sometimes we would ride our bicycles downtown along Main Street, but only because there wasn't anything else we could think of doing. Mostly, these days we just stuck around my yard, suspiciously watching Mr. Wyatt Edward Farrow's house across the street, and pondering the disappearance of all the roadkill. I didn't even miss our school walks overly much.

Carry, on the other hand, was a different case entirely, but that was to be expected. This new Carry—the one who recently "shifted her interests to boys"—turned everything into a federal case, and my mother's rule about not walking alone was no exception.

"I'm almost fifteen, Mother," Carry snapped. "I think I can walk a half mile to the bus stop by myself."

"You're just making my case for me," my mother replied. "Mary Ann Dailey is a month *older* than you, and look what happened to *her*."

"I'm *not* Mary Ann Dailey," Carry said. "And I happen to *like* walking. And besides, do you really want to get up at four thirty every morning?"

A brief silence fell into the kitchen and I thought I was on the verge of witnessing a rare phenomenon. My sister actually had a chance of winning this particular argument on account of her having to be on Main Street by five in the morning and my mother not usually getting up until just after six.

But I was wrong.

Uncle Henry picked that minute to come in from the living room. "I'll get up and walk with you," he said to Carry. "How does that sound?"

I saw relief on my mother's face. I saw consternation on Carry's. She knew she was licked. As I said before, we both really liked Uncle Henry, and so her argument's sails ran completely out of wind.

"Thank you, Hank," my mother said.

"That okay with you, my little sugarplum?" he asked my sister.

Carry looked up, sighed, and said, "Fine. As long as you promise not to call me that in front of anybody I know."

Uncle Henry nodded. "It's a deal."

On account of our house having only three bedrooms, Uncle Henry had to spend his nights sleeping on the sofa in our living room. He didn't seem to mind, though. He told my mother and me that we had possibly the most comfortable sofa in Alabama and that it was far more comfortable than his own bed back home in Mobile. I doubted the honesty of this statement. Our sofa was a very worn piece of furniture that probably should have been replaced years ago. My mother had even patched it in places with silver duct tape.

Most days, it was Uncle Henry who picked us up from school. This was good because it was one thing to be waiting around for my mother, wasting time that would otherwise be spent sitting at my desk learning, and another thing entirely to be wasting time that belonged to me. Even if I didn't use it for much, I valued my personal time. I think that's important.

Later on when Carry's bus was due home, Uncle Henry would go get her. Although they would walk in the mornings, he would usually drive in the afternoons, and I never heard Carry once complain about not getting in the second part of her daily walk. If my mother wasn't home, Uncle Henry gave me and Dewey a choice. We could go inside, lock the doors, and wait thirty minutes until he got back, or we could come with. Usually we came with and spent the whole trip talking or listening to Uncle Henry's stories. He had a lot of them, and most were funny, although I am not certain how much stock I put in their validity. I asked my mother about this once.

"Well," she asked, "do you enjoy them?"

I told her I most certainly did. Dewey, too.

"Then why does it matter how much truth are in them?"

I thought of this awhile and finally figured Uncle Henry's stories were a little like a magic show. When you're really little, you just think it's real magic you're watching, and you're amazed. Then, when you get older, you realize there's tricks to everything, only you don't see the tricks, so you're *still* amazed, just for a different reason than before. It's only when you figure out the tricks that the show stops being amazing.

After that, I quit worrying about how much of Uncle Henry's stories were based on his real-life experiences and how much of them were just pulled out of a secret lining in his sleeve and just enjoyed listening instead.

Rarely was Carry in a good disposition after school. During the ride back home, me and Dewey and Uncle Henry knew enough to just leave her be and continue discussing stuff amongst ourselves, but one afternoon her mood was particularly foul. Rain had been pounding Alvin to varying degrees nonstop since those first few drops fell onto our heads during the search for Mary Ann Dailey, but it hit its worst on Wednesday. Carry's bus dropped her off early that day, and we arrived to find her standing there under a steel gray sky full of thunderheads, with her pants soaking wet from nearly the waist down. Apparently due to our tardiness, she became the victim of a drive-by puddle splash. By the looks of things, it must have been a tsunami.

She sat in the backseat, her arms tightly crossed, her lips pressed hard together, staring out at the smudgy wet streets. Nobody had said a word once she got in the car. Her wet bangs hung limply on either side of her face, and she looked ready to kill someone. I think even Uncle Henry was afraid of her. Poor Dewey was stuck beside her in the backseat. I was sure thankful it was him though, and not me.

I decided the tension needed breaking. "I bet you got a good deal on this car, Uncle Henry, workin' at the plant an' all." Uncle Henry had spent the better part of his life working for Toyota. And that's the only car I'd known him to drive. His was blue. I didn't know how old it was or anything, but to me it seemed pretty nice.

A slight smile came to his lips. "You bet I did. Guess what this car cost me?"

I shrugged and looked back at Dewey. He still looked a little freaked out having to sit beside my sister and all her anger. You see, at this time in her life, Carry was so unpredictable you never knew what to expect. And that was just during her regular moods. Something like this? Who knew? She could suddenly pull a pen out of her pocket or something and shove it in Dewey's eye.

Well, to be perfectly honest, nothing like that ever happened. But we didn't know back then that it wouldn't.

Shaking my head, I said to Uncle Henry, "To be right honest, I don't really know the cost of cars."

"Fair enough," he said. "Well, you'll be amazed to know that I got this fine automobile for absolutely nothing." His voice was changing, and I could tell he was off on one of his stories. "I betcha don't believe me, hey? But it's the God's honest truth." He was always saying his stories were the God's honest truth. I don't think Uncle Henry maybe believed so much in God.

"Really?" I asked.

He nodded. "That's right. Absolutely nothing. Except it took me ten years to do it." One of his trademark dramatic pauses followed.

"How come?" I asked. "Why ten years?"

One of his eyebrows lifted and he grinned sneakily at me. "Because I *stole* it."

My eyes widened. In the backseat, the fear on Dewey's face hadn't changed. His fearful eyes set into his round freckled face surrounded by all his thick red hair made him look like an alarm bell ready to go off at any second. I looked back to Uncle Henry.

"You *stole* this car?" I asked. "Does my mom know? That's grand theft auto." I knew these things on account of my mother being a police officer and all.

"No, she don't," Uncle Henry said. "And let's keep it our secret, okay?"

Narrowing my eyes, I considered this. "I don't rightly know if it's ethical for me to keep somethin' like this from her. Frankly, Uncle Henry, I find this quite disturbin'." And I did. I couldn't believe he was a car thief.

"Why don't you ask why it took me ten years?" he asked.

"Okay," I said. "Why did it take you ten years?"

"Because I took it one piece at a time. Smugglin' them out in my lunch pail, or under my jacket. My tailpipe's seven years older than my muffler, which is two years older than the rearview right here."

He tapped the mirror as we pulled into our driveway.

"Wow," I said. "That's amazing."

"No, it isn't, ass facc," Carry said, opening her door and getting out. "It's a stupid Johnny Cash song. I can't believe how gullible you are."

She slammed her door as Uncle Henry turned off the ignition. "Well, at least she talked to us," he said, and smiled. Dewey let out a loud sigh, almost like he had been holding his breath the last five miles. The normal color was creeping back into his face as we all got out of Uncle Henry's car.

A heavy wind had set into the storm. The rain now fell slanted and the few tall pines along the sidewalk looked about ready to snap while their upper branches tossed like kite tails. We were halfway to the front door of the house when one of Mr. Farrow's tools roared to life across the street. Both me and Dewey stopped midstep and turned to look at his garage and that strip of bright white light beneath it, shining like a shark tooth in the middle of such a dark and gloomy afternoon.

"What is it about that house that catches you boys' interest so much?" Uncle Henry asked. He was on the top step, protected from most of the rain by the over-hanging roof. Me and Dewey were still out in the elements, getting wetter by the minute, but neither of us cared. Our eyes met and we both knew what the other one was thinking, and that was: *How do we answer such a question?*

After a moment of silent consideration, I decided that when in doubt, honesty was almost always the best policy and most certainly the safest way of keeping out of trouble (yet more advice handed down from my mother). So I took up the initiative.

"Well, Uncle Henry," I said. "We've been noticing somethin' peculiar about the roadkill lately."

He just stood there, looking at me expectantly. But it was Dewey who finished the observation. "There ain't none no more," he said. "Not a one. Not *any*where."

Uncle Henry stared back at each of us a moment longer. Then he nodded his head without so much of a smile or anything and said, "I see. You know, this sounds like the kind of thing we need to discuss more inside the house, out of all this rain. And probably best done over hot cocoa, I figure."

Twenty minutes later in the living room, with me and Dewey on the sofa and Uncle Henry in the big stuffed chair beside the television, three empty cocoa mugs were on the coffee table, and our concerns about Mr. Wyatt Edward Farrow and the sudden disappearance of Alvin roadkill had all been completely laid out. I was worried at first we were going to sound crazy, but the more we talked, the more I realized we were on to something.

Even Uncle Henry seemed to think so. "You're

pretty sure this Farrow fellow is up to no good?" he asked, sitting back in the chair. Like the sofa, the chair was also in bad need of replacing. Uncle Henry rubbed his chin with his fingers.

"I definitely got a bad feelin' from him when we brung over them apples," I said. "He's the sneaky type."

Uncle Henry's eyes narrowed and he nodded solemnly. "Well, if you got a feelin', you got a feelin'. We all gotta trust our feelings. What do you think he's up to?"

Me and Dewey looked at each other and shrugged. "That's the part we been tryin' to figure out."

"And the roadkill bein' gone," Uncle Henry said. "That's definitely a mite disturbin', I'd say."

"That's exactly what I said," Dewey said.

Uncle Henry's fingers tapped a rhythm out on his cheek. "I wonder . . ." he said. "Do you think by any chance—I mean, you boys must've already considered this possibility—that maybe the two things are somehow connected?"

It was like a fork of lightning jolted into my brain the minute he said it. How could we not have seen this ourselves? I thought we were just too close to the problem to make out the entire forest, as my mother would say.

Just then Carry came in, slurping soup from a white-handled bowl. I had no idea how long she had been in the kitchen, but obviously long enough to have heard some of our discussion. "Why are you encouragin' them, Uncle Henry?" she asked. It was a relief to see her disposition had brightened since getting home.

Uncle Henry shook his head and turned his palms upward. "I'm not encouragin' nor discouragin', I'm simply pointin' out facts and connectin' the dots."

"You're encouragin' them to keep stalkin' the new neighbor."

"We ain't stalkin'," I said. Then I looked at Uncle Henry and asked, "Are we?"

He rubbed his nose with his thumb. "I don't reckon so. So far you've just been inquisitive from a distance. Not sure where the line between inquisitive and stalkin' is, but I'm pretty sure you're still on the winnin' side at this point."

"Well, you're encouragin' them to be strange, then," Carry said, making one of her new faces she only recently came up with.

"You're just ornery cuz you discovered boys," I said, quoting my mother as best I could without really understanding what it was I was saying.

"Oh, you got a boyfriend now?" Uncle Henry asked. "Anyone I know?"

"He lives in Satsuma," I said, before Carry could answer. This was the first time I connected the boy problem with an actual boy *friend,* but it made sense. It also made sense that any boy my sister was seeing was living in Satsuma on account of I hadn't seen her with one here in Alvin. Of course, I was just hypothesizing.

Uncle Henry's eyebrows went up. "Satsuma? I thought all you young girls were after that farm boy." He snapped his fingers, trying to recall who he was thinking of. "That Allen kid, what was his name?" The Allens had a soy and corn farm out along Highway Seventeen.

"Jesse Allen?" Dewey asked.

With another snap, Uncle Henry pointed at him. "Bingo." He looked up to Carry. "Thought he was the dreamboat round these parts?"

"Jesse *James* Allen," I clarified. A half dozen years ago, the Allens' farmhouse burned to the ground. Jesse James lost his mother, his father, and his grandma in that fire.

I knew all this because, on the day after the fire, Jesse James Allen had become the most famous kid in Alvin when the *Alvin Alerter* ran a picture of him and his grandpa on the front page asking folks to do what they could to help with food and clothing. I'm not sure how old he was in that picture, probably around my age.

He was still going to school back then, although he'd repeated a few grades. He wasn't much good at school. I guess that's why his grandpa pulled him out after the fire because Jesse and school didn't mix, and because he needed Jesse's help on the farm.

I didn't know what all the fuss was about when it came to Jesse and girls, but they all seemed to like him. Especially during those years right after he dropped out of school. Maybe it was on account of him looking so much older than most of the boys his age, I didn't know. Or maybe it had something to do with him not having to go to school. All I knew was that even Carry seemed to develop a crush on Jesse as she got older. I still remembered a conversation we had had not that long ago. Maybe just a little more than two and a half years.

Carry had told me she reckoned Jesse looked like he should be in a band, either as a singer or a drummer. I wasn't sure why she picked those two choices. "Why not a guitar player?" I asked her. "Or one of them guys who plays keyboards?" We had just come home from school that day. I hadn't even taken off my sneakers yet.

"Nope," she'd said, all dreamy-eyed. "Jesse James is definitely the singer or drummer type. Don't you think he looks like Rick Springfield?"

I didn't rightly know what Rick Springfield looked like, but if he had a mess of black hair that hung down over his eyes so far he could barely see past it, and wore the same ripped denim jacket every single day of his life over top of a dirty white T-shirt, then I guessed she was right. "Isn't Rick Springfield a singer, though?" I asked.

"Yeah," my sister said. "And an actor."

"So, why should Jesse be a drummer, too?"

"Because drummers are cool. Maybe even cooler than singers."

"No, they're not," I said. "All they do is sit behind the band and hit stuff. They don't even really make music."

She just gave me a look like I didn't have the slightest clue what I was talking about, and maybe she was right. She walked off down the hall to her room, leaving me standing in the kitchen, where my mom was cooking soup.

"That *is* what drummers do, ain't it, Mom? Just sit around and hit stuff?"

"Last time I checked, honey," she said.

"How is that cooler than playing a guitar?"

"Can't help you there." She had shrugged. "I lost track of what was cool many years ago, I'm afraid."

I related all this to my Uncle Henry, Dewey, and Carry as I remembered it, but as I said, this memory was from two and a half years ago, and Jesse James Allen's popularity had diminished with time. These days, Jesse still lived on the farm with his grandpa, only in a new farmhouse they built the summer following the great Allen fire, with the help of the Mexicans who came up to work.

Carry laughed sarcastically at Uncle Henry's comment about Jesse being a dreamboat. I guess time had taken away her crush on him, too. She probably didn't like Rick Springfield anymore, neither. "Maybe back when I was ten," she said. "Now he's just weird." Then she sneered at me. "And you know nothin' 'bout my life, so quit pretendin' you do." With that, she turned on her heel and stomped back to the kitchen.

"At least she didn't call you ass face," Dewey said.

"Hey," Uncle Henry said, "language."

"Sorry," Dewey said.

But I kept thinking about what Uncle Henry had said, about there being maybe a connection between the roadkill disappearing and Mr. Farrow moving into the neighborhood. This thought continued long after Dewey had gone home for supper.

My mother returned from work in time to cook dinner and, as she set a plate of fried chicken and mashed potatoes on the table in front of me, all sorts of possible connections still tumbled through my mind.

"You're awfully quiet there, soldier," Uncle Henry said, picking up a drumstick.

"Thinkin' 'bout stuff," I said.

He nodded, chewing.

Carry's attitude had made a strange about-face since we picked her up at the bus stop, and for the first time in as long as I could remember, she almost felt like the old Carry again. She dove into her dinner without any complaining. She even said *please* and *thank you* just as polite as could be. Of course I was immediately suspicious. Then, a few minutes after my mother finished serving and had sat down herself, I heard Carry twice catch her breath, as though she were about to say something and then, at the last minute, thought better of it.

"Mama?" she asked, finally. Now I was *really* suspicious. Carry never called my mother *Mama* unless she wanted something.

"Yes, honey?"

Carry hesitated slightly. Then when she spoke, she did so quickly, as though she wanted to get all the words out onto the table in a single breath. "This Saturday mornin', a bunch of my friends are getting together in Satsuma for pizza and an afternoon movie."

My mother swallowed, but didn't say nothing.

Carry took the opportunity to continue. "I was wonderin' if I could go along with 'em. You know, on the bus and all that." Her words kept speeding up. Pretty soon, I thought, she'd sound like the channel six weather guy. "I won't be late," she promised. "I'll be home before supper."

"Is Jessica going?" my mother asked. Jessica Thompson had been Carry's best friend since seventh grade.

Carry paused, and in that second, I saw the doubt in her eyes. Without question, my mother and Uncle Henry saw it, too. "Yeah, sure," Carry said. "I think so."

My mother and Uncle Henry gave each other a quick look. "Let me think on it," my mother said. Carry gave her plate a frustrated frown.

"Oh!" I said. "Me and Dewey was wonderin' if he could sleep over on Saturday. His mama already said it's fine."

"I'm working the night shift on Saturday," my mother said, "so I suppose it's up to Uncle Henry."

Uncle Henry wiped his hands with his napkin. "Well, I guess if you soldiers promise to stay in line, I'm up to it."

"Thanks, Uncle Henry."

Carry tossed the chicken wing in her hand back onto her plate. "How come he always gets everythin' he wants?"

"He doesn't get everythin' he wants," my mother said.

"Whatever. I just asked to go to Satsuma and you have to 'think on it.' He asks for somethin', and just *poof,* you say sure." She made the *poof* motion with her hands. I thought she was getting a bit crazy.

"Honey, it's a bit different," my mother said. "It's not that I'm tryin' to be mean or nothin', it's just . . . we still haven't found Mary Ann Dailey, and until we do . . ."

Carry burst from her seat. "What if you *never* find her, Mom? Do I *never* get to leave the house again? I am *so sick* of Mary Ann Dailey." She stomped out of the kitchen. Her bedroom door slammed shut a few seconds later.

My mother and Uncle Henry continued eating in silence, as though nothing had happened. I kept looking from one to the other, waiting for them to say something.

Finally my mother did. "I don't know what to do with her anymore, Hank."

Uncle Henry finished chewing and swallowed. "You askin' my advice?"

"I always want your advice."

"Well, I would never assume to know better at parentin' than a mother, especially when that mother is you."

"Yeah, but you managed to raise them two boys of yours, and they turned into fine adults," my mother replied. "Somehow you made it through okay. So, yes, I'm askin' your advice, because I don't think I'm gonna be so okay if this goes on much longer."

"Well," Uncle Henry said, "first, you gotta remember mine were boys." He nodded across the table at me. "This fine fellow here? He ain't gonna give you near the troubles that girl down the hall is. And if I had to place a bet, I don't think your troubles with her have nearly even started yet."

My mother pressed her palm over her eyes. "Oh, don't say that. Please don't say that."

Uncle Henry touched her arm. "She's a girl turnin' into a woman. You gotta expect some upheaval through that. And you can survive it if you learn how to roll with it. But I don't think you're gonna have any luck at tryin' to avoid it."

"So you think I should let her go to Satsuma on Saturday?"

Behind his glasses, Uncle Henry's blue eyes gleamed. "She was rude and out of place, but what she said had some truth in it. You can't stop her life because of one missing girl. Eventually everyone has to—"

My mother cut him off. "We're gonna find her," she said curtly, staring intensely back at him.

I didn't quite understand her reaction, but Uncle Henry just nodded solemnly and looked down at the table. "I reckon you will, sooner or later," he said.

"It'll be sooner," my mother said. She sounded almost angry.

Uncle Henry nodded again, but said nothing in reply. I had noticed my mother growing progressively more anxious with each passing day since Mary Ann Dailey went missing. She didn't talk about it much in front of me, but what little I heard made it sound like there wasn't a lot of progress in the case. There was a frustrating lack of clues and she was quickly running out of people to question. She had even made at least two trips I knew of down to Satsuma to talk to kids and teachers at Mary Ann's school.

She let out a sigh. "Okay, so I let her go to Satsuma. Now my second question: How much of what she's tellin' us that she's going to Satsuma for do I trust? You saw her face when I asked about Jessica Thompson. She ain't goin'."

"Ah," Uncle Henry said, obviously happy to have moved to a new part in the conversation. "Now that's a different question entirely. I reckon the *spirit* of what she's sayin' is true. I reckon she is goin' for pizza and a movie, but it's with a *friend*. Singular."

One eyebrow lifted on my mother's face. "So, you're thinkin' the same as me, then."

"Probably. And you're right. The Thompson girl ain't goin'. Caroline's hopin' you won't call and check up. She's hopin' you won't call her bluff."

"I don't get it," I said. "What are y'all talkin' 'bout?"

"Mind your business," my mother said, and turned back to Uncle Henry. "So do I still let her go?"

"As I said, I can't assume to offer better parentin' advice than—"

"Just tell me, damn it."

Uncle Henry shot me a glance. "Gets a mite testy, don't she?"

I laughed.

"Leah," he said, "she's headin' into an age where you're about to lose pretty near all control you ever had over her. Right now, she's still askin', and that's a *good* thing. You wanna keep that up as long as possible. So, yes, I say you let her go, and you trust that you've done a good enough job these last fourteen odd years that she's got enough judgment to stay on the good side of stupid. And you *don't* check up on her story, no matter how much you'll want to. That'll just put her on the spot. That's the cop in you thinking— not the parent. She'll be fifteen in a couple months. That's only two years younger than you were when you *had* her."

"Well, that's exactly my point," my mother said.

Uncle Henry shrugged. "You turned out okay. Everything happens for a reason."

She laughed. "I was the other side of stupid, that was the reason. The bad side."

"That could be."

We all laughed then and went back to eating. My

thoughts returned to Mr. Wyatt Edward Farrow and something new occurred to me. "Mom? Do you think maybe Mr. Farrow might have snatched up Mary Ann Dailey?"

Confusion fell over her face. "Now, where in the world would you get an idea like that?"

"Well, he's just suspicious, is all," I said. "He's doin' somethin' sneaky."

"Why do you think he's doin' somethin' sneaky?" she asked.

I looked across at Uncle Henry for backup, but he wasn't even looking at me. "Well, me and Dewey . . . we've sorta been watchin' him, and there's some disturbin' things we've noticed. You know, he never leaves that garage, not even to go to the bathroom?"

My mother wiped her mouth and set down her napkin. "How in the Lord's name would you boys know anythin' 'bout that man's bathroom schedule?"

"We watch from the lawn. The lights never come on in the rest of the house. Dewey thinks maybe he goes to the toilet in the dark, though."

She shook her head. Her eyes were full of disbelief. "Do you boys go to the bathroom while you're spyin' on the neighbor?"

I furrowed my brow, thinking about this, and realized that we didn't. Then I realized if we could go that long without going, probably so could Mr. Farrow. My mother noticed the revelation on my face. "Stop thinkin' bad things about the neighbors. It ain't neighborly," she said.

Uncle Henry still refused to offer even a smidgeon of support. "But, Mama, he *never* leaves that house. Ever."

"What does he eat?" she asked.

"What do you mean?"

"He told us he works *nights*. And I've seen him walkin' in the early mornings many times. I think he goes for walks after finishing workin' all night and then comes back and sleeps all day. But for cryin' out loud, Abe, he has to buy groceries. You should be able to figure out for yourself that he must leave the house sometimes. Just not the times you boys are stakin' it out."

All this made perfect sense when she laid it out like that. I couldn't figure out why Uncle Henry was keeping so quiet, though. Only a couple hours earlier he had been telling me and Dewey that we were on to something. Even in light of this new information, I still knew we were. In fact, it was all starting to add up and make some kind of sense in my head. When we finally finished dinner and I helped clean up and dry the dishes, I phoned Dewey and quietly told him my new theory.

"I figured it all out," I said. "Mr. Farrow goes out every mornin' and collects all the roadkill. My mom's even seen him leavin' many times."

I could sense Dewey's excitement even through the telephone line. "What does he do with it?" he asked. "You reckon he eats it like old Newt Parker?"

"Nah, Mr. Farrow buys groceries to eat," I said. Then I looked around to make sure my mother and Uncle Henry weren't in listening distance and said, "I reckon Mr. Farrow is using that roadkill to make himself some sort of monster."

Dewey gasped. "Like Frankenstein."

"Exactly like Frankenstein," I said. "Only *Roadkill* Frankenstein."

I think we both knew then we had hit the hammer straight down onto the spike. A moment of silent awe transpired.

"Oh," I said, before hanging up, "and I asked my mom about Saturday. She said it would be fine if you slept over."

CHAPTER 6

The Alvin Police Station was a small brick building pretty much indistinguishable among the rest of the buildings along Main Street. The only two structures downtown that really stood out as being impressive were the library and the courthouse. They stood at opposite ends and opposite sides of the street. Towering a good story above everything else, they both had white marbled columns and expansive steps that led up to huge wooden doors. The courthouse even had a couple of marble lions sitting on brick platforms out front of it.

But the police station where my mother worked was just a one-story building set slightly back from the street. Inside were two gray desks separated by a partition. The desks belonged to my mother and Officer Christopher Jackson. A computer and a telephone sat on each one. My mother's desk had a stuffed dog with a blue ribbon wrapped around its neck sitting beside her computer screen. I bought her that dog two years ago for Mother's Day. She gave me the money, but I went downtown and bought it myself. Carry gave her a cactus, but it died.

On the back wall was a locked door that led to the jail.

I'd seen the jail a couple times. There's a photograph in my bedroom of me and Dewey locked inside, gripping the bars and trying to push our faces between them. The jail was very small. I could almost reach from front to back, and probably if me and Dewey touched fingers, we could reach across the other way. A single lightbulb lit the room very dimly and the walls were an ugly mustard color. Being locked up was fun for the fifteen minutes Officer Jackson kept us there for, pretending we were legendary train robbers, but I figured for most people, the fun started running out pretty quickly after that. It would get a mite depressing.

The thick metal door (that from this side looked like a normal door) hid the claustrophobic cell pretty near completely from the rest of the station. Fluorescents in the ceiling brightly bounced off the white office walls and tiled floor. Compared to the jail, everything out here was cheery.

At the other end of the room from the jail door was Police Chief Ethan Montgomery's office. It had glass walls covered by venetian blinds. I had only been in Chief Montgomery's office a few times. It seemed to me much too small for his large cherry desk and high-backed burgundy chair. They pretty near filled most of the whole thing. I'm not even a hundred percent sure how that desk came in through his office door.

Chief Montgomery's office had everything, even satellite television. The TV hung from the ceiling. Chief Montgomery rarely missed a game. It didn't matter which sport it was, he followed everything.

Today was Friday morning. Mary Ann Dailey had been gone exactly one week, and me and my mother picked up Dewey for school twenty minutes earlier than usual on account of my mother having to go to the station first and talk to Chief Montgomery. He had called bright and early and woke us up. I heard my mother take the call just as Uncle Henry came back in from walking Carry to her bus stop.

The Mary Ann Dailey incident had thrown everybody's life into a twist and nobody's life was more twisted than my mother's. I rarely saw her anymore. Even though, from what I could tell, the trail to solving the case dead-ended days ago, she still spent most nearly all her time at work. I didn't know when she slept. By how she looked, I guessed she didn't do it much. Her eyes had dark rings beneath them and there were creases in her face that weren't usually there. In one week, she seemed to have aged ten years. And she had grown irritable. So much so that, even those times when she was home, I tried to stay out of her way. Last night she had even snapped at Uncle Henry.

I had been in bed maybe thirty minutes when I heard my mother come home. Barely ten minutes after that, she went off on him.

"You're investin' way too much personal emotion in your work, Leah," I had heard him say. Uncle Henry had a deep voice that reverberated through walls, so I could always hear him from my room. Normally, I wasn't privy to my mother's side of the conversations, but lately she talked in a raised, clipped voice that sailed across floors and down halls like a sparrow going through barn rafters.

"What do you suggest I do, Hank?"

"I suggest you take a break. Get some sleep. Get some distance."

"Well, tomorrow that little girl will've been gone one week," my mother said. "Do you understand how much lower our odds of finding her are *now* than they were five or six days ago?"

"I understand your odds are lower with you looking like shit and not sleeping," he had responded. Hearing Uncle Henry curse surprised me.

"Every day I don't find that girl is one day closer to her becoming a statistic, Hank. I'm not gonna have that on my conscience again."

"You're taking this whole goddamn thing personally, Leah. You can't do that. You're not responsible for that girl."

"Then who is? If *I'm* not responsible, who the *hell* is? I'm the person everybody's expectin' to find her. Look around you, Hank. Ain't nobody else searchin' her out. You told me not to give up. Well, guess what? I ain't givin' up."

"I didn't tell you to become obsessed."

"I ain't obsessed."

"Leah, listen to me. This whole thing has clutched you by the throat. It's dredged up emotions still lingerin' from what happened to Ruby Mae Vickers. You *are* obsessed, you just don't see it. You're trying to settle a twelve-year-old score with yourself for what happened to Ruby Mae. But you didn't *let* that happen."

"Then who the hell *did,* Hank? Who did? I had three months to find her. Three goddamn months. Then she gets delivered to me, and I *still* couldn't figure out who did it. You saw the autopsy report. You know what that girl went through those three months I failed to find her. Whoever had her used her every way they could think of. By the looks of things, she became part of their daily schedule." My mother's voice had started cracking, but even still she was on the verge of hollering it had risen so loud.

"You did your best, Leah."

"Well, my best wasn't goddamn good enough, was it? I think about Ruby Mae and then I think, what if the same thing's happenin' to Mary Ann Dailey? What if every day I don't find her is another day of her havin' to endure . . ." Then my mother had begun crying, unable to finish her sentence.

"See?" Uncle Henry said, with no compassion in his voice. "You're obsessed. You've been obsessed for twelve years. And no matter what happens. No matter if you find Mary Ann Dailey, or if she never turns up, or if she turns up the same way Ruby Mae did. None of it's gonna change what happened twelve years ago."

My mother choked back her tears. "She won't end up the—"

But Uncle Henry cut her off, loudly and angrily. "She might! She goddamn very well could, and you better be prepared for that. It's your *job* to be prepared for that. At this point, from where I'm standin', odds are lookin' in favor of her either not turnin' up or turnin' up dead."

"Go to hell!" my mother said. And I heard her stomp down the hall into her room and slam her door. She reminded me exactly of Carry, only Carry had been happy yesterday because she came home to find a note from my mother magneted to the fridge saying it would be fine for her to go to Satsuma for a movie and pizza with her friends, so long as she made sure to get home by five in time for supper.

Earlier is better, my mother had written at the bottom.

All I knew when I turned over and pulled my blanket up to my chin was that I sure hoped this case would be over soon. I didn't know if any of us were going to survive it much longer, never mind Mary Ann Dailey.

But, this morning as we drove to the station, my mother seemed to have gotten over all her agitation from last night, though I could tell it hadn't gone very far. It was just behind her eyes, looking for any chance to pop out again. I hoped for Dewey's sake that chance wouldn't come. I was growing used to having to treat the women of my household as though they were crates of dynamite, but I had the feeling Dewey would be awfully surprised to see my mother blow up.

"You guys stay in here and don't touch anything on the desks," my mother said. Chris Jackson wasn't at work yet, so the office was empty. The door into Chief Montgomery's office was open and I could hear him shuffling about, but couldn't see him on account of the blinds being closed over the windows.

Along with the desks, the office had a photocopier, and a table with a coffeemaker and stuff like that on it. A potted palm sat beside the table. There was also a watercooler.

Dewey immediately started playing with the watercooler, pulling out one of the paper cups that nobody ever used and filling it in spurts. Sometimes it amazed me how easily amused he was. But then we both liked balancing rocks on sticks, so what did I know?

My mother pushed Chief Montgomery's door closed, but it didn't close all the way, so I wandered across and pretended to be fascinated with the coffee machine while I did my best to listen to their conversation. I missed all the formalities and came in straight on what was the crux of the matter, I figured.

"I'm thinkin' I made a mistake givin' you this case," Chief Montgomery said.

"You never gave me this case," my mother answered. "Mrs. Dailey called me directly at home. *She* gave me this case."

"Well, you know what I mean. I'm thinkin' maybe you should step back and give this one to Jackson."

I heard my mother let out a loud huff. "What is it with you people? Why does everyone think my tryin' as hard as I can to find this Dailey girl is a bad thing?"

"I don't rightly know who us 'people' are, Leah, but it's not what you're doin' that's worryin' me, it's *how* you're doin' it."

"I'm taking responsibility."

There was a squeak. I guessed Chief Montgomery sat back in his chair, probably to take a sip of coffee. When he spoke again, his voice was low and calm. "You take too much responsibility. You always have. Ever since . . ." He drifted off into a whisper.

"Oh, don't start that shit, Ethan. Don't go not mentionin' things just because you think they're gonna wind me up."

"That's not what I'm doin', Leah. Trust me, you're

upset enough. I don't know if you could get much more upset."

"Yeah? Well, start tellin' me how I've taken on too much responsibility since Billy died and just *watch*. What did you expect me to do? He left me alone with a brand-new baby and not even a pot to piss in, and you're tellin' me *I took on too much responsibility*? Give your head a shake. I didn't see anybody else stepping up to the plate."

"First, it's almost like you still blame Billy for dying and leaving you alone to raise those kids, Leah. You've got to get over that. Shit happens. And second, your parents were there for you. You could've leaned on them much more than you did."

"It wasn't their job to be there for me, Ethan. *I'm* the one who got pregnant at seventeen. It was *my* mess. It still is."

"I'm just saying you take on too much because you're *used* to taking on too much."

Across the room, binders were stuffed into shelves that ran along one of the office walls. I had no idea what sort of things were in the binders. Dewey finally tired of the watercooler and moved on to them. Starting at the left, one by one he pulled them out halfway and then pushed them back in with a clunk. I wished he could find something quieter to entertain himself with.

"Yeah," my mother said, "well, look at my life, Ethan. It hasn't really been full of consistent support for me and my children. And when I finally did find a guy who didn't run out on me? We have two babies, and then two years later he's killed in a car crash. Then Ma goes. Then Pa goes. There comes a point where you kinda stop and realize there ain't nobody you can depend on for the long haul 'cept yourself."

"Your pa was there for you right up until the end, Leah," Chief Montgomery said. "He may have had to retire from the force, but he never retired from his responsibility to you and those kids."

My mother sighed. "Yeah, it was great, Ethan. Abe got to spend the first six years of his life falling in love with his grandpa, while watching him deteriorate away to nothing. I think I would've rather had Pa go quickly the way Ma did."

Chief Montgomery said nothing.

"I think in some ways he *did* go the day Mom did," my mother said. "At least part of him did."

"Of course that's true," Mr. Montgomery said. "Christ, Leah, they were married for near on their whole lives. All they *had* was each other."

There was another pause, then my mother said, "Until I came along and messed it all up."

"Now, how in your mind did you mess everything up? Sometimes I wonder how you think."

"I got myself pregnant at seventeen, Ethan."

"Sure you did. And your pa was right pissed about it. I remember him telling me he was gonna shoot the little bastard who did that to his daughter. But you know what? He *didn't*. And that little bastard turned out to actually be a decent guy. Billy did right by you. And, even though you don't need me to tell you how dead set against you marrying Billy your daddy was, both your ma and your pa showed up at your wedding, and they smiled like they was proud as peacocks to see their little girl looking so beautiful. On account of they *was,* Leah. And I ain't *never* seen a man love his grandchildren the way your pa did. That man would've redirected the Mississippi if he thought it would've put a smile on little Caroline Josephine's face."

"You're right. They was even nice to Billy *after* the wedding."

"Of course they was. That's the way your folks were. Your pa only hated Billy on account of he reckoned he was taking you away from him."

"You think?"

"I do. When it came down to it, your pa would always be there for you, no matter *who* you married. I remember how concerned he was for you when Billy died. It was *real* concern, Leah. He worried about you and those kids *constantly*. You could've relied on him much more than you did."

"He was in no shape to worry about me," my mother said. "I should've been worrying more about *him*."

"He got *sick*, Leah. There's nothing you could've done differently to save him. Be happy Abe got to spend as much time with him as he did. He has good memories of his grandpa. Happy ones. Nobody can ever take those away from him."

Silence followed and I had to come in close to hear my mother when she spoke again, because her voice was so quiet. "You're right, Ethan. I know you're right. It's just so hard. Sometimes I miss him so much." I heard tears in my mother's voice. I always hated it when she cried, and lately she'd been crying more than ever.

But Chief Montgomery didn't let up. "And your pa made certain you were financially okay," he said. "He made *damn* sure of that. Christ, Leah, he got you this job."

"Yeah, but you know? It's not always about the money, Ethan. And even if it was, when you're blindsided a half dozen times in as many years, you learn to look out for yourself. And your kids. And if that's taking on too much responsibility, well, then I guess I'm guilty."

I heard Chief Montgomery's mug settle onto his desk. "Leah, nobody's ever gonna accuse you of not being a good mother to those kids. That's not what I'm talkin' 'bout and you know it. I'm talkin' 'bout the way it's all spilled over into this case. I'm talking about Ruby Mae Vickers. And don't you even try to tell me you don't think Ruby Mae had nothin' to do with your pa dyin'."

There was a pause and then my mother's voice rose a good octave. "What the hell are you talkin' 'bout now?"

"You've never forgiven yourself for Ruby Mae because she was your first big case and you've always felt you let your father down. You were promoted to detective and you botched your first case and never got over it. I was there, Leah, remember? I know you thought you disappointed your pa, and that disappointment put some distance between you. Distance I know now that you regret."

"You're crazy. There was no distance between us."

"There was so, and that's why you were so hellbent on raisin' them kids yourself.

"No, Leah, I'm not crazy. What you tend to forget is that you ain't really no detective. Alvin is too small for a detective. You were given this position only so that we could raise your salary, not because anyone expected you to suddenly be some kind of super crime solver. If it weren't for the county regulations, you'd just be a cop like the rest of us. You *are* just a cop like the rest of us. You have no extra responsibilities, so stop pretendin' you do."

Another long pause and then I heard my mom sniffling. "I miss Dad a lot sometimes."

Chief Montgomery's chair squeaked again as I heard him get up and come around his desk. "Oh, honey, we all do. Your dad was a great cop. And a great father. And he'd be nothing but proud of you. I know you don't believe that, but I knew your dad better than anyone. For over twenty-three years I worked with Joe. I was there for him when you got pregnant with Carry. Had you been my daughter? I'da been swearing a side off a greased-up hog, but your pa? He never once said a bad word about it. He was nothin' but proud."

I heard more crying from my mother.

Chief Montgomery continued talking. "Oh, he was ready to hunt down and kill that Billy Cunningham kid, don't get me wrong. I had to talk him down a few times. But not because he didn't love you or Carry. See, you come by this responsibility thing naturally. Your pa never once left a mistake without fixing it up one way or another. But if he were here right now, I can promise you this: He'd tell you it's time to stop blaming the world on yourself. There are things you can control and things you cannot. Focus on the right ones, cuz the others are like bashing your head against a wall of bricks. You follow?"

I heard more sniffles.

"I'm serious, Leah. If you don't understand this, I'm pullin' you off this case."

"I understand," my mother said quietly.

Dewey finished his game with the binders and came over to where I stood. "What're you doing?" he whispered.

I shushed him.

"What?" he asked.

"Listenin'," I said.

"What're they sayin'?" he whispered back.

I shushed him again. That's when we both looked up and found Ethan Montgomery standing over us with the door open.

He leveled his eyes directly at me. "You boys need to learn to mind your business," he said. I could tell he was mad, but not real mad.

"My mom tells me that all the time," I said.

This almost made him smile, but he held it back. "Your mom's a smart woman. Do you good to listen to her instead of eavesdroppin' on our conversations. You got that?"

I said I most certainly did as I tried to look around the doorway to where my mother was standing holding a Kleenex up at her face, but Chief Montgomery stepped sideways, blocking my view. "What did I just tell you?" he asked.

I was about to question why my mom wasn't my business, but Dewey interrupted, pointing to the gun on Chief Montgomery's hip. "That real?" he asked.

"What do you think?" I asked him back. "Now why would the chief of police carry around a fake gun?" I looked up at Chief Montgomery and smiled.

"Think you're pretty smart, hey?" he asked back. I thought about replying, telling him how I didn't think it took a lot of brains to figure that one out (which would really be a remark directed at Dewey), but decided things were too strange lately and I might not be the best judge of what's permissible for me to say and what's not at this particular point in time. So I just let it go.

My mother stepped to the door. "You okay?" Chief Montgomery asked her.

She nodded. She wasn't crying, but her eyes were red. The Kleenex was gone from her hand.

"You're gonna remember what I said?" Chief Montgomery asked.

She nodded.

"All right. Then for now, you're still on the case. But I'm watchin' you." He did the "I'm watching you" sign with his two fingers by pointing them first at his eyes and then at her. Then he gave me a wink, making things feel almost normal again.

CHAPTER 7

The next afternoon was the afternoon Carry was meant to go to Satsuma to meet her friends for a pizza and a movie. I was still uncertain about what she was really doing and what she was saying she was doing and how the two things were different in the minds of my mother and Uncle Henry, but I gave up trying to sort it out. There were more important things to think about.

Like how Mr. Wyatt Edward Farrow and the missing roadkill was connected. I was still clinging to my theory of the Roadkill Frankenstein monster. It was a good one, I thought. One that made a lot of sense when you plugged in all the different variables.

My mother drove Carry to the bus stop for Satsuma. On the weekends the bus came to the top of Main Street, almost all the way up to the courthouse building. I came along for the ride. Once we got back home, Dewey would be coming over and spending the night, so I decided to get as much non-Dewey family time in as I could.

My mother pulled up to the curb in front of the bus

stop and Carry got out, dragging her backpack from the floor of her seat and hefting it onto her shoulder. She had been sitting in the passenger front seat of the car and the window was rolled down. The day was exceptionally mild, a nice change from all our recent rain. Carry shut the door and said good-bye before going over to the bench beside the stop and having a seat.

The car remained at the curb. Both me and Carry looked at my mother expectantly. After a few seconds, Carry closed her eyes, stood and, leaving her backpack on the bench, came over to the open window. "You're not gonna sit here and wait until the bus comes, are you?"

My mother sighed.

"Why don't you just follow me all around Satsuma?" Carry asked with a defiant gleam in her eyes.

"I would if I thought I could get away with it."

"Mother," Carry said, "either you're okay with me going on my own or you aren't. This is ridiculous."

My mother took two deep breaths before responding. "You're right. I'll leave you to wait for the bus. Remember: home by five."

"Bye, Mother," Carry said, turning her back and returning to the bench.

Pulling away from the curb, my mother turned down the first side street, turned the car around, and headed back down Main Street toward our house, taking one last glance at Carry as we went past. "I hope you never go through this, Abe," she said to me.

I was about to make a snide remark, asking if she meant she hoped I was never going to discover boys, when something darted out in front of us from between two buildings. For a brief second, I saw it, frozen in place like a picture. It was a possum. Then there was the unmistakable double bump as the car ran it over.

I turned around and looked out the back window at the brown lump of dead possum lying in our wake. I couldn't believe it.

I couldn't wait to tell Dewey. The roadkill was back.

Then we stopped at the intersection in front of where the new sushi restaurant was being built. Well, the building was already there, they were just putting a new front on it. That was pretty much all the construction that happened on Main Street. The buildings were all brick and stone so they weren't going anywhere anytime soon. Shops would just redress the front and sometimes add new walls inside.

This restaurant had intrigued me and Dewey since they first started hanging the plywood signs from the top. A big purple fish arched above the main window with an army of Japanese people spewing from its open mouth, carrying thick swords and big silver shields. I laughed again now as we drove past.

"What?" Mom asked.

"That place looks funny."

"Why?"

"Because it's called the Happy Shogun Sushi Palace and I don't think the fish or the guys with the swords look very happy. And is the fish swallowing them? Or are they coming out of his stomach?"

"Sounds like you've put a lot of thought into this already."

A week ago the name had appeared along the bottom of the window, and me and Dewey nearly split a gut when we saw it. We'd heard about sushi, of course, but neither of us had ever tried it. "Isn't sushi like raw fish? Who wants to eat that? It doesn't sound very good," I said.

"You have no idea how good it is until you try it. You shouldn't judge things like that. Millions of people around the world love sushi."

"Not people in Alabama."

"Not yet. We're only startin' to see the sort of immigration that brings people to our town who will offer us new food like this. You should be happy about it." The Japanese family who owned the restaurant were called the Takahashis. They had moved to Alvin at the beginning of summer and were the topic of conversation for most of July.

I looked back at the fish. It had sharp teeth and the sword guys looked pretty mean. "Maybe the Takahashis took Mary Ann Dailey," I said. For all I knew, Japanese people might eat little girls. If you ate raw fish, you probably ate anything.

"Now why do you say that?"

"Well, they just moved in a few months ago and then Mary Ann disappears. Just the timin' is all."

"Listen, Abe, I don't want you accusing people just because of no reason. That's twice you've done that. I don't want you accusing our neighbor because he works all night in his garage, and I especially don't want no accusing because people are Japanese or any culture different than yours. That's racist. And I am not raising no racist. Not under my roof."

"Well, they all have names that sound like Power Rangers," I said, ignoring her comment about Mr. Wyatt Edward Farrow, who, secretly, was still my prime suspect. Not just in the case of Mary Ann Dailey, but in everything.

"What? I'm gonna pretend I didn't even hear that."

"Why? Saying their names sound like a cartoon is racist?"

"Of course it's racist, Abe. Don't you even know? Remind me to get your Uncle Henry to discuss this with you."

I didn't see how something true could be racist. I didn't say having cartoon names was a bad thing or nothing. I would actually like a weird name. Especially if it came with super powers of some sort. I decided to keep this thought to myself.

"What's sushi like?" I asked instead.

"I don't know, but I'm gonna try it before I say I don't like it. I think it's great that we get a chance to broaden our horizons without even leaving Alvin. This is one of the reasons for the outreach program."

The outreach program was sponsored by our church in an effort to bring more immigration to Alvin. Me and my mother donated money once a week. The church had helped the Takahashis move here. So, in a way, I guess we're partly responsible for them and their new sushi restaurant.

"Okay, I'll try it too, then, before I say I hate it," I said.

She sighed. "Well, that's a start."

"What's a shogun?" I asked.

"Actually, I don't rightly know that, either. Some kind of Japanese warrior. I bet this is another good question for Uncle Henry. Then, after you find out, you can tell me and we'll both learn something. Or, better yet, next time you see Mr. Takahashi, why don't you ask *him*? Just don't say anything racist."

"I reckon I don't know what's racist and what isn't," I said.

"Okay, stick with plan A," she said. "Ask Uncle Henry. That was a better idea."

CHAPTER 8

As soon as Mom pulled into the drive, I raced inside to call Dewey and tell him about the roadkill. He was skeptical. "Did you actually *hit* it? Or just see it?"

"Both. I mean, we hit it and then I looked back and there it was."

"You're *sure*?"

"Dewey, I'm telling you we ran over a possum. It's splattered across Main Street."

I could hear him sigh through the phone. "Okay, I'm bringing my bike over. Let's go check it out."

Mom stopped me on the way outside. "Where are you going?"

"With Dewey for a bike ride."

She did a weird thing then. She just stood there like she almost wasn't going to let me go. "Mom, I'll be with *Dewey*. On a *bike*." I knew she was thinking about Carry off by herself for the day in Satsuma. I felt like telling her: *I'm not going to Satsuma, I'm going down the street a mile*. But I decided not to.

With a big breath, she looked away and came to a decision. "Okay, but don't be long, all right? An hour?"

"I don't have a watch."

"We'll have to get you one."

"Okay, but I don't have one today."

Uncle Henry must've been listening from the living room where he was watching television. He came in and handed me his Timex. "Here, now you have a watch," he said. "Please, for your mother's sake, don't be late?"

His seriousness almost scared me. "I won't," I said. "We're just going downtown to check somethin' out. Then we'll be right back."

Mom looked puzzled. "Check what out?"

I looked to Uncle Henry. "Mom hit a possum on the way home from droppin' off Carry. Dewey doesn't believe me."

Uncle Henry's eyebrows went up. "Really?" He looked at my mother. "You really hit a possum?"

She shook her head, shrugging. "I dunno, I might have. Why? Since when is hitting a possum such a big deal?"

"Oh," Uncle Henry said, nodding, "it's a big deal to some people right now." He gave me a wink. "I'll explain it to her. You go make sure it's still there and actually dead. Then come home and tell me how this affects the overall theory."

My mother looked at him like he'd lost his marbles. I thanked him for the watch and went out the door.

"One hour!" my mother called after me. "Or less. Less is okay, too."

We weren't even halfway to Main Street when we found a dead raccoon lying on the side of the road. By the looks of things, it had probably been there near on a week. We got off our bikes and inspected it thoroughly. Dewey even poked it with a stick. "It's over." He sighed.

I frowned. I hadn't realized how much more interesting life was with an unsolved roadkill mystery hanging over it. This was like someone had set a giant piece of birthday cake in front of us, then laid down a big ol' fork, and then, at the last minute, took away the cake. All we had was forks.

And dead animals on the road.

Still, we continued on to Main Street to double-check that the possum my mother killed on our way home was actually dead. It was. Pretty much in the same state of deadness as the raccoon, only more fresh.

"Well, this ain't the way I wanted this to end," Dewey said. Neither of us did.

"After what Uncle Henry said, I really thought it had something to do with Mr. Wyatt Edward Farrow," I said.

"I still think he's up to no good," Dewey said. "Could be he just hasn't gone collectin' for a while."

"Dewey, that raccoon has been there at least four or five days."

"Maybe he's saved up so much he's got a stockpile," Dewey offered, but I could tell he was scrambling.

"Could be," I said. We wanted to believe it, that's for sure.

"Even if he isn't stockpiling roadkill, I still think he's up to no good," Dewey said.

"Oh, I know he is," I said. "It's just some kind of no

good that ain't got nothing to do with disappearing roadkill. At least not no more."

"So we still have a mystery." Dewey smiled.

"He's still at the top of my suspect list," I said.

"Mine, too."

For what, neither of us knew. I pulled Uncle Henry's watch from my pocket. It was too big to wear around my wrist. "My mom told me to be home in an hour. We still got twenty-seven minutes, not countin' the fifteen it'll take to get back."

That was when Tiffany Michelle Yates came out of Igloo's with an ice cream cone in her hand nearly as big as my head. It was one of those waffle cones and the ice cream was pink.

"What kind of ice cream is pink?" Dewey asked.

"Bubble gum," she said with a big grin. Her teeth looked especially white against her dark face.

"Looks girlie to me," I said.

"I'm a girl," Tiffany Michelle Yates said. And she was. A black girl two years younger than Carry that Carry used to sometimes play with. That was back before Carry discovered boys and what Mom called *cliques*. Now Carry wouldn't be seen as dead as this possum playing with a thirteen-year-old.

"What're y'all doing?" she asked. She wore a pretty pink dress that matched her ice cream, and her hair looked freshly washed with a bright yellow ribbon tying it back. She looked as though she belonged on a postcard for Alvin with that giant ice cream cone in her hand.

"The roadkill came back," Dewey explained.

She lifted an eyebrow. "What?"

"It had all disappeared for the longest time, but now it's back." He pointed to the possum on the road. "Abe's mom killed this one."

"Okay," she said, looking at us like we fell off the back of a nut truck. We watched her continue down the sidewalk, eating her ice cream.

"Girls can be so weird," Dewey said, mounting his bike. "I doubt I'll ever understand them."

I thought of Carry and agreed. "I know you never will. They're not understandable. I think that's their reason for existin'. Uncle Henry told me somethin' like that once."

We rode down the sidewalk, showing off by going no hands and saying, "Bye," to Tiffany Michelle and her giant ice cream cone as we went past.

From what my mother would later find out, it was the last thing anybody said to her before she disappeared.

CHAPTER 9

We made it back home with ten minutes to spare. My mother was happy about that, and when I returned the watch to Uncle Henry, he promised to buy me my own next time he was in town. I could tell my mother was still a little concerned about Carry, even though she still had three hours to go until the time she had promised to be back home.

Mom made us some chicken noodle soup and we ate it in the living room while watching television. Cooking and television were nice distractions for her, but every time a show ended I saw her glance over at the clock on the mantel and get a bit more antsy.

"Stop worryin'," Uncle Henry said at four. "She promised to be home at five, she'll be home by five. Besides, I thought you was goin' into work this afternoon?"

"What if she ain't back by five?" my mother asked.

"Then we'll deal with that then. Don't make up problems ahead of time that don't even exist yet." He flipped through the channels, stopping at some fishing show.

"You're not gonna make us watch people fish, are you?" I asked.

"It's kind of relaxin'," he said. "I think your mom could use some relaxin'." He looked at my mother. "That is, if she ain't goin' to work like she says she was gonna. Are you goin' in or not?"

"So far I've decided to take the day off. I'll make an official decision come five."

"Fishin's relaxin' like watchin' paint peel's relaxin'," Dewey said. We all laughed until the telephone rang, interrupting us. The sound of it made my mother nearly jump out of her skin.

"Quit thinkin' the worst," Uncle Henry said, watching her get up to answer it. "It's got nothing to do with Caroline."

He was right. It didn't.

But I could tell my mother was still terrified when she hung up the phone after taking the call.

Uncle Henry could tell, too. It was in his voice. "Who was it?" He was out of his chair, out of the living room, and standing right beside her. I was behind him. Dewey was still in the living room watching people fish.

"Mrs. Yates. Tiffany . . . her daughter. She's missing."

"*Missing* missing?" Uncle Henry asked. "Or just ten minutes late coming home?"

My mother looked stunned. "*Missing* missing. Goin' on near three hours, Mrs. Yates said. Tiffany Michelle was supposed to meet her friend at the movie house at two. She never showed up."

I thought this over and then spoke up. "Dewey and

me saw her right before then," I said. "She was on Main Street with the biggest ice cream cone I ever seen. One of those big ol' waffle cones. The ice cream was pink just like her dress. She asked us what we was doin' and we told her studyin' the roadkill that all came back. We even showed her the possum you runned over, but she didn't seem to care so much about it, just that big waffle cone. I swear it was the biggest one I ever seen."

Uncle Henry held up his palm. "Slow down there, son. We don't care so much about the ice cream. Are you sure it was Tiffany Yates?"

I nodded. "Tiffany Michelle Yates. She had a bright yellow bow in her hair and looked like she'd just had a shampoo. I reckoned the way she looked she belonged on some sort of postcard or jigsaw puzzle or somethin'." I thought all my details were helpful, but nobody seemed to want to hear about them so much.

"Are you sure it was right before that time? How do you know?"

"Cuz I was wearin' your watch, remember?"

"Put on your shoes and coat," my mother said to me. "Dewey, you, too."

"How come?" I asked.

"Cuz you're witnesses. You could be the last people who saw this girl before she disappeared."

I frowned; something in my stomach clenched. "Where are you takin' us? We ain't goin' to jail or nothin' like that, is we?"

My mother shook her head, giving Uncle Henry as much of a half smile as she could in her state. "Of course not. You're coming with me to see Mr. and Mrs.

Yates. They're gonna wanna talk to you. Then we're gonna go to Main Street and you're gonna explain exactly where you saw her and what she said and everything else."

I thought I'd already explained it pretty thoroughly, but I didn't mind doing it again. It made it seem like Dewey and me were kind of special now that we were witnesses and all. We put on our shoes while my mother went into the bedroom and changed into her uniform. She came out wearing her gun and everything.

The Yateses lived in the same area as Luther Willard King. In fact, I had ridden my bike past their house the last time I brought Luther Willard the ten dollars from my mother for not mowing our lawn. I remembered back to the first time I made that trip. Back to those two girls practically naked playing in the dirt in front of the house and how I'd heard Luther Willard's father wheezing and coughing in the back, as close near death as a rat in a gator swamp. We drove slowly up Oakdale Road, my mother checking the house numbers. Six older black kids rode past my side of the car on bikes. They all smiled with big white grins.

The Yates didn't live in a rundown shotgun house like Luther Willard King, but their place wasn't a whole lot nicer than the Kings', either. It was cramped and gray. I couldn't tell if it once was painted or if that was the color it was supposed to be. They had a bit more lawn in the front, but it was patchy and mostly moss, especially around the concrete steps that led up to the screen door. At least the house's roof wasn't caved in. The garage, separated from the house, wasn't quite so lucky.

"That thing's gonna fall over right onto that car," I said as we parked at the end of the drive. "But by the looks of that car, I doubt anybody'll notice afterward."

Dewey laughed.

With a sigh, my mother shut off the engine and turned to me. "What's wrong with you? Why do you say stupid things like that?"

Dewey stopped laughing.

"Like what?" I asked. "Look at that car. I doubt it even runs without at least three or four of them black kids pushing it." Dewey laughed again. I thought I was being honest. Normally my mother valued honesty. Today, apparently, things were different. Right away, I knew I'd made a mistake.

Her face actually grew red and I could tell she was really mad. Dewey shut up again. I even flinched, thinking she might swat me one. "What? What'd I do?" I asked.

"That is the most racist thing I've ever heard come out of your mouth. I have a mind to go home and make you suck on a bar of Ivory soap."

"For what? What part of what I said was racist?" I looked back at Dewey, but he just shrugged.

"*All* of it, Abe. First off, where do you get off criticizin' other people's houses? You're lucky you have one to live in. You could very well have grown up far poorer than them."

"Like the Kings?" I asked. "Have you seen Luther Willard's place? It makes this one look like the Grand Hyatt down in Satsuma."

"You interrupted me, Abe; I wasn't finished. And you interrupted with yet another near racist comment. But we hadn't gotten to your worst one. The one about them boys pushin' that car around."

I sighed. "I guess I don't understand racism."

"I guess you should learn."

"How?" I asked.

"Well, there's two ways. The easy one and the hard one. I'd advise the easy one: Just figure it out for yourself, and when in doubt, keep quiet."

"What's the hard one?"

"Having some of them black kids give you a little reminder whenever you say something offensive. I don't reckon they'd have much understandin' for a little no-account white boy like yourself."

Narrowing my eyes, I studied my mother, trying to tell if she was kidding or not. I couldn't be sure, so I decided to err on the safe side and go with trying to figure things out the easy way.

Mr. Yates answered the door and invited us into the front room, which he referred to as the parlor. A tall, thin man, he wore an unbuttoned yellow shirt over a white T-shirt and brown pants. His chin was stubbly, as though he hadn't shaved in a couple days. He directed us to a flowered couch with worn cushions that sat in front of the window.

I ran my toe over the green shag carpet, trying not to notice Mrs. Yates crying. She was sitting in a mustard-colored chair in the corner by the fireplace, holding a hankie to her cheek, wiping back tears as she tried to talk about Tiffany Michelle. Mrs. Yates wasn't a thin women. She was short and stout, but carried herself with much grace. Her bright brown eyes gleamed behind her tears.

Mr. Yates brought in a pot of coffee and four mugs. I couldn't figure out why there were four, given there was only three adults in the room, but it turned out Mr. Yates didn't drink coffee. The extra two were for Dewey and me. I looked to my mother, but she shook her head. "It'll stunt your growth. And trust me, you two need every inch you can get."

Mr. Yates laughed at this, even though I could tell it was a forced laugh. He wasn't crying, but he was obviously just as upset about his daughter as his wife was.

My mom told them how Dewey and me had seen Tiffany on Main Street with the ice cream cone. They listened to me tell it a few minutes. I told them Tiffany was very pretty in her pink dress and yellow bow and that she looked like a postcard. This seemed to make them happy.

Dewey kept completely silent the whole time. It was certainly a change from his regular behavior.

"You don't think she's been taken like Mary Ann Dailey?" Mrs. Yates asked my mother. Mr. Yates, squatting beside her chair, put his hand up on her leg.

My mother sighed. I knew she didn't like the insinuation being made by someone else that Mary Ann Dailey had been nabbed by someone. My mother had come to this conclusion on her own very early on, but for some reason she took exception with anyone else having the same opinion. This time, she managed to keep her thoughts hidden away. I was glad of that. I think everyone in Alvin had resolved themselves to the fact that Mary Ann hadn't just wandered off and would turn up walking aimlessly down Main Street any moment. Even the kids at school knew most likely someone was responsible for her disappearance.

"She's been gone barely three hours," my mother said. "Normally we don't even consider people missing until forty-eight, so right now I wouldn't worry too much. She could be lost, she could have gotten distracted, she could be out with friends. At this point, there are still many possibilities. I wouldn't be too worried."

"Our Tiffany always goes where she says she's going," Mr. Yates said. "And she's never late comin' home."

I thought of Carry and looked over at my mother, but she was intently listening to the Yateses, nodding and taking notes. "Well, we're gonna go check Main Street where Abe and his friend here saw your daughter and ask around and see if anybody else saw her. I'll let you know as soon as I find anything out."

Tears welled in Mrs. Yates's eyes. "Please bring my baby home."

I felt my mother grow tense and she hesitated. Her breath caught in her throat. "I'll do my best, ma'am."

We drove up Main Street to Igloo's, where me and Dewey told Tiffany Michelle about the possum. After questioning everyone in the local stores and finding nobody who remembered seeing the girl, my mother made me go over the whole thing again, twice. Both times I made a big deal out of the roadkill she runned over still being there.

"Okay, Abe?" she said. "I'm not so interested in the

dead possum. Concentrate on the parts of the story involving Tiffany."

I tried explaining that the roadkill was the whole reason we were talking to Tiffany Michelle in the first place, but she didn't seem to care. I showed her where Tiffany had walked, and told her what she had said and how we rode past her with no hands and said, "Bye."

"You was showin' off for a girl?" my mother asked.

My eyes widened. "No."

My mother looked to Dewey. He was looking at his feet.

"Yes," she said. "You were. You were doing tricks, trying to impress Tiffany Michelle Yates."

I glanced away, wondering out loud: "Was that racist?"

My mother smiled slightly, shaking her head. "You really are clueless. Good thing you're cute. No, Abe, that was completely *not* racist. Just surprisin', is all. Didn't think you and Dewey noticed girls."

I considered this as we got back into the car. "I didn't, neither."

Dewey continued being unusually quiet.

My mother radioed Officer Chris Jackson at the station and told him about Tiffany Michelle Yates. She told him it was too early to tell if this had anything to do with Mary Ann Dailey. Then she said she was dropping me and Dewey at home and going to have a quick bite before coming in. "That is, providin' my daughter's back from her field trip to Satsuma."

I noticed the clock on her dash read 5:11. Carry should've walked in the door eleven minutes ago, but

Uncle Henry hadn't called my mother's car phone, so I wondered if maybe she hadn't.

"Oh, and, Chris," my mother said, "one last thing. What do you think about the idea of a curfew?"

He thought it wasn't a bad idea and they ended up deciding that, until Mary Ann Dailey and Tiffany Michelle Yates were found, everyone younger than eighteen had to be off the streets by seven o'clock.

"Get Montgomery to clear it with the mayor," my mother said. "Then get the local television and radios to put it out. And I think you'd do well to suggest they consider canceling the Harvest Fair." The Alvin Harvest Fair was probably the biggest event our town had all year. I couldn't believe my mother was considering canceling it. I couldn't believe she even had the *ability* to cancel it.

"You're canceling the fair?" I asked after she finished talking. Even Dewey found that surprising.

"Well, puttin' it on hold for now," she said. "We just can't have something like the fair going on when there's potentially people taking young girls; it's just too risky."

"I think a lot of people might be upset to hear there'll be no fair this year," I said.

"Well, those people should be more upset that there's little girls missing," my mother said.

I thought that over and decided it made sense. Then I asked, "What good's a seven o'clock curfew if Tiffany Michelle went missing at two o'clock in the afternoon?"

My mother picked at her teeth as she drove. I thought she either didn't hear me or was ignoring my question, but it turned out she was thinking it over. "It doesn't really do much good at all, I suspect," she finally replied. "But sometimes it's not about trying to keep kids safe. Sometimes it's about sending out a message."

She checked the clock on the dash. "And it's nearly quarter past five, so if your sister isn't home when we get there, the curfew won't do her much good either, because she'll be grounded forever."

CHAPTER 10

Apparently Carry would be grounded forever. She wasn't home yet. It was half past five and she had promised to be back from Satsuma *inside the door* (as my mom specified) by five.

Uncle Henry made his "world famous" jambalaya for dinner that night. I don't think it was famous outside of my mother, Carry, me, and maybe Dewey, but he claimed it was. He claimed lots of things. Growing up, I always assumed everything he said was true, but now that I had started questioning things, I was beginning to see a lot of it was likely him just pulling my leg or seeing how far he could go in making me believe things.

My mother was only home for a quick bite. With Tiffany Michelle Yates missing, she now had two girls to look for. Well, maybe three, counting her own daughter.

"I'm gonna wring her neck," my mother said as she began cleaning up the pots Uncle Henry used to cook with. "I cannot believe that girl's not home. I'm gonna *kill* her."

She was talking like she was mad, but I could hear more worry than anger in her voice. *Real* worry. Uncle Henry heard it too, I could tell. He kept saying to her that Carry was fine and that she was probably just waiting for a bus or testing out her limits by a half hour here or there.

"I'll show her limits," my mother said. I was thinking tonight would've been a better day for her to cook on account of it would've given her something to do. As it was, she just sort of followed Uncle Henry aimlessly around the kitchen.

"Why don't you go sit down and relax?" he asked.

"Because I don't relax."

He nodded. "You think about all the bad things in the world. You need to fix that."

"Hank, my daughter is *missing*."

Uncle Henry stopped stirring at the stove, turned, and grabbed her by the shoulders. "No, Leah, she is *not*. Your daughter is *late*. It's important that you distinguish the two in your head. Find somethin' to do while I finish up here."

She began shaking her head when Dewey offered help. "You could show me your gun!" he said.

I could see she was about to tell him no when Uncle Henry said, "That's a good idea, Leah. Show the boys your gun. Give them a lesson in weapon safety."

As she considered this, I saw it flash across her face: She was going to give in. Dewey saw it, too. His face lit up like a lightnin' bug. "Okay, fine," my mother said. "But we're learning gun *safety,* not how to shoot up a liquor store gangland style."

"Really?" asked Dewey, his grin widening into a broad smile. "I used to have an air rifle, but I ain't never held a *real* gun before. Is yours like them ones in the movies?" I saw excitement glimmer in his green eyes. This even filled me with anticipation. My mother rarely liked to discuss that aspect of her job, especially not specifics about her gun, and *never* had she given any sort of actual demonstration of how it worked.

My mother kept her gun in the drawer beside her bed. It had a device on the end called a gunlock that stuck down the barrel, making it impossible to shoot unless you had the key. "You have to unlock it like that every time?" Dewey asked. "Doesn't that take a long while if you're chasing someone?"

I rolled my eyes. "She just keeps it like that at home."

With a nod, my mother added, "So as I don't accidentally take it out and shoot Carry."

We were sitting on the edge of my mother's bed, with her closest to the drawer and Dewey in the middle. "Well, that's not exactly the reason," she said. "It's just safer if it's locked."

"Can't you just hide the bullets?" Dewey asked.

"Oh, I do that, too," she said. "You can't be too safe when it comes to guns."

"What kind of gun is it?" Dewey asked.

"It's a Smith and Wesson," my mother answered. "Thirty-six caliber."

"What does thirty-six caliber mean?" Dewey asked. I realized he asked a lot of questions sometimes. Obviously, we had left the unusually quiet version of Dewey behind somewhere on Main Street.

"It's the size of bullets it takes."

"Where are the bullets?" Dewey asked.

"That's a secret," she said.

"How big are they?" Dewey asked.

She held her fingers apart maybe the size of a quarter. "About that long. You sure are interested in guns, Dewey. Hopefully that'll evolve into a career in law enforcement and not slide the other direction." My mother finished unlocking the gun and handed it across Dewey's lap to me. I looked at her eagerly. She nodded. "Go ahead, Abe. Hold it."

My eyes widened as I took it in my hand. I stretched out my arm and pointed it at the closet beside the bed. She pushed my arm, swinging it in the other direction, back toward the door. I looked at her, puzzled. "Why does it matter if there's no bullets?"

"You just don't take chances."

I didn't see what sort of chance you could take without bullets. "Can I pull the trigger?"

"You could try, but first you need to click this." She showed me something just above the handle. "It's the safety. When it's on, you can't shoot. It's another way to avoid accidents."

"Wow, there's lots of them. Ways to stop accidents, I mean."

She shook her head. "No, there's not nearly enough."

I pretended to take some shots at the hallway through the open bedroom door. The gun felt solid in my hand, the grip comfortable. "It's not very heavy," I said.

"It's a lot heavier when it's loaded."

"Can I have a turn?" Dewey asked.

"Sure," my mother said. Then to me: "First, click on the safety, then pass it to him handle first. Always facing away from people."

I did. Dewey took it, immediately clicked off the safety, turned his hand sideways, and started shooting at the door with the barrel pointing slightly downward, making *kapow!* sounds with each pull of the trigger.

My mother reached across and grabbed the gun. "Stop," she said, turning it right way up. "First, we don't shoot sideways. Gangsters, drug dealers, and other bad guys shoot sideways. Second, you don't just fire off shots like you're in *Scarface.* You carefully aim and make sure every time you pull that trigger you've thought through exactly what you're doing. Remember you might be killing people. Especially if you don't know what you're doing. And, unfortunately, most people with guns have no idea what they're doing."

"Who's Scarface?" Dewey asked. He carefully lined up and took two shots, still making the *kapow!* sound.

"One of those guys who probably holds the gun sideways," my mother said. She took the gun back.

Dewey's face fell. "Can we see you load it?"

"No."

It fell further.

"Tell you what. If you guys are really interested, I'll take you to the shooting range for Abe's birthday when he turns fourteen. That's how old I was when my dad took me."

My eyebrows shot up. "Seriously? That'll be awesome!"

"Where's the shooting range?" Dewey asked. I could tell as soon as he did it had been a mistake. We had almost made my mother forget about Carry.

"Satsuma," she said. "Now go wash up for dinner. It's going to be an early night for you two."

*   *   *

That night after the dishes had been cleared away, me and Dewey were sent to my room for an early night. We lay in my bed and I listened as my mother called into the station to tell them she'd be staying at home and they should consider her "on call" because of Carry still being gone. She told whoever was on the other end (I assumed it was Officer Jackson) that she didn't want to leave the house other than for an emergency until she knew her daughter was safe. She hung up and I heard her keys jingle as she told Uncle Henry she was going to drive around and look for Carry. "Call my car phone immediately, Hank, if she comes home, or phones, or . . . or *anything*."

"Of course," Uncle Henry said. He didn't try talking her out of going. Carry was near on four hours late, and I think even *he* was starting to get worried something bad had happened.

It was a clear night and my bedroom curtains were open. Me and Dewey lay there while the purples and violets of twilight painted my room, turning gradually to dark blue and then to black. Beside me, Dewey held his arm straight out with his index finger and thumb forming a gun. He pretended to shoot out first my light fixture and then the speckles sprayed across my ceiling. His utter lack of worry was starting to annoy me. "What if my mom's right?" I asked him. "What if something horrible *has* happened to Carry?"

"She's likely fine," Dewey said, taking a shot at my chest of drawers. "What could possibly happen?"

I was stunned; it's like he thought it was a real gun he was forming with his hand and that he now had the power to protect the world from all its problems. "Have you suddenly developed amnesia?" I asked. "Two girls are missing, and right across the road—maybe a couple hundred yards away—we have Mr. Wyatt Edward Farrow making Roadkill Frankenstein. You was terrified about it yesterday. Now we're just idly lying here doing nothin' while Carry's out there alone, possibly being attacked by one of his garage creations. Well, *I'm* doing nothin', you're doing as close to nothin' as someone can without actually doing nothin'. That's not a *real* gun, you know. Nothin's goin' to die if you *kapow!* them to death with your finger."

"I'm sure your sister's fine," he said. "She's scary enough that nothin's gonna go near her."

I laughed, but still I wasn't so sure. Then I heard something outside.

Awkwardly, I climbed up over top of Dewey and peered out my window, through the scattered branches of the trees growing on the other side. What I saw in that broken light of stars and streetlamps made my heart come to a complete stop in my chest: two bright golden eyes stared straight back into mine, only inches from the other side.

I knew immediately it could be one thing and one thing only.

I was staring straight into the eyes of Mr. Wyatt Edward Farrow's Roadkill Frankenstein.

CHAPTER 11

My heart started again as the eyes transformed into those of my sister, and Carry's hand came up and gently knocked on the glass. Unlatching my window, I slid it open, filling my room with the moist smell of pine on the night air and the singing of cicadas.

"What's going on?" Dewey asked me. Carry shushed him.

"It's Carry," I whispered back. "Where've you been?" I asked her. "Mom's livid."

"Her car ain't here," Carry said.

"That's cuz she's out lookin' for you," Dewey said. We both shushed him. He went back to his pretend gun.

Carry pushed my window all the way open. "What're you doing?" I asked.

"Comin' in."

"Like heck," I said. "Come in through the front door."

"No, Mom might see me. I want to be in bed before she gets back."

I looked at her sharply. "I'm not helpin' you. You're like five hours late. You deserve to get in trouble."

"What are you? The Carry Police?" She glanced at Dewey shooting out my ceiling. "What the hell's he doing?"

"Mom showed him her gun. He's been like this ever since."

I watched while she digested what I had just told her. "She must really be mad if she showed you her gun."

"You'll be lucky if she doesn't shoot you with it."

Right then the headlights of my mother's car swept across the yard, lighting up the area outside my window as she pulled into the drive. "It's Mom! Let me in!" Carry demanded.

"No!" I tried to push the window back closed, but Carry was stronger than me. Dewey was no help. He just kept make-believe shooting stuff. "It doesn't matter," I said, struggling. "Four hours or four and a half hours. Both are late enough that she's gonna kill you, and you know it."

"You're right about that," came a voice from the hall. It was my mother. I turned to see her silhouetted in the doorway of my bedroom.

"Shit," I heard Carry say beneath her breath. Under normal circumstances, I'd tell my mother if I heard my sister cuss, but I figured she was in it deep enough already. I didn't want my mother to *actually* kill her.

"Go round to the front door," my mother said. Her voice was eerily calm and hollow. It scared me, and I wasn't even the one in trouble. Dewey stopped shooting. Carry stood there frozen with one foot on my window ledge. She looked like that possum on Main Street squatting in the middle of the lane just before my mother runned it over.

"Now!" my mother yelled.

This time Carry moved. She ducked back outside and, I assume, headed for the front door.

My mother looked at me and Dewey. "Now shut your window and go to sleep," she said. I slid it closed and crawled underneath the covers beside Dewey. "I don't want to hear another word from either of you two." She closed my door completely by pulling it shut with a solid crack.

Neither of us said a thing for a long while. Finally, Dewey whispered, "Okay, now I'm worried about Carry."

I told him to shut up.

Carry's door slammed twice. Both were loud and not far apart. The first was Carry and the second was, without question, my mother, whose voice was at least an entire octave and ten decibels higher than usual. She screamed so loud that every single word easily pushed its way under Carry's closed door (or, more likely, right through it) and on into my room. It sounded as though my mother was standing right beside my bed, that's how loud she was.

"How dare you?" she asked Carry. "How dare you take advantage of me like that? Against my better judgment, I give you the benefit of the doubt and let you go into Satsuma, knowing damn well you ain't goin' to no movie with no 'friends'!"

I still wasn't sure what she meant by that, but I didn't say nothing to Dewey. Both of us were kind of shell-shocked, lying there frozen with the blankets pulled up to our chins. He'd even stopped shooting off finger rounds.

"Oh, don't even give me that look! Do you think I'm stupid? You must! Well, you're gonna find out who's the stupid one, because you're not leavin' this house except to go to and from school. Otherwise, you're grounded. And you're grounded right through to January!"

I blinked. Carry had stayed out well past her assigned time, but even to me this seemed a little extreme. Carry thought so, too. We heard her telling my mother so.

"You can't ground me that long. Nobody's grounded for near on three months! That's not even close to bein' fair!"

"You don't decide fair, young lady, *I* do. And from now on, I'm not even listenin' to you no more. You're a liar, and you can't be trusted. There are girls being *taken* on the streets! Girls your age! And here I am, waiting up all hours at home, worried that you've become one of them. And you don't even have the decency to come back on *time*. I *trusted* you. You're lucky you ain't grounded all the way to summer."

"You know what, Mother?" Carry had started yelling now too, nearly as loud as my mother. "This isn't about me. This is about *you* and your insecurities and the fact that you failed to save Ruby Mae Vickers!"

And that's when we heard it. The unmistakable sound of my mother's palm slapping hard against Carry's face. After that, the doors, the hallway, my room, everything just fell silent. After a good five seconds, one of them said something. It wasn't loud enough to tell who or what. Then I heard Carry's door open and my mother come out of it before pulling it gently closed behind her.

A long while later, I heard my mother talking to Uncle Henry in the living room, but with my door firmly shut, it all just sounded like mumbles from my bed. I got the feeling Uncle Henry was concerned about what he had just heard transpire.

I decided then that maybe I needed to step in. Carry seemed to be completely out of control. My mother was completely irrational. I was beginning to feel like the most sane one in the house—other than Uncle Henry—and he didn't do much parenting on account of he didn't think anybody should parent other people's kids except their own parents.

"Where're you going?" Dewey whispered as I got out of bed. His voice was shaky. He sounded frightened.

"To talk to Carry," I said.

"What if your mom catches you?"

"Catches me what?"

"I don't know. But she seems a little . . . scary tonight. I reckon if she finds you out of bed, she'll hit you, too."

"I'll be fine," I said. "Go to sleep."

Quietly, I stepped across the hardwood, trying to make as little noise as possible. The door squeaked when I opened it, and I could almost feel Dewey tense up in the bed behind me. I glanced down the hall toward the kitchen. My mother and Uncle Henry were still safely in the living room at the other end of the house.

"She needed disciplinin', Hank," I heard my mother say. "All kids need disciplinin'."

"I can't disagree with you there. And nobody knew how to discipline children better than your pa, but I never knew him to slap one of ya."

I never heard my mother's response as I quietly opened Carry's door and slipped inside her room. The light beside her bed was on, casting a dim, warm glow across her chest of drawers, baby blue drapes, and the navy comforter strewn across her mattress. She was sitting on the end of her bed, still clothed in pink capris and a blue shirt. Her feet were bare.

She looked up from gazing at the floor as I came in. Immediately, my eyes were drawn to the red mark on her cheek. Tears stood in her eyes. I think she believed I was my mother returning when I first came in, because she kind of flinched, but then she just sneered and said, "What do *you* want?"

"Wonderin' if maybe we can talk," I said, trying to sound as grown up as possible.

She wiped her eyes and gave me a look as though I'd just told her we were going swimming with the gators in Skeeter Swamp outside Mr. Robert Lee Garner's ranch. "What the hell about?" she asked.

Tentatively, I took a seat beside her. Unlike her, my bare feet didn't touch the floor and I felt very small in my red pajamas. "You wearing perfume?" I asked.

She gave me another one of them looks. "Of course. What's it matter to you?"

"Just never noticed you smellin' before. You smell good."

"You're weird."

"You're behavin' badly."

She closed her eyes and let out a deep breath. "Oh, dear God. Please tell me Mother didn't send you in here for a pep talk?"

"No, I came in here on my own accord. I reckon she's a bit too out of control right now to talk to you proper."

This seemed to calm her down a little. She even gave me the briefest of smiles as she looked into my face. "So you're gonna talk to me proper? 'Bout my behavior?"

I nodded. Remembering back to what I overheard my mother say to Chief Montgomery in his office, I said, "You know Mom's always been there for us. With money and support and all that."

"You sound like a commercial for one of them insurance companies. What's your point? It's her *job* to support us. Do you think that's something special? Like most parents just leave their kids out in the woods and let the coyotes raise 'em?"

I breathed deeply, trying to figure out what to say next. Until now, I thought I was doing a fairly good job at talking at her level, but she brought up a good point. Then I remembered my trip into Cloverdale earlier. "Well," I said, "a lot of folk ain't got nearly as good a life as we do. Think of all them black kids livin' up in Cloverdale. They got garages about to fall in on their cars and some of their kids play naked in the dirt."

"What're you talkin' about?"

"I seen 'em. I ride to Luther Willard King's every two weeks to give him ten dollars, and he has two little sisters with no shoes or shirts in his front yard sometimes. They're nearly always all covered in mud from their knees right up to their asses."

She laughed at that.

"And someone in the house wheezes and hacks so loud, every time I go there I expect to arrive at a funeral. It's Luther's father, I think."

The laughing stopped but she stayed smiling, so I continued my little speech.

"And here, Mom makes sure we have clothes and food and all that. You don't have to sit around outside buck-ass naked in the dirt."

"Okay, you made a point," she said. "*Somehow*. I'm not exactly sure how you managed, but *somehow* you did. That still don't give her the right to hit me."

"No, it don't. And I think Uncle Henry's tellin' her that right now. But she's been under a lot of stress. You know she's worried about those two missin' girls."

"Two?" my sister asked. "You mean one. Ruby Mae don't count. She went missin' twelve years ago."

"No, I mean two. While you was gone *out to the movies*"—I said it the same way my mother had even though I didn't understand why we was saying it that way—"Tiffany Michelle Yates turned up gone. Me and Dewey saw her about ten minutes before she disappeared. Mom thinks we might be the last ones to talk to her. We're witnesses in the case." I stuck my chest out slightly when I said that last part.

It was like a lightning bug suddenly flew into Carry's ear and lit up her brain. With a deep breath, she went back to staring at her feet. "So that's why Mom's so upset."

"Hell yes, I'd say so. Also because you were so

goddamn late and didn't have to be. You could've just shown up on time like a normal person. Especially on your first time out by yourself like that. Me and Dewey went biking today and came back ten minutes early."

"Yeah, well, I ain't you and Dewey." She studied me a second, then asked, "When did you start cussin'?"

"That ain't no business of yours," I said. "But anyway, you could've at least phoned."

She thought on that a bit. "You're right," she said. "I could've phoned."

I smiled. I felt I'd made some real progress. "All I'm sayin' is that, at least until Mom finishes with this case, I think you should try to act a bit nicer."

"Well, thank you for your concern," she said. "I'll take your advice under advisement."

I nodded. "That sounds good," I said. Even though I didn't quite know what *advisement* meant, it sure did sound like she understood. I stood up. "Now I think you should get to sleep and probably Mom'll have calmed down by morning."

"Probably," Carry said, bringing her hand to the red mark on her cheek.

I left her room and tiptoed across the hall, realizing I'd left my bedroom door open. Closing it now, I clambered back under the covers beside Dewey. "I think I really got through to her," I told him.

"From here it sounded to me like she was making fun of you," Dewey said.

"That's cuz you don't understand families and keepin' them together the way I do. You don't have a sister."

"I think your sister's crazy."

"I think she'll be better from now on. She's just going through a bad patch, is all."

"Well," Dewey said, yawning and turning over, pulling most of the covers with him, "don't worry about her so much. You'll always have me."

I smiled, looking up at my ceiling. I missed Carry—the way she used to be. The way we used to play together. She taught me to read before anyone at school ever did. If it turned out I somehow didn't fix her tonight, I sure hoped the bad part my mother had told me about was near on over.

I could still recall with quite some accuracy the time shortly after my grandpa died when Carry announced that she was taking me outside and showing me how to build a tree fort. I had been feeling pretty bad ever since losing Grandpa. I think she knew it. I was pretty sure everybody knew it, on account of I never left the house much, even on weekends. In fact, I rarely left my room. Death was something I found hard to understand.

"Did Mom tell you to play with me?" I asked her.

"No," she said, indignantly. "Why would you even *ask* that? Don't I always play with you?"

She had a point. Normally, Carry and I played together like that cat and that mouse from that cartoon. I can't remember what it was called. It made no sense on account of in real life the cat would've just ate the mouse and figured that was it. We played. Game over. But the TV cat and the mouse got along as great as me and Carry did.

Back before Carry discovered boys, that was.

"So, what do you say? You comin' or not?" she asked.

"Comin' where?" I asked back.

"Outside to build a tree fort."

"We don't have no trees," I pointed out. Least none capable of sustaining no forts.

"That don't matter none," she said. "We'll build a non-tree tree fort."

"What the heck's a non-tree tree fort?"

"A tree fort without a tree, dummy," she said.

Reluctantly, I put on my shoes and let her drag me outside.

From what I knew about my pa, he had considered himself a bit of a carpenter, and the whole time I'd spent growing up, our garage had been full of wood that had been there ever since he died. It was so full of wood and tools and junk that my mother couldn't even park her car inside of it. Now Carry and I rummaged through the stockpile. Well, she rummaged, I more or less watched, not having the slightest idea what it was she was looking for. But she seemed to know. Every so often she'd pull a piece of wood out and set it aside, saying, "Aha!" or, "Perfect!" or, "Exactly what we'll need!"

"Isn't Mom going to kill us when she gets home from work?" I asked.

"Mom is going to be ecstatic that you're not moping around the house like a ghost," she said. "Besides, I think she'll be secretly happy to see some of this wood taken away."

"But where are we taking it to?" I asked.

"The backyard," she said. "Where else would we build a fort?"

I wasn't so sure my mother would be so happy coming home to a backyard full of wood. I thought she'd rather have it hidden away in the garage.

When Carry was finished extracting all the correct pieces of lumber, her and I lugged them outside, making our way around the house to the backyard. The lawn still felt wet with dew from the morning. I noticed the grass was getting pretty long. Usually, my grandpa had kept it mowed for my mother, but ever since he had gone into the hospital, the responsibility had fallen back to her, and she had more important things in her life to worry about. The state of our yard was a constant reminder that my grandpa was gone from my life forever.

I tried not to think about it too much.

The air had the crisp smell of dandelions and wild-flowers in it. We dumped the wood into a pile right between two small cherry trees that just happened to place it almost dead center with my bedroom window. This was back before Carry and me swapped rooms. Our first batch fell with such a large clatter it scared four or five swallows out of the tall oaks lining the backside of our property.

As we brought load after load of wood out of the garage, my arms and legs began to grow more and more weary. "This is exhausting," I said to Carry. "I don't know if I can build a fort. I can barely even move the pieces of one."

"We're almost done."

We finally got all the wood out. Then we realized we had a problem. Well, I noticed it after watching Carry search around the garage aimlessly for near on twenty minutes. "What're you lookin' for?" I asked. She had a hammer in her hand.

"Nails. I can't find any."

"Why would Pa have a hammer without nails?" I asked. "That would be like having a car without wheels. Makes no sense."

"I know. Still, I can't find any. This place is a mess, though." It had been a mess when we walked in this morning. It was even more of a mess now, since we started going through all the stuff. Once again, I considered the possibility of my mother killing us both when she got home from work.

Things were scattered everywhere. There were tools in drawers and boxes, on the floor, and on shelves. There were little boxes of screws, nuts, and bolts, round plastic things, hooks, all kinds of stuff. I had no clue what any of it was.

But none of it was nails.

Finally, using a stepladder, Carry found a cardboard box full of nails on a very high shelf. "Okay, now all we need is the saw and a measuring tape. And there's a handsaw right there on the workbench, and I'm pretty sure I saw a measuring tape underneath that pile of shingles on the floor by your feet."

We brought the hammer, the nails, the saw, and the measuring tape outside and set them all by our large pile of wood. The pile nearly reached the height of my bedroom window.

"Do you honestly know what you're doing?" I asked Carry.

"Sure I do," she said. "Pa used to let me in the garage with him while he built stuff all the time."

I felt a twinge of jealousy then that she had known our pa and even got to do stuff with him, and I never did. It just didn't feel fair. I wanted to ask her some questions about him, but I thought her answers might just make me feel worse.

I pushed the feeling away. There would be better days to ask Carry more questions about him. Today we were building the fort.

"So what do we do first?" I asked, still exhausted from getting ready to start building the fort. So far, we'd been outside nearly two hours, and what we had looked nothing at all like a tree fort to me. To me it resembled some sort of building that had been hit by a small bomb.

Carry brought two chairs from inside along with a small pad of paper and a pencil. She made some quick sketches and calculations. She didn't show me what she was sketching or calculating, and I didn't ask. I just wanted to get going so we could finish up and get back inside.

After double-checking her calculations, she got me to help her place the wood across the chairs so she could measure out a length and draw a line before sawing off a piece.

She did this to two pieces.

Then she handed me one of the cut pieces and said, "Hold up this one right here. I'll hold this piece up and I'll nail them together."

I did, and she did.

We worked for five more hours like this on that fort, with her doing all the calculating, measuring, cutting, and nailing, and me doing all the holding. I grew more and more tired. Three hours into the ordeal, my mother came home and I felt like rejoicing. I figured she'd yell and scream about us taking the wood out of the garage and we'd be ordered to come inside and probably spend the rest of the day in our rooms—an opportunity for a break that I'd leap at! But instead, my mother took one look at Carry's fort and laughed, telling her to keep going. "I can't wait to see what you come up with in the end."

I wanted to kill her. I was starving. But I wasn't about to let my sister think I couldn't keep up with her when it came to building forts, so I sweated it out.

The sun was down behind the trees when Carry finally pronounced the fort complete. We stepped back from it and took it all in, the structure lit by the purple and orange glow of the fading light of dusk. The sweet smell of the neighbor's magnolias floated on the air.

"Well, what do you think?" she asked.

"Is it supposed to be leanin'?" I asked.

"It's not leanin' much."

"Ain't it supposed to have walls?" I asked.

"Think of it as having many doors," she said.

"Doesn't seem very safe."

She glared at me. "Do you have anything positive to say?"

I smiled. "We're done?"

She smiled back. "We're done. Let's go eat."

We raced into the house and my mother fixed us hot dogs and French fries. Nothing ever tasted as good as those hot dogs that night.

I remembered lying in bed later on, trying to fall asleep with my arms aching something fierce. Our construction efforts stood—well, *leaned*—conspicuously right outside my bedroom window. That night had a slight wind in it. I heard the shrubs rustle outside, and every so often I could make out the squeak of wood against wood.

When I woke up in the morning, the first thing I did was look outside. Carry's fort had completely collapsed, folded in on itself like an accordion.

I had smiled then, realizing it hadn't been about the fort at all. It had all been about the process of building it with my sister. And it *had* been fun. And I also realized she'd done it because she knew I needed to get out of the house, and get my mind off of my grandpa. And, for a while, it had worked.

My sister had been there when I needed her.

And now, tonight, I was there for my sister because she needed me. It had all come around full circle the way I was finding so many things in life often did.

From beside me, Dewey piped up, interrupting my thoughts. Dewey was always interrupting something. "By the way," he said, "when *did* you start cussing?"

"Oh, shut the hell up and get some goddamn sleep," I said.

And we laughed.

CHAPTER 12

We attended service at the Clover Creek First Baptist Church the following Wednesday. My mother told most everyone we went to the house of the Lord twice a week—Wednesday and Sunday—like all the *real* God-fearing people of Alvin, but the truth was, today would actually only be our *second* visit since Mary Ann Dailey disappeared. My mother had just been too busy with the case and, I think, had other things on her mind besides God.

Even still, Carry put up a fuss about having to go.

"Thought I was grounded for the next three months?" she whined when my mother told her to put on her dress shoes.

"Groundin' means doin' whatever and goin' wherever I tell you to," my mother said, pointing a finger straight at Carry. I saw an intensity flash in my mother's eyes, reminding me of how loud that slap had been the other night. Carry saw it too, I figured, on account of her putting on those shoes right quick without saying another word.

The Clover Creek First Baptist Church squatted amongst a garden of roses, the bushes bursting of pinks and yellows. It occupied a thirty-acre or so nearly square patch of land, nestled between Clover Creek Drive, the curve of Finley Circle, and the very eastern end of Main Street. Most of the churchyard was taken up by the cemetery, which was nicely landscaped with stone paths that led through the crosses and gravestones, sometimes stopping at small wooden benches. All these rest areas had gardens of their own and the nicely mown lawn was broken up by the odd fig and hickory tree. Tall oaks edged the outside of the property, making it feel very contained other than from the front. There were even a couple of silver-leafed maples, the leaves of which were now starting to rust a deep red as autumn wound on.

The church was by no means a tall building, but it did have a tall steeple containing a real bell. That bell had been the original bell from the first church ever built in Alvin over a hundred years ago. Since then, the church had been rebuilt twicc, and both times the old bell was kept. I'd never heard it rung in all my life.

Reverend Matthew and his wife, Hazel, looked after the church and had done so for as long as I could remember. Reverend Matthew made sure it was painted at least every two years, making its outside wooden paneling the brightest and cleanest color of white I'd ever seen. It was nearly completely white, other than the arched stained glass windows that were set on either side.

I used to go to Sunday school at Clover Creek First Baptist when I was younger, and sometimes we'd even have lock-ins, where we'd spend the night and play games, but my mother let me stop going to Sunday school when I turned ten. Dewey's mother followed suit. All the Sunday school classes were taught in downstairs rooms that I hadn't been anywhere near since my tenth birthday.

I followed Uncle Henry up the steps with the rest of the people filing inside. Overhead, the sun played hide-and-seek with a sky full of white fluffy clouds. Reverend Matthew was at the door shaking everyone's hand, the way he always was. He was a nice man, not very tall and without much hair, but he had a kind face. I believe he must've been nearly sixty, but his face made him almost look like a baby. He spoke very quiet and gentle. "Hi, Abe," he said, taking my hand lightly. "I'm so glad you made it this afternoon."

"I'm glad, too," I said. "Even though my shoes aren't so comfortable."

This made Reverend Matthew laugh, but it also brought a swat to the back of my head from my mother, who was behind me with Carry. Fact was, the shoes I was wearing weren't comfortable because I only wore them to church and so they never really got properly worn in, especially given our spotty attendance record. But they were polished black and matched the black pants and checkered collared shirt I had on. Sometimes, for particularly formal church functions, my mother made me wear an actual tie and jacket, but thankfully that wasn't today. I doubt the jacket still fit me anyway. Getting the shoes on had been enough of a struggle. I could already feel my feet beginning to blister.

My mother and Carry were both in dresses that had been freshly washed, and were wearing elegant shoes. My mother's shoes were black. Carry's shoes were red. I once again noticed Carry smelled better than usual. She must've been wearing perfume again. I followed Uncle Henry up the row of pews until he found a seat and then I slid in beside him. He was also dressed up—in much the same fashion as me, only with a red pin-striped shirt and navy pants. He was even wearing a hat, which he now took off and put in his lap.

My mother and Carry sat next to me, and I heard my sister still whispering her discontentment under her breath and my mother telling her she not dare make a scene under hers.

"I noticed on the way in that the parishioners have done a nice job on the gardens this fall," Uncle Henry pointed out. I think he said it more to drown out my mother and Carry than for any other reason. I agreed with him, though.

We were eight pews from the front of the church. The light falling inside felt magical to me, the way it always did. I believe it was a combination of the way the sun fell through the delicate stained glass windows and how everything reflected off the polished wooden floors and pews. It was all made out of pine with a layer of varnish so thick you could actually see your reflection in it if you squinted hard enough.

Once everyone was seated, Reverend Matthew started up to the front. On the wall behind the altar hung an empty cross (at least that's how Reverend Matthews referred to it). I imagined Jesus hanging from it by his wrists, his head limp with that crown of thorns. I can't imagine being nailed to a cross like that. According to Reverend Matthew, Jesus suffered all our pain, so right there you know it must've been really bad.

Mrs. Williams started up with the organ and we all stood and sang hymns, the same way we always did at the beginning of church. After the hymns, Reverend Matthew started his preaching and it sure didn't take long for him to get to Mary Ann Dailey. I'd been wondering if he was gonna say something about her. I figured missing girls would be something pretty important to the Lord.

"With recent events," Reverend Matthew said, stepping out from behind his pulpit, "many of you may be looking to your Bibles and seeing that children are never seen to 'accept Christ.' Therefore, they cannot get right with God. And this information might lead us to believe it is our job to keep our children safe, which, of course, it is. And yet, He never tells us how to keep our children safe.

"So it would not be unreasonable to ask yourself: Did He just forget an important point? Did it slip His mind somehow and, now, because of this minor exclusion, the souls of many children are all gonna end up suffering eternally in hell? Is that what we think when we look at our Bibles?"

He paused and there was a murmur through the crowd. Reverend Matthew always liked to put a twist on things to make you have to think. I liked it, since it made his sermons at least slightly interesting.

Reverend Matthew chuckled to himself and slowly

shook his head. "The answer, of course, is no. A child is completely safe, wrapped and tightly held in the arms of God until they are able to understand for themselves what it means to accept Jesus Christ as their savior. God protects them while nurturing their ability to make their own decision to be saved.

"We must read two Samuel chapter twelve, verses twenty-two and twenty-three, along with Matthew chapter eighteen, verse ten. It is only the adults and older children, those who can understand the concept of sin resulting from the separation of God, who are at the age when acceptance of Christ is possible.

"So we must not worry about Mary Ann Dailey and this other girl. Both are still under God's protection. Wherever Mary Ann and Tiffany are, God is there watching. He is listening. He is leading them toward salvation in His own way. We must stand as one and keep our faith and know that God is providing the candle to light their way home."

Reverend Matthew went on like this for a considerable time, but I noticed a distinct difference between how he talked about Mary Ann Dailey and Tiffany Michelle Yates. He barely mentioned Tiffany Michelle by name. He certainly spent a lot more time telling God about Mary Ann Dailey and asking for Him to give her a candle and whatever else to help guide her safely home than he did for Tiffany Michelle Yates. This struck me as rather odd, as I had no idea why he would do something like this.

I decided it would be a good question to ask my mother later on, or maybe Uncle Henry would be better, as I had a sneaking suspicion the answer had something to do with Tiffany Michelle being black and I didn't want to get my mother angry by saying something racist. I was still struggling with what, exactly, was racist and what wasn't. To me it seemed that Reverend Matthew must've thought God was racist and cared to hear more about Mary Ann, but then I was most likely wrong. I was finding more and more when it came to racism I nearly always was.

It took me twenty minutes of discreetly glancing around before I found Dewey and his parents. They were on the other side of the church, a half-dozen pews behind us, right near the back. It was odd seeing Dewey's pa. He worked for the railroad and was nearly never around. It was almost as though Dewey was like me, and didn't have no pa. Mine was killed when I was very young, and I didn't remember him at all.

Most folks didn't like to talk about what happened to my pa, or at least if they did, they didn't seem to particularly like doing it in front of me. That especially went for my mother. But from what I'd heard over the years, he used to work at a gas station down the other side of Main Street, right near the end of town. It wasn't there no more—the Brookside Mall was put up in its place a long time ago.

Anyhow, my pa used to work nights and get off in the really early mornings, like before the sun rose. One particular morning he was driving home and came up behind a large truck—one of them ones with all the wheels—a *semi,* I thought they was called. I guess my pa decided the semi was going too slow, so he decided to go around it. Only, he didn't check the road good enough before changing lanes, and there was another car coming from the other direction that hit him head-on.

I heard the other driver lived, but my pa never even managed to make it to a hospital. My mother got a phone call telling her what had happened. Most of this I know from the few discussions I'd had with Carry about it.

She told me she could remember being woken up by my mother just as the sun was starting to come up outside. The sky was still dark, but had just begun to turn that soft shade of pink, and in that light, she could tell my mother had been crying.

"What's wrong?" she'd asked.

She said my mother had smiled at her, but it was one of those transparent smiles that was easy to see right through. "Nothing," she had said. "You need to get up and get dressed. Uncle Henry's coming to get you."

"Why?"

"You're going to stay with him a couple days."

She rubbed her eyes, she told me. It was all so confusing. "What about Abe?"

"He's coming, too."

She said she remembered Uncle Henry showing up and him and my mother talking in the living room for quite a long time before Carry and me were finally told to get in his car. Then we drove to his house, where we stayed almost an entire week.

I was pretty young, so I didn't remember any of this. It's funny, because in my head there were little details, but I think they all came from Carry's retelling it to me, not from when it actually happened.

That's probably why I don't really miss my pa—because I never really got to know him very well. Sometimes I felt a little guilty about that.

Here's a secret, though: One day I was looking for some wrapping paper for a Christmas present I had for my mother. It was something dumb I had made at school; I can't even remember now what it was. But I looked all over the house for some paper until I finally decided to look in her bedroom closet. I had to bring a chair in from the kitchen so I could see up on the top shelf.

I didn't find any wrapping paper up there, but I did find an old white shoe box. It had been there so long, the top was covered in dust. It didn't look like anyone had opened it for quite a while.

My mother was at work, and I didn't think she'd care if I looked in a shoe box anyway, so I carefully took it down from the shelf, and held it tightly while I jumped down from the chair and sat on it instead. Then, with the box in my lap, I carefully slipped off the top.

The box was full of pictures. Pictures I had never seen before in my life.

Almost every one of them was of my pa. I knew they were of my pa because of the only picture of him my mother kept on display since he died: their wedding picture that sat on a shelf in the living room. I had no idea why she had kept all these ones hidden away in a dusty old box in her closet. There were probably fifty pictures in that box, maybe even more.

There were so many, in fact, that I knew she'd never miss one of them being gone. And so I took one.

I kind of felt bad about it later, on account of I was raised not to steal (least that's what my mother always told me), but I also thought I deserved to have a picture of my pa.

That must have been four or five years ago. I never told her I had it, and she ain't never found it in all that time. I kept it in an envelope in one of the drawers in my bedroom, and sometimes I carried it around in my pocket for good luck. It seemed to work. Every time I had it with me, something lucky happened. Once I even found a five-dollar bill lying on the sidewalk while carrying my pa's picture around.

It made Dewey want to keep a picture of his pa in his pocket.

"But you don't need a picture," I had told him. "Your pa's still alive."

"Yeah," he said. "I guess you're right."

"You should feel lucky for that."

"Yeah," he said, "I guess."

But seeing Dewey now with his pa, I realized how awkward they looked together and reckoned having a pa who was never around was probably just as bad or maybe even worse than having one who was dead.

Anyway, now that I'd found Dewey in this church full of people, I kept sneaking looks over my shoulder at him and making faces, trying to get him to laugh. Every time I did, my mother gave me an elbow and told me to shush.

Another thing came to my attention near the end of the service, and that was a disturbing absence of the presence of Mr. Wyatt Edward Farrow. But then, I didn't know why I was surprised. I never really had him pegged as the churchgoing type. He was more like the kind of guy who stayed locked away in his garage, making all sorts of roadkill monsters and possibly doing things far, far worse.

Most of the clouds had disappeared from the sky by the time church came to an end and we walked out to find a yellow sparkling sun shining happily in a sky of deep sea blue. Something about the sun reminded me of hope. It beamed brightly down across the colorful rose bushes and all the rest of the well-tended gardens, making even the grave markers and the crosses seem happy, sort of like a nice park for all the dead people to play Frisbee with their dead dogs, or sit and feed dead pigeons.

My mother and Uncle Henry began to stroll along the stone paths that wound through the grounds. I tagged along behind them, taking in the sweet smell of flowers. "Mom?" I asked after a short bit.

She looked back at me, her eyebrows raised.

"I still think you should consider the chance that it's Mr. Farrow from across the street taking them girls," I said. I said it quietly so nobody else would hear.

She stopped walking and, with a sigh, squatted down in front of me, taking a glance at Carry, who was lingering at least ten yards behind. "Now why do you say that?" my mother asked, pushing a hair lick away from where it had fallen in front of my eye. "You obviously feel very strongly about it to have brought it up twice now. Tell me why."

I kicked the grass with the toe of my shoe. "I don't know, there's just something about him I find distrustful." I looked up at her, squinting into the sun. "Why wasn't he in church?"

"Maybe he's not a Baptist. Could be a Methodist," she said, very matter-of-factly.

"Yeah," I pointed out. "He *could* even be atheist." I reconsidered, adding: "Or worse, Catholic."

Mom smiled, dismissing my point. "Abe, you can't judge people by the way they look or because of some 'weird feeling' you happen to get from them. The feeling is *your* issue, not Mr. Farrow's. He seems nice enough to me."

But, by the way she said it, I could tell I'd managed to plant maybe the smallest seed of suspicion inside her. "How come there hasn't been a big hunt by all the folks in Alvin for Tiffany Michelle Yates?" I asked. "There was one for Mary Ann Dailey."

Mom took a deep breath. At first I thought I'd said something wrong again, but then I realized I'd just said something tough for her to answer. "Remember our talk about racism the other day?" she asked. "How I told you it was important you figured out how to never judge people by their race?"

I nodded.

"Not all people have mothers like you do, Abe. There's a lot of folk around who still don't think with their hearts or their brains."

"Then what do they think with?"

"Something much lower and around the backside," she said.

It took me a minute, but I got it. I laughed. "But, Mom," I said, "does that mean Reverend Matthew's racist, too? He talked far more about Mary Ann Dailey than Tiffany Michelle. I was starting to wonder if maybe God was a racist."

She looked away, scratching under her chin before looking back. "I know one thing for absolute certain, Abe. God judges us on only one thing: our actions. How we treat each other. That's what's important to Him. Reverend Matthew spent more time talkin' about Mary Ann because he knew that's who his parishioners are most worried about. She's been gone the longest."

Her voice sort of hung there as though there were more to say. I figured I knew what it was, so I said it. "And his parishioners are nearly all white folk."

Again she turned her gaze from mine, this time answering without looking back. "I'm sure Reverend Starks over at the Full Gospel is asking God for Tiffany Michelle's fair share."

That was when Sheryl Davis came stomping across the lawn right up to my mother. "What's this I hear about the Harvest Fair possibly bein' canceled?" she asked, although the way she said it was less like a question and more like some kind of demand. It was obvious she was quite upset by the news.

Sheryl was a plump woman, with a high, nasally voice. Nearly always, she showed up to things like church or the Harvest Fair looking like some kind of wrapped present. Today was no exception. She wore a white dress with a flower pattern all over it and a red bow in her hair.

"Well," my mother replied, "with the girls going missing and such, I just don't think something like the fair would be safe. Too many people in one place makes it too easy for a little one to go astray."

"I don't see how that has any effect on the fair," Sheryl said. "You *know* how important the fair is to this town. Especially the pie contest." Sheryl Davis won the pie-baking contest going back every year I could remember. She always made the same pie, a strawberry rhubarb one. I'd never tasted it, on account of I didn't so much like rhubarb, but from what I heard, she made a pretty good pie.

"I think we can go without the fair and without a pie contest for one season," my mother said.

Sheryl harrumphed. "I'm gonna get a petition goin'."

"Go ahead," my mother said calmly, "still won't make any difference, though. If the Alvin Police Department says there's no Harvest Fair this year, then there will be no Harvest Fair this season, petition or no petition. While you're at it, maybe get a petition goin' to stop little girls from bein' taken away. See if that works at all."

With a final glare at my mother, Sheryl marched off back toward the way she had come, where a group of other plump women wrapped up as presents stood waiting to hear about the outcome of her complaint.

"She's just mad because she won't get a chance to enter the pie contest," my mother whispered to me. "I don't know why she even cares so much. She wins every year anyway. You'd think by now it would stop meaning anything to the woman."

"Maybe that's all she has to look forward to," I said.

My mother regarded me a good full second before

responding. "That was a very adult point to make, Abe. And you're right. Maybe that *is* all she has, but it still doesn't take priority over this town's children. It does make me a little sad for her, though."

It made me a little sad for her, too.

CHAPTER 13

We were well into autumn now, and the leaves on the trees had started to turn all kinds of burnt oranges and firehouse red and most had already fallen to the ground. It was a time of year that normally made the town look especially pretty, and this year was no different except my mother's case put a dark slant on everything, autumn included. The two missing girls had her completely wound up. It was as though she kept waiting for another one to disappear at any moment. She seemed especially worried about me and Carry.

Actually, it was probably the trip to and from school that made her most nervous. It was a time, I suppose, that children were particularly vulnerable.

Nevertheless, the changes in the season seemed to bring a substantial change to my mother's attitude, at least for a while. There were a few days when she wasn't working that she appeared to be almost downright happy. That was until her mind once again started fixating on her case.

I liked those happy days. I hadn't seen her actually smile a real, honest, and true smile for as long as I could remember.

It was on one of those rare occasions that she announced: "I'm taking y'all out for a nice lunch today. And that includes you too, Hank."

"I actually gotta drive way up to Franklin later this afternoon. Have a cribbage match booked with an old friend of mine who's in the hospital for her kidneys."

"Well, we can go sooner rather than later."

Going out for food *always* made me happy. "Can we go to Tex's Barbecue?" I asked. Tex's served the best chili on the planet. At least that's what the menu said, and judging from my limited experience with chili, I had to agree. Carry was seated at the kitchen table, her head in her hands, her fingers pulling up on her hair like it was dog's ears or something. She didn't seem too thrilled to be going out. Maybe she wouldn't be coming, being grounded and all.

"Is Carry coming, too?" I asked.

"Yep, and we're not going to Tex's. I promised Mr. Takahashi we'd all come to his new sushi restaurant."

Happy Shogun Sushi Palace had officially opened its doors two days ago. I hadn't heard any reviews as of yet.

Carry's head fell into her arms and clumped loudly onto the tabletop. "Can't I just stay home? After all, I *am* grounded, right?" she asked.

"No," my mother said. "We're all going to Happy Samurai Sand Castle, and that's final."

"Happy Shogun Sushi Palace," I corrected.

"Whatever," my mother said.

Uncle Henry edged in: "You know, Leah, Carry really *is* grounded. Maybe she should stay home. I don't mind sticking around and keeping an eye on her."

My mother rolled her eyes. "I can't believe you guys. You're all scared to try something new. It's just food, for cryin' out loud."

"Raw food!" Carry said. "You're trying to kill me, aren't you?"

"I'm a police officer, honey. If I wanted to kill you, I know much better ways than this."

"You know, Leah," Uncle Henry chimed in, "round here, what you're talkin' 'bout really isn't 'just food.' It's more like bait." He laughed, but I could tell he was just as wary as my sister about those Happy Shoguns.

No other customers sat inside Happy Shogun Sushi Palace when we arrived. Mr. Takahashi greeted us at the door with a bow from his waist. He wore a red jacket with gold buttons and trim. "Welcome to my fine establishment," he said, smiling. With a sweep of his hand, he gestured to the array of empty tables. "Please sit wherever you wish."

We took a seat in the corner by the window. I sat across from Carry, whose disposition hadn't improved the slightest since leaving home. Mr. Takahashi handed us each a menu while his wife poured tea in clear glasses.

"What's that floatin' in it?" I asked.

"Tea leaves," Mrs. Takahashi said. "It's green tea.

Good for the stomach." She was dressed similarly to Mr. Takahashi and had her hair up in a bun on top of her head, held together with a crossed pair of black and gold chopsticks. I noticed she was wearing a lot of makeup on her face. It made her look almost like a cat.

Uncle Henry lifted his cup and sniffed his tea before taking a sip. He looked across the table to my mother. "It's not bad."

"See?" she said.

Mr. and Mrs. Takahashi left us alone with our menus and a heavy silence fell over the table as each of us realized we had absolutely no idea what we were looking at. "I don't understand any of this," I said.

"It all sounds disgusting," Carry said.

"How can you tell?" I asked. "Most of the words aren't even in English."

My mother sighed. Uncle Henry laughed.

Standing across the restaurant, his hands clasped behind his back, Mr. Takahashi witnessed all this take place. He came over and asked, "Is there something I may be able to help with?"

"I don't think we're quite ready to start orderin' as of yet," my mother said, trying to be as polite as possible.

With another bow, Mr. Takahashi abruptly turned and marched back to his position across the room with his hands behind his back, patiently waiting for us to decide which cast members of a Jacques Cousteau adventure show we wanted to ingest for dinner.

I looked up at my mother. "Is it okay if I drink this tea, or will it stunt my growth like Mr. Yates's coffee?"

"I think the tea's fine," she said. "Didn't you hear Mrs. Takahashi? It's good for your stomach."

Cautiously, I brought the cup up to my nose and sniffed it the way Uncle Henry had. The glass was hot and hard to hold on to, and I wondered why Japanese people didn't know about handles. But the tea didn't smell too bad so I took a taste. "It's all right," I said.

Carry ignored her tea.

I set down my cup. "There's somethin' I don't understand," I said.

"Here we go," my mother said. Uncle Henry's hand reached across the tabletop and came down on hers.

"Some folk keep talkin' like Mary Ann Dailey and Tiffany Michelle Yates are gonna show up again any day now," I said. "And some of 'em say that might not be a good thing, that they might show up the same way Ruby Mae Vickers did." I paused a minute, gauging my mother's reaction. I was starting to figure things out a bit when it came to talking to my mother.

Her eyes fell away to the floor, but Uncle Henry tapped her hand and she lifted them back to mine. "What is it you don't understand, honey?" she asked resignedly.

"Why would anyone want to take some girl away? And especially why would anyone want to take some girl away just to hurt 'em? It makes no sense to me."

Mr. Takahashi approached the table. "You ready to order?"

My mother quickly scanned the menu, as though his interruption was the happiest event in recent history. "Oh, well, I dunno," she said.

"I don't rightly understand most of this," Uncle Henry said.

Mr. Takahashi raised an index finger to his lips.

"How about I bring you special sushi surprise. A little bit of this, a little bit of that. You can taste some of everything."

With a glance at Uncle Henry, my mother nodded. "That sounds like a fine idea," Uncle Henry said.

"Very well." Mr. Takahashi grinned, collecting the menus. He disappeared into the kitchen.

"So, Hank," my mother said, "why don't you tell us about this friend of yours in the hospital in Franklin?"

Uncle Henry gave her a half grin. "Why don't you address your boy's concern, Leah?" I was relieved to hear him ask that question, as I was beginning to wonder if everyone just forgot about me talking.

Mom took a deep breath and pushed her hair back up on her head. She stared at Uncle Henry for a long while, with a look in her eyes like she wanted to strangle the breath out of him. When she finally turned her attention back to me, she seemed calmer. "Well, honey, I don't rightly know. I guess the answer to your question is that some people just ain't right in the head."

"You mean folk like Newt Parker, who used to eat roadkill?" I asked. Roadkill was still on my mind. Mr. Wyatt Edward Farrow had yet to drop off the end of my suspect list.

My mother shook her head. "No, Newt Parker wasn't right in his head a different way—a harmless way. Well, I guess except for the roadkill he ate. But it was already dead, so I don't think that's so bad, really."

Mr. Takahashi brought a dish covered in slices of raw fish laid across rolls of rice. Some were white, some were pink, some were yellow. He also laid chopsticks down in front of all of us. I had never used chopsticks before. I didn't think my mother or Carry had, either. I had no idea about Uncle Henry.

As Mr. Takahashi walked away, my mother whispered to Uncle Henry, "Do you think we should ask what each of these are before we try them?"

"I think it's best not to know," Uncle Henry said. He fumbled with the chopsticks, dropping one of the pink slices of fish four times on the way to his mouth. Finally, he just used his fingers. I assumed he hadn't used chopsticks before, either.

My mother tried a white piece, and I tried a pink one like Uncle Henry. It tasted slimy in my mouth, and I found it best not to chew it. It was far better to just let it slide down my throat and then quickly chase it with the tea.

Smiling, Mom tried to convince us it didn't taste too bad at all.

"I didn't really taste anything," I said. "Just felt it slide across my tongue."

"You gonna try some, Caroline?" my mother asked.

Carry just shook her head, her arms still crossed defiantly over her chest. Uncle Henry caught my mother's eye and gently shook his head. I could hear his thoughts: *Leave her be, Leah.*

I decided to fill in the silence. "Anyway," I continued with my previous line of thinking, "when you say people who ain't right in the head, you mean like some kinda cougar?"

My mother's eyebrows came together confused. She shook her head. "I have no idea what you're talkin' about."

"Mr. Garner told Dewey and me that he reckoned it was some sorta cougar that got Ruby Mae Vickers. Only, he said, not the sort of cougar me and Dewey was picturin' in our heads. I figured he meant a person."

I saw my mother nodding absently, deep in thought. "That's a fairly reasonable way of putting it. The thing to remember, Abe, is that not all people are nice. Some people are sick in ways that make them hurt other people. They might not even mean to do it."

I stared out at Main Street, considering this. "I think I understand."

"Mr. Takahashi?" I called across the restaurant, hoping I wasn't about to say anything racist. "What's a shogun, anyway?"

He smiled, showing a mouthful of white teeth and once again approached our table. "Shogun fearsome Japanese warrior with big sword. You eat lots of sushi, you become like him." Mrs. Takahashi came out of the kitchen with a big round plate that she set down on our table. It was full of slimy sea creatures, each a variety of different colors. Two of them were purple with actual tentacles attached to them. The tentacles had suction cups. I picked one up and made it wiggle in my fingers while I hummed a little tune. Even Carry smiled at that.

"Stop it!" my mother said, slapping me on the hand with one of her chopsticks. "Eat it, don't dance with it."

At that point, Uncle Henry started laughing.

I decided I wanted to eat it. I shoved the whole thing into my mouth and realized near on immediately it was a huge mistake. It tasted exactly the way it looked, like some purple creature with suction cups and tentacles. I barely managed to swallow it. It took the entire rest of my tea to wash it down my throat. Carry looked at me like I'd just done the most disgusting thing she'd ever seen though, and that made the whole thing worth it.

"How was it?" my mother asked.

"Tentacley."

"Yeah, I think I'll pass on that one," she said.

"Mom?" I asked. "Can I ask another question about the case?" Lately, she'd not wanted to talk much about it, so I didn't want to get her angry by just launching into my badgering.

She let out a big sigh. "Yes, Abe?"

"You reckon you'll catch whoever took Mary Ann and Tiffany Michelle?"

She gave Uncle Henry another long look. This time, it lasted so long I started wishing I hadn't asked my question. It was Uncle Henry who finally answered it. "Your mama's gonna do her best, Abe. That's all any-one in this world can do—their best." He turned back to my mother. "Nobody expects perfection from anyone. Or maybe they do—sometimes from *themselves*—but those are false expectations that can never be met. All we can hope to do during our life, Abe, is to be honest and try our damndest not to hurt the ones we love. Try to find a place inside us where we have integrity."

"What's integrity?" I asked.

"Integrity's how you know what the right thing to do is, even when you don't," Uncle Henry said.

I looked to my mother. "You mean like when I say things that are racist even though I don't realize they are? Does that mean I have no integrity?"

My mother's eyes grew wet. She shook her head.

"No, that's just ignorance. There's a difference. You're too young to understand that difference yet. But one day you will."

"And when you do," Uncle Henry added, "it will be up to you whether or not you want to live your life with integrity or not."

I smiled. "I want to be full of integrity."

Uncle Henry smiled back. "Then you will be."

Mr. Takahashi brought yet another plate of stuff. This one was full of short rolled-up rice with more raw fishy things hiding inside.

"My gosh," my mother said, "how much food are you bringing us?"

"This is last course," he said. He looked at the other two plates still sitting practically untouched on the table. "What's wrong? You no like?"

"No, it's delicious," my mother said. "We're just . . . we just ate before we came. Dumb, I know."

Mr. Takahashi looked perplexed. "Eat. Food is good for you." He walked back to get the teapot and refill our glasses. When he finally left, I looked at my mother and said, "I thought integrity meant you were honest?"

"About the *important* things," she said. "And to the people important to us. Sometimes integrity means telling little white lies so that you don't hurt people's feelings."

"The main point of it all, Abe," Uncle Henry said, "is that you don't intentionally hurt people. Or you at least try not to. You can't avoid hurting people sometimes. As you grow older you will make mistakes and people will get hurt because of them. But if you have integrity, you try your best to fix those mistakes. You take ownership of them, and then you fix them. Do you understand?"

"Not really," I said, poking at one of the rice things with my chopstick.

"You're only eleven," he said. "Give it time. I think you have lots of potential." He gave me a wink, and it made me feel good.

Carry still hadn't spoken or eaten a single thing since we sat down. Now, for the first time, she opened her mouth. "Am I the only one who thinks we should get this all in a doggy bag and stop at Willie's Fried Chicken on the way home?"

Uncle Henry tried to hold back his smile, unsuccessfully. Sheepishly, he looked across the table to my mother. "No, you ain't the only one. In fact, I'm quite sure there's four of us."

After finally bagging up our three courses of questionable creatures, Mr. Takahashi presented us with our bill. He bowed seven times to us on our way out, his face spread in a huge grin. I'd never known anyone to be so happy to have customers in my life. In her hand, Mom held two bags to take home, holding all the stuff we didn't eat during dinner, which was pretty near all of it.

"Now was that so bad?" my mother said, once we were out on the sidewalk with the door to Happy Shogun Sushi Palace closed firmly behind us.

"Mom, I'm still starving," Carry said.

"That's because you refused to eat anything," Mom said.

Uncle Henry hesitated. "I'm sort of hungry, too. I thought we really were headed to Willie's Chicken."

With a big sigh, Mom said, "Okay, I'm no longer gonna try to instill any sort of culture into this family. How about you, Abe? Are you starving, too?"

I patted my stomach. "No, those four pieces of whatever slimy things I ate filled me up pretty good. In fact, I think two of them may be wrestlin' down there and the other two might be tryin' to crawl their way back up."

"Oh, don't," Carry said, "you're gonna make me puke."

"What time is it?" I asked Uncle Henry.

"Just before three. Let's get the chicken to go. I gotta take off to Franklin soon as we get back."

I looked up at my mother. "Is it okay if I go on a bike ride with Dewey after we eat? You know, to wear off all the tentacles and stuff?"

My mother's shoulders dropped. She glanced at Uncle Henry.

He shrugged. "We're still well under your curfew," he said.

"Okay," she told me, "but only for an hour and a half. Promise to be home in an hour?"

I started reminding her that I didn't have a watch when Uncle Henry reached into his pocket and pulled out a brown box with a silver ribbon. "This, my friend, is for you." He handed it to me, smiling.

My eyes widened. "What is it?

"Open it," Uncle Henry said, standing back on his heels.

I did, carefully removing the ribbon before sliding the top off the box. Inside was my very own watch. "Wow!" I said, gently prying it from its holder in the box's bottom. It had a bright white face with a shiny chrome ring around it and a leather band much smaller than Uncle Henry's. But just like Uncle Henry's, top center on the watch's face was the word Timex.

I gave him a big grin. "Thank you! It's just like yours."

"It's just like mine was ten years ago," he said.

"Here," my mother said, "let me help you put it on." She did, fitting it snugly around my left wrist.

I turned my arm, watching the dim light of the overcast day play in the chrome. "It's awesome!"

Uncle Henry beamed. "Glad you like it. It's even set to the right time already."

"So now you have *no* excuse not to be home on time," my mother said, unlocking the car. But I was too busy admiring my new gift to really pay much attention.

After eating my fill of Willie's Fried Chicken, me and Dewey hit Cottonwood Lane with our bikes and headed south down Hunter Road. At first we didn't really have any clear destination, but something seemed to be guiding us or pulling us in a certain direction, because we both made the same turns and headed down the same side streets without either of us saying a word to each other.

It soon became obvious where we were headed, and I felt a dark coldness creep over me when the realization came. We were headed to that willow tree, the one just the other side of Skeeter Swamp by Robert Lee Garner's ranch, where he said he had found the body of Ruby Mae Vickers twelve years ago. Neither of us said a word until we were on Thompson Drive, about to turn down the trail that followed the northern edge of the swamp. That trail would take us right past the small hill where Ruby Mae's willow stood.

"What are we doin'?" I asked.

"I was just about to ask you the same thing," Dewey said. "I've been followin' you."

"No, I've been followin' you."

"Guess we've both been followin' each other."

I thought about this. It made sense, somehow. As much as most anything Dewey said did, anyway. "I think we're headed to that place where Mr. Robert Lee Garner told us he found Ruby Mae."

"Would seem that way," Dewey said.

I skidded to a sideways stop right at the top of Huckleberry Trail. Dewey pulled up beside me. "You think these girls being gone might be affectin' us more than we think?" I asked.

Dewey looked like he was tryin' hard to think that one out. "How do you mean?"

"I mean, I think about them all the time. Well, not so much Mary Ann, I guess, but Tiffany Michelle. We were the *last* people to talk to her before she disappeared, and far as the police can tell, she disappeared maybe ten or fifteen minutes after we rode away. What if we hadn't taken off on her?"

"Then you'da been late gettin' home and your mom would likely've grounded you for life like she has Carry."

"Yeah, but Tiffany Michelle might not be gone. We could have *saved* her, Dewey. I even think sometimes that maybe we're sorta to blame."

Dewey thought this over. "Another way of lookin' at it maybe is that we might be gone, too."

That particular thought hadn't crossed my mind. Now that Dewey said it, it made enough sense that I felt slightly better about not being there for Tiffany Michelle Yates. "Anyway," I said, "my point is, we both seem to have come down this way without thinking, heading straight to the spot Mr. Garner told us that other girl's body turned up twelve years ago. I think maybe our brains might be thinkin' stuff on their own without really tellin' us 'bout it."

Dewey laughed. "I think mine does that all the time."

I looked away, thinking hard. "So, are we going to go to that tree?"

"I reckon we are."

Nodding slowly, I stared at a pinecone lying in the patchy grass on the edge of the trail. Although the swamp was still a fair ride down the curved path, the stagnant water hung in the air like the smell of pungent death. After a few seconds, I checked my new watch and turned back to Dewey. "I guess we best be gettin', then. I've only got forty minutes before Mom expects me home."

We both mounted our bikes and sped off down the twisting trail, banked by scrabbly pines and thick, knotted oaks whose boughs hung over our heads like a canopy of green draped with Spanish moss.

The trees wove closer together as we came to the

swamp, with the odd cypress digging its wide clawlike roots into the loamy ground like some gnarled hand with a thick arm branching off into twisted fingers. Those fingers reached out and wrapped around any trees that happened to grow in the vicinity, almost as though the cypress was trying to strangle the life out of its neighbors.

Occasionally, we'd pass gaps between trunks with enough room to see the black green of the swamp lying in a bed of reeds, looking deceptively peaceful. Deceptive because, under that murky stillness, we knew there was a host of gators just waiting for their next meal. And nothing had the patience of a gator. I thought then that patience maybe was the secret to nabbing your prey. Maybe whoever took Mary Ann Dailey and Tiffany Michelle Yates was someone with extreme patience. I would try to remember to bring that up with my mother. It sure seemed to work for gators.

We pulled to a stop beside the willow on the small hill. It was an old tree with lots of bulging roots digging deep down into the dirt. The boughs reached way up above our heads, curving around each other in places, ending in bursts of green and yellow that shook gently in the afternoon breeze, sounding almost like little rattlesnakes.

Wild grass growing around the bottom of the hill became more sparse as it neared the top. A handful of white daisies had been carefully clipped and tied together with a pink bow, and laid at the base of the willow's trunk. Both Dewey and I knew they'd been placed there by Mr. Garner. They appeared near fresh, probably less than a day or two old. Neither of us mentioned them, we just stood there silently looking at the tree for some time.

Finally Dewey broke the quiet. "You think that's where her body was?" he asked, pointing to the flowers. "Right there?"

"Maybe," I said. "Probably."

Our attention was pulled away by the sound of hammering across the Anikawa. Through the trees, we could just barely make out the toolshed Mr. Garner was building, maybe five hundred yards on the other side. "He must be nearly done," Dewey said.

"Let's go see," I said, and hopped back onto my bike.

We rode over the arched stone bridge with the river laughing ominously beneath us and headed down the narrow and unkempt path to where Mr. Garner knelt on the top of his shed. He had four rafters in place and was working on the fifth, which looked to be about exactly the halfway point. When we skidded to a stop, he was sitting with one leg over the last rafter he built and his other stretched out so that his foot pushed against the back wall of the shed. His hammer was in one hand, a nail in the other. He had three other nails in his mouth.

Mr. Garner didn't hear us pull up, but Dixie saw us and exploded in a cacophony of barks and yelps. She frightened a group of maybe a dozen hens. They ran off in a burst of squawks, followed by one of the biggest cocks I've ever seen in my life, all of them ducking under the white wooden fence that separated the cattle from the small area Mr. Garner actually lived in.

Sitting up on the half-framed roof of his new toolshed, Mr. Garner placed his hammer on the top of the front wall and set the nails that were in his mouth carefully beside it before looking down at us and saying, "Hey, what brings you boys my way?"

Dewey and me exchanged glances. "Don't rightly know," I said at last, looking back up. "We just kinda rode out this way."

He nodded knowingly, his eyes briefly cutting in the direction of the willow. He was wearing a Florida Panthers cap and had a light raincoat on. I noticed his boots looked almost new. They were a tan color with thick soles, the sort of thing you used for hunting or hiking. "Been thinkin' 'bout things?" he asked.

I shrugged.

He nodded again. "Yeah, me too. These girls disappearing is the worst tragedy this town's had since the Allen fire back in eighty-one."

I was so young when Jesse James lost near on all his family in that blaze that it never really affected me so much. I realized now it probably affected most folk a lot more. "What happened to that farmhouse, anyway?" I asked Mr. Garner, realizing I didn't rightly know how the fire even got started.

He scratched the back of his head. "Authorities investigated that question for a couple weeks afterward," he said. "Your mother wasn't involved in that case at all, if I recall correctly. In the end, they decided it was accidental. Something in the basement, either faulty electrical or an untended open flame like a candle or somethin'."

"Why did they have a candle goin'?" I asked.

He shrugged. "It was the middle of the night. That's

why James and Laura didn't have a chance. Their bedroom was right above where the flames started."

"What about Jesse James's grandma?"

"Reckon she slept through most of it. Her and George didn't sleep together anymore. She was in their room, he was on the sofa. He claims he got up to use the facilities and found the house engulfed. Couldn't save his wife. Though he sure tried, the poor man." Mr. Garner's eyes averted away from mine. I could tell recalling this tale was upsetting him and wished I hadn't asked about it.

"He managed to get out alive, though. The real miracle was Jesse. How he lived, nobody will ever know. He slept in the basement, just one room away from where the whole thing started."

"Good thing he did survive," Dewey said. "At least there's two of them left now. Be awfully lonely otherwise."

I was about to get mad at him for saying something so insensitive when I saw that his words had touched Mr. Garner. "That's true," Mr. Garner said. "Hadn't looked at it that way, son. I guess we have to be thankful for what we have, not regretful for what we've lost."

I thought I'd be pretty regretful if I lost my mother, father, and grandma all in one night. Wouldn't matter whether I still had a grandpa or not. I kept this to myself though, hoping our conversation might turn to something happier. I'd had enough sadness the past few weeks to last me the rest of my life.

"So," Dewey said, oblivious, "how much longer until you get this ol' shed done, anyway?" I didn't think Dewey could be sad if you killed Bambi's mom right in front of him. Dewey didn't seem to have the capacity to be sad.

Mr. Garner wiped his forehead with the back of his hand. "Oh, I should be able to get the roof finished tonight, I hope." He looked up at the dark, pregnant clouds hanging low overhead. "Looks like rain, and I really want to get it covered before any rain. After that, there's just a bit of trim and some paint. It's pretty much there." He went back to working on that fifth rafter while we watched.

"What about the door?" Dewey asked.

"No point in puttin' on a door if there ain't no roof," Mr. Garner said. "The raccoons'll just climb up over top."

"Looks nice," I said.

"Thank you, Abe."

We talked a bit more, but I realized the day was darkening and checked my new watch. "I really need to get goin'," I told Dewey. "I promised my mom we'd be home in twenty-seven minutes."

"That's a nice watch," Mr. Garner said. "It new?" He finished rafter number six. I'd reckon, given my new judge of time, that it had taken just over four minutes for him to complete it.

I beamed, proudly displaying the timepiece strapped to the back of my wrist. "Yep," I said. "My Uncle Henry bought it for me. Gave it to me earlier today."

Mr. Garner smiled. "That certainly is a nice watch you got there. And it's very responsible of you to listen to your mama, Abe. Makes you a good person."

I nodded and again I thought about Carry and how *I* was able to tell her the way she should act and actually *change* her. She was still full of anger and all that, but she sure seemed better since our talk. "Well," I said, "we best be going."

We said good-bye and headed back home, this time going around the other way, completely avoiding Ruby Mae's willow.

I checked my watch as we turned onto Cottonwood Lane. The small area of brightness in the darkening sky was still high enough that I knew we were okay. It turned out we were still inside of our hour and a half. Barely. That made me happy. In some ways, I felt almost obligated to make up all the extra time Carry had stayed late in Satsuma that night.

Dewey waved good-bye and kept on riding down the sidewalk to his own house while I coasted up my driveway, dumping my bike beside the garage before walking across to the front steps. I was whistling when I came through the door. Not any specific song, just whistling. Something about what Mr. Garner said about being grateful for what we have instead of regretting what we didn't struck some sort of chord with me. Well, I guess technically Dewey had said it, but I hadn't noticed until Mr. Garner rephrased it. Dewey hadn't, either. I refused to give Dewey any credit for saying something he didn't mean to say in the first place. Either way though, it had left me feeling more peaceful than I had in a while.

That peace was about to be broken as my mother came rushing out of the kitchen to meet me.

"Thank God you're home," she said.

"What?" I asked. I even smiled. "I'm *early,* reckonin' by my brand-new watch, and Uncle Henry said this here watch tells the time better than those super atomic clocks they got up there in outer space."

But something in her face made me stop talking and stop smiling. And then I found out why.

It was Mary Ann Dailey.

She'd shown back up.

CHAPTER 14

"Where is she?" I asked excitedly as my mother strapped on her boots. She was already in uniform. Uncle Henry was standing in the doorway, seeing her off.

"Abe," she said, "I can't talk right now. I gotta get goin'."

"Is she all right?"

My mother purposely avoided looking at me after I posed that question, so I cast a glance to Uncle Henry. By the sol-emn, slow shake of his head, I knew immediately Mary Ann Dailey was *not* all right.

"Is she alive?" I looked to my mother and then to Uncle Henry. They both quickly looked at each other and then looked away. My mother put on her jacket and went for the door. "Tell me," I said. "Please? Is she alive?"

"No, Abe," Uncle Henry said quietly. "She's dead."

"Who found her?"

"Robert Garner," he said.

"Mr. Robert Lee Garner?" I asked. "Holly Berry Ranch Mr. Garner?"

"Yes, Abe. How many other Mr. Garners do you know?"

My mother was out the door, about to close it, when I shouted, "Wait!"

She paused, staring at me. "Abe, I really have to go." She was obviously very upset. Her fingers trembled.

"But . . ." I tried to think this all through as quickly as I could. Dewey and me . . . we'd . . . "I just saw Mr. Garner," I said. "Couldn't been not more than thirty minutes ago. Maybe even less. *Probably* even less."

Confusion swept across my mother's face. "What? What are you talkin' about? Where did you see Mr. Garner?"

"At his ranch. That's where me and Dewey rode our bikes to."

"Why?"

I couldn't answer this one, because the God's honest truth was neither me nor Dewey had any clue what brought us there. "I don't know," I said. "We went to look at the willow where he found Ruby Mae Vickers."

Tears filled my mother's eyes.

"What?" I asked.

She turned away. Uncle Henry's hand came down on my shoulder. "They found Mary Ann Dailey at the same place," he said in my ear.

"But . . . that's impossible. We was just there. There wasn't no girl's body anywhere. Just that willow and Mr. Garner hammering away on his toolshed."

Wiping her eyes with the back of her hand, my

mother said, "Okay, Abe, that's fine. I really have to go now." She tried to push the door closed, but I blocked it with my foot.

"You have to bring me with you," I said.

"No, Abe. You can't come to a murder scene. I'm sorry."

"But, Mom, I'm tellin' you, we was just there. Not even fifteen minutes ago. That makes me a witness, don't it? Doesn't that mean you have to bring me?"

"No," she said sternly.

"I'm coming," I said. I don't know what inside me wanted so badly to see the dead body of Mary Ann Dailey, but something sure as heck did.

"No, and that's final."

"I'm a witness. I'm coming."

"No."

"Yes."

"No."

Then, from behind me, Uncle Henry's quiet voice said, "Leah?"

Her eyes flickered up to his face.

"Maybe . . . maybe you should take him."

"What? Are you crazy?"

"Think about it, Leah. If he really was there fifteen or twenty minutes ago, he very well may be your only witness. Take him. If it was anybody else, you wouldn't hesitate."

"I most certainly would. If they was eleven years old. Hank, this is a murder scene."

"He needs to go. Can't you tell?"

She looked at me and, for the first time in a long

time, I felt my mother actually see me for who I really was. I wasn't the same person I had been the last time it happened.

With a sigh, she said, "We could be out there for hours."

"That's fine," I said.

She heaved a deep breath. "Okay, get in the car." Her eyes once again locked with Uncle Henry's as she closed the door.

I felt the first drops of rain hit the top of my head as I made my way into the passenger seat. My mother got in behind the wheel and put the key in the ignition. She paused before turning it, looking at me. "You sure about this?"

I nodded. "I am, Mom. Seriously."

"All right, then. I need you to obey me completely throughout this entire procedure, you understand me? This is vitally important, Abe. It's very easy to contaminate a murder scene. Even officers who've been in the force a long time make mistakes during these kinds of things. I don't need you mucking anything up."

"I understand," I said.

"Okay." She pulled out onto Cottonwood Lane and picked up her heavy car phone. "Here, dial the station for me," she said, handing it over to me. "It's speed dial number one. Give me back the phone when Chris answers. Don't say anything to him."

"Okay," I said, and did as she requested, handing her back the phone the second I heard Mr. Jackson pick up the line at his end.

At first, I guessed she was using the phone instead

of her radio so that I didn't hear the entire conversation. As she spoke, I reconsidered. I think she chose the phone because it felt more private. And somehow possibly more safe.

"Chris, it's Leah. Bad news. The Dailey girl turned up dead. Guess who found her? Bob Garner. Nearly the exact same place he found Ruby Mae. Nearly the same condition too, from what he described on the phone." I heard her choking back tears as she spoke. The longer she went, the more obvious it was. "I need you to meet me at the Holly Berry Ranch immediately. I am en route now." A tear rolled down her cheek as she handed me back the phone.

"Hang this up for me, honey," she said, and wiped her face with the sleeve of her jacket.

I did as she asked. Under her breath, I heard her talking to herself. "He said it was just like Ruby Mae all over again. Oh, God, I can't do this. I thought I could, but I can't." Her hand reached up and grabbed the Lord Jesus hanging around her neck. She began twisting it in her fingers. "I can't go through this again."

She hadn't realized she'd been speaking out loud until I reached over and touched her arm. "Yes, you can, Mom. Twelve years ago you were still pretty much a kid. You're not anymore. You can do this. I know you can. I have faith in you."

She looked straight at me for a second, her eyes completely red and full of tears. "Oh, Abe," she said and then they all just started flowing.

"Right now, Mom, you need to pull yourself together. You can cry 'bout it later, but I don't reckon this is the way a detective should show up at a murder scene, do you?"

"No," she said, wiping her face dry and riveting her courage, "you're right. You're absolutely right. When did you get so smart?"

"I've been gettin' smart all along, you just didn't really notice it happenin'. 'Course I learned it all from you."

She forced a tearful smile, reached over, and squeezed my hand.

CHAPTER 15

By the time we pulled into Holly Berry Ranch, my mother had fully regained her composure. She got out of the car and put on her hat. My hand was going for my door handle when she said, "You stay here, you understand? If I need you, I'll come get you."

I began to object, but she cut me off. "You told me you'd listen and obey me, Abe. Don't disappoint me now."

I stopped objecting and resigned myself to being stuck in the car.

My mother went around to the trunk and pulled out her hip waders and rain gear. I had no idea why she needed them waders unless she planned on walking through Skeeter Swamp and, in my opinion, nobody in their right mind would ever walk through Skeeter Swamp. Of course, lately my mother hadn't been in her right mind so much, so I wouldn't put anything past her.

She carried the hip waders over to where Mr. Robert Lee Garner waited, leaning against a pine tree, smoking one of his cigars. He was still wearing the Panther cap and the rain jacket, which was now coming in handy, as the small drizzle that had started when we left my house had now turned into real rain.

I waited until my mother was a good fifty yards away before rolling down my window and reaching across the center console to roll down hers. She said I had to stay in the car. She didn't say I couldn't listen.

It wasn't easy to hear them though, not with them being a good hundred yards away and the rain coming down on the swamp and leaves and all. I strained and did the best I could. According to what little I did make out, Mr. Garner found Mary Ann's body in nearly the exact same spot and position he had found Ruby Mae's in twelve years ago.

My mother looked over her shoulder toward the willow across the river and swamp. By the look on her face, I could tell she could see enough even from that far away to disturb her. I leaned as far forward as I could and tried to see the base of that willow tree, but the best I got was the edge of the leaves overhanging the stone bridge.

"Her body's in nearly the same shape Ruby Mae's was," Mr. Garner said. I had no idea what that meant, or what he was referring to when he clarified by saying she was "well used" before she was killed.

Off in the distance, I heard a siren coming closer. No doubt, it was Officer Jackson. I saw relief flood over my mother when she heard the same sound. It was obvious to me that she didn't want to be the one to have to go look at Mary Ann Dailey. Instead, she stalled for time by asking Mr. Garner some standard questions.

He told her he had just finished working on his tool-shed for the night and gone in for a beer when Dixie started barking like some kind of crazy wolfhound. I knew what he meant. She had barked the same way when Dewey and me showed up here less than a half hour ago. He said he came outside to see what had her in such a state, expecting to find a raccoon or maybe a coyote, but there was nothing nowhere. That's when he got suspicious and went back for his rifle and did a more thorough examination of his immediate property.

And that's when he found Mary Ann Dailey.

Across the way, I could see Mr. Garner's toolshed. He had indeed managed to get the roof on in time for the rain, it appeared. There were no shingles yet, but all the rafters must've gone up because he now had it covered with plywood and tar paper. It actually looked like a proper roof.

Officer Jackson pulled up beside me and brought his car to a stop. The siren quieted, but the red and blue lights continued flashing, bouncing off the trees and Mr. Garner's toolshed. Officer Jackson got out of his car, put on his hat, and cast a questioning look at me through my open window.

"I'm a witness," I said, but he ignored me and continued on to where my mother and Mr. Garner were standing.

That's when I realized I was still holding my mother's car phone in my lap. I stared at it well over a full minute, trying to decide whether or not what I was considering doing fell under the caption of incredibly stupid or just slightly stupid. One thing was that I was pretty sure it had nothing at all to do with not upholding my integrity, and so far my mother's only order for me to obey was to stay in the car, so I wasn't breaking that rule at all.

I decided to execute my plan. With a careful glance out the windshield, which was blurred and slicked with rain, I made sure my mother was in no danger of witnessing what I was about to do. Then I took her phone and dialed Dewey's number.

His mother answered, but put him on when I asked her to.

"Why're you using your mother's car phone?" he asked.

"Now how did you know that?" I asked.

"You keep cutting out. It's terrible. Besides, isn't that property of the Alvin Police Department?"

"You don't care, so quit pretending," I said. "Guess where I am."

"That's easy. Your mom's car."

I paused, thinking he was joking and realizing he wasn't. "Yeah, but guess where that is. You'll never guess."

"Then I'm not gonna try. Why should I try if I never will?" he asked abruptly. "Just tell me right off."

I sighed. "Fine."

So I did. I told him everything. About how I came home and found out Mr. Robert Lee Garner had discovered the body of Mary Ann Dailey in the exact same place as he had found Ruby Mae's and how I convinced my mother into bringing me to the crime scene on account of I was a witness and all that.

"But you're stuck in the car?" he asked. I had told him that part, too.

"Yeah," I said.

"So, what's the point of being a witness, then? I don't see how you can be witnessin' much from the car."

I wanted to say something sarcastic, but I couldn't on account of him being absolutely right. Through the rain-smudged windshield, I saw Mr. Garner point toward the willow and watched Officer Jackson head in that direction. "I think Chris Jackson's goin' over to look at the body," I whispered to Dewey into the phone.

"What's your mom doin'?" he asked.

"She's puttin' on her hip waders."

"Now why in God's name would she be . . . she's not thinkin' of goin' into Skeeter Swamp, is she? She wouldn't be that crazy, would she?"

It occurred to me why she might consider doing just that. "I bet she's wonderin' if Tiffany Michelle Yates is somewhere in that swamp," I said to Dewey. "I bet she's gonna go search it."

"She'll get eaten by gators!" he screamed into the phone. "You gotta stop her!"

"I can't. She told me to stay in the car and obey her orders." Outside the car, my mother slowly followed in nearly the same direction Officer Jackson had gone. Mr. Robert Lee Garner came along behind her. Sure enough, she started into Skeeter Swamp, one slow step at a time. "Jesus, I can't look. She's wadin' into the swamp," I said.

Dewey tried to placate me. "She's got that gun, remember? She'll be fine."

He was right, my mother did have her gun and it was out of its holster and in her hand, pointing up at the rain clouds as she cautiously went farther into the swamp with her elbow bent near on ninety degrees. Her gaze never left the surface of that stale, murky water. My heart began pounding in my throat and sweat tickled the back of my neck. I thought she must've been at least as scared as me, likely more so.

"You just be careful in there," Mr. Garner called out to her. "That thing's full of gators. Even if the other girl had been thrown in, I doubt there'd be anything left of her by now. Those bastards are fast and they're hungry."

I shivered, feeling a cold steel ice pick at the base of my spine as outside the car the rain hammered down harder than ever. It was as though the sky was beginning to open up.

"I'll be fine," my mother called back, never once taking her eyes off that water.

Officer Jackson came back over the stone bridge. "I'm gonna grab the camera and the CSI kit," he said to my mother. "I think I may be able to get a boot print. Hard to tell. I'll also try to get a proper forensics team as quick as possible. Hopefully there's somebody available in Mobile."

"What do you think's gonna happen?" Dewey asked, but I shushed him.

"I'm tryin' to listen to 'em talkin'," I said.

"Think someone's gonna get shot?" he asked.

"Just be quiet a sec."

"Okay," I heard my mother say to Officer Jackson. Then, tentatively she added, "And once you've done that, I need you to bring Abe out of the car and show him the body. Get a sworn statement from him that it hadn't been there when he was here fifteen minutes be-fore Bob called me."

Officer Jackson stopped, nearly midstep. "You seri-ous, Leah? You want me to show your boy . . . ?"

She sighed. "He's a witness, Chris. He wants to see it. He's offered to help. I think it'll be fine."

"You're sure 'bout this?"

"I'm sure."

"You're his mama."

"That I am. That I am." She took a few more steps before saying, "I don't think there's much to be gained by me wadin' through much more of this swamp. Like Bob said, if Tiffany Michelle's body got dumped in here, it's likely been digested, and frankly, I don't want to lose either of my legs."

"I think that sounds reasonable," Officer Jackson said, opening his trunk and removing the CSI kit and camera. My mother slowly made her way out of the swamp, coming up on the other side, and I breathed a sigh of relief as both her feet once again touched on solid ground. I'm sure she did the same.

"Dewey," I said into the phone. "My mom's out of the swamp and I just heard her tell Officer Jackson that, once he's taken pictures and stuff, he's supposed to bring me out and show me the body. I gotta swear it wasn't there when we was here."

"What about me?" he asked. "Don't I need to swear, too?"

"Dunno," I said. "I guess they only need one wit-ness for somethin' like this."

It wasn't fifteen minutes later that Officer Jackson

approached my mother's car. "I gotta go," I said, and quickly hung up the phone.

"I'm supposed to show you the murder scene," Officer Jackson said, bending so as he could talk to me through my open window. "You sure you're up for this? It's probably not entirely necessary."

I nodded. "I'm okay."

He shook his head. "All right." He clicked open my door. I swung my legs out of the car and stood on the hard ground of Mr. Robert Lee Garner's ranch. The rain pelted me, but I was already half soaked on account of having my window wide open. I barely even noticed as I followed Officer Jackson toward that stone bridge. A mixture of emotions built up inside me as we drew closer, and I wasn't even sure what half of them were. I was excited, I was scared, I was sad, I was . . . I don't know what I was. I purposely didn't look at that willow as we walked. My eyes stayed locked on the back of Officer Jackson's boots until we were across the stone bridge and stopped at the base of the small hill that led up to the trunk of the willow tree.

"You sure you're okay?" Officer Jackson asked. I think he knew I hadn't looked away from the ground yet.

I nodded. "I think I'm fine," I said. But really, I wasn't sure.

"Okay, then look up, Abe. There's Mary Ann Dailey."

I don't know what I was expecting to see, but obviously it was something different than what lay before me, because near on immediately I felt what I could only assume was the first panic attack of my life trying to overtake me. With two deep breaths, I managed to fight it off as I looked at Mary Ann's dead body lying limp and lifeless, propped up against the trunk of that tree.

She was practically naked, and her skin had a blueish color to it. A cut ran all the way across the front of her throat, right below her chin. Her eyes were wide open, but there was no life behind them. That was the part that was hardest for me, seeing those eyes. You get so used to seeing eyes full of life that when you finally see dead ones, they aren't like anything you could ever have imagined.

The body was strewn across the rise of the roots, some of it partially buried in a shallow hole that obviously had been dug in a hurry. There was loose dirt on her skin and what little clothing she wore. I think it may have only been a large blue T-shirt full of shreds, but I could be mistaken. So much of the details blurred together in my head very quickly after seeing her. The hole was far too shallow to be of any use, and it made me wonder why anybody would even go to the trouble of digging it. It didn't nearly hide her from view from any possible angle. It was almost as though whoever placed her here just knew in the back of his head that the dead are supposed to be buried and it didn't matter how deeply, provided they were somewhat beneath the ground.

"Nearly exactly like I found Ruby Mae," Mr. Garner said from behind me. His voice made me jump.

"Seen enough?" Officer Jackson asked me, resting his arm across my shoulders.

I nodded, but found it hard to look away from Mary Ann. It was those eyes. They had me gripped.

"Okay, then," he said and gently turned me around. I noticed a shovel lying in the dirt between the small hill the tree stood on and the swamp as Officer Jackson guided me back to the car, where I sat on the seat while he squatted outside the open door and took my report, asking me things like what time approximately had I been at the Holly Berry Ranch and was I definitely sure there was no body under that tree and then he asked a whole bunch of questions about Mr. Garner. What he had been doing, what he had been wearing, what he talked about. Officer Jackson asked me more questions about Mr. Robert Lee Garner than anything else.

"Now you're sure about the time and that?" Officer Jackson said.

"One hundred percent," I said. "See, my Uncle Henry bought me a new watch today." I showed him my exquisite timepiece.

"And you're certain the body wasn't there already?"

"Yes, sir," I said. "In fact, that was why Dewey and I came in the first place. To look at the tree where they found Ruby Mae twelve years ago."

He tapped his pencil against his pad and stared at me a few seconds. "Livin' with your mama really has an effect on you, don't it?"

"I think everyone's mama has an effect on them, don't you?" I asked.

He nodded and looked away, scratching the back of his head. "I suppose you're right. How about you roll up those windows now and try to stay warm. Your mama's probably gonna be here another couple hours. If you want, I can try to get someone to come pick you up."

"No, sir," I said. "I'd like to stay, if that's all right."

He shook his head. "It's fine with me."

CHAPTER 16

About an hour or so later, another two squad cars pulled into the ranch. Since Alvin only had two of their own cars, these were obviously from some other town. I suspected this was the forensics team Officer Jackson had called in.

Two officers got out of each car. Of the four, two of them each carried some sort of kit, much bigger than the CSI kits that Officer Jackson and my mother kept in the trunks of their cars. All four of the men had short-cropped hair. Two were blond with goatees. The other two had dark features and no facial hair.

One of the pair of experts went in the direction of the body; the other started taking samples of things from around Mr. Garner's ranch: leaf and branch cuttings, dirt specimens, and something that looked remarkably like chicken dung to me. All of it was collected and put into clear plastic bags. Some of it, like the chicken dung, was taken using a pair of tweezers and placed in a test tube full of liquid that was then shaken and brought back to their cars. I had no idea what they were doing with any of it. All I knew about forensic experts was that they were way too high-tech as far as Alvin police work went and that they were the ones who tried to solve crimes by running scientific tests on things like blood and stuff like that. We were just learning about blood cells in school.

I called Dewey back and reported with an update.

"They're testing chicken shit?" he asked in disbelief. "Why the heck would they be doin' that?"

"I don't have the slightest idea," I said. "Maybe they think it's possible Mary Ann Dailey was taken by a chicken."

Dewey laughed and I wished I hadn't made the joke. After seeing her body, laughing just didn't seem right.

"Wow, I can't believe all this," Dewey said after a period of silence.

One of the forensic experts called out to Mr. Garner. "Is this here your shovel?" he asked, pointing to the spade I had seen on my way back to the car.

Mr. Garner's hands went to his hips. He barely gave the shovel a glance. "Could be," he said. "Sorta looks like it could be anyone's shovel. Most shovels look the same, don't they?" He sounded mad, and I couldn't figure out why.

"You being a smart ass?" the man asked.

"You're the expert, you tell me," Mr. Garner said.

"Detective Teal, I'm finding your friend here rather uncooperative," the forensic officer said to my mother.

She came over to where Mr. Garner was standing, his big arms crossed across his chest. "Something wrong, Bob?"

"I don't know, Leah. You tell me. You bring these 'forensic experts' in and suddenly they all askin' me if that's my shovel or not. Sounds to me almost like an accusation."

"Bob, please just answer their questions. They're only doing their job, just like the rest of us."

"Okay, then," Mr. Garner said. "*You* ask me."

"Ask you what?"

"Ask me if that's my shovel."

"Is it?" my mother asked. I didn't remember seeing that shovel when Dewey and I had been here earlier. Not lying on the other side of the river or anywhere else for that matter.

"Are you asking me if I killed a little girl and left her body partially buried beside the creek?" Mr. Garner asked back instead of answering my mother's question. I couldn't see how he mixed those two things up.

But my mother paused and I saw her swallow. "Did you?" she asked.

I couldn't believe I heard what I heard. "My mom just asked Mr. Garner if he did it," I told Dewey in a fast whisper. "If he was the one who killed Mary Ann."

"We know he wasn't," Dewey said.

I shushed him and told him I couldn't hear with him jabbering and the rain and all.

Mr. Garner's face grew slightly red. "What do you think, Leah?" he asked. "Let me tell you what *I* think. I think you're makin' some really bad decisions right now and you don't want to be askin' me things like that."

My mother took a very deep breath. She was frustrated. After a hesitation, she asked, "How come your tools ain't locked up?"

"Jesus *Christ,* Leah, I only *just* got the roof on the shed. Like less than ten minutes before I found Mary

Ann. I haven't even gone down to Jim's for the hardware for the door yet. The last thing I expected was someone to come lookin' for a shovel to dig a hole for a little girl."

My mother considered this, looking over at the willow, where I assumed Mary Ann's body was being bagged, since I saw them take the necessary equipment in that direction. "Three little girls go missing," she said. "Funny, how two of 'em show up right outside your ranch."

Mr. Garner was quick to respond. "Yeah, you'd think I'd be smarter than that if it were me."

"That's not helping your case."

"My case? *What?* I'm actually a suspect? Shouldn't you be reading me my rights?"

"No," my mother said, nodding to Officer Jackson. "*He* will. I have to get my kid home." She turned and started walking toward the car.

"Dewey, I gotta go," I quickly said and hung up the phone.

"You're not serious?" Mr. Garner called out behind my mother just as Officer Jackson told him about his right to remain silent and all that.

Mr. Garner apparently didn't care about that right. "Leah, your pa and I were friends, for Christ's sake." I watched Officer Jackson bring Mr. Garner's hands behind his back and cuff him.

"Jeez!" I said, remembering the windows. Quickly I reached across and started winding my mother's up. Her seat and steering wheel were drenched from incoming rain, but she barely seemed to notice as she opened the door and got inside.

"You think Mr. Garner killed Mary Ann Dailey?" I asked.

"Mind your business and do up your belt." She glanced at my open window. "And do that up. And give me that." She pointed to the car phone lying on the floor at my feet. I handed it to her and started rolling the window up. She went through the phone's call log. I swallowed hard, knowing she was seeing my two calls to Dewey. "I figured as much," she said. "Abe, you got about as much sense as a dew worm."

"You only told me to stay in the car, nothing else."

"You know what?" she asked. "Right now, I don't even care."

I could tell by her tone not to ask any more questions about nothing. I didn't think it was Mr. Garner who killed Mary Ann Dailey, though. I still had Mr. Farrow at the top of my list.

She backed out, leaving tire trails in the swampy mud before turning back onto the dirt road. "Is Mr. Garner gonna go to jail?" I asked after a few miles of silence.

"I said, mind your business." She lifted her phone and speed dialed Chief Montgomery at home without even pulling over to do it. This was very unusual behavior for my mother, who was generally overly cautious about such things. I listened to her describe what had happened.

". . . and we found tape marks over her mouth, rope marks on her wrists, strained ligaments in her feet. Yeah. Very much like the Vickers girl. No, Ethan, I'm fine. Seriously." She threw me a sideways glance. "Nearly exact same indications of sexual abuse. Yes. No,

I'm seriously fine. I don't care *how* I sound. If you saw what I just did, you wouldn't sound so perfect, either. Yeah, they're bagging her. Found extensive DNA evidence on Bob Garner's shovel. Not sure yet. Yeah, we're bringing him in."

She hung up the phone. I started to say something, but she quickly snapped at me, "I said, mind your business," so I closed my mouth tight.

All the way home, I kept glancing at her every couple minutes. It was a very long time for me to have to mind my business.

Back at home, I tried talking to my mother about Mary Ann Dailey, but I could tell right away she really had no desire to discuss it. "Why don't you go and find something to do in your room?" she said. Carry was already in her own room with the door closed, where she'd spent most of her time since her grounding. That is, other than the foray into Japanese raw fish, which was almost like cruel and unusual punishment as far as she was concerned.

It wasn't even near on bedtime, but I stayed in my room anyway, sitting on my hardwood floor and playing with my LEGO blocks. Really, it was just an excuse to listen to my mother and Uncle Henry talking down the hall, a good three rooms away. I was starting to get pretty good at picking up their conversations.

"The killings were almost identical," I heard my mother say. "Mary Ann was even killed the same way—slit right across her throat." I cringed, remembering that slash.

"Did they find the knife?" Uncle Henry asked.

"No, but whoever dumped her walked in from the road. They found traces of blood leading back to where she must have been taken from a truck or a car, so she was killed somewhere else and brought to the swamp."

"Well," Uncle Henry said, "there must be a heckuva lot of blood somewhere, don'tcha think? Can't you just look in every car seat, trunk seat, vehicle trunk, and truck bed in town for blood?"

"You know we already arrested Bob Garner. They found evidence linking him to the shovel used to dig the shallow grave the body was laying in."

"Yeah," Uncle Henry said, "but do you really think it was him?"

"She was found on his property. *His* shovel was used to try and bury her. It's pretty cut and dried, Hank. Least the forensics guys think so. They've still got some more test work to do, but for the time being, Bob Garner's being held for the murder."

"You know that man was a good friend of your daddy's."

"That's got nothin' to do with nothin'."

"Maybe, maybe not. I always thought he was a pretty smart man, though."

"What're you sayin'?" my mother asked.

"I'm sayin' a smart man don't leave a shovel round with evidence on it settin' him up for murder."

"Maybe he was in some kind of hurry."

"Or maybe—" Uncle Henry cut off his sentence.

There was a pause and then I heard my mother, her voice choked with tears: "She was laying in almost the exact same place as Ruby Mae. Almost *exactly,* Hank. It's too much of a coincidence, ain't it?"

"It's been twelve years, Leah. Coincidences generally happen faster than that."

I heard her sigh. It almost sounded as though she was going to break down completely. "I told the Daileys today that their little girl was gone forever," she said. "It was horrible. It was Ruby Mae Vickers all over again."

"Oh, come here," I heard Uncle Henry say.

And then my mother's sobs wound their way down the hall, echoing off the bare yellow of our kitchen walls.

I sat on the floor of my room, listening to them talk, piecing together LEGOs in seemingly random ways. I had no idea what it was I was building, I was just doing stuff to pass away the time, sorta like the way me and Dewey used to kill off afternoons in the front yard balancing rocks on the ends of sticks. But as I assembled what looked to me like some sort of strange molecule, I began to think about how Dewey and me were the last two people to see Tiffany Michelle Yates alive that afternoon and how weird that was and all.

That coldness came back, only this time it started at my feet and rose right up to my neck as I realized Dewey had been right. It could very easily have been him or me that went missing that day. What if one of us had ended up beneath that willow?

The image of Mr. Robert Lee Garner being handcuffed by Officer Jackson flashed in my mind and a sour feeling came to my stomach. I remembered what Mr. Garner said about Ruby Mae and how bad he seemed to feel about finding her body all them years ago. I remembered him telling me and Dewey how he still left flowers for her. I remembered the fresh flowers we had seen earlier today when we rode our bikes to his ranch. I was near on positive he didn't have anything to do with Mary Ann Dailey's death, yet he was now sitting in the Alvin jail for it. Then I remembered the fifteen minutes I spent in that cell and the sourness in my stomach grew worse. I checked my watch. Mr. Garner would have already been there at least two hours.

I don't think I could've survived another fifteen minutes in that sickly mustard-colored room.

It occurred to me that since Ruby Mae was killed twelve years ago, in all likelihood, Mr. Wyatt Edward Farrow wasn't behind this on account of him just moving to Alvin at the end of last summer. From what little I knew of him, his interests leaned more toward roadkill than young girls anyway.

So if it wasn't Mr. Garner and it wasn't Mr. Farrow, who was it?

It was a mystery I didn't find nearly as fascinating as the disappearing roadkill, so I finally stopped thinking about it, figuring it was one of those things best left to grown-ups to work out.

CHAPTER 17

Nearly a week later, my delusion that the little talk I had with Carry the night she came home four and a half hours late had somehow changed her came crumbling down to the ground, leaving me with an ethical quandary for which Carry was entirely to blame.

After the heart-to-heart we'd had that night, I had really hoped she would now second-think the way she had been acting, especially with Tiffany Michelle Yates still being gone and Mary Ann Dailey showing up dead and all. Mr. Garner was still in the Alvin jail, and I couldn't imagine how bored he must be. He continued giving no indication of knowing anything about the whereabouts of Tiffany Michelle. In fact, after that first day, he pretty near stopped talking altogether except for occasionally telling my mother how disappointed her pa would be in her if he was still alive.

I figured that wasn't helping his case much.

Tonight, I lay in bed with the light from the occasional star barely managing to find its way through my window and into my bedroom, and I listened to my mother and Uncle Henry talking while I drifted off to sleep. I couldn't understand what they were saying tonight, it was all just murmurs, but the fact that they weren't loud or hysterical was comforting, especially given how things had been lately.

After seeing Mary Ann Dailey's lifeless body beneath that tree, I worried I might have nightmares about it for the rest of my life, but surprisingly, the incident didn't seem to plague my sleep much. If it did, I must have forgotten any dreams I had recounting that day by the time I woke up. What it did do, however, was make it harder for me to fall asleep. I kept thinking about Mary Ann's eyes, and how lifeless they looked. How they were wide open, but staring at nothing.

It made me think of my own life and how lucky I was to be alive and still able to look at things. To still have life in my eyes. And those thoughts always led to others, like maybe I wasn't always living the way I should be. Maybe I should spend every day thinking tomorrow might be the one where I end up under a tree like Mary Ann. I sure as heck wouldn't spend the day balancing rocks on the ends of sticks if I knew I only had one day left.

So these days, I spent a lot more time awake in my bed thinking about stuff I really hadn't paid much attention to before. Maybe this was a good thing, I wondered. Maybe that's why my mother didn't put up quite the fight about me coming along as, now that I thought back, she probably should have. Maybe she was considerably smarter than I had been giving her credit for over the years.

At any rate, tonight my mother and Uncle Henry

were having what appeared to be a relatively *normal* conversation again for once, and the quiet mumbles reverberating through the house calmed my mind immensely. I was nearly asleep when I heard a different sound entirely. This one filled my stomach with fire because, as soon as I heard it, I realized how stupid and heartless my own sister actually was.

I thought I had somehow made her understand it was important to stick together and help each other, the way I had heard my mother tell Chief Montgomery she wished *her* family had supported *her* during those years after she had Carry. Honestly, I had thought I had somehow gotten through to her, that she now knew that if she looked out for me and my mother, I'd look out for her.

But now I realized Carry had just written me off as a little kid and told me what I wanted to hear. Either that, or she was already testing how well I'd watch out for her.

The noise had come from her room: the unmistakable sound of her window gently sliding open, followed by her climbing out through it and dropping down into the shrubs on the other side. Just to be sure, I got up on my knees and watched out my own window as she came creeping around the house and snuck like a shadow through the pin light darkness of our front yard.

She left me not knowing what to do. I had spent a half hour that night telling her I would be there for her, but now I couldn't figure out what the best way to do that was. Should I just let her go and pretend I never saw her? That would be easiest. But what if something happened to her?

I don't think I had fully understood how Ruby Mae

Vickers had haunted my mother's life the past twelve years until that day I saw Mary Ann Dailey's dead body. But now I think I did, and if there was one thing I knew, it was that I didn't want my own Ruby Mae. And if something *did* happen to Carry on account of me not tellin' anyone I saw her leave, she very well could become just that.

That thought cinched my decision. I got out of bed, feeling the hardwood cold on my bare feet, and shuffled down the hall in my pajamas. Passing through the kitchen, I went straight on to the living room, spending the whole trip trying to figure out how I was gonna say it. I thought of at least ten different ways, but when I got there, it didn't make any difference because I just blurted it out anyway.

"Carry snuck out her window," I said.

Uncle Henry's eyes closed and he took a deep breath. My mother's face went through a range of emotions until finally settling on anger. Uncle Henry started talking, but my mother wheeled on him after bolting off the sofa to her feet, immediately cutting him off. "Not a word!" she said. Then to me: "Get your coat on. You're coming along."

"Now, why is he—" Uncle Henry started, but again she cut him off, this time with just a sharp glare. My uncle raised up his palms in surrender.

Uncle Henry followed me to the door as I quickly struggled into my boots and slipped my big green winter coat over top of my pajamas. My mother went to get her own coat. She came out of the bedroom wearing it. "Seriously, Leah, why is Abe—"

"Because I'm his goddamn mother and I *say* he's

coming, that's why," she snapped. "Is that good enough for you?"

Again Uncle Henry raised his palms, this time with a shrug. "Fair enough." He looked at me. "Take notes. This is what you *don't* do to stay out of trouble. Be smarter than your sister."

I was still sort of in shock, wondering if somehow I *was* in trouble. It kind of felt like it. But once we were in the car, my mother assured me I wasn't and that I did the right thing by telling. I think the real reason she brought me was to make sure she kept at least some semblance of calmness as she hunted the streets of Alvin for her daughter. She couldn't bring Uncle Henry and leave me alone, and she knew she wouldn't be completely irrational with me in the car.

It was a dark night, and some of Alvin's roads didn't have streetlights. Others were eerily lit under their yellow sodium glow. Once we drove maybe a mile or so, going up and down the neighborhood streets, my mother almost seemed calm. "At least this time I know she's actually *gone* somewhere," she said. "She wasn't *taken* by anyone."

"Maybe she went out to meet her boyfriend?" I offered.

Mom clucked her tongue. "That's the part that still scares me."

"You think he might kill her?"

She sighed, shaking her head. "Ironically, it's not death on my mind this time, but life."

"What do you mean?"

"Nothing. I'm just ramblin'."

We drove the circle from Cottonwood Lane down

Hunter Road and Blackberry Trail. I saw the yellow eyes of an owl sitting on the branch of a large oak tree go by out my window. "Well," my mother said, "if she was on foot, we'd have passed her by now. Which means she's in a car." She pulled over and grabbed her car phone from the stand on the console.

"Who're you calling?"

"Jessica Thompson." Jessica Thompson had been Carry's best friend since sixth grade. I listened to my mother's end of the conversation as she talked to Jessica's mother. It was full of frustrating pauses and I could tell my mother was fighting to remain calm. "Yes, I understand, Mrs. Thompson, but I would really appreciate it if you could get your daughter out of bed for three minutes so I can ask her a question . . . See, mine's snuck out and I need to find her . . . No, I'm not insinuating anything . . . I'm sorry Jess has the flu, but I really . . . Okay, thank you so much. Yes, of course, I'll hang on."

There had always been some weird tension between Jessica's family and ours that I never understood, as though both families waited for the day when one of their daughters would corrupt the other. You would think Mrs. Thompson would be happy to hear it was Carry and not Jessica on the Alvin Police Department's most-wanted list tonight.

My mother was still waiting for Jessica to come to the phone. I searched the trees outside my window for more owls, but saw none. Then my mother started speaking again.

"Hi, Jessica? Listen, it's Mrs. Teal. I need you to tell me what make and color of car Carry's boyfriend drives . . . Jess? Don't cover, please? I promise I won't flip out on her . . . I just have to find her . . . Yes, it's an emergency . . . Red? What make? You sure? That's fine. Okay, thank you . . . Oh, and just so I don't have to bother you again, on the off chance his vehicle doesn't turn up, what's his name? Thank you, Jess. Thank your mother for me, too. I hope you're feeling better tomorrow. No, I won't tell her it was you."

My mother always kept a notepad by her steering wheel. She wrote all the information down as Jessica told it to her.

She hung up and immediately hit a number on her speed dial.

"Who're you calling now?" I asked.

"Mind your business. Hi, Chris? I need you to run a name for me. Stephen McFarren, lives in Satsuma." She waited. I looked for more owls. "Okay, give me all twenty-seven. No, on second thought, scratch that. Check if any of them happen to have a red Pontiac, most likely a Firebird, registered in their name or their father's name. No, I don't have a year." She waited some more. "1982? That sounds about right."

She wrote down some information and then said to Officer Jackson, "Okay, he sounds too old. At least he *better* be too old. Any chance he's got a *son* named Stephen? Perfect. How old is the son? Jesus Christ. Okay, give me the phone number." She was about to hang up when she stopped and said, "Chris, one last thing. Do me a favor? If you aren't too busy, forward the office phones to your car number and help me look for that vehicle. It's somewhere here in Alvin or within three miles of the city limits right now. No, actually, scratch that, too. He's nineteen years old, which means speed zones mean nothin' to him. That vehicle could be *six* miles outside city limits by now. Odds are, though, it's parked down some dark alley. Yeah, I'm on the east side. If you take west, that should cover things pretty well."

There was a pause while I assumed Officer Jackson asked my mother why she wanted this particular vehicle hunted down in such an emergency.

"Because my daughter's in that car," my mother said. "That's why."

She hung up and looked at me. "I've got one last call to make." She smiled. "This one's the fun one."

I didn't dare ask as she dialed the number she had written on her pad.

"Hello, Mr. McFarren. Hi, this is Detective Teal from the Alvin Police Department. I was just wondering if you happened to know the whereabouts of your son? I see. And you know his girlfriend? You've met her? Mmm-hmm. Well, funny thing. It turns out your son is dating *my* daughter." She made a fake laugh, only most people other than me wouldn't know it was fake. "Yes, nice to meet you, too. I am just wondering if Stephen told you that Caroline's only fourteen years old . . . ?" I noticed she avoided pointing out that she'd be fifteen in less than two months.

There was a long period of silence after she said that.

"Yeah, no, she's not seventeen, she's fourteen . . . I dunno, I guess your son lied. No, Mr. McFarren, I am quite sure of my daughter's age."

She paused to cough and roll her eyes at me.

"Actually, Mr. McFarren, I'm wondering if you are familiar with the statutory rape laws in Alabama? No, no, you're probably right . . . but just in case, let me educate you so you can make your son aware. You know, for next time.

"There actually *are* no statutory rape laws in this state. The age of consent is sixteen. If the person is under sixteen years of age it is *automatically* considered rape in the second degree whether it was consensual or not and can carry a prison sentence of up to twenty years. You may want to sit your son down and make certain he is aware of these facts. You probably also heard someone has been taking young girls from our town? One was found butchered just days ago . . . No, I'm not accusing your son of having anything to do with it, I'm only sayin', if I were him, I wouldn't want to throw that kind of suspicion out there by being found with fourteen-year-old girls in the backseat of his car. You know what I mean."

A hesitation while she listened. "Oh, don't worry, I'll be doing the same with my daughter. I'm in no way pinning the blame completely on your boy. But remember, hc *is* the one that could be convicted if things went the wrong way. And I've visited the jails in this state. They are not the nicest in the country. No, I am actually out looking for them now. Don't worry, I will be sure to let him know you wish him home at his earliest convenience. I trust this won't be a problem any longer? Thank you, Mr. McFarren."

She hung up, sat back, and took a big breath. "Okay, I actually enjoyed that a bit too much."

"Is Carry's boyfriend going to jail?" I asked.

"No, probably not. Probably he's just going out to the woodshed."

"What does that mean?"

"Nothing you'll ever have to worry about." She turned and even smiled at me before pulling back onto the street. We drove down all the clumpy gravel roads following the basin where Stillwater Creek and Clover Creek ran. These weren't even roads at all, just ruddy patches of hard-packed mud where nobody but fishermen and truck drivers generally come. Occasionally, me and Dewcy rode through here on our bikes, but not very often.

Eventually, my mother turned up Main Street, which, compared to most other streets in town, was rather brightly lit. We went slow, stopping to look down each intersection we went by.

From the console between us, my mother's car phone sprang to life. She hefted it up and answered the call. "Hey, Chris. Oh, thank God. No, no. Have they seen you? Okay, just leave them . . . let me take care of it." A long pause followed. Afterward, Mom sighed. "No, I'm fine. I have Abe with me. Yes . . . yes, of course that's why." She laughed. "I already called Stephen McFarren's father and read him the riot act on second-degree rape. No, it won't escalate from there . . . No, Chris? Seriously. Just go back to the station. Please? Let me handle this? I'm calm. Here, listen." She held the phone toward me. "Am I calm?"

"She seems fairly calm," I said, although she'd never asked me to vouch like this before, so I suddenly felt she might be less calm than I had thought a few seconds earlier. "Okay, thanks, Chris," she said into the phone. "Yes, I will call you immediately after I send him on his way. Thanks again."

Ending the call, she tossed the phone onto the mat at her feet. It landed with a thump as she accelerated west on Main Street. I glanced at the speedometer. "Aren't we going a bit fast?" I asked.

"I'm a cop. I'm allowed to speed."

"Okay."

CHAPTER 18

We came to the end of Main Street and kept going, the buildings on either side of us breaking to knotted forests of oak and hemlock. They loomed far above the street, blocking out what little night light there was. Even the streetlamps were spaced farther apart out here. We crossed over Blackberry Creek and I realized we were headed way out of Alvin.

"Where are we going?"

"A few miles outside of town. It's exactly how I guessed it. They're parked at the side of some back-ass dirt road running along one of the ranches. It just better not be *exactly* like I guessed it."

"What do you mean?"

"Nothing."

Main Street split off into Old Highway Seventeen and New Highway Seventeen, which folks just called Highway Seventeen. That's the way we went. The only things out here were ranch houses, farms, old barns, and lots and lots of crops and cattle. On either side of us, a mist blanketed the fields. Out my window, I saw the tall barn of the old Hunter place barely rising above it.

Old Man Hunter no longer owned the ranch; he had sold it years ago. Back when he did have it, he grew soy and corn. Now it was just cattle. On the other side of the car, the Shearers' cotton farm sat nearly invisible in the white fog.

The road came up out of the fog as we went past the Allen farm. There were two farmhouses on the farm, an old one set closer to the road (it had been built back before New Highway Seventeen came through their land) and a new one. The old one was barely a husk of what it once was. Jesse James Allen and his grandfather built the new one after the one they lived in burned almost all the way to the ground six years ago. Jesse's grandfather liked to say they built it practically by hand, but the truth, according to my mother, was that they got a lot of help from the hired hands that came up from Mexico that year.

I couldn't believe the old farmhouse was still standing. I only caught a glimpse of it. It was an ugly sight, standing there like some hollow-eyed creature scarred and black amidst a sca of fog. It made me shiver as the road dipped back into the mist, hiding it again.

Jesse James Allen wasn't much older than Carry. He was eighteen, which apparently put him a year younger than her new boyfriend. "How come I never see Jesse James Allen no more?" I asked.

My mother thought this over. "After the fire, he wasn't the same. He lost his mother, father, and grandmother, remember? Think of how that would affect you."

"I *did* lose them," I said. "Although to be right honest, I don't much remember Grandma or my pa."

"Well, you were young," my mother said. "And true enough, you have experienced a lot of death for such a little person. But it was different for you—you didn't lose them all at once. And like you said, you hardly knew your pa."

"Sometimes I wish I had," I said. "Known my pa, I mean."

She frowned. "Well, I'm afraid we're going to have to postpone *this* conversation for another day. Right now I'll be giving you answers I'll regret later on." Why did I always get the feeling my mother was mad at my pa for dying on her? It didn't make any sense to me. I didn't think he *meant* to die. Probably, if he had the choice, he'd still be here with us cooking up barbecue for dinner every night like most pas did.

I realized I had my photo of my pa in my pocket. It made me feel good, knowing my lucky picture was with us. Things would work out okay, no matter what. I just knew it.

"I'm sorry, Abe," she said. "I didn't mean . . . It's just . . . I don't like talking about your pa."

"I know," I said. I *did* know this. I just didn't know why. Again, I wondered if it was because she was mad at him for up and dying on us. Maybe I wasn't supposed to be missing him if she was upset with him. I didn't rightly know. Then I thought about my grandpa. Unlike my pa, I got to know my grandpa very well before he died. He was fun. I really enjoyed it when we were together. Grandpa taught me how to play checkers. We used to play all the time, even after he went into the hospital, and I'd win most of the games. Although, when I thought back on it now, I couldn't help but wonder if he'd let me win some of them on purpose.

I remembered when I found out he died. I don't think I ever cried so much in my whole entire life. I still missed him a lot, and sometimes found myself crying because of it. Usually, only when I was alone in my bed.

I wondered if my mother felt the same way about my grandpa as she did about my pa.

"Am I allowed to miss Grandma and Grandpa?" I asked her. Like my pa, we rarely spoke of my grandparents. My mother didn't like talking about them, either. Maybe it was just dead people in general that made her uncomfortable, I didn't rightly know. I did know that I couldn't remember when we last visited their graves. We'd gone a couple of times after Grandpa first died, but hadn't been since.

I thought Grandpa deserved a visit.

My mother's face fell. She reached over and touched the side of my head. "Oh, honey, you're allowed to miss anybody you want. Even your father. I just—I have Carry to worry about right now. And for the record? I miss Grandma and Grandpa, too. They were taken from us too early." Tears touched her eyes. She tried to keep me from seeing them as she reached up and let the Lord Jesus play in her fingers. The silver chain bounced on her throat. I knew that necklace meant a lot to her. My grandpa gave it to her before he died, and it was one of the few things she kept in her life to remind her of him. In fact, I never once saw her take it off. "Your grandpa would be so proud at what a great boy you've turned into," she said.

"What about Carry?" I asked.

"What do you . . . Oh—" She wiped her face, realizing what I meant. "Honey, they would both be so proud of *both* of you. You know, your sister isn't really doing anything wrong. I mean she *is*, but she ain't doin' nothin' every other fourteen-year-old doesn't do. At least the headstrong ones. The others all *think* about doing it. At least you gotta give Caroline that—she's got guts and initiative. Probably at this point they outweigh her brains."

We turned down a dark gravel road. My mother drove slowly. Neither of us spoke. I had no idea why, but I felt excited anticipation building inside me. It was almost like *I* was the one who snuck out and was about to get caught.

Sure enough, a few blocks later, a red car came into sight. Parked at the side of the road, it was barely visible in the misty night.

Mom pulled over immediately. "Okay, you're going to stay here. Understand? Sit quietly in this seat and do not move."

I nodded. I was getting used to waiting in the car. Mom sat back in her seat for a second with both hands on the wheel and took a big deep breath. "Calm, happy thoughts, Leah," she said, and got out.

As soon as she was far enough away, I rolled both windows down. There was no way I was missing this. Dewey would want a full report in the morning.

My mother approached the car slowly and quietly on the passenger side. She even crept the last part of the way. I felt like I was actually getting to watch her do her job—something I'd always wanted to do, but something she constantly refused to allow except for the other day when she brought me along to the murder scene of Mary Ann Dailey. But that was only on account of me being a witness and all. Even though, since then, I had started suspecting my mother had other motives for wanting me to see the body that day, like maybe I was supposed to learn something from it. One thing was for sure: I would never forget looking into Mary Ann Dailey's dead eyes. They'd be with me until I died myself.

Through the dark mist hanging along the road between our car and Stephen McFarren's Firebird, I saw my mother's hand go up and try the door. Apparently it was unlocked because in the next instant she slammed it open and, in one motion, pulled Carry right out from the backseat. My sister got tangled in the shoulder belt from the front and I could see her dealing with that while simultaneously trying desperately to get her shirt back on. She was wearing her bra though, and her bottom parts were, from where I sat anyway, still clothed. That was a detail Dewey would want to know for sure.

With Carry mainly dressed and free of the shoulder belt, my mother began walking her back toward our car when Carry's boyfriend stumbled from the driver's side of his Firebird. My guess was that he had been delayed on account of having to put whatever clothes had been removed from his body back onto it before getting out.

Even in the misty darkness, Stephen McFarren looked like one of those tall, goofy senior guys you always saw with skateboards or in movies. His hair was dark and curly, his body seemed too thin to support his height, and his teeth shone white even on this dark street, appearing way too big for his mouth. I figured Carry could do a lot better.

Stephen McFarren started shouting at my mother. I couldn't hear what he was saying, but he wasn't at all happy with her pulling Carry away from him and his backseat. Then I heard him say something about calling the police on her.

Which, of course, I immediately knew was a huge mistake. I just didn't know exactly *how* huge until I saw what happened next.

I don't even know where she'd had it, but suddenly my mother's gun was in her hands and she had both arms held straight out, pointing the barrel of her weapon directly at Stephen McFarren, exactly the way she told me and Dewey to never hold a gun unless we wanted someone to get hurt. Somehow, while pulling out her gun, my mother had also managed to push Carry down to a kneeling position on the street at her feet. It all took place in one instantaneous movement that I must have blinked through, because I missed it entirely.

"If I was you, young man," she said, "I'd get back into my vehicle right this instant and head for home." Her voice had risen in volume and was commanding in a way I had never heard before.

Stephen McFarren's hands shot straight up over his head. "Whoa, lady. Hold on. There's some mistake . . ."

"There's no mistake," my mother said. "Get back in your car right now, or I'll blow your fucking head off. And if you ever go near my daughter again, I will blow your fucking *testicles* off. Do I make myself clear?"

Stephen McFarren just stood there stunned. Or maybe

he was frozen with fear. Or maybe he peed himself. I know I very well could have in his position.

"I said, do I make myself clear?" my mother yelled.

He nodded. "Yes, ma'am."

"Then why are you still standing there? Go. Get in your goddamn car and drive away."

Stephen McFarren leaped behind the wheel of his red Firebird and slammed the door. Starting the car, he drove off with the passenger door still open. Half a block away he stopped, reached across, and closed that. Then he continued on in a peel of rubber.

"You okay, baby?" my mother asked Carry as she helped her into the backseat of our car. She sounded completely calm once more. It was as though she had some magical switch that she could just flip on and off.

I sat there in the front with my mouth hanging open. Never in my life had I heard my mother use those words. Of course, I'd never seen her threaten to kill someone, either. I started thinking back to all the times she ever got mad and yelled at me and realized I probably hadn't been that bad after all.

My mother turned the car around and headed back toward the highway. Carry still hadn't said a word yet. She was just sitting there in the backseat, her arms folded tightly across her chest. Finally she said, "I can't believe you, Mother. All the girls date older guys. I don't know what your problem is."

"You're not 'all the girls,' " my mother said.

"I can't believe you pulled your gun," I said.

"I can't believe I didn't pull the trigger."

We drove in silence awhile. My mother turned onto

Highway Seventeen and once again we started passing all the farms on the outskirts of town. "Guess I'm pretty grounded," Carry said.

"Let's talk in the morning," my mother said. "When I don't have a loaded gun this close to my hand."

CHAPTER 19

The next day was Saturday.

I always woke early on Saturday mornings, and this Saturday wasn't any exception. The clock in the kitchen said twenty minutes to seven when I padded out wearing my pajamas. This morning I even had socks on. I decided the weather had gotten too cold for bare feet on my hardwood floor in the morning anymore.

Sometimes, Uncle Henry had the same sleeping habits I did. Usually, by the time I got up, the smell of coffee brewing would already be filling the kitchen and the hall when I opened my bedroom door. This morning though, I could still hear him sawing logs from the living room sofa. It was a bit of a disappointment, to be honest. I liked getting up early, but it was awfully boring when you were the only one awake. Besides, I especially liked having the smell of coffee drifting through the house while I wiped the sleep from my eyes. This morning, all I got was the cold tile kitchen floor (that even felt cold through my socks) and the feeling that the entire rest of the world was

sound asleep just waiting for me to make some sort of
noise to bring it to life.

I tiptoed into the living room, thinking that just my
standing there looking at him might make Uncle Henry
open his eyes, but he did not. The thick gold drapes
were pulled mostly shut across the picture window
above the sofa, but there was a gap of a few inches between them, and the morning sun glowed through it,
casting the room in a magical pink and gold that really
made me wish I wasn't the only one wandering around
awake.

Then I noticed something move outside through that
gap in the drapes. At first I couldn't believe what I
thought I saw, so I had to creep closer, and near on lean
right over top of Uncle Henry to get a better look. My
heart flipped up into my throat when my initial guess
turned out to be absolutely correct.

It turned out I actually wasn't the only person in the
world awake this morning. I wasn't even the only person
awake on our block. Across the street, in plain morning
daylight, Mr. Wyatt Edward Farrow had just left his
house and was headed down Cottonwood Lane, taking
the sidewalk in the direction of Hunter Road.

He looked like some sort of cowboy from those old
movies, with a cowboy hat, boots, and everything. He
even had a leather vest over his checked shirt. Under
one of his arms was a long, rectangular cardboard box.
It looked to me like the perfect size and shape of box
someone might use to carry something like a shotgun
in. Squinting into the morning sun barely topping the
tree line behind the row of houses across our street, I

continued watching him shuffle down the lane until he was out of my line of sight.

I couldn't believe it. It was the first time I had ever seen him leave his house since he moved in. There was only one thing to do. I had to call Dewey, and we had to follow him.

Now I was very happy that nobody else in the house was awake. It made it much easier for me to discreetly use the phone, and I would be able to get out without having to answer a whole slew of questions. Probably Uncle Henry wouldn't have been so bad, but my mother would most likely frown upon the idea of me and Dewey sneaking around after our neighbor, even though I was near on positive he was up to no good. I couldn't understand why she didn't see it. To me, it was so clear. Even Uncle Henry thought the man seemed at least a mite suspicious after me and Dewey told him everything we saw.

At any rate, I was starting to learn forgiveness was generally easier to get than permission. Besides, I *really* didn't think my mother would be all that upset anyway; she would just have something to say about it. Mainly because she *always* had things to say about stuff I did.

Dewey turned out to already be up. He answered the phone on the first ring, which was good, because I didn't want to wake up his ma. She would have her own concerns, although through the years I had discovered Dewey's mother didn't seem nearly as thorough as my own when it came to worrying about or monitoring her son's business.

"I'll meet you outside on my bike in fifteen minutes," I whispered excitedly into the phone after telling him about what I saw.

"Why was he dressed like a cowboy?" Dewey asked. I heard him yawn right before he said it. It annoyed me that he wasn't already off the phone and getting his shoes on.

"How the heck should I know? Why is he walking down Cottonwood Lane before seven on a Saturday? And the biggest question is why is he carrying a shotgun with him?" I was getting frustrated, because it was questions like these that were exactly the reason we had to follow him. If we knew all the answers, we could just stay home and Dewey could go back to bed the way it sure seemed like he wanted to right now.

"You said the box just *looked* like it could carry a shotgun," Dewey said.

"Yeah, but what else would you put in a box like that? Come on, Dewey. It was a cardboard shotgun box if I ever seen one."

"Have you ever seen one? I never even heard've one."

I thought that over. "No, I suppose I haven't. Not until this morning, anyway."

"I'm not sure I should leave," Dewey said. "My mom's still asleep."

"Leave her a note. Tell her you'll be back before nine." I reminded him I now had my very own watch.

"I'm still thinking that maybe we should wait . . ."

"Wait for what? We've been watchin' his house going on . . . I don't even know how long. Now, out of nowhere, I actually see him leave and we have the opportunity to find out what he's *really* up to. And you're worried about your mom because she's sleepin'?"

"We know he ain't taking roadkill," Dewey said. "It came back, remember?"

"We know he ain't taking it no *more,*" I corrected him. "We have no idea *what* he does. *This* is what we have to find out." I sighed, trying not to get too angry and raise my voice too loud. I didn't want to wake anybody.

Finally, I convinced Dewey that going after Mr. Wyatt Edward Farrow was not only the right thing to do, it was, by all intents, the *only* thing to do.

"All right," he said. "Give me twenty minutes."

"Twenty minutes? You already used up ten on the phone. We need to catch up with him. You got ten to get here."

"All right."

It took him more like seventeen. In fact, I was on the verge of calling him back when I saw his bike pull up outside my yard through that gap in them drapes. I already had my boots on and quietly headed outside using the back door, being careful to shut it slowly so it didn't slam the way it normally did. I grabbed my bike from beside the garage and pushed it gently down the driveway in the still quiet of the early morning.

"What took you so long?" I asked, still keeping my voice down.

"I was in my pajamas when you called."

"So was I."

"I was hungry."

I rolled my eyes. "Fine time to think about eating. Anyway, let's go before someone wakes up and finds us."

"Did you leave *your* mom a note?" Dewey asked.

I nodded.

"What'd it say?"

"Said I was going biking with you and I'd be home by nine. What did yours say?"

Dewey's cheeks pinkened under the golden morning light. The sun twinkled off the chrome of his handlebars. A few puffy white clouds were stretched across an otherwise light blue sky the color of a dipped Easter egg. "I said we was going after your neighbor to see what it is he does on Saturday mornings dressed as a cowboy."

I stared at him for what felt like a full-on minute, wondering if he was pulling my leg. He wasn't. "Now, why would you go say somethin' dumb like that?" I asked.

"Cuz it's the truth, ain't it?"

"So? What if your mom calls my mom?"

"I always tell the truth."

I bit my tongue and thought before responding. "I do too, but just because I left out part of the *why* doesn't mean I wasn't being truthful. Anyway, it's too late now to worry 'bout it; we ain't goin' back to your house to rewrite your note. Let's go, before we lose any chance of findin' him. Christ, Dewey, it's been nearly half an hour since he left."

We kicked off in the same direction Mr. Wyatt Edward Farrow had been walking. "I figure he's likely gone downtown," I said. "Although I doubt too many shops or anythin' is open so early on a Saturday morning." I said this, although I didn't rightly know whether or not it was true. Maybe all this time I'd been thinking I was one of the only people who woke up bright and early on Saturday mornings when the truth was it actually turned out *most* folk were just like me, and my mother and Carry were the exceptions. I guess me and Dewey were about to find out.

While we rode, I told Dewey about me and my

mother finding Carry and her boyfriend the night before. Most of the story I went over rather quickly, but
he made me slow down at several key areas. The first
was when I described what Carry was wearing in the
back of that car. I knew he'd be interested in hearing
that, I just never realized *how* interested. He must have
asked me nearly ten different things about it. Finally, I
just got mad.

"She was in her bra. What else do you need to
know? Why is this so important?"

Dewey shrugged. He was coasting beside me. "I
dunno," he said.

"Well, let's get past it, then, all right? I mean heck,
you can either imagine what she looked like, or you
can't. I don't see how I can provide any more details
than I already have."

He stopped me again when I got to the end and told
him about how my mother pulled out her gun, pointed
it straight at Carry's boyfriend, and—the most important part, I thought—used *the* word. Not once, but
twice.

"Really?" Dewey asked. This interested him even
more than Carry's undergarments. "Was the gun
loaded?"

It was my turn to shrug. "I'm assuming so. My mom
said it was."

"And she used all them words?"

I nodded. We both swerved around a parked Chevy
truck. "I couldn't believe what I heard," I said. "She
even said she was gonna blow his balls off, or something to that effect."

"Wow."

When Dewey was finally satisfied that he'd wrung

every detail of the story he could from me, we fell into silence for a while. I rode the lead, taking us up to Main Street.

"How do you know this is the way Mr. Farrow went?" Dewey asked.

"I don't," I said. "I just figure if you're gonna go out on a Saturday morning and get dressed up, you're probably headed downtown. I doubt he was going to the swamp or any of the mud roads or anything like that. He certainly didn't look dressed for roadkill collectin'."

Dewey considered this and seemed to be satisfied that it made some sort of sense, because he never asked any more about it. "So," he said after a bit, "did your mom really arrest Mr. Garner?"

This question didn't sit well with me, but I answered with the truth. "Yep. Far as I know, he's still in jail."

"You don't sound too happy about it," he said.

I hesitated. Truth was, I wasn't happy about it, but I didn't exactly know why. Something about the whole thing felt very wrong to me. Like there was something I should understand but didn't, or maybe something I should be remembering but forgot. "Tell me somethin', Dewey; you were there that afternoon in the rain when we went searching for Mary Ann Dailey. Remember all the stuff Mr. Robert Lee Garner said? Remember the way he talked about Ruby Mae Vickers? How he put flowers out for her?"

Dewey said he did. "He didn't seem as though he wanted to talk much 'bout them flowers, though."

I nodded. "But we saw more flowers that day we rode over to his ranch, remember?" I asked. "The day they found Mary Ann? Those flowers seemed fresh to me."

"Yup," Dewey said. "Me too."

I backpedaled slightly, slowing a bit. "Dewey, do you think Mr. Garner could do something like this to Mary Ann?"

"If the police think so, I don't see why my opinion would rightly matter. I'm only eleven years old," he said. This was a slightly different opinion than the one he had expressed the night Mary Ann Dailey showed up dead and Mr. Garner was first taken into custody.

"But—" I wanted to keep talking, yet I really didn't know where to go with it. Problem was the details surrounding everything to do with Mary Ann Dailey nearly exactly matched those of Ruby Mae Vickers. This meant, at least in my mother's eyes, that the two cases weren't just likely related, they *were* related. They *had* to be related.

I had figured nothing downtown would be open this early on a Saturday, but I was wrong. As we came up on the Mercantile (which everyone as old as my mother referred to as Mr. Harrison's five-and-dime), I saw Jesse James Allen coming up the sidewalk and turning in. I couldn't believe how many people were up so early. As the door opened, I slowed down to get a glimpse inside to make sure Mr. Farrow wasn't there.

I squinted into the dark interior. I didn't see any customers, just Mr. Harrison stocking shelves. My concentration was fixed so much on the store that I nearly ran into Jesse James where he was still holding the door open. Smiling, I backpedaled, skidding my bike to a stop. "I reckon I near on hit you," I said. "Sorry about that."

It had been at least a year since I'd last seen Jesse James, but he knew me well enough. At least usually. This time, it was like he'd never seen me before in his life. He just stared at me without saying a word.

"You okay?" I asked.

He looked terrible, like he was sick or something. His clothes didn't help. He had on a T-shirt that looked like it should have seen the bottom of a garbage can a long time ago. It was smudged with dirt and ripped along one of the seams. It hung untucked over a pair of jeans that were only in slightly better shape. His black hair probably hadn't been cut since at least Easter and was in need of a good combing. It hung over his soft gray eyes in a way that made it impossible to guess what he might be thinking.

As I looked at him, I couldn't help but remember those twins sitting in front of Luther Willard King's house. In my head, I gave myself a good talking to for these thoughts, assuming they had to be racist.

Awkwardly, Jesse James Allen gave me the briefest of nods before ducking into the Mercantile. Dewey pulled up beside me as the door closed, the bell attached to its top ringing.

"Never mind him," Dewey said to me. "My pa says he ain't been right since the fire."

"He used to say hi to me," I said, feeling a bit dejected.

"Looked to me like he ain't sayin' *nothing* today."

I gave the door one last consideration.

"Are we lookin' for Mr. Farrow or not?" Dewey asked. He'd started slowly down the sidewalk again.

I nodded. "I'm coming." I began pedaling, leaving all thoughts of the store and Jesse's rudeness behind me.

It didn't take me long to catch back up to Dewey. He wasn't nearly as fast a rider as I was. "Let me ask you something else," I said as I coasted up to his side. I wanted to get back to my issues about the Ruby Mae case being related to Mary Ann Dailey and whether or not Mr. Garner was innocent. I decided to try approaching the problem from the opposite direction. "Do you think Mr. Garner might have killed Ruby Mae Vickers all them years ago?"

Dewey glanced away from the street and looked at me, confused. "No, 'course not. Why would he be puttin' flowers out for her if he did that?"

I nodded slowly, more to myself than to Dewey. That was the main question that had been rattling around inside my head ever since I'd seen Officer Jackson pull out his handcuffs and bring Mr. Garner's hands behind his back out there on Holly Berry Ranch.

But there *was* something else, too. Something I *knew* I had forgotten. Something *important*. But, no matter how hard I thought about it, I couldn't quite put my finger on it. It was as though it was just waiting there, hovering in the corner of my mind just outside of reach.

"Look!" Dewey shouted, interrupting my thoughts. We had just turned down Main Street, and two blocks ahead of us was none other than Mr. Wyatt Edward Farrow himself. There was no mistaking those cowboy boots, vest, and hat. He was still carrying what I was now completely convinced could *only* be a shotgun box. He was walking in the same direction we were going, so he didn't see us behind him.

We hit our brakes, slowing nearly to a stop. "We

gotta keep back at least a block or two," I said quietly. I knew something about tailing a suspect from all the years growing up with my mother.

"I'm not so sure that looks like a shotgun box to me," Dewey said.

"What else could it be?"

"I dunno. Roses, maybe?"

"Now, why in heck would Mr. Wyatt Edward Farrow be carryin' a cardboard box full of roses down Main Street at seven in the mornin' on a Saturday?" I asked.

"I dunno," Dewey said. "Why would he be carrryin' a shotgun in a box down Main Street at seven in the mornin'?"

"Because he's up to no good," I said. That one was easy.

"There could be anythin' in that box," Dewey pointed out. "Maybe a baseball bat."

"That makes even less sense than the roses. At any rate, we'll never know unless we follow him and find out."

Mr. Farrow walked another six blocks or so until he came to the post office. He tried the door but, of course, the Alvin Post Office is *never* open before nine o'clock, *especially* on Saturdays, when I figured it probably stayed closed until noon. We pulled up to a stop a few blocks away, trying not to look conspicuous.

"What's he doin'?" Dewey asked.

"I dunno," I said. "Maybe he was goin' to start shooting everyone working at the post office, but showed up too early."

"You think if he were gonna do somethin' like that, he'd be smart enough to check up on their hours first."

We watched him ponder the dilemma of the not-yet-open post office for a few minutes until he took a card and a pen from the pocket of his jeans and wrote something on the card before tucking it into the top of the shotgun box. Then, with a suspicious glance up and down the street, he propped the box against the post office door. Luckily, he didn't see us when he looked around. With one final consideration of the box and the locked door, he started walking back our way, whistling to himself.

"Let's turn around," Dewey whispered.

"No," I said. "Let's wait until he's long past and go see what he wrote on that card. Maybe we can even open the box."

"I don't think that's a very good idea," Dewey said.

"You don't think any of my good ideas are very good. It's part of why you never . . ."

I started explaining all this to Dewey when I heard a car pull up beside us. I nearly ignored it completely, even when I heard the door open. But seconds later, my mother was yelling at us in a way that, had I not heard her screaming all them cusswords at Carry's boyfriend last night, might have actually scared me. She was telling us to get in the goddamn car and that we don't go stalking neighbors and we *especially* don't sneak out of the house without asking permission first.

I saw the color drain from Dewey's face as she came around and held the door open and we clambered into the backseat.

"She's really mad," he said.

"It was your stupid note," I snapped back.

"Hope she didn't bring her gun," he said.

Outside, my mother was throwing our bikes into the trunk of her car. She wasn't being too gentle about it.

"Didn't you learn nothin' last night?" she asked me after she got inside the car and pulled her door shut.

"What do you mean?" I asked.

"With Carry and her boyfriend? Did you not learn anythin'?"

"I learned that you don't take kindly to boys parking with Carry, and that when you pull out your gun, you tend to use some words I never heard you use before."

She hesitated then, and I wasn't sure if I'd maybe said something really wrong. But I saw her struggle not to smile, and my stomach calmed a bit. "Well, that's not what you were supposed to learn," she said. "You were supposed to learn that you don't sneak out of the house. And I already told you about how you should be treatin' our neighbors."

"But—" I started, but stopped when she held up her finger. Her face was red and I could tell she was angry. Dewey, on the other hand, obviously didn't know my mother as well as I did.

"Ma'am, we saw Mr. Farrow carrying a box that may or may not have contained a shotgun. It could have had roses in it, I thought, but Abe pointed out that my idea made less sense and that it probably *was* a shotgun. Then I figured it maybe was something like a baseball bat, but again, Abe—"

"Dewey," she said, turning right around to him.

"Do yourself a huge favor right now and just stop talkin', all right?"

Nodding, Dewey said very matter-of-factly, "All right, ma'am, I will do just that. I was only tryin' to point out that if someone actually was walkin' around with what could possibly be a loaded firearm and perhaps—and this again was Abe's theory—had planned on shooting up the post office, I think it's somethin' that—"

My mother's eyes closed and her head came down on the top of her steering wheel.

I turned to Dewey. "Dewey. Seriously. Shut up."

He nodded. "All right," he said.

My mother sighed, shaking her head. "And next time you leave a note, Dewey? Don't incriminate yourself if you don't have to. It's just . . . stupid."

"I was being honest," he said, again, very matter-of-factly.

"There's honest, Dewey, and there's stupid. Learn the difference, or you'll end up in my jail or dead or somethin' one of these days."

Seriousness fell over Dewey's face. "All right, I will do that. I will learn the difference." He was keeping his own, I'll give him that much. I heard not even the slightest hint of shakiness in his voice.

My mother shook her head again. "You're a very strange boy, Dewey."

He gave another nod.

My mother pulled the car out onto the street. I gave Dewey an elbow. "Told you your note sucked," I whispered, but my mother shushed me and told us both not to say another word.

We didn't.

CHAPTER 20

Shortly after starting back home after apprehending me and Dewey, my mother's car phone rang. I was beginning to suspect maybe my theory was right. Maybe most folk *do* keep the same early-morning Saturday schedule as me, except they just don't go to work. They just walked around with shotguns in cardboard boxes or called people on the telephone.

"Chris?" my mother asked after she answered. "What is it?"

"It's Officer Jackson," I whispered to Dewey.

"I'm not dumb," he said. "I know that."

"Great," my mother said into the phone. "I'll be right there."

She hung up and set the phone on its stand. "What did Officer Jackson want?" I asked.

Surprisingly, she didn't answer by telling me to mind my business. "The initial forensics report on Mary Ann Dailey's in."

"And . . . ?" I asked.

"And we're gonna stop at the station on our way home," she said. "Chris and Ethan are already there, along with one of the experts from Mobile. Apparently he showed up before sunrise this morning. I assume that won't mess up your boys' schedule or nothin'?" she asked.

I could tell she was being sarcastic, but I don't think Dewey did. "No, ma'am," he said. "That should be fine."

She nearly laughed. "What about your mother, Dewey? Think she'll be okay with you bein' out a bit longer?"

"I reckon she won't care either way," he said. "Most likely she's back to sleepin'. She don't normally get up before noon on the weekends. She must've gone to the bathroom or somethin' if she saw my note." It sounded cold the way he said it, but I knew it was true. I saw in my mother's eyes that she did, too.

"I can't believe the expert from Mobile works on Saturdays," I said. "And so early, too. He must've started on the road before five."

"Police work ain't like normal work," my mother said. "Sometimes you gotta work odd hours."

As we pulled up to the station, I thought my mother was about to tell us to wait in the car, but even the short drive up Main Street had calmed her down considerably. By the time the car was in PARK, she hardly even seemed upset anymore.

"Can we come in and say hi to Chief Montgomery?" I asked my mother.

She thought this over, closed her eyes, and answered with a deep breath. "Fine. Just tell me you two actually learned somethin' today. I still can't believe last night didn't open your eyes all the way, Abe."

"I already told you I *did* learn somethin' last night," I said. "It just weren't the thing you thought I did."

"It wasn't the thing I *wanted* you to learn, would be more precise," she said.

"Well, next time maybe you should tell me what I should be learnin' upfront. I think maybe that might make it easier for everyone."

She pretended to understand this. "Maybe. Do you at least know what you were supposed to have learned this morning?"

"That I don't sneak out of the house?" I asked.

"So far so good," my mother said hesitantly. "And?"

"And that me and Dewey don't follow our neighbors tryin' to figure out what it is they're doin' that's so suspicious."

My mother shook her head. "You should've just stopped with that 'I don't follow our neighbors'; the rest of it is all some sort of figment of you boys' overactive imagination. Which, I might add, I'm beginnin' to find a mite disturbin'."

"But," I started, "what if—"

"Abe," she said, "just drop it. Understand? Trust me, this is somethin' you should've done a long time ago."

Out my window, two old men strolled past on the sidewalk. Seemed like the whole town was awake. Except probably Carry and Dewey's mother.

I searched my mind for some way to make my mother see that it wasn't our imaginations at all and that *she* was just being blind because of some silly rule she had about neighbors, but I came up completely empty.

"You know what I learned?" Dewey asked.

My mother tilted her head back and stared at the car's ceiling. "What's that, Dewey?"

"That I should be as untruthful as possible from now on," he said with complete, utter confidence.

My mother looked at me over her shoulder, her eyes meeting mine. She gave me a look of exasperation that near on made me laugh. I could tell she was close to giving up on trying to get anything through to Dewey. "Do me a favor, Dewey?" she asked.

"What's that, ma'am?" Dewey asked back.

"Just . . . just don't tell your mother what it is you think you learned. And maybe go back to havin' learned nothin' this morning. How does that sound?"

"Confusing."

"Good enough," my mother said, and opened her door.

"So, are we coming, too?" I asked.

She bent and stuck her head back inside, looking over the seat at Dewey. "Well, I don't rightly trust you two alone in my vehicle, so I guess that's the only option I got." She winked at me and I knew we werc no longer in any sort of trouble. I started wondering if we really ever were. I think my mother might have used up all the anger she had on Carry's boyfriend last night.

"Don't touch anything," she said as we followed her inside the station. "Or at least please *try* not to?" She watched Dewey head straight across the room to the water cooler just as he'd done the last time she brought us here together and added, "Or at least nothing important."

Dewey looked back at her.

"No, Dewey." She sighed. "The water cooler ain't important. You're fine."

Officer Jackson and Chief Montgomery leaned over what was usually my mother's desk. One of the forensic officers I recognized from the swamp that day in the rain sat between them on my mother's chair. His hair looked freshly cut, even shorter than it had been then. Even his goatee looked trimmed. Up close, he looked much older than he had that day in the rain. His eyes were a dull blue that looked up from the pictures and file folders strewn across the desk as my mother approached.

"Leah," Chief Montgomery said, "you remember Officer Philip Diamond from Mobile? Officer Diamond, this is Detective Leah Teal."

Officer Diamond half stood from his chair and shook my mother's hand. "Nice to see you again," he said. Not only did he look older, but when he rose from his seat, he also seemed much taller than I recalled.

A black hardcover notebook was lying off to the side. I hadn't seen it before and guessed it belonged to Officer Diamond. It was almost as though he had completely taken over, although if my mother minded at all, she didn't show it.

Officer Jackson and Chief Montgomery were both in uniform. My mother, of course, was not. Neither was Officer Diamond, who wore a black collared shirt and tan pants. As he once again fell back into my mother's chair, a musty cologne wafted through the room, nearly making me cough. He didn't smell nearly as pretty as Carry did now that she wore perfume.

My attention was drawn to a gurgling and bubbling across the room, where Dewey was slowly filling up one of the paper cups that I'd never seen anybody but him actually use. I looked back to the four officers crowded around the files and pictures, keeping a few steps behind my mother so as not to look conspicuous. I guess I did all right, because they ignored me while they talked about Mary Ann Dailey.

I had a pretty good view of the stuff scattered across the gray desktop, but I purposely avoided looking at them photos. From the slight glimpse I did catch, I knew right away they weren't the sort of pictures I wanted in my head. It was already hard enough getting to sleep having to deal with the image of Mary Ann Dailey lying in that shallow hollow of dirt beneath that beautiful willow out there in the mud.

"So what do we have?" my mother asked.

Officer Diamond slid the black book across the desk and lifted it in his hands, flipping through a few pages before finally answering. "Well," he said, "for starters, we found a nice assortment of food in her stomach, most of it only partially digested. She had eaten shortly before her death, probably within a couple hours. Three maybe, at most."

"What sort of food?" my mother asked.

"Let's see," Officer Diamond said. "Biscuits, blueberry jam, potato chips, garlic dip, and a chocolate bar." He glanced up. "Most likely, we figure it was a Three Musketeers."

My mother's hand came up and rubbed her eyes. "Sorry," she said, "I'm usually more awake than this, but doesn't all that sound more like she was at some slumber party, sittin' round watchin' movies? It certainly don't seem like she was bein' raped and made ready for killin'."

Officer Diamond nodded. "Exactly. And it's all pretty much like that. We even found traces of ice cream and cake in her intestines that had been consumed earlier on."

"All we're missin' is the soda pop and pizza," Officer Jackson said.

Officer Diamond looked up at him. "No, we even found that, too. Well, the soda pop, anyway. Traces of root beer coating the lining of her bladder. 'Course other than that, the rest of her bladder and bowels were pretty much empty."

"Right," my mother said, as though this made perfect sense to her. None of it made any sense to me, other than that it sounded like Mary Ann Dailey got to eat much better than me. "What sort of physical evidence have you uncovered?" my mother asked.

"Not a helluva lot," Officer Diamond said. "Three hairs other than her own on her entire body. Two of 'em belonged to Garner's dog, and the other came from Garner himself. Then, of course, there's all that blood of the victim on Garner's shovel, as well as dried skin matching that of the suspect."

My mother picked up a pen from the desk and tapped it against her lower lip. I think it was the only thing still on the desk that actually belonged to her. That and the stuffed dog I bought her for Mother's Day. Across the room, Dewey finished filling the paper cup and placed it on top of the cooler before beginning to fill a second one. Nobody but me noticed.

"Anybody else's blood on that shovel?" my mother asked.

Officer Diamond shook his head. "Just the girl's."

Frowning, my mother tapped her lip some more. I could tell she was disappointed about this information. She cast a glance to Officer Jackson. "What about the boot prints you were tryin' to get?"

He shook his head. "Wasn't enough definition to get anything worthwhile. The downpour washed all the details away. Even any tire tracks we may have hoped for were too messed up by the time we got there. What little we did manage to get seemed to be congruent with Garner's work boots."

My mother let out a deep breath. "Well, I suppose, given what we've got, so far it sounds like we got the right man."

"Oh, there *was* one more thing," Officer Diamond said. "We found light traces of organochlorine compounds and ammonium nitrate on the victim's skin. That's not a huge surprise, mind you—these are basic chemicals regularly found in farm-use insecticide and fertilizer. All very consistent with her being kept on a farm or a ranch of some kind. We even found light particles of hay dust in her lungs and hair, even though her hair had been recently washed."

Dewey placed cup number two on top of the cooler and started on number three. Sometimes I had no clue what went through his mind.

My mother shook her head, confused. "He washed her hair?"

"Quite often, judging by the soap residue left on her scalp and the rest of her body," Officer Diamond said. "Bathed her and washed her hair, probably once every two days or so." He looked back down at his book. "Oh, and there were a few boll weevil bites at the base of her neck. We also discovered traces of chicken feces particulate on her skin. Our theory is that she was dragged from wherever he kept her to whatever vehicle he brought her to the murder scene in after her last bath. At that point, she was likely already dead." He paused. "So, as I said, everything points to her being kept on some kind of farm or ranch."

"Well, we already knew that," Officer Jackson said.

My mother stared off at the far wall. "Does Bob Garner still have chickens?" she asked.

They all looked at each other, waiting for one to answer. After a few awkward seconds, I took the initiative. "Yes, he most certainly does. At least a dozen and a big ol' cock. Me and Dewey saw 'em that afternoon we showed up and Mr. Garner was working on his tool shed."

I think my voice startled them. Until now, they had forgot I was standing there listening.

"Abe," my mother said, "why don't you go play with Dewey?" She looked over at the three full cups of water precariously balancing on top of the cooler while he filled number four. ". . . Or find something else to entertain yourself with."

"Why?" I asked. "I was the only one of all of you who knew about the chickens. And you know what? I can tell you right now, she wasn't kept on Mr. Garner's ranch."

"I agree with the boy on that one," Chief Montgomery said, looking up from the series of photographs he'd been going through. He gave my mother a look I took to indicate his displeasure at having me present. "Or, if she was, Tiffany Michelle Yates certainly isn't. We searched that entire ranch, every square foot of it, going through it with a fine-toothed comb."

"Unless she's well hidden," Officer Diamond said.

"She'd have to be *very* well hidden, Phil," Chief Montgomery said. "Seriously, there's no way. We went through that place from top to bottom. Twice."

"I already told you," I said. "Mary Ann Dailey wasn't kept there, so why would Tiffany Michelle be there?"

With an exasperated sigh, Chief Montgomery leveled his gaze at my mother. "Why is your boy here, Leah?"

"Hang on a sec, Ethan." She turned to me. "Why do you say Mary Ann Dailey wasn't kept at Mr. Garner's ranch?"

"Didn't you listen to what Officer Diamond said?" I asked. "There were *boll weevil* bites on her neck. Since when do boll weevils go anywhere near cattle ranches? They attack cotton fields. Everyone knows that. I can't *believe* none of you do."

"Watch your tone, young man," my mother said.

Chief Montgomery scratched the back of his neck. When he spoke, his voice was quieter than before. "Actually, the boy's right, Leah. There are no cotton farms anywhere near Bob Garner's place. The chance of there being boll weevils is pretty much zero."

A mess of emotions swelled in my chest. I felt as though I were suddenly important. I also suspected I would be getting a firm talking-to the moment we returned to the car. After a few seconds of struggling between the two, I decided it was worth speaking out for.

"So Garner had the girl somewhere else, hidden on the property of one of the outlying farmlands, most likely," Officer Jackson said. "Then, when the time came, he moved her to where we found her last Saturday."

"I assume Bob's still not talking?" my mother asked Chief Montgomery.

He shook his head solemnly. "Not about anythin' important, anyway. Just about how disappointed your daddy'd be if he knew what was going on."

My mother's gaze dropped to the floor.

Chief Montgomery leaned across the desk and reached out his big arm and put a firm hand on her shoulder. "Leah, he's playin' the only card he has left. Don't let it get to you. Problem is though, without a confession, we're stuck runnin' with whatever clues we can dig up. Which, as of now, means we gotta start lookin' for Tiffany Michelle Yates on some piece of farmland in or around Alvin."

"And if we don't find her then?" my mother asked.

"We make a decision at that point about what to do next. We may have to widen our search to neighboring towns, I dunno. Hopefully, it won't come to that. Hopefully, new evidence will show up just by searching our own town."

My mother looked over to Officer Jackson. "Alvin has like, what? Eight thousand or so acres of surrounding farmland?"

"Actually," he replied, frowning, "it's closer to twelve."

"Great," she said, sarcastically. "Thanks, Chris, you just made me feel a lot better. Anyway, I gotta get these boys home." She looked over at Dewey, just about to place cup number five on top of the water cooler. "You better drink all them, or I'm gonna make you ride in the trunk."

Dewey's eyes grew wide. I think he feared my mother because, next thing I knew, he had quickly downed every single cup.

My mother smiled at me. "Now we really have to get him home before he has to go to the bathroom."

CHAPTER 21

Mom drove Dewey straight to our house after our stop at the police station. It was a good thing too, because by the time we got there, Dewey had already started wriggling around in the backseat. My mother noticed in the rearview mirror. "Dewey, you want me to drive you straight home instead of making you ride your bike?"

"No, ma'am," he said, "I'm fine."

"Dewey, you look ready to pee your pants any minute," she said.

"Think of waterfalls," I whispered to him.

"Shut up," he whispered back.

"Well, then," my mother said, "how 'bout coming in and using our toilet before headin' home. Will you at least do that?"

He considered it a minute. I couldn't figure out why he was so opposed to admitting he had to go. I know if I had just downed five full cups of water, I wouldn't hesitate to take up an offer like that. Most likely, I'd have already made my mother pull over so I could go in the woods. Finally, after more wriggling, Dewey conceded. "Okay, ma'am. I will do just that. And I appreciate the offer very much."

"It's not a problem, Dewey," she said. By the way she said it, I could tell she wanted to once again add something to the effect of *you really are a strange boy,* but she didn't.

"I'll get your boys' bikes out of the trunk. You go ahead and go inside and"—she looked at Dewey nearly bending over now that he was standing outside the car—"and do your business."

I ain't never seen Dewey run as fast as he did then. He barely said thanks as he tore up the front steps, flung open our door, and raced down the hallway. I came in shortly afterward to find Uncle Henry standing there questioningly. "What's going on with Dewey?" he asked.

"It's a long story," I said.

Uncle Henry nodded knowingly. I think he was growing accustomed to my and Dewey's stories always being long and sometimes unusual. Outside, I heard my mother's trunk slam shut and, a few minutes later, she came in and took off her boots. "Is he still in there?" she asked.

"Yup," I said.

"What's going on?" Uncle Henry asked her.

"It's a long story," my mother said.

"Yeah, that's the part I've heard so far," he replied.

"Trust me," my mother said, "it's really enough. The rest ain't so interestin'. What is interestin' though, is that the initial forensic reports on Mary Ann Dailey came back this morning."

"Oh, is that what took you so long?" Uncle Henry asked.

"Yeah, we had to make a pit stop at the station," my mother said.

Just then Dewey came out of the washroom with a look of utter relief and contentment smattered across his face.

"Better?" my mother asked.

Dewey nodded.

"Your mama's been callin' for you ever since Leah left to pick you boys up," Uncle Henry told him. "She's called three times so far. I think you better be gettin' home."

Dewey's eyes widened. "Did she sound mad?"

Uncle Henry shrugged. "I don't rightly know, but three calls in an hour and a half would generally indicate to me she isn't exactly happy."

Dewey looked at me. "I think I'm in for it."

"Then get goin'," my mother said. "Your bike's just outside in the driveway."

In his marathon run to the washroom, Dewey hadn't even bothered taking his shoes off or nothing. "Okay," he said. "Bye, Abe. Bye, Miss Teal. Bye, Uncle Henry."

We all said bye as he ran out the door, slamming it shut behind him.

"I think he's in for it," I said to my mom after a few seconds.

"Oh, he'll be fine. I bet his mom's not even sure she knows exactly what to be mad 'bout. Most likely, she's really only mad cuz I was, and that makes her think that bein' mad's the right thing to do."

"I don't understand."

Shaking her head, my mother said, "To be honest, Abe, I don't, either. But you know? At least Dewey was honest. I have to give him that. And he was willin' to back it up and admit it when I called him on it."

"Mom," I said, "you called him stupid."

She let out a deep breath. "Yeah," she said, "I probably shouldn'ta done that. Dewey is Dewey. He's got a good heart. He'll get along fine in life. Everybody's different, and sometimes even I forget that. Different doesn't matter. This is the thing you need to learn about what color people are and where they come from, Abe. What matters is how good your heart is. There's never, *ever* nothin' wrong with being too honest, so please forget what I said to him earlier. I'll make a point of tellin' Dewey the same thing next time I see him."

I didn't reply, but something about what she just said struck a chord somewhere inside of me.

Then the smell hit. I hadn't noticed it until now, but Uncle Henry had the coffee on and I was willing to bet the smell of crackling bacon would soon be following. "You makin' eggs?" I asked him.

Uncle Henry smiled. "Figured if I waited long enough, you'd show up hungry."

"Where's Caroline?" my mother asked.

"Where do you think?" Uncle Henry asked back. "It's not even ten. She's still sound asleep." We followed him into the kitchen, where he started pulling out pans and took the eggs and bacon from the refrigerator. My mother opened the bread box and pulled out a loaf of white bread, setting it beside the toaster.

I turned one of the kitchen chairs around so it faced toward them instead of the table. Our kitchen chairs were white with small yellow daisies, much too light for the dark brown table they surrounded, my mother always said. For as long as I could remember, she wanted to replace that table. She had an ongoing dream to replace nearly all the furniture in our house one day. I took a seat. "Mom, can I talk to you about Mr. Robert Lee Garner?" I asked.

She sighed. "What?"

"Well, I have some questions," I said.

"Actually, I'd like to hear how some of this morning went, too," Uncle Henry said as the first strips of bacon hit the pan with a loud pop. Almost instantly the two smells, coffee and bacon, intertwined and, along with the bright morning light beaming in through the small window over the sink, it suddenly felt exactly the way a Saturday was *supposed* to.

"Oh, Hank, don't *you* start," my mother said.

"Leah, there ain't no big secrets no more," Uncle Henry said. "Least none that I can tell. You've started lettin' other people into this whole mess, and that's a good thing. Surely even you must've noticed the changes in yourself. I know me and the little soldier here sure have."

That caught me by surprise, but as soon as he said it, I realized Uncle Henry was right. My mother had been gettin' less anxious lately, even though by all indications, the case was worse off than ever. I hadn't noticed though, so I doubted if maybe my mother had, either.

"You don't feel like part of the burden's been lifted from your back?" he asked her.

Placing both palms on the countertop, she looked down and thought a minute. "I don't know what I feel, Hank. I think maybe I'm just exhausted. Maybe I'm starting to wear out. Maybe I'm starting to just not care anymore."

Uncle Henry came over and turned her around. "No, honey, that ain't it at all. You're just too close to it all to see it. You're going through a transition and I really can't wait to see what comes out the other end. I think it's gonna be a thing of beauty. Anyway, tell me about the forensics report."

"No big surprises. Lots of evidence backing up what we already know. Everything still points to Bob Garner. We just need to sort out the details of exactly how he did it, and hope we do it fast enough to save Tiffany Michelle Yates, if she's still in need of savin'." She cast me a look, as though she wished she hadn't said that last part, and part of me wished she hadn't, either. It was funny how Mary Ann Dailey and Tiffany Michelle were different in my head. I think it was because me and Dewey were the last people to see Tiffany Michelle, and I couldn't stop picturing how pretty she looked in that dress with that ribbon in her hair and how happy she was to have that big pink ice cream cone. Like I said before, I had been thinking a lot about how maybe we could have saved her, or maybe it could have been us instead of her. Mary Ann Dailey wasn't like that at all. When Officer Jackson showed me her lying in the dirt beneath that tree, that had been the first time I had seen her in near on two years.

Uncle Henry frowned. "I still don't believe he did it."

"Well, believe it, Hank. Evidence doesn't lie."

"You can say that, Leah," he said, looking her square in the face, "but it still won't change my mind. I *know* the man. He knew your pa. He didn't do it."

Tears came to my mother's eyes. "Hank, stop it! What do you want from me? It's not even *me* saying he did. It's these experts they got from Mobile. They got computers and all sorts of tests they run. They *know* he's guilty."

"And *I* know he's not. And I don't even need a computer or tests. Anyway, my bacon's about to burn."

"Mom?" I asked.

"What?" she asked back, distractedly.

"Can I ask you a few things about Mr. Garner?"

She heaved a big sigh. "Okay, Abe. Let me just grab a cup of coffee and we'll go sit in the living room, all right?" I watched her pour a mug and then she did something she never had before. She turned to me and asked, "Would you like one, too?"

I hesitated, unsure of what she meant. "Coffee?"

"Yeah. I think you're old enough for the odd cup."

Even Uncle Henry paused at the stove where he was putting the fried strips of bacon on a piece of white bread to sop up the extra grease and looked back to see my reaction.

"Okay," I said after a bit of thought.

She poured me my own mug and put in two spoons of sugar and a splash of cream. After she handed it to me, I carefully followed her to the living room, trying not to spill while also attempting to carry the mug by only its handle, because the edge of the cup was too hot to touch.

We both sat on the sofa and set our mugs on the coffee table in front of us. Uncle Henry's blankets were neatly folded with his pillow on top at one end. I sat at the other. The drapes were now pulled open and the day shone brightly through the window, filling the room with light. I could hear Uncle Henry starting a new pan of bacon in the kitchen. The eggs would soon be following.

"Do you know why I brought you to the station with me today?" she asked.

I had just figured it was because we were already out and it was convenient, but obviously there was another reason so I said, "I guess not."

"Because I decided a while back that I can't shield you from the world anymore, Abe. I know you're only eleven, but Mary Ann Dailey was only fourteen and look what happened to her. Maybe if she had been better prepared for the way the world really was, things might not have turned out the way they did. That's why I finally agreed to let you come to Bob Garner's ranch and see her body when you asked to. Not because you were a witness, although that does help a bit, but mainly because you seemed to want to come so badly, and I couldn't figure out why. Do you know why?"

I thought about this a long while, watching the steam rise from my red mug still on the table in front of me. My mother sat beside me sipping from hers. "I actually *don't* know," I said finally. "But something inside me really did want to come. I felt almost like I *had* to come. It still doesn't make any sense to me."

From the kitchen, pots clanged as the bacon sizzled.

"If I had to guess," my mother said, "I'd say your subconscious knows you're growin' up and is tryin' its best to do so with whatever tools it has available. Now, you're in a special situation on account of having a police officer for a mother. I'm sure, despite all my efforts to be careful about not doing it, you've heard many things throughout your childhood most children don't even have a clue about until they're in their mid-teens. You probably didn't always understand it all, but it got stored away inside your head, and as you got older, the pieces slowly came together one way or another. I think because of that, you have a much different view of the world than most kids your age. I'm not sure that's a good thing or not. In fact, it's most likely not, but it would be stupid of me to just pretend it wasn't true, because avoiding issues is nearly always a bad thing to do. At least by my experience."

"You mean like the way you don't like talkin' 'bout Grandma and Grandpa?" I asked. "Or my father?"

My mother winced at this. I saw her hand reach for the Lord Jesus dangling from the silver chain around her neck the way she always did when she thought about Grandma and Grandpa, only this time she caught herself and set her hand back in her lap. Her other hand put her mug back on the table. "See?" she replied. "You've just turned my own argument against me in a way I cannot possibly defend. That is not something an average eleven-year-old boy would ever think of doin', or even have the ability to. Take Dewey, for example."

"I don't think Dewey's average," I said.

"Oh, you'd be surprised," she said. "But Dewey don't think like you. And I'm willing to bet there are parts of what you saw that day out at Holly Berry Ranch regarding Mary Ann Dailey that you purposely didn't tell him. Am I correct?"

Slowly, I nodded. "Parts," I said.

"How come?"

"Because there was stuff he just didn't need to know about. Why tell him things that are just gonna scare him?"

"But they didn't scare you so much, did they?" she asked. "I mean, they probably upset you—and I would be worried if they didn't—but you've slowly learned, simply by virtue of living under the same roof as me and really having no other full-time role model, that the world isn't always a nice place. You don't expect it to be. Dewey still does. If it rained gumdrops tomorrow, Dewey'd be outside with his mouth open, tryin' to catch every one he possibly could. Whereas you—"

"Whereas I'd be wonderin' why there was gumdrops fallin' from the sky, and since there were, it would seem mighty suspicious, and my first thought would be that they might possibly be poisonous."

Both my mother's eyebrows went up. "Wow. You're even further along on this than I thought," she said. "I hope to God I haven't messed you up, Abe. Aren't you going to try your coffee?"

I had forgotten about it completely. Now I gently lifted it to my mouth, smelling that delicious aroma before taking my first sip. It tasted exactly like it smelled, although as a taste, it wasn't quite as fulfilling as an aroma, but still it wasn't bad. And I felt very grown up drinking it. I set my mug back down on the table and said, "It's good. I think I like coffee."

"You just don't drink too much of it, okay? How 'bout we keep it special for Saturdays for now?"

"Okay," I agreed. "What did you mean about messing me up?"

My mother shuffled uncomfortably on her cushion. "You've grown up so fast. In some ways, I think you're older than your sister. You're far more cynical, that's for sure. I just . . . sometimes I think I robbed you out of experiencing all the fairy-tale parts of life. You seem to have a better handle on the horrible parts."

I had no idea what *cynical* meant, but didn't bother asking. "I don't think life is horrible. I mean, some parts are. I think it's just confusin' at times. Like tryin' to figure out what sort of comments are racist and what ones aren't."

"I've noticed you seem to be gettin' better at that," she said. "I suppose my biggest worry is that you could fall one of two ways. Growing up the way you have could make you more wary and keep you safer, or it could make you . . ." She trailed off.

"What?" I asked.

"Nothing."

"No, what?"

"Well, sometimes when you grow up differently than other people, you can have strange thoughts that cause you to behave in ways you don't understand or even mean. Like, say you started stealin' from Mr. Harrison's five-and-dime."

"I ain't never stole a thing in my life!" I said, finding that a mite insulting.

She patted my leg. "I know, honey, I'm just using that as an example. Anyway, I think we've gone off on a trail we shouldn't have. I was more talking to myself with that last part. Anyway, you had some questions about Mr. Garner?"

I opened my mouth to speak, but just as I was about to, Uncle Henry called from the kitchen. "Breakfast is pretty near done, guys!"

My mother smiled. "Is it okay if we talk more later? I'm starving."

"Sure," I said. After everything she'd just told me, I was actually relieved. I needed to do some thinking before I said what I was going to say.

My mother stood, finishing her coffee. "Actually, how about you stay in here a few more minutes," she said. "Finish up your coffee while I go help Hank finish up breakfast. We'll call you when it's ready. Shouldn't be long."

"Okay," I said. I only said it because I could tell she wanted to talk with Uncle Henry alone.

"You think that was a smart conversation to have?" he asked her. His voice was flat and I couldn't tell what his opinion on the matter was.

"I don't know," my mother answered. "But it's one I felt needed havin'. You think it was a mistake, right?"

There was a pause before he answered. "They're your children. You raise them as you see fit. Some of it I think was good. Some of it started gettin' into dangerous territory. But I'm sure you know what you're doin'."

"Thank you. Now I'm gonna go tell my boy his breakfast is ready while you go down the hall and brave the danger of wakin' his sister up and draggin' her lazy ass out to this table."

"This is revenge for me questioning your little conversation with Abe, isn't it?"

"No," my mother said, "this is actually my survival skills training kicking in. The best altercation is one you avoid altogether."

CHAPTER 22

Breakfast turned out as delicious as it always did on Saturday mornings. Even Carry didn't seem to be in the moldy, rotted-up mood she had been stuck in going on four months now. I figured my mother had completely forgotten about my request to ask some questions about Mr. Garner, but I turned out to be wrong. She surprised me as we were just finishing cleaning up from the meal by saying, "Hank? Any chance you could take Carry into town? I think she could use a new set of clothes for school, and I know there's some things Abe wants to discuss with me."

Uncle Henry and Carry seemed equally surprised. A wide smile spread across my sister's lips. "What about my groundin'?"

"I told you already," my mother said. "Groundin' means you do what I say. Christ, if I had to put up with you at home twenty-four hours a day that would be more like grounding myself."

Carry frowned. "I ain't got no money."

Fishing twenty dollars from her purse, my mother handed it to Carry, then looked at Hank. "Do you mind? If you have any other plans at all, I completely understand."

Uncle Hank put on his cap. "I would love nothing better than to take my little sugarplum out shopping."

"Thank you," my mother said. "Now, that money's for clothes, and clothes only. And, Hank? Make sure they're practical. The sort of thing that might attract *fourteen*-year-old boys, not nineteen-year-old ones, you got me?"

"Yes, sir," he said, saluting her.

My mother and I finished washing and drying dishes while Uncle Henry and Carry got ready before heading outside to where Uncle Henry's supposedly stolen car sat parked in front of our house.

"There, all done," my mother said, folding her dish-towel and hanging it over the handle of the stove. "You ready for another coffee?"

"Sure," I said slowly, wondering if this was some sort of test. "Am I gonna stop growing, though?"

She laughed. "I actually don't think that's true."

"Then why did you say it in front of Mr. and Mrs. Yates?"

"Because some people wouldn't think it's proper for me to allow my eleven-year-old son to drink coffee. I'm not really entirely sure why, but I'm quite positive the bit about it stunting your growth is an old wives' tale."

"Like whistling when you walk past a graveyard so the spirits don't think you're scared?" I asked.

"Actually," my mother said, "that one may be true. I still do it." She shrugged. "Usually I find it's better to err on the side of caution with things like that. Being short ain't that big of a deal if I turn out wrong. Being attacked by someone's dead ghost is another thing entirely."

I laughed as my mother handed me the second cup of coffee I had ever been given in my life. Once again we went into the living room, taking the same places on the sofa we had before. I set my mug on the table. This time, she held hers in her lap and sat back, crossing her legs.

"So," she said, "you wanted to ask me something about Mr. Garner?" I could tell she was a little worried about what it was I wanted to know. Likely it had to do with our conversation earlier.

"Well, I have some questions and stuff," I said, not liking how awkward it all felt. It felt so awkward that I came close to telling her to just forget about it, but I couldn't on account of some things were really bothering me and needed to be gotten off my chest.

"Well, then," she said, "go ahead and ask me, Abe. I'll do my best to answer as honestly as possible."

I took a deep breath. She could tell I was a bit wary. "Well," I said, "if Mr. Garner killed Mary Ann Dailey, does that mean he also took Tiffany Michelle Yates?"

She thought about this a minute, then leaned forward, her hands coming around her cup, placing it between her knees. Steam rose from the top. I had no idea how she could grasp the sides of the mug that way; her fingers must have been burning. "Yes, honey, I think so."

"Then, where is she?"

"That's a good question, Abe. It's the one we're all asking. And it's something we have to figure out soon, because wherever she is, she probably doesn't have any food or water. You were there at the station today—I'm not sure how much you heard or how much you understood, but we *do* have some new evidence and clues to follow up on, and we're hoping it will help us uncover her whereabouts."

"So you don't think Tiffany Michelle is dead?" I asked.

She sipped her coffee. "I'll be honest," she said, "I truly don't know. What I do know is that we haven't seen her body, so I'm hoping that's a good sign."

I stared at my coffee on the table in front of me. Then I noticed the table. It was old and brown and chipped. We had had it for as long as I could remember. It was yet another piece of furniture that would one day be replaced with something brand-new, according to my mother. I didn't see why it was so important to replace old things if they still worked fine. All the furniture in our house seemed as reliable as always to me.

"Do you *really* think he did it?" I asked without looking up. "Mr. Garner, I mean."

"Them experts from Mobile found lots of forensic evidence supporting that he did, Abe."

"Yeah, but what does that mean?"

"It means they found *his* prints on her body and nobody else's. Fingerprints are like snowflakes. Everybody's is completely different than everyone else's. And they're tiny. You can only see them under a microscope."

"I know," I said. "We studied them in school. But couldn't they have come from when Mr. Garner found Mary Ann Dailey's body? I mean, they said they found Dixie's hair on her, too. Do you think Dixie killed her?"

My mother gave me a patronizing smile. "Come on,

Abe. The important fact is that *nobody else's* prints were found."

"What if the real killer wore gloves? And a hairnet? Or some kind of space suit?"

"Okay, maybe you aren't old enough for this conversation," she said.

I regretted mentioning the space suit. With a sip of my coffee, I continued, ignoring her comment. "All right, but Mr. Garner's fingerprints could easily have already been on that shovel, right? I mean it *was* his shovel. And it could have already been by that tree. He goes to that tree a lot. You guys saw the flowers underneath Mary Ann's body, right?"

Mom leaned forward and set her mug on the coffee table. "How do you know about the flowers?" she asked, looking at me until I rose my face up to meet hers. "We were holding that evidence back in case of false confessions."

"What's a false confession?" I asked.

She sat back. "Well, as strange as this sounds, some people want to be noticed so much that, when they hear about somethin' like this happenin', they'll tell the police they were the ones who did it, just so they feel important."

"That's crazy," I said.

"It's a crazy world, Abe," my mother said. "Anyway, what we normally do is hold back at least one pertinent piece of evidence from everyone, especially the newspapers, so that nobody but the real killer could possibly know 'bout it. That way we know whether or not the person really did it. In this case, it was the fresh flowers we found when we removed Mary Ann Dailey's body. They had been placed right beneath her."

"Yeah, I know. White daisies, clipped and tied in a bunch with a pink ribbon," I said.

This grabbed my mother's attention in a way I had seen nothing do before. "Now, how in the name of the Lord do you know that?"

It took me a few seconds to figure out why she was so surprised. "Wait," I said. "You think the *killer* put them there?"

"Who else would've, Abe?"

"Mr. Garner. Those daisies were there when we rode our bikes over earlier that day. Mr. Garner always puts flowers around that tree. He's done so ever since finding Ruby Mae Vickers."

"And you know this how?"

"He told us during the time we walked along the river lookin' for Mary Ann Dailey the day after she disappeared. Remember? The day it rained somethin' awful and most everyone in the town went out searching for her. Well, except Mr. Farrow from across the street," I said, letting that fact sink in. "We saw flowers then and asked him about them and he said he put them there, but I got the distinct feeling he didn't much like discussin' them too much. But when me and Dewey rode up that day right before he found Mary Ann's body, those daisies was already there. You can ask Dewey if you don't believe me."

"Now, why would I believe Dewey over you, Abe?" she asked. "Of course I believe you. But why didn't you tell me this before? You didn't even tell Chris when he took your report."

I shrugged. "Guess I forgot about them. Seeing Mary Ann Dailey's body just thrown away like that made it hard for me to think properly."

Closing her eyes, she let out a shallow breath, then opened them again. "Do you wish you hadn't seen it? Did I make a mistake bringing you along?"

"Sometimes I wish I hadn't. But I don't think you made a mistake. It's like you said earlier, I already thought about things like that a lot. Sometimes what you picture in your mind can be worse than it turns out to be in real life."

"Was this one of those times?" she asked, looking as though she hoped my answer would be yes.

But I shook my head. I figured there was no point in not being honest now. "I never expected her eyes to look the way they did. All the life was gone, yet they was still open. It was like seeing a puppet without a hand inside."

Her head dropped, and I wished I would have said it different. I touched her hand. "Mom, I'm glad I got to see it. It didn't mess me up, like you said earlier. I promise." She brought her eyes back up to mine. "But there's something you need to understand," I said. "Maybe you're right about Mr. Garner killing Mary Ann Dailey, although I don't rightly think you are, but you sure as heck aren't right about him doin' the same to Ruby Mae Vickers. Me and Dewey listened to the way he talked about her. It was almost as though he had found his *own* daughter dead by that tree, he felt so bad." A wetness was coming to my mother's eyes, making them look like pools of blue. "Mom, for twelve years he's been putting flowers out for her. Do you think he'd do that if he *killed* her? I sure as heck don't."

Now normally, I would be expecting a slap for using an almost cussword like *heck* once in front of my mother, and here I had done it twice. But today was special and I could sense it. Maybe it was the coffee, maybe it was the way she was treating me, but I felt more grown up than ever.

She may not have even noticed I did so. Her head turned toward the window. Outside, a bluebird perched on a branch of one of the two fig trees that grew along the edge of our property. Across the street, Mr. Wyatt Edward Farrow's house sat dark and quiet, as though it were asleep. I guessed my mother had been right. He probably did spend most early parts of the days sleeping and then used the nights for working. I found it strange that some people worked at night. But then, Mr. Wyatt Edward Farrow apparently built stuff for a living, although where he found a market for Roadkill Frankensteins was a problem for another day.

What was it Mr. Garner had said that day we went huntin' for Mary Ann Dailey? That he just built stuff to keep busy because "the devil finds work for idle hands to do." So he didn't have to work nights. In fact, he had just been finishing up his work on that toolshed that afternoon Dewey and I pulled up on our bikes. The day Mary Ann Dailey's body turned up.

It was then that I realized what it was that'd been bothering me the last few days. The thing I kept feeling like I should be remembering but couldn't. "Mom?" I asked.

She seemed distracted, and I nearly repeated the question until she tore herself away from the view outside and looked at me. "Yes, Abe?"

"How long does it take to put a roof on a toolshed?"

She shook her head. "I have no idea, why?"

"Because it took us, say, twenty-five minutes or so

to ride home that afternoon from Mr. Garner's ranch. Then it probably took another fifteen or twenty before you and I got back there in the car. It took almost as long in the car on account of me and Dewey know some shortcuts, and it took me a good five minutes or so to convince you to let me come along, remember?"

From her eyes, I could tell she was completely lost as to where I was going with this. "Abe, what's your point?"

"My point's this. Mr. Garner claims he had just finished the roof of his toolshed and gone in for a beer when but five minutes later Dixie's barking brought him back outside and, maybe five minutes after that, he found Mary Ann Dailey. It probably took him a couple more minutes to run back to the house and call you."

She nodded. "And what evidence we have supports his claim that the body had only been under that tree maybe ten minutes or so, so I will agree with you that on this particular point, Mr. Garner is probably not lying."

"Good," I said, feeling myself get on a roll. "And then there's the very shallow hole someone dug. I mean, it wasn't even a hole. It couldn't have been more than three or four shovels of dirt."

"Right."

"So, why even dig that much? Unless you planned on diggin' more, only what you didn't plan on was to have some coon dog spot you and start raisin' up such a fuss. So you drop the diggin' idea completely and just toss the body down. I mean, if Mr. Garner wanted to dig a hole, he could dig all day, and Dixie wouldn't even raise an ear."

"Okay, now you're speculatin', but go on. If you have more, I mean."

"Oh, I do," I said. "Okay, so say the total time between me and Dewey leaving Mr. Garner's ranch and you and me getting back there was forty minutes. Mr. Garner had just finished putting his sixth rafter up when we left. It took him four minutes and maybe twenty-two seconds to get it done."

"Now how do you know that?"

I showed her my wrist. "On account of my new timepiece Uncle Henry gave me. I time everythin' now. You know I can run from here to Dewey's house in less than fifty-six seconds. Well, I did it once."

"Abe, please go back to Mr. Garner's toolshed."

"Right. Anyway, he had four more rafters to go when we left. If he spent that much time on the rest, that means it would have taken him about fifteen minutes or so to finish. Then he had to nail up the plywood over top of those to make the actual roof and then that had to be covered with tar paper that he stapled onto that plywood."

"Why do you suddenly know so much about construction work and what the hell does this have to do with anything?"

"Because, Mom? When you and I got back there less than an hour later, that roof was done. He had finished all the rafters, put on the plywood, and stapled the tar paper on. Now, I'm assumin' he must've previously cut everythin' to size or there's no way he had time to do it. As it is, he must've just worked at lightnin' speed if he had been inside five minutes with his beer before hearing Dixie," I said.

I paused for a breath and another sip of coffee. "My

guess is that I'm probably a little low in how long of a stretch occurred between us leavin' and returning and, more likely, Mr. Garner's probably off on how long he was inside before Dixie brought him back out. I mean, I saw Mary Ann Dailey's body. It messes up your perspective on things a bit. But one thing I know for sure. There's no way he had any time to finish that tool shed and then go get her body from someplace else, dig a quick hole that makes absolutely no sense anyway, throw her body in it, and then call you on the phone.

"And my biggest problem with this whole thing— and one that I can't believe I never heard none of you talk about in the station this mornin'—is why in tarnation would he call *you*? At least right away? Especially if he's left a shovel with whatever they found on it out there by her body. How does that make any sense to any of you? I don't care if you're an expert whatever the heck from Mobile or what." I stopped then, realizing my hand was trembling. I took a few deep breaths. Never before had I spoken to my mother so abruptly.

"Okay, your tone's gettin' a bit disrespectful there, Abe," she said, but I could tell she said it more out of reflex. I had her thinking. And she was thinking hard.

"Sorry," I said. "But really, why would he go to all that bother of finishing his work before putting her by the tree? And then there was that thing he said about cougars. Why say something like that if you're talkin' 'bout yourself? Far as I can tell, nobody'd want to think of himself as bein' that way."

Gears were spinning in my mother's mind, but my last comment brought her back to the topic at hand. "Cougars? What did he say about cougars?"

"I told you already," I said with a sigh, then caught

myself. I really did have to watch out for being disrespectful. This was new and dangerous territory for me. "That day we all went searching for Mary Ann Dailey in the rain? Dewey asked Mr. Garner if he reckoned maybe it was a cougar or something that got her. And Mr. Garner said he reckoned so, just not the sorta cougar we was thinkin' 'bout."

"Oh, right, I remember you sayin' that now."

"Do you really think he'd say that if *he* were the cougar, Mom?"

My mother looked into her coffee cup.

I remembered the conversation we had in the sushi restaurant. "Mr. Garner has integrity, Mom. I know it. I feel it."

My mother went still for a long time, and I wondered if this whole talk had been one huge mistake I might never come back from. Her fingers played with the Lord Jesus dangling from her neck. She looked out the window, her eyes focused on something very, very far away. Eventually, her lips moved, but I barely heard the two words that came out: "Oh, shit."

"And, Mom?"

"Yes, Abe?"

"That shovel hadn't been in his shed. When we left, there were no tools in that shed. It was empty on account of it had no roof on it."

She turned and looked me square in the face. "Now, why are you just telling me all this now?"

"I tried to tell you the day Mary Ann showed back up, but you kept telling me to mind my business."

She closed her eyes.

"Mom?"

She kept her eyes closed. "Yes, Abe?"

"I *really* don't think Mr. Robert Lee Garner killed Mary Ann Dailey. I don't think he killed no one. I maybe don't know people as good as I will when I'm older, but everything inside me says he didn't do it. Mr. Garner was near on as upset as you when she went missing. You weren't with me and Dewey in the forest that day in the rain. He was angry and upset and I don't think he killed no one."

Reaching out, she pulled me over to her, nearly sloshing coffee out of my cup and onto my hand. Putting her arms around me, she rocked me back and forth, holding me tightly to her chest. "Oh, honey," she said. "I think maybe I made a big mistake."

I looked up at her face. "What're you goin' to do?"

Her jaw tightened. "What I should've done weeks ago. I'm gonna find Tiffany Michelle Yates before it's too late."

"And, Mom?"

"Yes?"

"What about Mr. Garner?"

Slowly, she shook her head. "That one's gonna be a little more complicated, but I'll figure it out."

CHAPTER 23

Two days later, my mother drove me and Dewey to school, but stopped me when I was about to leave the car.

"What?" I asked.

"You're gonna be late today," she said.

"I am? Why?"

"Because I want you to come with me to the station and tell Chief Montgomery what you told me," she said.

"Can I come, too?" Dewey asked. He was already outside, but hadn't yet closed his door.

"No. One of you's gotta learn somethin'," my mother said.

With a grumble, he shut the door and skulked off to the school entrance while I returned to my seat in the front, sitting taller and more proudly than ever. Boy, did I feel important.

That feeling disappeared pretty fast once we were in Chief Montgomery's office. Truth was, I never even got to say a single word.

"You're not listenin' to me, Ethan," my mother said

after trying to set up the point of our little meeting twice. "I'm telling you, I made a mistake. Bob Garner didn't kill anyone."

Above our heads, a very slow wooden fan turned. To our right was a wall of law books that reached all the way from the floor to the ceiling. I'd been in this office before, but always alone with my attention centered on the television hanging from the ceiling opposite Chief Montgomery's desk. This was the first time I actually took the time to notice the rest of the room. Then I noticed Chief Montgomery as he gave me yet another look I couldn't read before putting all his attention on my mother.

"No, Leah," Chief Montgomery said, "that's where you're wrong. I'm listenin' to you just fine. I'm just havin' a real hard time findin' any sort of actual evidence to back up this little change of heart you've suddenly had." He looked over and pointed his thumb at me. "And why in God's name is he in here?"

"Because it's . . . it's something Abe said that made me realize we've got the wrong man in custody, Ethan. Ever since Ruby Mae's death, Bob Garner holds that willow tree nearly in reverence. Her death affected him so deeply it was as though he found his own daughter lying dead that day. He told my son whoever was responsible for takin' that girl's life was a cougar. He—" I couldn't believe my mother was tellin' the chief of police that I was the one who changed her mind.

Apparently, neither could Chief Montgomery.

"Leah," he said, cutting her off. "Do you have even the slightest inkling of how crazy you're soundin' right now?" Chief Montgomery looked at me, his lips forming a thin line. "I'm sorry, Abe, but I'm gonna have to ask you to step outside my office while me and your ma finish this little conversation. I mean absolutely no offense to you. Is that okay?"

"Yes, sir," I said.

I walked out into the main room, hearing Chief Montgomery's chair squeak as he got up and closed the door firmly behind me before they continued talking. Luckily, neither of them kept their voices down and, without Dewey banging binders or gurgling water coolers, I was able to pretty much hear the whole thing, especially since I discreetly stayed just outside the door.

"Leah," he said, "listen to yourself." I heard him get back into that big ol' chair of his. "You're putting something your eleven-year-old son told you above the results of an entire team of professional forensic experts in Mobile. Think about that a minute." I reckoned he did have a point.

"No, Ethan, I'm putting his *feelings* above them."

There was another squeak and a pause before Chief Montgomery spoke again. "I reckon that's even worse. Leah, more than ever, you're showing me that you've gotten way too close to this damn thing. It's become so personal your family's now part of your investigation process. You're coming to me and telling me we've got to let our prime suspect go because your eleven-year-old boy is 'pretty sure he didn't do it.' "

I wasn't too certain I liked how that sounded.

"He didn't do it, Ethan. It's not just Abe. *I* know it. I've known it all along, I've just been afraid to admit it. Hank knows it, too. He's been saying so since the beginning. Christ, I think even *you* know it. Just nobody wants to stand up and take responsibility for putting an innocent man behind bars."

"Funny thing is, Leah, we've got them experts who say he did do it. And they ain't never met the man before, so their opinion is completely unbiased, which takes it right out of your hands and *frees* you from all that responsibility. This time it actually isn't you, Leah. Even if we do have the wrong man, you can rest easy. You had nothing to do with him going to jail."

After another hesitation, I worried they were going to open the door and find me listening, but then my mother spoke up.

"It's my fault," she said. "I arrested him."

Chief Montgomery must have sat way back in his chair and probably put his hands behind his head the way he does sometimes, because I heard a really loud squeak this time before he responded. When he did, there was almost a laugh in his voice. "No, actually you got Jackson to do it, which was probably one of the smarter moves you've made on this case because this way it really *is* completely out of your hands."

My mother's voice went quiet. I took a chance and moved closer to Chief Montgomery's office door. "How can I get him free?" I heard her ask.

Chief Montgomery spoke very matter-of-factly, almost like he was placing an order at the drive-through window at Aunt Bella's Burger Hut. "Find me another child murderer," he said. "Preferably one with Tiffany Michelle Yates still alive and well along for the ride." There was a window framed in the door leading into Chief Montgomery's office. The glass was gold and beveled, making it impossible to see any details through it, but through that smoked glass, I saw the blurred shadow of Chief Montgomery lean forward, bringing his big arms onto the top of his desk.

"And, Leah," he said, "if there *is* any truth to what you're tellin' me, there's only one way you're ever gonna do that, and that's to finally figure out this ain't about *you*. And that really shouldn't be too hard, because this time? It really isn't."

My mother's tone changed completely. She almost sounded like a wounded dog. "I see I've worn out my welcome when it comes to your sensitivity." She was hurt, and I could tell she was trying hard to hide the fact from Chief Montgomery. I'm pretty sure though that if *I* could tell, most likely he could, too.

"You want sensitivity?" he asked. "Then earn it. Go do your goddamn job."

I heard her footsteps coming loudly toward the door and I barely managed to take a couple big steps back before she opened it and marched out of Chief Montgomery's office. I don't think she actually noticed me at all, she was so upset. She stomped straight past me, through the rest of the office, and out onto the street, letting the station door slam closed behind her. I was just about to follow when I felt Chief Montgomery in the doorway of his office right behind me. I turned around and, in the brief second our eyes met, I could tell he had just done one of the most painful things he'd ever had to do in his life.

"Go take care of her," he said, and gave me a partial smile.

"I always do," I said.

He winked at me. "I know," he said, and patted my back.

*   *   *

My mother didn't talk as we drove away. I didn't even question when she took a wrong turn, leading us in the complete opposite direction of my school. I just sat there watching the pines and oaks slowly break to oaks and cypress trees until we were almost completely surrounded on both sides of the street by cypress. Their eerie, twisted branches reached up into the sky like gnarled fingers as we sped past.

Then I figured out where we were going.

We were traveling just south of Skeeter Swamp, headed to Mr. Garner's ranch. My mother pulled to a stop on the gravel road barely a block away from where Mary Ann Dailey's body had been left strewn under that tree on the south side of the Anikawa. Without a word or even a glance my way, she got out of the car, closed her door, and headed toward the willow tree. Since she never said otherwise, I cautiously tagged along behind her.

Yellow police tape marked off the area. My mother ducked beneath it, and I did the same. There were markers where the body had been, indicating its exact position. Other items, like Mr. Garner's shovel, had also been marked off. "Touch nothin'," she said to me, without even a glance back to where I stood watching.

I had no intention of doing any such thing. It felt weird just being here again. I stood a good ten feet back from where that small hill began to rise, where the golden wild grass still grew long, bending in the morning wind. As the hill rose, the grass shortened until it finally broke to dirt at the top. That was, except for the one area that someone had recently dug out, revealing the willow's thick wooded roots beneath. In my head, I once again saw Mary Ann Dailey strewn in that patch of dirt, partially clothed. It was a horrible picture.

My mother squatted beside where the body was marked, intently studying something in the dirt. "What're you looking at?" I asked.

"The indentations in the ground from where those daises had been," she said.

After a few minutes she got up and walked carefully around the base of the hill, calling me over when she found some old dried-up daffodils that had been blown into the thrush and wild grass on the south side. "What're these, do you think?" she asked me.

"Old flowers Mr. Garner had placed for Ruby Mae," I said. "He didn't always tie 'em. That day we were all searchin' for Mary Ann Dailey, he'd tossed roses over the whole hill, scattering them around the bottom of the willow. Least I think they was roses. I don't know my flowers that good."

My mother once again squattcd down, this time in the long grass a few feet away from where she discovered the dried-up daffodils. "What color were they?"

I tried to remember. "Red, pink, and yellow, I think. It was a while ago, remember. And it was rainin' somethin' fierce."

She reached into the tall weeds and pulled out a dead yellow rose. Only two or three petals were left, and they looked ready to fall off at any time.

My mother's hand not holding the dead flower came up to her mouth.

"What?" I asked.

She shook her head, biting her lip in a way that made it look like she was holding back crying. "I really did arrest an innocent man. Not only that, he was one of your grandpa's best friends."

Tears really did come then, so I approached her, being careful not to disrupt anything that had been marked off by the police. I wrapped my arms around her. "It's okay, Mom. Everyone makes mistakes. *You* told me that."

She kept shaking her head. "*I* don't. I *can't*."

"Yeah, you *can*. You just gotta fix 'em once you realized what you done. You told me that, too."

Her hand came off my shoulder and wiped her cheek. "I have no idea if I can fix this."

I didn't bother telling her that everything's fixable. She already knew, because she'd told me *that,* too.

CHAPTER 24

We managed to make it to church the following Sunday.

Immediately afterward, in what I considered a very unchristian-like fashion, my mother started suspecting all sorts of people that I considered she probably should not be suspecting anything about. Mainly, I noticed, she was targeting farmers. When they inquired as to why they were being asked so many questions, she actually told them she wasn't suspecting nobody of nothing, she was just looking for information. But I knew different. I'd known her my whole life. Of course, I think the farmers knew different too, since they all seemed to take offense at her asking them anything at all.

The first vehicle she approached in the church parking lot belonged to Glen Nelson. "Do you mind if I take a quick look?" she asked him.

"Now, why would you wanna be lookin' in my truck?" asked Mr. Nelson. "If this is about that Dailey girl, I heard you caught your man. If this is 'bout anythin' else, I think you better tell me what, before I say whether or not it's all right to be searchin' my stuff."

"We still have one missin' girl, Mr. Nelson," my mother said. "And just because we have Mr. Garner in custody don't necessarily mean he's the one who did it. We're keepin' our options open." She walked around his big white pickup, looking at the tires and glancing in the truck bed.

"What you think you're gonna find?" Glen Nelson asked. "Bunch of little girl's blood all over my vehicle?"

"Dunno what exactly it is I'm lookin' for," my mother clarified. "I'm just lookin'. Don't worry, it's not just you. I'll be checkin' out lots of trucks over the next few days."

They started arguing, but I knew my mother would get her way. I had seen her work like this before, so I left them in the parking lot and walked around the back of the churchyard, following the stone path that led through the gardens and graves. Dewey followed right behind me. "Whatcha doin'?" he asked.

"You mean 'sides gettin' away from my mom?"

Dewey laughed. "She sure likes confrontation."

I stopped and wheeled around on him. "What do you know about confrontation?" I asked.

With a shrug, Dewey answered, "Not much, only that your mom seems to like gettin' her nose where some people don't think it belongs."

I scrunched up my own nose. "Who told you that?"

Dewey crossed his arms. "Thought of it myself."

"You most certainly did *not*." I laughed. "You don't even know what that all means."

After some consideration, Dewey kinda agreed with me. "Okay, maybe I just heard rumors, is all. Anyway, you never answered me. Whatcha doin'? Why're we going over to the gravesites? They give me the willies."

"Just wanna see somethin', is all." I actually wasn't sure *why* I wanted to see it, but for some reason, a part of me did. That part had kept tugging my pant legs toward the small cemetery tucked in behind the parish even during Reverend Matthew's service.

Me and Dewey both walked straight over to the new headstone marking the grave of Mary Ann Dailey. A few other folks were already standing around looking at it. One of them was Mrs. Dailey. She was dressed all in black, wearing a veil, and sobbing into a tissue. When her husband saw me and Dewey, he gave us a not-so-nice look and led his wife back toward the parking lot and, I assume, their car.

"Why'd he do that?" Dewey asked. I ignored him.

Mary Ann Dailey's grave felt almost peaceful, especially compared to the last way I had seen her. The plot was obviously fresh, with brown dirt still marking the dug-out rectangle. I wondered how long it would take before that got hidden by grass. The dirt was compensated for by bouquets of beautiful flowers and balloons and teddy bears. In some ways, it looked like a hospital room the day a new baby was born. In other ways it seemed desperately sad.

The headstone was a simple stone arc. I read the words carved into it, accidentally saying them aloud but, luckily, only so loud that Dewey heard. " 'Mary Ann Dailey,' " I read. " 'Beloved daughter taken too soon from this life, dream with little angels.' "

"I can't begin to understand why you wanna be lookin' at that for," Dewey said.

"I dunno," I said. "It just feels like I should. You reckon she's really with the angels now?"

"I reckon so," Dewey said. "Reverend Matthew told us children are safe in the arms of God until they're old enough to understand 'bout acceptin' Jesus an' all that."

"I hope she's someplace nice," I said.

"I bet no matter where she is," Dewey said, "it's most likely nicer than the swamp. And if you ask me, that willow tree she was under is much too close to Skeeter Swamp for comfort. At least here, there's no gators."

I agreed. We walked back around to the front of the church. Most folks had already left, and I noticed Uncle Henry had taken my mother aside and was talking quietly to her as we came up. "So what're you gonna do tomorrow, Leah?" Uncle Henry asked her. "Track down every farmer in Alvin and go through his truck lookin' for God only knows what you might find that could possibly turn out to support your case?"

"I *have* to, Hank," my mother said.

He patted her shoulder. "I know. I'm through with all my chidin'—for now. You do what you gotta do."

She smiled sadly. It was nice to see her smile for a change, even if it did have that element of sadness to it.

Dewey and me had rode our bicycles to church the way we did sometimes and now we asked my mother if it'd be okay if we didn't go straight home, but rode around town a bit instead. She thought this over a long time until Uncle Henry took up the initiative. "It'll be fine, boys. Just don't be longer than an hour or so. You still got that watch, right, Abe?"

I said I sure did and showed him the back of my wrist to prove it.

"Good boy." Then, putting his arm around my mother, he led her back to her car. "Come on, Leah. Let's get you home. I think you need a stomach full o' comfort food for lunch."

"Let's go," I said to Dewey, pulling my front tire up over the small curb and onto the sidewalk.

"Where're we going? Thought we was going into town?"

"Nah, I wanna go talk to Reverend Starks at the Full Gospel. I reckon it's time we figured out the difference 'tween a white girl missin' and a black girl missin', because it seems to me there shouldn't be no difference. But if you listen to folk round here, there certainly tends to be."

We rode our bikes along Thompson Drive, which more or less followed the Anikawa, only on the town side of it instead of Mr. Garner's ranch side. We weren't nearly close enough to the river to even hear the water, but that made little matter, for I still sensed that place of death gnawing at me, despite it being probably a mile from where we were. I thought of the way Mary Ann's body had been left, just tossed there like somebody's discarded sack of trash.

Services at the Full Gospel always ran longer than they did at Clover Creek on account of all the singing and stuff they did. We set our bikes against the worn white siding of the church and tiptoed up the steps, quietly slipping inside through the open doors. We stood in the very back, behind everyone else. The whole congregation was standing and singing as loud as they could, so at first I thought nobody was going to see us until, barely a second later, Reverend Starks's eyes locked on mine. Even though he didn't miss a single note, I suddenly felt a mite conspicuous and wished maybe we hadn't come after all.

But, in spite of that, we continued standing there, awkwardly watching and listening, until five songs later, Reverend Starks said some final words about *both* girls.

He then asked his congregation to all bow their heads and pray that poor little Mary Ann Dailey had found peace in heaven and that the good Lord found His way to returning Tiffany Michelle back to her loving parents. Even from our position at the back of the church, I could hear Mrs. Yates sobbing from somewhere up in the front pews. Then more people started crying. By the time Reverend Starks dismissed everyone and they all filed out, most folk were dabbing their eyes with handkerchiefs, or simply letting the tears stream down their faces. It was a much more emotional experience than I had ever felt at Clover Creek First Baptist.

Some of the folk going by gave me and Dewey strange looks, but most were too upset to even care that we were there. Reverend Starks followed behind everyone and, when he finally made it to where we stood, he took off his glasses, held them up to the sunlight washing down through the open doors, and wiped them clean with a handkerchief he pulled from his pocket. "So, what brings two white boys like yourselves to my congregation this afternoon?" he asked. He had a deep, soothing voice that bellowed even when he talked quietly, like he was doing now.

I explained what my mother had told me about why

Clover Creek hadn't really spoken of Tiffany Michelle and that Tiffany would be getting her share of praying down here at Full Gospel, and that I wanted to come see so for myself, because I couldn't rightly figure out the difference between a white girl missing and a black one.

"But you said just as much about Mary Ann Dailey as you did about Tiffany Michelle," I told him. "Least while we was standing here."

The reverend replaced his glasses on his wide nose and looked both of us in the eyes one at a time before answering. When he did, he answered slowly, but his voice still seemed to thunder through that small church. "God don't see no color, boys," he said. "It's only man who sees color."

"You mean He's colorblind, like Jacob Rivers in my class?" Dewey asked. "You can hold a green crayon and a black crayon up to Jacob, and that kid will swear up and down they both the exact same."

The reverend cracked a smile. It was missing a few teeth, and I noticed one had been capped with gold. "Sorta, son. Although I reckon the Lord knows the difference between black and green. He certainly knows the difference between black and white, but He don't care about that difference. If He did, He wouldn't have put us all here on this planet together all them years ago."

"I don't understand," said Dewey.

I wanted to punch him. "He don't understand much," I said.

Dewey glared at me.

"No, it's fine," Reverend Starks said, holding up a large palm. His fingertips were nearly bright pink. "Most folks don't understand, to be honest. Even some of my own congregation have trouble when it comes to graspin' this point. And really, it's probably the easiest yet most important thing the Bible has to teach us." He squatted down in front of Dewey, reached out, and clutched his arm. "You see, son, God made us all different for a reason. It's like a sort of test. He put us all down here together to see if we could work things out by ourselves and somehow figure out how to get along."

"So, how do you think we's doin'?" Dewey asked.

The reverend looked away for a second, thinking. "Some days, I believe we manage to pull it off a mite better than others. But I'll tell you what. I believe we all got a whole lotta learnin' to do."

"Reverend Starks?" I asked. "Do you think Mr. Garner killed Mary Ann Dailey?"

He looked genuinely surprised by this question. "Now, that sounds more like somethin' you should be askin' your ma. She's the one who arrested him, ain't she?"

I scratched my head. "Not technically," I said. "Technically, it was Officer Jackson. But she *did* think Mr. Garner was probably the one who did it originally. And evidence brought back from Mobile, well, it . . ."

Reverend Starks waved my discussion about evidence away with his hand. Both his knees popped like bottle rockets as he stood. "I don't give a rat's ass about that science stuff. You say she *originally* thought it was Robert Garner? I'm guessin' that means she's had a change of mind since?"

I wasn't sure I should be talking about what my mother thought about the case and told the reverend so.

He nodded slowly. "That's fine. But between you an' me? I'm glad she's on a different path. I know Robert

Lee Garner. I remember when he found Ruby Mae's body going on, what? Ten years ago now?"

"Twelve," I told him.

He shook his head and gave a low whistle. "Time certainly does not wait for no man now, does it? Doesn't matter, to me it will always feel like yesterday. I remember how discovering Ruby Mae's little body affected Robert Garner. A man who reacts like that from findin' a dead girl by a tree near his swamp? There ain't no way he did somethin' like this. And you can even tell your mother I said so if you find it in your heart to do so."

I told him I wasn't sure if that would happen or not.

He arched an eyebrow. "You boys didn't tell your mas you was comin' here today, did you?"

Dewey gestured to me. "His mom knows we're out on our bikes, just not exactly where."

"I see," Reverend Starks said, eyeing me suspiciously. "Maybe you should think of becoming a lawyer instead of following in your ma's footsteps when you get older."

"Why's that?" I asked.

"Never mind," he said, and a big grin spread across his face. "Best you both be running along though, I imagine."

I looked at my watch. "He's right, Dewey. We've only got twenty minutes to make it home."

"That's a nice watch you got there, boy," the reverend said. "It new?"

"It was a present from my Uncle Henry."

"I remember your Uncle Henry. From what I know of him, he's a good man. And now that I think about it, haven't I seen him round town lately? He stayin' with you and your ma?"

I nodded. "And my sister. Just 'til this thing with Tiffany Michelle Yates gets solved."

"That's good. Awfully nice thing of him to do. Like I said, he's a good man. Maybe you should ask *him* how he feels about Mr. Garner."

I already knew the answer to that, but I didn't tell the reverend. Instead, I thanked him for his time, and me and Dewey headed off.

CHAPTER 25

The next day was a Monday and school got out early on account of there being a teachers' meeting after lunch. Dewey's mother had to go into Satsuma for some shopping. She had insisted that an actual mall was in order (the closest thing we had to a mall in Alvin was a small strip of outlet stores along Old Highway Seventeen). Uncle Henry had gone down to Mobile for the afternoon to take care of something to do with renewing the mortgage on his property, so that meant one of two things. Either my mother let me brave the afternoon streets of Alvin home alone on foot, or she had to take time out of her day of suspecting farmers and come pick me up. I'm willing to bet the farmers were happy with the choice she made. I told her this as I climbed into her car.

"I was almost done anyway, smart mouth," she said. "Do up your belt."

I did. "Did you find anythin'?"

She frowned. "No. Nothin' worth mentionin'. Seems the farmers of this town are 'bout the most honest people in the whole place." I thought about mentioning that Mr.

Wyatt Edward Farrow not being a farmer tended to support her point as far as I was concerned, but I held my tongue.

"Which farms you got left to investigate?" I asked. The sun was a pale yellow today, not nearly as hot as it had been lately.

"A couple on the outskirts," she said. "The Allen farm's up next."

With a shiver, I remembered how that farm had loomed past my side of the car the night we drove out of town to threaten the life of Carry's boyfriend. Both Allen farmhouses, but particularly the old one—the one that burned up and killed nearly all of Jesse James Allen's family—had squatted there in the dark mist and felt as though it was staring back at me as we went past, its black insides like a gaping mouth ready to gobble up anyone who might dare go near it. I hoped my mother wasn't about to suggest we go together now and finish up that part of her investigation.

My hope dissolved fast.

"How 'bout we just take one small detour down Highway Seventeen so I can check on Jesse James and his grandpa before heading back to the station?" she asked. "Then you can wait with Officer Jackson while I file my paperwork. We might even make it home in time for me to wrestle up some burgers for supper."

Burgers almost made any proposition worthwhile, for I certainly did like them. Especially my mother's, which she always fried with mushrooms and onions. "Okay," I said. Besides, sometimes when Chief Montgomery wasn't at the station (and he just might not be if we showed up around suppertime), my mother and Officer Jackson let me sit in his office and watch satellite television. The screen wasn't very big or nothing, but the fact that I could watch over three hundred channels more than made up for that. It sure as heck beat what we had at home.

The drive to the Allen farm went much faster than it had that night in the dark. At least it sure *felt* like it did. I figured it was that way with lots of stuff. Nighttime, especially when it's dark and misty like it had been then, makes everything feel slower and scarier.

Soon we were on Highway Seventeen, driving past fields of cotton and corn. The pungent smell of manure filled the car as, outside my window, the corn broke into a field of cattle. Then there was the old Hunter barn tall in the center surrounded by all them cows. They looked hot, even on this autumn afternoon, swishing away flies with their tails while they stood and chewed.

There wasn't much left of the cotton crops going by on the other side of the street. Harvesting was now over. The fields passing by outside my window began to slow as my mother came up the rise connecting to the dirt driveway that led off into the Allen farm. Even in the daytime, the burnt-out husk of the original farmhouse gave me a bit of the willies. It sat very close to the road, but no longer had a driveway connecting it to the highway. The gate that used to be in front had been replaced by a stretch of fence continuing up to the new driveway that led through to the main gate of the farm.

Turning in, my mother pulled to a stop outside the gate and honked her horn. When nobody made any indication of coming out to open it for us, she stepped out of the car and swung it open herself. It wasn't locked. Then, after driving through, she got out once again, and closed it behind us. The wide, dusty lane be-

yond the gate took us to the new farmhouse that Jesse
James and his grandpa had built all by themselves, not
counting the help they got from them Mexicans.

My mother parked well in front of an old, red Chevy
truck. It was caked with dried dirt and mud and parked
facing toward the street.

"How come the new farmhouse is so much smaller
than the old one?" I asked.

"Well, remember," my mother answered, "Jesse
James and his grandpa built this one all by themselves."

"I thought you said they got help from them Mexicans?" I asked.

"I reckon they likely did," she said, "but you just
keep that tidbit of information to yourself, you understand me? Under no circumstances do you say such a
thing in front of *anyone,* especially not Jesse or his
grandpa. If they like people to think otherwise, that's
fine and their business. You got that?"

I told her I did.

"Besides," she said, "there are only two of them
now. They don't need as much room as before." She
got out of the car and put on her hat.

"Can I come, too?" I asked.

She thought this over and decided it would be okay.
I followed her across the dusty drive and then over the
walkway that ran along the front of the farmhouse and
up to the front door. The walkway was overgrown with
weeds, wild grass, and bunches of wildflowers, including some of the tallest dandelions I'd ever seen; nearly
all of them had gone to seed already. I thought about
how it would feel to lose my whole family, or near on all
of it—the way Jesse had—and another shiver twisted its
way up my backbone.

"And," my mother said, "I don't think they keep animals in the back the way they used to. They used to have goats and stuff."

"They still have chickens," I said, pointing out two hens that had come from around the side of the farmhouse. They stood at the end of the walkway, cocking their heads sideways as though trying to figure out who we were and what we wanted. I laughed.

"Chickens don't take much room, Abe," my mother said. She knocked on the front door and waited for someone to answer. Nobody did, so she knocked again, only louder this time.

"That's strange," she said, stepping back and looking up at the house and then over at the old Chevy in the driveway. "George Allen's truck's here."

"It don't look much like it's been driven in a while, I reckon," I said. "Look at the windshield, it's covered in dust. I doubt you could even see out of it well enough to drive."

"Well, I don't reckon they do much drivin' no more," my mother said. " 'Cept maybe into town every now and then for food and supplies and stuff. They keep mostly to themselves."

I almost told my mother about seeing Jesse James Allen in town that Saturday morning me and Dewey were following Mr. Farrow, but decided any recollection of that day was best left alone.

I followed her back around to where we was parked. She made a big circle, rounding the side of the red pickup farthest from the farmhouse. "Mr. Allen!" she called out, cupping her hands around her mouth. "Mr. Allen, are you out here somewhere? It's Leah Teal from the Alvin Police Department."

The only response she got was the clucking of chickens. Maybe five or six more were on the driveway behind the pickup, pecking through the gravel and patches of dried grass while being led around by a rather stern cock.

"The place seems dead," I pointed out. A small wooden shed had been built against the side of the farmhouse on the other side of the pickup. Probably it was full of things like chicken feed, axes, shovels, and other basic farming tools. It was much too small for the big equipment—the stuff they used for harvesting. That would all be stored somewhere else.

A slight breeze picked up, blowing from the back fields. It carried with it the unmistakable smell of farm. There were several varieties when it came to the smell and, living in Alvin, you got to know them all. Thankfully, the Allens didn't farm cattle. That one was the worst, by far.

From here, the acres of land owned by the Allens seemed to stretch on forever. All of the crops had been harvested, of course, but way off in the back (it may have been two hundred yards away, it may have been more; crops tend to throw off your sense of distance completely) the cornfield still did its best to stay standing. It waved in the breeze like the slight ripple of waves in a sea of bright green.

"How come the corn hasn't been harvested?" I asked.

My mother hushed me. "Maybe George Allen had to sell the combine," she whispered back. "Jesse and him don't have a lot of money."

"You mean all them Mexicans harvested the corn by hand?"

She shushed me. I tried to figure out if I had said something racist.

My mother cupped her hands around her mouth. "Mr. Allen!" she called again.

"I reckon the only things here are the chickens," I said. They hardly looked overly well fed. "And even *they* look hungry."

"Mr. Allen!" My mother was hollering in all directions now. "George Allen? Are you out here *any*where?"

"They gotta be *some*where," I said.

My mother cut me a sideways glance. "That's very astute of you."

I had no idea what *astute* meant, but decided she had just called me smart. "Thank you," I said. "Maybe Jesse and his grandpa walked into town?"

"Abe, George Allen's gotta be eighty-five if he's a day. I doubt he's walking much these days, never mind the two and a half miles it is each way into town. Especially not in this heat."

I was about to point out that today actually wasn't really that hot when my mother walked over to the truck and ran her finger along the inside of the bed, examining the dirt on it afterward. Then she opened the door on the driver's side and carefully examined the seats, looking behind and underneath them. She even checked out the mats and the steering wheel. The last thing she did was pop the glove box, but all she found inside were the registration papers.

"Find anything?" I asked.

She shook her head. "Seems pretty clean to me," she said.

A squawk drew my attention away as the cock decided to attack three of the straggling hens. I decided to teach it a lesson, so with a squawk of my own, I chased it around the back of the farmhouse, running through the unkempt grass that looked as though it hadn't been mowed in months. The cock fled as fast as it could, bobbing along on its tiny stick-feet. The falling sun intensified the splashes of red on its outstretched wings. Its beak opened in a way that made it look like it was screaming.

It looked so ridiculous I couldn't help but laugh as I chased it.

My mother was still examining the truck. "Abe!" she called out. "Please don't. This isn't our—"

But I didn't hear whatever she finished saying, because around the back of the farmhouse I discovered something that made my legs, my arms, and even my ears stop working. I skidded to an immediate halt, my heart racing so hard in my chest I thought it might burst right through my rib cage.

A wheelbarrow leaned up against the back porch, positioned so its bed faced outward. Like the cock's wings, the handles and bed of that barrow were red, only *completely* red, and even *I* could tell it wasn't paint I was looking at glistening under that pale yellow sun.

It felt like an eternity went by before I managed to regain control of my mouth. When I spoke my voice came out shaky and quiet. "Mom," I said, "you better come here."

CHAPTER 26

My mother came around, both anxiously and cautiously at the same time. "Abe, what—" she started to ask, but stopped at the sight of the wheelbarrow. Without even looking down, her hand pulled her gun from its holster, something I had only seen her do once before.

"Mr. Allen!" she yelled, her fingers gripped tightly around her weapon's handle. "Mr. Allen, are you out here?" Then, lowering her voice almost to a whisper, she said, "Abe, go get back in the car. Right now! Get back in the car, and lock the doors."

Three hens pecked the ground around the bloody wheelbarrow. "Mom," I said, trying to keep things calm. "Maybe it's just animal blood." I figured this wasn't such a bad assumption, considering we were on a farm and all.

My mother ignored me completely. "Abe," she said again, her voice low and commanding, "listen to me. Get back in the goddamn car, right this instant. Lock the doors. Do it. *Now*."

Grudgingly, I headed back to the car, slightly annoyed, but also a bit relieved. Annoyed because it was me who found the wheelbarrow in the first place, and I didn't see why a wheelbarrow full of blood meant I had to go wait in the car yet again. Besides, I really thought my hypothesis of animal blood was a good one. As I slinked away, I heard my mother unclip the walkie-talkie she had brought along for the day and call the station for backup. I made a wide turn toward the car so I could see everything as long as possible. Every two or three steps, I looked over my shoulder and watched while my mother scanned the entire farmyard slowly, her gaze locked on the horizon. Both her hands gripped her gun, which she had pointed toward the ground at waist height.

"Mr. Allen!" she yelled again, this time so loud it made me jump. "Mr. Allen, if you're out here, you must make yourself known now, before I make a mistake and accidentally shoot you!"

I stopped between the truck and the farmhouse as, far beyond the red pickup, the shadow of a figure emerged from the old burnt-out building. From the angle I was at, I don't think my mother could see me, but she did see whoever it was that had come out into the sunlight from the old barn's dark insides. She recognized him immediately. From the look of surprise and fear on his face, I don't think he had heard my mother yelling at all or had any idea we were here.

"Jesse!" my mother called out. "Is your grandpa around here somewhere?"

He shook his head, but said nothing.

"Where might I be able to find him?" she asked. I stepped back, cautiously sneaking another peek at my mother. She still held her weapon tightly at her side. It wasn't pointed at Jesse James Allen, but by her posture, she was anything but relaxed.

Jesse had yet to say a word. He just stood there. I could make out his face more clearly now. It was filled with fear and confusion. From here, he looked pretty near exactly as he had that morning on the street. I didn't think a comb had touched that mess of hair at any point in time in the interim.

"Jesse!" my mother said. "I need you to tell me where your grandpa is, and I need you to do it *now*. Jesse, I have a gun in my hand. Do you understand that?"

I returned to my position just far enough around the edge of the house to be out of my mother's line of sight. Only, Jesse James Allen *did* see me. His head turned and looked dead straight at me. Something in his eyes threw a chill through my blood I doubted I would ever forget. I took two steps back, putting myself between the red pickup and the toolshed.

It was then that I noticed the smell. A horrible smell, like the one that used to come out of the old mink farm that had been in operation down Old Mill Road before the townsfolk signed a petition to get them to shut it down. Only, this smell actually seemed worse, something that, until today, I wouldn't have thought possible.

The smell confused me, and it took a good couple seconds for me to pinpoint the source of it. Then I figured it out. It was coming from the toolshed. The shed had a pair of double doors, with a fairly thick chain threaded several times through the hasps of each door. Normally, the chain was secured with a padlock, and the padlock was there now, but it was open. I took a step closer, holding my breath as best I could, unsure whether I really wanted to know what was creating that horrible stench. Part of me, that eleven-year-old-boy part, knew I *needed* to find out, or I would forever regret not knowing.

I glanced back to Jesse, seeing his attention rapidly alternate between me and my mother. The color was draining from his face.

"Jesse, I need you to put your hands in the air and walk slowly toward me," I heard my mother say. I knew she was too busy to pay me much attention, so I lifted off the lock and carefully slipped the chain from the hasps in the doors. The whole time, I did my best not to breathe through my nose, but breathing through my mouth only made it worse because, whether or not it was actually true, I imagined I could now taste that smell.

When the chain was free, I set it quietly on the dusty ground and swung open the wooden doors. At that moment, I saw exactly where that smell was coming from.

Propped up on the slatted wooden floor was the decaying remains of Jesse's grandpa. There wasn't much left of him— his body looked nearly skeletal. Maggots covered near on all the skin he had remaining, and my stomach churned so hard I had to look away before I got sick.

"Mom!" I called out.

"Abe! I thought I told you to get in the goddamn car and lock the door?" she asked. "You're getting worse than your goddamn sister!"

"But, Mom," I pleaded, "you really need to see this."

I heard her slowly start stepping around in my direction. "Jesse, put your hands up, do you hear me? Put them up *now!*"

My mother came up beside where I stood, walking sideways, her back to the farmhouse, her gun now aimed directly at Jesse James Allen just the same way I'd seen it aimed at Stephen McFarren, only now I realized that night with Carry and her boyfriend had been just an act compared to the real thing. "Why aren't you in—" She made a fast shoulder check, glancing into the shed, and I watched the second it took for her brain to throw it all together. "Jesus Christ."

That's when Jesse James began running toward the back fields where the cornstalks were doing their best to keep standing. "Abe, I'm *begging* you. Get in the car now! I'm seriously not kidding around." She took off on foot after Jesse, running as fast as I'd ever seen anyone go. A few hens in her way quickly scattered as her boots left the dusty driveway and hit the dead wild grass of the outlying farmland. "Jesse! Stop right now, or so help me God, I'll shoot you!"

But Jesse didn't stop. My mother did, though. She stopped and carefully took aim before pulling off a shot. I could not believe how loud it was. My ears were still ringing as I watched it miss, hitting the hard ground right near Jesse's foot. The dirt beside his shoe flew up in an explosion of dark brown powder.

My mother started off after him again, still gaining fast, especially once Jesse hit the cornfield. The stalks slowed him down substantially and, since it was so late in the season with harvest over and all, the corn gave easily to his weight, leaving an open trail behind him. When my mother wasn't more than thirty yards away, she stopped again, yelling, "Jesse, I'm givin' you one last chance. Stop, or you *will* be shot."

I guess Jesse James Allen didn't believe her, because he kept trudging as fast as he could through that corn, and this time my mother did not miss. Even though I was somewhat more prepared for the thunderclap of sound made by her gun, I still jumped as she pulled the trigger and got off her shot, putting a bullet right in the back of Jesse's leg. Jesse James Allen went down, falling into a clump on the tilled ground, amidst a cradle of green stalks all on their way to dying or going to seed.

While this all happened, I had stood frozen, not even noticing the smell from the shed anymore. Something about it captivated me. It was like watching a movie, only different on account of it was real life with my very own mother in the starring role.

Strange feelings swept through me that I hadn't felt before, but I was starting to get used to that. Maybe this was part of becoming a grown-up.

Seeing Jesse lying there, all crumpled up in the dirt, made me wonder if my mother might have killed him, but I figured it was probably unlikely anyone could die from a bullet wound to the back of the leg. At least not right away. At least my mother didn't think he was dead. I heard her yelling at him over and over while she patted him down: "Where is she? Where is she?"

When Jesse James Allen answered, his voice was strained and the words seemed to come out in a flood of pain.

"The old farmhouse," he said, and once again fell still.

CHAPTER 27

I wasn't entirely sure what to do. In all the commotion, my mother seemed to have completely forgot about me and, from what I could tell, I was no longer in any danger from either Jesse James or his grandpa on account of one lying close to death in the cornfield and the other being eaten by maggots in the shed behind me while he rotted away in the waning heat of late afternoon.

Officer Jackson's cruiser pulled up. Just like that day at Robert Lee Garner's, he shut down his siren, but left the red and blue lights flashing. "Jesse's in the cornfield, Chris!" my mother yelled to him as she ran to the burned-out husk of the old barn. "I had to put one in the back of his knee. He's unarmed."

Pausing upon seeing me, Officer Jackson asked, "What're you doing here?"

"Helpin'," I said.

He gave me a dubious look. "Bet you are," he said, then jogged out to the field, where Jesse James Allen had begun screaming in pain amidst the broken patch of corn.

I once again fell back on my theory that forgiveness came easier than permission and started toward the old barn, reaching it barely after my mother did on account of the cornfield being much farther from it than the new farmhouse.

"Abe!" my mother said in a clipped whisper. "What the hell are you doing? I told you to stay in that god-damn car!"

I was very aware of her gun and remembered quite clearly how she acted the night we caught Carry with the boy in the car, but I wasn't scared. There were some things a kid of eleven years just had to be part of. And I'd come way too far to give up now. I'd never forgive myself if I did. Dewey wouldn't, neither.

I could tell she wanted to give me a speech about listening to her when she told me to do something, but there were far more important things she had to deal with first. So instead, she said, "You are going to get *such* a talking-to when this is all over, let me tell you what. You're turning into your goddamn sister!"

Suddenly I had new admiration for Carry and her change in attitude. It took a lot of guts and bravery to keep up this sort of thing. But I was already heavily invested. There was no turning back.

Besides, from where I stood, *I* was the one who found Grandpa Allen *and* the wheelbarrow. I had played just as much a part in this as she had, possibly even more. Geez, I was even the one who convinced her Mr. Robert Lee Garner was actually innocent. In some ways, I was starting to think, without me, she might never have got this far in her investigation. Of course, that was the old eleven-year-old version of myself talking. I had started noticing lately that there were two different versions of me going on in my body—the little boy who was a lot like Dewey, and another one who was starting to be a lot more grown up.

"Oh my God," my mother gasped when we entered the dilapidated barn. At one time, it was a three-story structure with a hay loft, but much of it was now gone, mostly due to the fire, the rest due to time. Lengths of wooden boards that once ran along the outside had fallen away, leaving open rectangles to the outside. Those, combined with the gaping holes where doors and windows had once been, allowed the dusty light of the westerly sun to fall eerily through, casting weird patterns surrounded by even stranger shadows around them. It was like walking into the mouth of some sort of deformed clown. In some places, like the back corners, it was near on pitch-black.

Unfortunately, that wasn't the case in the center area of the back wall. Tiffany Michelle Yates stood there, her arms stretched straight above her head. Her hands were tied to a metal hook hanging from a thick black chain. The chain went right to the top of the barn, looping over one of the ceiling's crossbeams before coming back down where the rest of it wound around a rusted winch with a red handle. The winch was bolted to the wall barely three feet away from Tiffany.

Her head lulled limply forward. Her black hair, matted with hay and dirt, hung down over her chest. I'm pretty sure my mother and me had the same thought at nearly the same time: We were too late. There was no indication of life in the way Tiffany Michelle hung there. She wore a big, oversized gray T-shirt that came nearly to her knees, and for all I knew, there was not another stitch of clothing on her.

The sun's orange light poured down on her through an oddly shaped hole in the barn's roof, lighting her up in the middle of all that darkness as though she were under a spotlight. It kind of made her look like an angel, and I remembered asking Dewey if he thought Mary Ann Dailey was with the angels now after reading what it had said on her tombstone behind Clover Creek First Baptist.

Dream with little angels.

I hoped Reverend Starks was right and that God didn't see color so that Tiffany Michelle Yates could be with the angels now, too.

"Tiffany?" my mother asked softly. Apparently, she wasn't quite as positive as me about Tiffany's condition.

There was no reaction, though. Tiffany Michelle just continued hanging there from that rusty hook, her entire body limp.

My mother said Tiffany's name twice more, and I think she was about to give up when those strands of black hair moved slightly. "She's alive," I said, amazed.

"Tiffany," my mother said again. "It's okay. You're safe."

Slowly, Tiffany Michelle raised her head and I had to take a step back. It was her eyes. They terrified me. They were wide with fear and looked at us the same way a coyote looks at you when you happen upon it accidentally in the woods. She no longer appeared anything like the little girl with the big ice cream cone and that pink dress. Now she looked like some sort of wild animal.

Silver duct tape covered her mouth. In places, dried blood stained the gray T-shirt hanging over her. It looked like the blood in the wheelbarrow, only not nearly so thick.

My mother took a slow step forward. "Tiffany, honey, it's okay. You're safe now. Jesse James is in custody. He can't hurt you anymore."

Tiffany's eyes stayed wide.

From her belt, my mother removed her flashlight and played the beam across Tiffany, hesitating only slightly on the trickle of red running down the inside of her left leg. It looked fairly dry, but not nearly as old as the blood on her shirt, and ran all the way down to her toes, which barely managed to touch the hay-covered dirty barn floor. Jesse had tightened the winch just enough to keep her heels elevated. I couldn't imagine how uncomfortable she must have been hanging there like that.

My mind tried remembering back to how pretty she had looked that afternoon on Main Street, with her hair freshly washed and tied back with that thick yellow ribbon. Now she resembled something out of a horror movie. No matter how hard I tried, I could not overlay the two images inside my head.

"Tiffany, can you understand me?" my mother asked, keeping her voice quiet and soft.

Tiffany nodded, her eyes starting to focus normally again.

"Good. Jesse James is in handcuffs. I shot him in the leg. You're safe. He can't hurt you anymore." She looked straight into Tiffany's eyes and repeated this last part. "He can't hurt you anymore. Do you understand?"

Again, Tiffany nodded. Tears began to well in her eyes.

"I'm going to remove the tape from your mouth," my mother said. "Is that okay?"

Tiffany confirmed it was.

"This may sting a bit. I'll try to go slow," my mother said. She went slow enough. The tape left a sticky residue around Tiffany's mouth, and her lips were near on blue in color, but having the duct tape taken off seemed to bring her some relief.

Her chest heaved as she took several deep breaths, but otherwise she said nothing.

"That blood on your leg?" my mother asked. "Are you injured? Or . . ." She trailed off. My mother's blue eyes met with Tiffany's brown ones. They gleamed with an intensity that relayed some sort of information between them I had no way of grasping. But right away, my mother nodded in understanding and, with one more step, came close enough to wrap her arms around Tiffany's head and pull her gently against her chest. "It's okay," she said, patting the back of the girl's head. "He can't hurt you anymore. It's all going to be okay."

After a long hug, my mother inspected the winch holding the chain in place. It didn't take her long to figure out how to unlock it and turn the handle so the chain lowered enough that both of Tiffany's feet were flat on the barn floor. Then she removed her knife from her belt and cut the knot free that tied Tiffany Michelle's hands to the hook. Almost immediately, Tiffany's legs gave way and she collapsed. My mother managed to catch her just in time before she landed in the sawdust and dirt covering the wooden floor.

Officer Jackson came in the same way we had. "I've got Jesse James cuffed in the back of my car. I've already read him his rights," he said. He lowered his voice as he approached us. Tiffany Michelle Yates was still wrapped in my mother's arms. I was starting to feel awkward and in the way.

"How is she?" Officer Jackson asked.

My mother gave him a look similar to the one she'd shared with Tiffany. Again, I didn't understand it, but Officer Jackson replied with, "Jesus Christ."

"How's Jesse's leg?" my mother asked him.

"He'll live."

She frowned. "I almost wish I'd aimed higher."

"No, you don't," Officer Jackson said. "You did it *right*. And you saved her life."

"Yeah, well, I should have saved two *more* of them," she said.

Two dried pools of blood were on the floorboards farther along the wall. "Hey," I called out. One looked fairly recent—even the hay on the floor in that area was stained a brownish scarlet. The other one, even farther down, wouldn't even have been noticeable if the sun hadn't fallen since we arrived, stretching the odd-shaped span of now golden light far enough to show it. It was old and faded. Years of hay and dirt had all but covered it up except for those places where the floorboards happened to somehow be clean enough to see it. "What're they from?"

Right away, I saw Tiffany Michelle grow tense and look away. She had no desire to think about them stains and I pretty much figured she must know something about them.

My mother examined them with her flashlight. Her

face grew even more serious as she looked to Officer Jackson. "Get someone from Satsuma or Franklin down here to do some lab work," she said. "But my money's on that middle one matching the blood of Mary Ann Dailey." Tears were in her throat. You could hear them as she continued. "And I bet that far one?" Now the tears were in her eyes as she struggled to finish. "That far one's probably from Ruby Mae Vickers."

The setting sun had brightened the back corner of the barn enough that Officer Jackson noticed a large butcher knife leaning against the wall. He snapped on a pair of gloves and picked it up carefully by the handle using just two fingers. The blade had been sloppily wiped. Blood still caked its edges. The wooden handle was soaked in it.

Tiffany Michelle gripped my mother harder than ever. She buried her face in my mother's chest as Officer Jackson dropped the knife into an evidence bag.

"I gotta get this girl to the hospital," my mother said.

Officer Jackson nodded. "One thing, though," he said. "I'm having some problems followin' all this. I mean, sure, I'll give you Mary Ann Dailey, but Ruby Mae Vickers? Ruby Mae turned up *twelve years ago,* Leah. Jesse James would've been six years old back then. It makes no sense."

"None of this makes no sense, Chris," my mother said. "Look around you. What we walked in and found here today, this little girl the way she is"—she pulled Tiffany Michelle in even tighter—"*that* makes no sense. I mean, Christ, what's happened to this world?"

CHAPTER 28

My mother didn't say a word about the case for the next few days. Mainly she slept. I think everyone agreed the ordeal had put her close to dying of sheer exhaustion and frustration, so nobody bothered her while she spent most of that time in bed. Uncle Henry didn't even ask a single question about what happened.

Then, four nights later, with my door halfway open, she seemed to get some of her energy back. She'd gone to the station for a couple hours earlier on, and now, as I lay in my bed, I listened to her explain everything that happened to Uncle Henry. A lot of what she told him hadn't made sense to me back at the Allen farm, but hearing it again cleared things up a bit. There were still parts I didn't quite understand, but I resigned myself to the fact that I probably never would completely.

After Officer Jackson took Jesse into custody, a team of officers from Mobile came up and took Jesse James Allen back with them to some hospital in Birmingham, where he was currently under guard and being analyzed by psychiatric experts, or something like that.

I wasn't exactly sure what that meant. I mean, I knew that meant he was probably on the floor for mental patients, but usually the people who got sent there were somehow sick in the head. I had known Jesse James Allen when he was still in school, and he always seemed normal to me.

Then I remembered Dewey telling me what his pa had said about Jesse James not being right since the fire. I figured maybe there was some truth to that.

"So," I heard Uncle Henry ask. "The bloodstains. Were they—"

My mother cut him off. "Well, the middle one—the *fresh* one, although I hate sayin' it that way—turned out exactly how I thought. The blood belonged to Mary Ann Dailey. Jesse must've hung her a few feet farther along the wall from where we found Tiffany Michelle, and when it came time, he just slit her throat right there and waited until she bled out." She took a deep breath. "That's why we didn't find no blood in the truck. Well, that and the fact he used a hay bag to wrap her in before transporting her to where he left the body." Once again, I could hear tears in my mother's voice. I was getting used to the sound now.

"Seems awfully well thought out to me," Uncle Henry said. "Especially from what little I know about that kid. Jesse James Allen's always struck me as a bit simpleminded."

"Me too, Hank. But we found the bag he used. He even knew to wear gloves so he wouldn't leave any prints. We found those, too. They was with the bag."

"It's almost like he read a how-to book on murderin' or somethin'," Uncle Henry said.

" 'Cept the problem there is that Jesse James Allen don't know how to read," my mother said. "Other than real basic stuff."

"Then, how—" Uncle Henry started, but stopped halfway through his sentence and changed topics. "What about that other bloodstain. Did it come from Ruby Mae?"

My mother blew her nose. I assumed she was crying. "We're still waitin' for the official forensic reports, but initial analysis shows a probable match. The blood types are the same, and the team from Mobile have already put the age of the stain around the same time, so I think it's safe to say that it did." She hesitated, then added, "Poor little Ruby Mac Vickers, hanging there all by herself for three months a dozen years ago."

"Tiffany Michelle Yates disappeared before Mary Ann Dailey's body showed up. Were they both in that barn at the same time?" Uncle Henry asked. This was a question I hadn't thought of.

"That's something we don't know yet. Tiffany Michelle is in the Alvin Hospital Psychiatric Care Facility. They don't want to push her into answering any questions too quickly. But by the way she buried her face into me when Abe pointed out the blood, and especially her reaction to the knife when Chris picked it up from where it had been leanin' against the wall, I think it's a fair bet they were not only both there, but Jesse killed Mary Ann in front of Tiffany." Her final words broke into tears. "Can you imagine, Hank? Can you even *imagine*?"

"No, Leah, I can't. Not even for a second. But there's a big element to all this that doesn't make a heckuva lot of sense. I'm sure you've realized this. If that *is* Ruby Mae's blood on the floor of that barn, that means the three cases are connected. But Jesse James Allen . . ."

"Was six years old when Ruby Mae was killed," my mother said, interrupting him. "That one had everyone ponderin'. But the therapist in charge of interviewing Jesse at the facility in Birmingham has already managed to unroll most of that mystery. Even though it's only been barely three days. You remember, Hank, how six years or so ago, Jesse James Allen stopped going to school?"

"Yeah," Uncle Henry said. "Right after his family's farmhouse burned down. George Allen needed him on that farm after that and, like I said before, from what I heard, Jesse wasn't too good at school anyway. He was probably much more of an asset to Grandpa George, who was left with nobody 'cept those Mexicans during the harvestin' season."

"Right," my mother said.

"And I remember the two of them, George and Jesse, built that new farmhouse entirely by themselves," Uncle Henry said. "What's this got to do with anythin', Leah?"

My mother didn't correct him about the farmhouse construction. "Well, from what we've gathered so far," she said, "both George Allen and Jesse's father, James, molested Jesse. They started when he was really young, from about five or so."

"You're shittin' me."

"God's honest truth. They didn't stop, neither. It kept on goin' for years. Then, and this is the horrible part—not that the last part wasn't horrible, but this is . . . well . . . unspeakable—when Jesse was six, the two men kidnapped Ruby Mae Vickers and tied her up in the barn, exactly the same way we found Tiffany Michelle Yates, only a little farther down. I reckon they used that same winch and all, only that chain was looped over three or four rafters instead of just the one."

There was a pause and then my uncle said, "I don't believe it."

"It gets worse, Hank. For three months, they raped that girl every which way you can imagine. Many times they brought little Jesse in, makin' him watch and even participate while they did it. Then, one day, somethin' happened and they got nervous, I guess, 'bout being caught."

"I know what happened," Uncle Henry said. "*You* happened, Leah. They got scared because you refused to let up on that case, and you scared them."

"Hank, *don't*. Sayin' that is the same as sayin' I killed her."

"No, sayin' that is sayin' you came a lot closer to savin' her life than you've ever given yourself credit for."

I listened to another spate of tears before my mother spoke again. "At any rate," she said, "they got nervous and so they killed her. Slit her throat right there in the barn and let her hang there like a piece of beef until all the blood run out. Oh, Hank, it's just so awful. When she was finished bleeding, they wrapped her in a hay bag, drove her out to Skeeter Swamp in the dead of night, and dumped her beside that willow tree across from Bob Garner's ranch."

"Jesus," Uncle Henry said.

"They even made little Jesse come along for the ride, tellin' him if he ever breathed a word of anything that happened regardin' Ruby Mae Vickers to anyone, he'd end up just the same way she did, throat slit and all. Hank, the boy was barely two months out of his sixth birthday. What does somethin' like that do to a six-year-old?"

"Damned if I know, Leah," Uncle Henry said. "Nothin' good, that's for sure. So I guess this puts Bob Garner in the clear."

"Yeah, we let him go on Monday. I've never done so much apologizin' in my life. I told him he owes everything to Abe. Without my little boy, he might still be in jail."

"Abe?" Uncle Henry asked. "What could Abe possibly have had to do with it?"

"That's a long story. I reckon I best let him tell it. You can ask him in the morning."

"So, what's gonna happen to Jesse James Allen now?"

"He'll be institutionalized for a long while, maybe even the rest of his life. According to the doctor, even Jesse's mother and grandmother knew about the molestin' . . . well, at least about Jesse being molested anyway . . . they just pretended it wasn't happenin'. 'Course that left Jesse with absolutely no one to turn to, nobody he could trust. You put a child in a situation like that, I don't see how he can help but become some sort of sociopath. Then, on top of all that, he literally watches while everyone in his family except his grandfather, who was probably the worst goddamn bastard of the bunch, burn up in a farmhouse fire."

Mr. Garner told me and Dewey that when the fire

happened, the authorities investigating construed it as accidental. Now, listening to everything my mother and Uncle Henry was saying, I thought about poor Jesse James Allen and how scared he must've been growing up in that house, and started wondering how accidental the blaze really was.

"Do you know yet what happened to George Allen? Did Jesse kill him?" Uncle Henry asked.

"No, unfortunately," my mother said. "I reckon, somehow, there would be a weird sort of justice in it if he had, but the autopsy report said the man died of congestive heart failure over a month ago."

"And Jesse just stuck him in a toolshed?" Uncle Henry asked, his voice full of disbelief.

"I don't reckon the kid had any idea what to do with him. I'm surprised George Allen didn't end up down by that willow tree, to be honest."

"I can't imagine," Uncle Henry said.

"Neither can I. But when you think about it a certain way, it's hard not to feel at least a little bad for Jesse James Allen. He must have been so lonely on that farm after George died. And having to walk by that toolshed every day, knowing his grandpa was inside . . ." She paused. "So, I guess he decided to fix his problem the way he had been taught to do as a kid: Find somebody to make your life less lonely, use them all you can, then get rid of them. He only knew one way to do all that, and so he did it exactly the same way his father and grandpa had done with Ruby Mae Vickers."

A very long stretch of silence followed, finally broken by Uncle Henry. "Well, I suppose Sheryl Davis will be happy now."

"Why's that?" my mother asked.

"She'll once again get a chance to enter her straw-berry rhubarb pie in the bake-off after all this year. We've still got three weeks until Thanksgiving. Plenty of time to organize the fair."

"Yeah, I suppose," my mother said. "I almost want to keep it canceled just out of spite. Some people's pri-orities never cease to amaze me."

I started to nod off after that. Their conversation quickly dissolved into the normal type of conversation my mother and Uncle Henry used to have before little girls started going missing from Alvin, almost as though the whole incident never happened. But it wasn't like that for me. The experience of seeing Mary Ann Dailey dead beneath that tree, and then being there when my mother found Tiffany Michelle Yates alive, stayed with me and would for the rest of my life. I often dreamt of them. Sometimes the dreams were good, sometimes they were nightmares, but it didn't matter. Having gone through the ordeal and being nearly as close to the case as my mother was a life-changing experience I wouldn't trade for anything.

Some of the real gory details I never divulged to anyone, Dewey included. *Especially* Dewey, actually. I figured one of us having to go through life with something like this in his head was enough. I *did* tell him what my mother said about me being the one who helped free Mr. Robert Lee Garner from jail and how my mother shot Jesse James Allen in the back of the leg, though. That last part, Dewey made me go over at least ten times. I think he kept expecting me to change some detail or something and that would prove I had made the whole thing up.

But I never did.

My story always stayed the same, and continued to throughout the years. I would always remember every detail, right down to Jesse James lying there in the field, looking near on as dead as the cornstalks surrounding him.

CHAPTER 29

First thing in the morning the next day, Uncle Henry left for home. We all stood in the doorway, watching him put on his boots and coat. He'd already packed his suitcase the night before.

"Well," he said, gripping my shoulder firmly, "you take good care of your mama and sister now, soldier."

"Always do," I said.

"And maybe next time we see you, Hank," my mother said, "my little girl here will have developed a bit more common sense."

"Oh," Uncle Henry said, "I reckon she's well on her way to doin' fine." He gave Carry a hug and then hugged my mother.

"Take care of yourself, Leah."

Gripping the handle of his suitcase, he opened the door and followed the steps and driveway down to where his car was out on the street. We watched him pull away, waving from the doorstep until he was out of sight.

I looked at my watch. "I miss him already," I said.

Carry stood there, her arms crossed. I couldn't remember a time before this had become her usual stance. "Why do you say things like that, Mother?"

"What? That you have no sense? Caroline, honey, it's true. Sorry if I embarrassed you. Anyway, you're off your grounding. I figure at this point, I've either done my job with you, or I haven't. I just hope to God you're not stupid enough to continue dating nineteen-year-old boys after all this."

Carry's gaze dropped to the carpet. "Mother, there isn't one boy in Alvin *or* Satsuma that will even come near me since you pointed your gun at Stephen and told him you were gonna blow his nuts off."

That brought a smile to my mother. "Perfect."

"He peed his pants, by the way," Carry said, looking back up.

Me and my mother laughed. Carry went to the living room and turned on the television. My mother started pulling on her boots.

"Where you goin'?" I asked.

"I have to go into the station for a bit. Won't be too long, though. I'll be back in time to make supper."

"Can I tag along?"

"What for?"

"Nowhere else I know of 'cept Chief Montgomery's office has satellite," I said.

She laughed. "Problem is, I'm gonna be in that office *with* Chief Montgomery havin' a little meetin'. That's what I'm goin' for. So you can't watch TV anyway."

"Oh," I said, frowning.

She stood thinking a moment. "Abe, how 'bout you come into Chief Montgomery's office for this meetin' *with* me?"

My eyebrows went up in surprise. "Really?" Then I remembered the last time we tried that, and brought them down hard. "Why? So he can kick me out again?"

She finished with her boots. "I don't reckon that'll happen this time. Put on your shoes."

I did. "Why not?" I asked, doing up the laces.

"I just don't."

We walked outside and got into the car. I did up my belt and my mother backed out onto Cottonwood Lane and headed toward Main Street. Houses and trees swept past my window. The few clouds hanging overhead seemed thin and vulnerable. I figured they wouldn't last even another hour. The day was set to be a beautiful one. We passed a rather nice house with bushes of flowers out front, still in full bloom. Bursts of purple, blues, and reds. A nicely painted birdhouse hung from the branch of a tall oak in the yard.

Lately, I had found myself noticing details around me I had never paid attention to before. Things like trees, and flowers, and birds, and all. I suppose what I was noticing was life. "You know," I said, "I reckon we live in one of the prettiest places in the world."

"Where else have you ever been?" my mother asked.

I thought it over. "Satsuma."

"Well, that ain't much to compare with."

"You don't reckon Alvin's pretty?" I asked.

"Oh, I didn't say that. And besides, it's not my opinion that counts when it comes to something like that. It's your own."

"Good," I said. "Then it's settled. We live in the prettiest place in the world."

We pulled up to the curb in front of the Alvin Police

Station, and my mother and I got out of the car and went inside.

Officer Jackson was at his desk, talking on the phone when we came in. He waved hello to my mother and gave me a wink. Mr. Montgomery's office door was closed with the television on inside. It sounded like he was watching hockey or something. When my mother knocked, he lowered the volume considerably. Then, after a loud chair squeak, he opened the door. He wore brown pants and a brown checkered short-sleeved shirt. The top button was undone and his brown tie had been loosened.

"Hey, Ethan," my mother said. I could tell she was hesitant and worried he might still be upset with her.

"Hey, you," he replied.

"Mind if we come in?" my mother asked.

"*We,* Leah? You *and* your son? Haven't we played this scene already? I reckon that may have been one time too many."

My mother looked back at me, proudly. "No, Ethan, I reckon you're wrong. Abe deserves to be part of this discussion. If it starts to go beyond any boundaries I'm comfortable with, *I'll* send him out."

"And what I'm comfortable with doesn't matter?" Chief Montgomery asked.

"Not today, Ethan," she replied. Which not only startled me, but judging from the look on his face, it surprised Chief Montgomery, too. "Ethan, listen," she continued. "I've had some really hard months, so excuse me if I'm out of line, but I told Abe he could sit in today, and when it comes to my kids, I keep my promises. Of course, you could always fire me, which at this point, I'd welcome near on as much as winning the lottery."

Frustrated resignation fell over Chief Montgomery's face and he held the door open while she came inside and I followed. He shut it behind us.

My mother squeezed herself into one of the two chairs in front of Chief Montgomery's desk. He sat in his big leather chair on the other side as I flopped into the only remaining one. Above our heads, the wooden fan slowly turned. Behind us, on the television mounted from the ceiling, the Chicago Blackhawks quietly led the Vancouver Canucks five to two in the second period.

Awkward silence passed for a second.

"Funny thing, hey, Ethan?" my mother asked, breaking it. "All them forensics experts from Mobile? The ones sayin' Mr. Garner did it for sure? The ones with their unbiased opinions and all? Looks like they . . . well . . . looks like they was actually wrong."

Chief Montgomery nodded. "I know. I knew it when you told me the first time."

This caught my mother off guard. Confusion took over her face as she opened her mouth to ask him something, but he spoke before she could.

"I had to do what I did, Leah. You were startin' to rely too much on the people around you," he said. "You're a good cop. Good cops go with their guts." Keeping his eyes on my mother, he gestured to me. "And if that means listenin' to your eleven-year-old boy because what he says strikes you a certain way, then so be it, but don't bring shit like that to me. You go out and *make* it work. By your*self*."

"So you never lost faith in me after all?"

"Oh, don't give yourself so much credit," Chief Montgomery said. "I lose faith in everyone, constantly. You, Chris, the world. But I never thought you wasn't good at your job." With a squeak, his chair leaned forward as his heavy arms came down on his desk. His hands nearly touched the pictures standing along the outside edge of the desktop. Most of them were of his family, but there was one of my grandpa and my mother when she was younger.

I looked up over my shoulder, just in time to see Vancouver put one in Chicago's net with only thirty seconds left in the period. I quickly realized I was being rude and turned back to Chief Montgomery, who hadn't noticed my behavior on account of he was watching the game, too. "Yes!" he yelled, partially standing from his chair and bringing his fist down on his desk.

My mother looked at him like he'd lost his mind.

"My brother in Vancouver's had seasons tickets goin' far back as I can recall," Chief Montgomery explained. "Every time I go up there, we hit every game we can. Besides, I hate Chicago. I got stuck at that airport once for ten hours."

My mother shook her head. "Are you even interested in what I came here to talk 'bout? Maybe I should come back later, after the game's over?" She almost sounded angry.

"No, that'd make no difference. Pittsburgh plays Colorado after this one's done." He smiled and threw me a wink.

My mother sighed.

"Geez, Leah," he said. "Lighten up. You solved your case. It's just . . . how can I put this? You and me? We work different. My work never comes home with me. And it never gets personal. Ever. Yours does. I reckon maybe it makes you better at your job than I am, but just remember: It also makes you a potential casualty."

"I'm not sure I understand that," my mother said.

"Working the way you do, you run so many risks. The risk of burning yourself out. The risk of dragging your family through hell with you every time a case turns bad. The risk of potential self-destruction every single goddamn time you put your uniform on. Are those risks worth taking to be a better cop? I don't know. For me, they certainly aren't."

After a pause, my mother said, "For me, I reckon they are."

Chief Montgomery nodded. "And I'm fairly certain your father would've agreed with you one hundred percent. But try to remember this. You've finally managed to find some closure on the Ruby Mae case. But it took *twelve years* to do it. For twelve years, you let it cast a shadow over your life and the lives of those around you. You *can't* let that happen again. *Ever.* Your next twelve years cannot be dictated by some case you don't happen to solve. Sometimes the bad guys win. It doesn't happen often, but it *does* happen. And when it does, let it go. Don't keep it inside, eating away at you for a dozen years until it finally chews its way out. It's not fair to you, and it certainly ain't fair to these know-it-all kids of yours. And I know your *father'd* even agree with me on *this* one."

On the television, the buzzer went, ending the second period. Through the open blinds, I saw a bluebird land on the branch of a fig tree planted outside.

My mother responded to Chief Montgomery. "Thanks, Ethan," she said, her voice very quiet.

"What are you thanking me for?" he asked. "Treating you like crap?"

"For doing what needed to be done. I know it wasn't easy. I know it hurt you at least as much as it hurt me."

Chief Montgomery batted the idea out of the air with his palm. "Oh, just get the hell out of my office before I put you on parkin' ticket duty or something. Surely, you've got somethin' to do now that your big case is solved. You've finally closed the circle."

"Actually," she said. "it's more as though it's *come* full circle. And you're right, I do have somethin' in need of doin'." Her fingers rose to the Lord Jesus hanging around her neck.

"Well, I hope it involves takin' a few days off," Chief Montgomery said, standing from his seat and stepping to the door. "Your job'll be waitin' for you whenever you come back. I don't reckon we're gonna have a huge need for a crack detective in the immediate future."

I said good-bye and left his office. My mother followed, stopping at the last minute to look Chief Montgomery in the eyes. "Now I understand why Dad liked you so much," she said.

"Your father hated me."

"He called you an ornery bastard, but as a term of endearment. Trust me. I heard how he spoke about people he didn't like."

"Will you just *go*? I've reached my emotional quota for this week."

"Bye, Ethan."

"Bye, Leah."

I was about to say good-bye to Officer Jackson and walk out to the street when Chief Montgomery called out. "Oh, and, Abe?"

I turned, nervously. "Yes, sir?"

He was leaning in his doorway, smiling. "Forgot to say thanks. You'll make a fine officer one day."

I blushed. "You know, sir," I said. "I reckon maybe I might."

Everyone laughed.

After we left the station, my mind went into auto-pilot as cypress trees and strangler figs passed by my window. It wasn't until a good ten minutes or so later that I realized we were headed the wrong direction for home.

We were driving north, and soon came to Blackberry Trail, which wound its way through a dense wooded area full of all sorts of different trees. Spindly maples, tall oaks, and scrawny pines went by my window, along with a whole lot of blackberry bushes, too. Of course, I expected to see blackberries—be a silly name for a trail otherwise. It was too late in the season for berries, though. Autumn was nearly done. The bushes were just tangled thorns and the tree branches were just thin fingers. The maples looked particularly naked. Although from here I couldn't see it, the forest floor must've been a bed of color, soft and moist.

A massive cypress sped past. Its gnarled boughs, draped with Spanish moss, reached boldly toward the midday sun, as though trying to pluck it from the clear sky like a sparkling yellow diamond.

Neither of us said a word as we drove. I didn't bother

asking where we were going. I figured I would find out soon enough, and if my mother wanted me to know, she would've already told me.

Blackberry Trail ended just outside of Cornflower Lake, possibly the prettiest lake in all of Alvin. We slowed along the edge of the small copse of trees that bounded the lake, until pulling to a stop when my mother found a suitable place to park. The air outside the car was sweet and wet. It was the smell of trees, the smell of the lake, the smell of black dirt. As we followed the narrow path through the nest of oaks, I smelled everything. All of nature combined in my nose. The smell of life.

The path led to the lake, where everything was quiet and still. It was encircled by trees and there were no other people anywhere along the shore. The placid water shimmered, looking almost emerald as it reflected the sun shining down from the bright blue sky along with the boughs of the cypress wrapped around the other side. They were the largest cypress I'd ever seen. Their huge, muscular branches hung heavy with Spanish moss yet still seemed to reach higher than any skyscraper I could imagine.

I picked one of the stones up out of the gray sand near the water's edge. Smooth and black, it had a pattern of white salt lines running through it. Like everything else here, it was beautiful. I put it in my pocket.

Never before could I remember being in a place so beautiful, or one that felt so alive. I realized my mother and I still hadn't spoken since leaving the police station.

"Why are we here?" I asked. Three sparrows darted

from the trees behind us, the lake reflecting them like black darts as they flew across the sky.

"I need to get rid of something," she said. Carefully, she lifted the Lord Jesus off her neck, pulling the chain over her head. I had never seen her take it off before.

"What're you gonna do with that?" I asked.

"I don't need it anymore."

"How come?"

She squatted beside me with the Lord Jesus and her chain gripped in her right hand. A light wind broke the reflected sunlight into bright sparkles across the top of the lake, making me squint. "I don't know if you'll understand this, Abe," she said. "But I wore this because it kept my father—your grandpa—close to me. Now I realize he *is* close to me. He's part of me. He's here." She touched her chest above where her heart was. "I no longer need to wear *this* to know his strength and courage will always be alongside me."

"So you're just gonna throw it away?" I asked.

"Not away," she said, standing. "Into the lake. It's a beautiful lake, isn't it?"

I agreed it most certainly was.

"Then I can't think of any better place. It's a beautiful necklace and deserves to be in a place like this."

I wasn't exactly sure why she was throwing away something Grandpa gave her, but it seemed like she knew she had to do it, so I didn't bother asking any more questions.

She brought the hand holding the necklace behind her back as far as she could and, with all her strength, flung the Lord Jesus like a discus, as high and as far as she could over Cornflower Lake. Briefly, I saw the sunlight glint off the silver chain. It looked like a string of pearls, sparkling and tumbling against the robin's egg sky. Then I lost sight of it until a second later, when I heard a faraway *kerplop!* For a few seconds, the sunlight played in the ripples my mother's necklace broke in the lake's mirrorlike surface until, slowly, the water went back to being still.

When I looked back up at her, tears stood in my mother's eyes. She left them there and smiled at me. "Come on," she said. "Let's go home and make supper."

CHAPTER 30

The Friday before Thanksgiving came two weeks later. That was the traditional day of the Alvin Harvest Fair. Despite all the threats of being canceled, the fair went off as usual.

Near on all of Main Street was taken up by the fair, and we walked to it from our home. Me and my mother and (of course) Dewey but, most surprisingly, even Carry came along. For once, she decided to pretend to actually be part of our family again. I couldn't believe it. I decided not to press my luck, so I kept my thoughts to myself.

The Alvin Harvest Fair was one of the biggest fairs in the area, bigger by far than the one they threw right before Christmas in Satsuma. In fact, many people from Satsuma came down to Alvin specifically for our fair.

We had barely made it onto Main Street when somebody dressed as a clown rode right by us on a unicycle.

"I'm gonna get me one of those," Dewey said.

"A clown?" I asked.

"No, a bike with only one wheel."

The sun glinted off the chrome bar holding up the unicycle's seat as the clown rode past us. Today was yet another nice autumn day in Alvin. Although a few white clouds stretched high across the sky, the sun was out and the weather was perfect fair weather; not too hot, not too cold.

"I'm pretty sure I saw a bike with only one wheel at Luther Willard King's house," I said. " 'Course, it was supposed to have two." I thought I was being pretty funny, but my mother shushed me.

"Don't talk like that, Abe."

"Am I bein' racist again?"

"No, you're just bein' annoyin'," she said.

Dewey laughed at this.

Mr. Kensington from the Alvin bank walked by on stilts with at least thirty balloons floating above his head in all kinds of colors. He asked us if we wanted a balloon. I said no. Dewey said yes, he sure did.

Mr. Kensington gave Dewey a green balloon. "How come you don't want one?" Dewey asked me.

"I'm too old for balloons," I said.

"You ain't no older than me."

"Well, maybe you're too old for balloons too, then," I said.

"I don't feel too old for balloons."

"Well," I said, "lately I've been feeling older than usual, I guess."

Just before the library, a midway was set up featuring all kinds of games with prizes like stuffed animals and goldfish. We slowed down at each booth as we went past. The first one was a basketball game. "Sink three balls and win one of the big bears!" said Mrs. Grace. She was a teacher from our school. For some reason, today she was dressed as a pirate, with an eye patch and a black scarf wrapped around her head with a skull on the front. She even had a stuffed parrot on her shoulder. "Only one dollar to try!"

"You can't win that game," Dewey said. "They tilt the baskets so it's near on impossible to get the ball in."

"What the heck does a pirate have to do with basketball?" I asked.

"No clue," Dewey said.

We kept on going.

Three booths later we came to the shooting gallery. You had to knock down four wooden people with an air rifle to win a goldfish bowl with a fish. "Hey, it's only a dollar for eight shots," I said. "Mom, you should try it."

She scrunched up her nose. "I ain't so good with an air rifle, Abe."

"You're a pretty good shot with a normal gun, though," I said. "What's the difference?"

"I dunno." She shrugged. "Besides, I just don't feel it's right for me to play a game like this on account of what I do."

I was thinking those white wooden guys on the back wall reminded me a bit of Jesse James Allen running into that cornfield.

"Can I try?" Dewey asked.

"Did your mama give you any money?" I asked back.

My mother shushed me. "Of course you can, Dewey," she said. The man behind the counter had a handlebar moustache and bushy eyebrows. His head was the closest I'd ever seen to being perfectly square. He took my mother's dollar bill and handed Dewey a rifle. "You be careful with this, boy," he said.

"Don't you worry about me," Dewey said.

Dewey took the rifle, carefully lining up his shot before squeezing the trigger. He looked so serious I nearly laughed, but when he took the shot, it was followed by a loud *thunk* as the rightmost wooden man fell backward. I near on couldn't believe it.

"Good shot!" my mother said.

"Lucky shot," I said.

Still keeping very serious, Dewey lined up his second try and, as amazing as it sounds, he managed to take out the second wooden guy in line.

"Did you start some kinda new hobby and not tell anyone?" I asked.

"I told you already," Dewey said. "I used to have an air rifle when I was a kid."

I shook my head. "You're *still* a kid. You've got a balloon tied to your wrist, for cryin' out loud."

"I think you should maybe consider working in the police force when you're older," my mother said.

"You really think that's where he'll end up using this kinda skill?" Carry asked, sounding almost like the old Carry. She was even being funny again. "I think you're bein' overly optimistic."

Dewey managed to nail all four of them targets with only four tries. Every single shot he made with that rifle was deadly accurate. None of us could believe it as we walked away with him carrying that goldfish bowl in his hands. He had a big, stupid grin on his face. "I've been practicin'," he said.

"With what?" I asked.

"With my finger. Like that night in your room."

I couldn't see how that could possibly count as practice, but before I could tell him, my mother said, "That was some pretty impressive shootin' back there, Dewey. Seriously, I don't think I could've hit all four with even eight tries."

"Thank you, Mrs. Teal," Dewey said. He said it as though he himself wasn't at all surprised by how well he did, though. It all felt very strange to me—almost as if I just saw a part of Dewey I'd never seen before, and I'd known Dewey a long, long time.

My thoughts were interrupted by someone shouting through a blow horn that the pie contest would be commencing at the top of Main Street in ten minutes.

"After all her gripin'," my mother said, "Sheryl Davis better win."

"Doesn't she always win?" I asked.

We managed to get a spot within viewing of the judges. There were five of them in all, two of which were Chief Montgomery and Mr. Robert Lee Garner. All the judges wore big red bibs that said A WORD TO THE WISE, EAT ALVIN PIES on them in bright yellow letters.

This year, eight different pies were entered in the contest. Of course, one of them was strawberry rhubarb and belonged to Sheryl Davis, who brought hers to the judging table looking as proud as if she'd just saved the world from some kind of certain disaster like typhoid.

"They all gotta eat eight whole pies?" Dewey asked.

"I think they only gotta have a piece of each," I said.

"Probably more like a mouthful," my mother corrected.

"Oh," Dewey said. I think he was a bit let down they weren't gonna eat whole pies.

"For someone so good with a rifle," I said, "you're pretty dumb when it comes to normal stuff like pie contests."

My mother shushed me. Carry said, "You're just jealous because *you* ain't got no goldfish."

"I don't want no goldfish," I said.

"But you wish you could shoot like me," Dewey said. I didn't bother responding on account of I saw the potential of this conversation spiraling out of control.

One by one, each of the judges took a bite of each of the eight different pies, filling out a small form after every swallow. "I wonder what they're writing about," Dewey said.

"Probably making a list of groceries they need to remember to get," I said, sarcastically.

My mother smacked the back of my head lightly. "Will you quit the snide remarks? You really are jealous about that goldfish, aren't you?"

I said nothing.

"I think they're likely rating different aspects of the pies," my mother said. "Things like taste, texture . . . I dunno. Whatever you can rate pies on, I suppose."

When they were finished, all the forms were handed down to Mr. Greenwood, a strange-looking man with very pointy facial features (especially his nose and chin) and cheeks that curved inward instead of out. He'd always reminded me of a fish. He usually worked at the post office, but today he was in charge of tallying the pie votes. It took him only a few minutes before he announced, "We have a winner! And the winner of this year's Harvest Fair Pie Contest is . . ."

Sheryl Davis was beaming in her pink and white

checkered apron. I could tell she was on the verge of stepping up to the table.

". . . Nancy Tress's blueberry apple."

Everyone roared with applause as Nancy Tress, her face full of surprise and shock, walked up and accepted her certificate. She wore a bright yellow apron that said KICK THE COOK! on the front. The only person not clapping was Sheryl Lynn Davis, who now looked like she wished she had an air rifle full of pellets and that everyone in the crowd was white and made from wood.

"I bet she's wishin' you'd kept the fair canceled now," Dewey said.

"Justice is a wonderful thing," my mother said.

We walked back past the midway to the parts of the fair we hadn't been to yet. "Look at that," I said, pointing to Happy Shogun Sushi Palace. Except it was no longer Happy Shogun Sushi Palace. The restaurant had a completely new front, and the paint was so fresh you could smell it gleaming in the afternoon sun. The big fish swallowing the grumpy guys with the swords was gone from the window, replaced by a cowboy riding a bull with curved horns. The cowboy had a big ol' grin on his face and held his hat up in the air. The restaurant name painted above the cowboy said HAPPY COW BURGER SHACK.

Standing out front, Mr. Nobu Takahashi handed pink fliers to people passing by. Instead of the red jacket with gold buttons, he now wore a white collared shirt with a bolo tie, tucked into brown denims. His thick leather belt had one of the biggest buckles I'd ever seen in my life. A cowboy hat hung off the back of his head, held there by leather ties fastened around his neck. He gave my mother one of the brochures.

"What happened to Happy Shogun Sushi Palace?" I asked.

"Nobody in Alvin like sushi much," he said. "So we change. Come to second grand opening next week. Our specialty is French fries with bacon, smothered in cheese." He did a quick two-step in his snakeskin cowboy boots.

"Your specialty sounds awesome!" Dewey said.

"Do you want to eat his fish?" I asked Mr. Takahashi. As soon as I said it, I worried my mother was about to give me a lecture for being racist, but instead everyone laughed, including Mr. Takahashi.

"No, thank you," he said.

"Besides, it's *my* fish," Dewey said. "Only I can let other people eat it."

I read the brochure my mother was holding. "You have a triple burger?" I asked Mr. Takahashi. "How big is it?"

"Bigger than your head," he said.

"Sounds awesome," Dewey said again.

"No octopus burgers?" I asked.

Again, everyone laughed. Funny, I still wasn't entirely clear on what was racist and what was actually funny until after I said it, but it seemed to me I was doing a lot better sorting out the funny ones.

"No," Mr. Takahashi said, "no octopus burger. Unless if you want one special, I make exception just for you."

"No, that's fine."

We promised to be at the second grand opening and

continued on. "I reckon he'll do well with this one," I said.

"I reckon you're right," my mother said. "And who knows? Maybe in a year or two, Alvin will be ready for sushi."

I was about to add a bit of sarcasm that I'm sure would've resulted in another lecture on racism when I saw something up ahead that made me freeze on confusion and fear. Mr. Wyatt Edward Farrow was making his way through the crowd straight toward us, his gaze locked on me and Dewey.

"Oh, no," I whispered.

"What?" said Dewey.

"Look."

"We gotta get away," said Dewey. "He's going to kill us."

"He's got a sack," I said.

"What's in it?"

"How the heck should I know?" I whispered back. "I bet knives or something like that. Probably butcher knives."

"Wish I still had that rifle."

"Dewey," I said, "it was an *air* rifle."

"It was still a rifle."

We turned and walked in the other direction, but a group of people were blocking the way. In a burst of confusion, we tried going left, then right, then left again, until the next thing I knew, Mr. Wyatt Edward Farrow was standing right in front of us, barely a few feet away. Mr. Wyatt Edward Farrow—in the flesh. His long face was pinched. His mouth formed a thin frown.

"I've got something for you boys," he said, undoing the drawstring on his sack. The sack was big, like the sort of thing you see in Santa Claus displays through Christmas season, only it was canvas and gray in color. It was so large, it probably held lots of butcher knives or at least one really, really big one.

"Oh, God," I heard Dewey whimper.

"Please," I said to Mr. Farrow, "we . . ." But I stopped when he pulled out a wooden biplane with a wingspan near on as big as my arm. The whole thing was beautifully painted white with red and blue stars on the wings and tail. It even had wheels and a propeller. He handed it to me.

"Sorry it took so long for me to return my gratitude for the basket you brung over when I moved in. I had a dinin' room set that needed buildin'. I was doin' it on commission for an old woman up yonder in Jewelville. Then when I finally got *that* finished, it turned out one of the table legs broke durin' transit, so I had to make a new one and send it out parcel post."

He pulled out a second biplane, nearly identical to mine, only painted with different designs. He handed that one to Dewey, who accepted it with the same awe and surprise that I did.

"Anyhow, I figured you boys would probably like somethin' like these," he said.

"What do you guys say?" my mother asked.

"Thank you," both Dewey and I responded. Although it came out more like questions than statements of gratitude. We were still sort of stunned.

Mr. Farrow looked at Carry. "I made somethin' for you too, little lady, although I hope you aren't too old to appreciate it." He pulled out a small wooden rocking chair that was painted and polished to a bright cherry rose. It was the perfect size for one of Carry's dolls and, whether she would admit it to anyone or not, Carry still loved those dolls.

"Thank you!" she said, taking the chair with a big smile.

"That will look just beautiful in your bedroom," my mother said. Then to Mr. Wyatt Edward Farrow, she said, "You're a very gracious man, I can't imagine how much time all these took to build."

"It was my pleasure, ma'am. If nothin' else, I can't say I've ever had quite the audience as these two boys gave me those first couple months after I moved in. Kinda nice havin' all that attention."

I looked at Dewey and then back at Mr. Farrow. "You mean . . . you *saw* us?"

He grinned. "Every time I went to the toilet."

"Wait," Dewey said. "When did . . ." But I elbowed him, making him stop before he finished his sentence. It didn't matter. Everybody laughed anyway.

Mr. Farrow seemed to notice Dewey's fish for the first time. "Now, hey, how'd you win that?"

"Shot four people," Dewey said.

"He shot four *wooden* people with an *air* rifle," my mother corrected.

"And did it in just four shots," Carry added.

"Wow, that's some fine shootin'," Mr. Farrow said. "Anyhow, I best be heading off. See y'all later." He gave me a wink and disappeared into the crowd.

"I hope you learned something from that," my mother said.

"I sure did," Dewey said. "I learned it's possible to go to the toilet in the dark."

My mother lightly smacked him upside his head. I laughed.

"Mom?" I asked. "Is it okay if me and Dewey go home and play with our planes?" I figured she'd probably make us stay with her or make us wait so she could walk us home, but she surprised me.

"That'd be fine. I'm gonna stay here a while longer, though."

"Dewey? You wanna go play with our planes?" I asked.

"Sure," he said.

"Um," Carry said, "would y'all mind if I tagged along, too?"

I gave her a wide grin. "Not one single bit."

Me, Carry, and Dewey headed back toward the house. It felt good having the three of us together again. I guess my mother was worried all that time for nothing.

Carry's hard time hadn't lasted that long after all.

And to be completely honest, I was pretty glad about that.

In this riveting novel from Michael Hiebert, a killer's release is the catalyst for shocking revelations in a small Southern town . . .

At twenty-two, Sylvie Carson has known a lifetime's worth of trouble. When she was a child, her baby brother was shot to death by a man named Preacher Eli. Orphaned by her teens, Sylvie is now raising her own baby with no partner in sight. For all these reasons, Leah Teal, Alvin, Alabama's only detective, tries to stay patient when Sylvie calls the station day and night, always with some new false alarm. But now Preacher Eli is out of prison and moving back to town.

As far as the law is concerned, the old man has paid his dues—though Leah's twelve-year-old son, Abe, vehemently disagrees. Between that and his relentless curiosity about the daddy he hardly knew, Abe's imagination is running in all directions lately. While Leah struggles with how much of the past to reveal to Abe, she's also concerned about Sylvie's mounting panic. Something in her gut tells her the girl might be a target after all. For as Leah knows well, there's danger not just in the secrets others keep from us, but in the lies that corrupt from within. It's a hunch that will be tested soon enough, as tensions mount on both sides.

Evoking the South with depth and grace, Michael

Hiebert's poignant, gripping novel captures the strength wrought by heartache and lost innocence—and the transformative power of forgiveness, whenever it comes . . .

Please read on for an exciting sneak peek of Michael Hiebert's second Alvin, Alabama, novel

CLOSE TO THE BROKEN HEARTED

now on sale wherever print and e-books are sold!

PROLOGUE

Alvin, Alabama—1971

The spring sun is low in the sky outside the single-paned windows of the kitchen in the small farmhouse where the family has gathered to eat. Upon the table sits a roast chicken ready to be carved, a plate of mashed potatoes, and a bowl of peas and corn, both harvested last year but kept frozen through the winter months. The light falling in through the windows is a deep orange, almost red, as the father, Tom Carson, stands to say grace. His hat sits on the top newel of the short run of stairs that separates this room from the living room below.

The table, like the house, was built by his father. The chicken and the vegetables came from the farm. Unlike the house, the rest of the farm had once all belonged to his father's father. Tom Carson is a proud man even though he lives a modest life. He is proud of his work in the fields that starts at daybreak and ends at supper. He is proud of his two children: Caleb, barely three, with black hair and fair skin like his father, and

Sylvie, five and a half, with blond hair like her mother used to have. They are good kids. Respectful kids. Long ago they learned not to make noise or fuss about while their father says grace. Soon Caleb will start working with his father little by little out on the farm. Sylvie already does some jobs with her mother around the home.

Each of the kids clutches their mother's hands. Mother closes her eyes. She is a good woman. Tom is lucky to have all he has. There're wrinkles around his wife's eyes he hasn't noticed before, and he wonders how hard this life has been on her. It's a thought that hasn't occurred to him until now.

In his cracked voice, he delivers the blessing, thanking the Lord Jesus for this wonderful bounty He has bestowed upon their family. The Lord Jesus has been good to Tom Carson.

Tom finishes and takes his chair at the table, folding his napkin onto his lap. Mother's fingers let go of the children's hands. Her gray eyes open and she smiles across the table at Tom. Tom reaches for the platter of chicken so that he may start to carve.

Across the room, there's a loud knock at the door.

Mother jumps. "Who would be knockin' aroun' here at suppertime?" she asks.

"Dunno," Tom Carson says gruffly. He gently lifts the napkin from his lap and begins to rise from the table when the door swings open with a squeak. It wasn't locked. Tom and his family never lock their doors. Nobody around these parts ever locks their doors.

Tom freezes, half out of his chair, as Preacher Eli Brown steps into his home. The preacher man is dressed in a white shirt with black trousers and vest. Muddy boots cover his feet. His thin face is fixed and stern, but what's caught Tom's attention is the gun the preacher holds in his right hand. It is pointed at the floor, being held as though it wasn't there at all.

"Preacher Eli," Tom says, trying to keep his voice calm. "What brings you round here? We's just 'bout to sit down to supper, as you can see." He sits back down.

The preacher says nothing, just stomps across Tom's living room leaving a trail of dried mud on the wooden floor. He comes up the few stairs toward the small kitchen where the family squeezes around the table. With each of the man's footsteps, Caleb wiggles out of his chair and crawls under the table where he seeks out the safety of his father's legs.

Preacher Eli dangles over the rail along the top of the stairs, the gun hand waving conspicuously in the air as he speaks with a low, slow drawl. "Tom, you and I have quite a land dispute goin' on. This thing oughta be worked out soon or there could be some trouble comin'."

Tom Carson looks down at his empty plate. "There ain't no dispute, Eli. The land's mine. It belonged to my father, just as it belonged to his father. Been in my family at least three generations. Maybe even more."

"The church disagrees with you."

Tom turned back to the preacher, his face red. "The church has no jurisdiction here, Preacher. If the land belonged to you, you'd have a title to it. If you got a title, produce it. But you can't do that cuz you ain't got one, and since you ain't got no title, you ain't got no land."

"The title is *missing*. You can't produce one either."

"Yes, well, the title seems to have *gone* missing."

Tom clears his throat. "I'd say you had somethin' to do with that. Doesn't matter, Eli. Everyone knows the land belongs to me."

"You wanna start asking folk?"

"No. Folk is 'fraid of you."

Preacher Eli Brown's teeth form a thin V of a smile. They are more brown than white and less than straight.

"That how the church doin' things these days, Eli? Bit of a step backward ain't it?" Tom nods at the gun. "That why you here? To scare me into giving you my land so you can build your new 'facility' on it? I got news for you, Eli. I ain't afraid of you or your 'church.' "

This time it's Preacher Eli who reddens. "Well, you oughta be. You oughta be very 'fraid. It is a spiteful and vengeful God you forsake. One does not just turn his back on the will of the Lord Jesus without severe repercussions." His bony voice grows in anger and volume. From under the table, Caleb climbs up onto his father's lap.

For a minute, Tom Carson says nothing, just stares pathetically back at the tall preacher who looks somehow scarecrowlike bathed in the red-orange light of dusk. "You are a fool, Eli. Who said anything about forsakin' God? I ain't turned my back on the Lord Jesus. Your church has nothing to do with neither God nor Jesus. Least if it does, it sure ain't my Jesus. If it were, heaven help us all. There is absolutely nothing holy about your affairs, Eli. You oughta be ashamed of callin' yourself a man of the cloth. You've made a mockery of everything folk hold sacred."

Tom turns back to the chicken. He's done talking to the preacher. He's given this man too much time in his house already. But as soon as he picks up the knife to begin carving the bird, a strange feeling comes over him, and he hesitates, glancing back at the man with the gun.

Preacher Eli's eye twitches. His facial muscles tighten. When he talks again, it's with the same commanding voice he uses from the pulpit. "How dare you speak to me with such irreverence? It is *you* . . ." His hand holding the gun shakes. "*You,* Tom Carson. You who must . . . who *will* answer for your sins."

Something flashes in the preacher man's eyes: a flicker of insanity.

Tom Carson has never been much of a gambler, but in that instant when he sees that look in Preacher Eli's eyes, he knows he's made a grave mistake. Until now, Tom had thought Eli Brown was many things, but a killer was definitely not one of them. Sure, the man had brought a gun into his home, but Tom had never really been scared. At no time did he think he or his family were in jeopardy of being hurt. Tom had chalked up the weapon to being part of the preacher's game— part of his ploy to scare him into giving up what was rightfully his. Tom had decided almost immediately after the man entered that he wouldn't let himself be so easily duped.

Only now, in this split second, Tom knows he's played his cards all wrong. Everything is over. It's all about to come to an end at the hands of a madman he grossly underestimated.

That thought's the last thing to go through Tom's mind as Eli raises the gun and pulls the trigger.

The small room, suddenly gone dark, fills with the

smell and the sound of a gunshot. It echoes off the wooden walls and floor like a thunderous death knell. Tom hears nothing else, only that deadly explosion. It seems to last an eternity and fills everything, even his mind.

In fact, Tom has been so focused on Preacher Eli, he hadn't noticed when Caleb made his way up his pant legs onto his lap minutes ago.

Now, as the sound dies away, leaving only the smell of gunpowder in its wake, Tom looks down, expecting to see his own stomach blown open, expecting to see himself dying.

What he sees is far, far worse.

There in his lap lies what remains of his little boy.

His perfect little man who just turned three years old barely two weeks ago lies with half his head on Tom's leg and one arm wrapped around his papa's waist.

Tom's eyes fill with tears as he takes in the blood splattered across the table, the floor, the counters, and most of this side of the kitchen. Tom himself is covered in it. He begins to shake. He rubs his son's arm as the world grows very small, and he looks back up to the preacher. It takes a minute for the words to come. When they do, they barely escape his lips. "What . . . what have you done?" he asks quietly.

The preacher's eyes widen in surprise as he steps slowly back down the stairs. His hand holding the gun falls to his side, the weapon slipping off his fingers and falling to the floor. His head shakes. "No . . . ," he says. "No."

Across the table, Mother begins screaming, "My

baby! My baby!" She comes around to where Caleb lies dead in a bundle in his father's lap. "My poor sweet baby."

Their daughter, Sylvie, remains quiet. She just pulls her feet up onto her chair and, wrapping her arms around her knees, tries to make herself as small as possible. She watches her mother and father cry over their dead son. She sees the preacher man who came in right before supper and killed her baby brother in the name of Jesus leave by the same door he came in through. She watches it all like a movie, unable to really comprehend what it means. It's so emotionally confusing, she feels almost nothing.

Just an emptiness inside. All empty and hollow.

She begins rocking back and forth on the wooden chair, her long blond pigtails swinging against her face. In her mind, a voice screams, "No! No! No!" over and over, but it's only in her head. On the outside, she's quiet. In fact, she doesn't even hear her parents crying anymore. She sees them, but she doesn't really process what she's looking at.

Nothing makes any sense.

When she woke up this morning, she had been a happy five-year-old girl with a good family and a good life. For the last year, she always told her mom her biggest wish was to raise horses and have babies when she grew up. Three babies.

Those had been her dreams. Horses and babies.

Now, sitting in that kitchen of death, Sylvie Carson no longer cares about the horses or the babies. She no longer cares about life. Preacher Eli killed her baby brother and he also killed her dreams. And none of it made any sense.

What Sylvie doesn't know is that this is only the beginning.

Because for her, the world will never make sense ever again.

CHAPTER 1

"Dewey," I said, "if I say it was blue, it was blue. Why the heck would I say it was blue if it was some other color? It's not like the important part of the story has anything to do with it bein' blue."

"I just ain't never seen one that's blue," Dewey said. "That's all, Abe."

"You ever seen one any other color?" I asked.

"What do you mean?"

"I mean, have you ever even seen one at all, blue or not? This one was the first one *I'd* ever seen. I mean other than in movies and on TV an' all that. It's not like you see 'em every day."

This question seemed to stump Dewey for a bit as he thought it over. Least, I think he was thinking about it. He may have been pondering the aluminum foil he was unrolling around my mother's living room floor. "Not sure," he said. "Not that I can remember."

"I think that's enough aluminum foil, don't you?" I asked. "How much is in a roll?"

He read the side of the box. "Fifty feet."

"And you had four boxes? That's two hundred feet, Dewey."

"I know, but when I paced off your livin' room, it was ten by twelve. Right there we have a hundred and twenty feet. And it ain't like the foil's gonna be laid down flat. And I reckon for this to work, Abe, we're gonna need to go into your dinin' room, too."

"Well, there ain't no more foil," I said. "My mom's already gonna be mad we used up two brand-new rolls."

"I took two from my house, too," he said. "At least we're sharin' responsibility."

"But the difference is that you reckon this is gonna work. I don't."

"It'll work."

I sighed.

"We need two more rolls," he said.

"We ain't got two more rolls, Dewey. I reckon if two hundred feet don't do it, two thousand feet ain't gonna make no difference."

He thought this over. "You might have a point. At the very least we should see some indication of it workin'. Then we can show your mom and she'll gladly buy us two more rolls."

"My mom ain't gonna want aluminum foil runnin' around the inside of her house, Dewey."

"She is when she sees what it does for her television reception," he said. "Think of how much money we're savin' her."

"How do you figure?" I asked.

"On a satellite dish."

"She ain't buyin' no satellite dish."

"Exactly."

"*Why* aren't we doing this at your place?" I asked him.

"Abe, my mom's *home*. It's hard enough to do anythin' at my place when my mom *ain't* home," he said. "You're lucky your mom works all day shootin' people."

"She don't shoot people all day," I said. "I don't reckon she's ever actually shot *anyone*." My mother was the only detective the Alvin Police Department had, and, if she had shot anyone, she certainly hadn't told me about it. And it seemed like the sort of thing she'd probably mention.

"I reckon she has."

"She hasn't," I assured him.

"I bet she thinks about it, though," Dewey said. "A lot."

"Can we just get this finished so I can have it cleaned up 'fore she gets home?" I asked him.

Dewey was taking the aluminum foil and rolling it into a sort of shiny rope. He made sure all the new pieces fit tightly against the old ones, making one solid snake that ran around the inside of my living room, starting and ending at the back of the television set.

"So why was they *all* blue?" Dewey asked. "The knights, I mean. Or was there other colors, too? They can't *all* be on the same side. Be awful confusin' if they was all blue."

"The other ones were red. I saw one of them later."

"Which ones were the good guys?" Dewey asked.

"How do you mean?"

"There's always a good side and a bad side, Abe. Were the blue ones the good ones or the bad ones? These colors make it hard to know. Usually they use somethin' obvious like black and white. Then you know who you should be rootin' for."

"Do you root for the good guys or the bad guys?" I asked.

Dewey stopped laying down his aluminum foil pipeline and considered this. "That depends on when in my life you had asked me. When I was little I always wanted the good guys to win. Then I went through a phase where I secretly hoped for the bad guys."

"And?" I asked. "What about now?"

"Now I guess I just want to see a fair fight," he said. "Did the blues and the reds both have swords?"

I started to get excited. The swords had been the best part. "You shoulda seen the swords," I said. "The red blades actually glowed the same color as the knights, and they were huge. They looked so big I doubt I coulda lifted one off the ground. And each sword had a different gem in its pommel and smaller ones all over its hilt. They actually had *real* swords for sale in Sleeping Beauty's Castle, but Mom refused to buy me one. She told me I'd wind up takin' somebody's eye out with it or somethin'."

"Wow," Dewey said, looking off into the distance and seemingly speaking to himself. "A *real* sword. That would be somethin'." His attention came back to the living room and all the foil. He looked me straight in the eyes. "Especially if we *both* had one. We could have sword fights."

"Are you even listenin' to a word I'm sayin'?" I asked him. "These were *real* swords, Dewey. We couldn't have sword fights with 'em. We'd wind up killin' each other."

"Still, it's fun to think about."

I hesitated. "You're right. It *is* fun to think about."

Dewey's aluminum foil rope ran along the walls of the entire living room, running behind the big stuffed chair and coming right up to the back of the TV. We'd even pushed the sofa away from the wall so that we could make sure it was as long as possible.

"Okay," I said, just in case Dewey had other ideas, "I think we've done as much as we're doin' with the foil. Now what?"

"Now I unhook the cable from your TV and attach the foil antenna with these alligator clips," he said.

"Can I ask where you got this idea?"

He shrugged. "While you was at Disney World I started an inventor's notebook. Turns out I'm pretty smart. I got lots of great ideas. They're probably worth a million dollars."

I glanced around the room. My mother was going to have a conniption when she saw what we'd done to it, and especially when she found out we'd used up two brand-new rolls of her aluminum foil. "Probably," I said. "You give off a glow of genius, that's for certain."

The light falling in through the window above the sofa was starting to turn purple and orange, which meant it was getting late. This further meant my mother would probably be home soon—unless she wound up working late like she sometimes did. I took another look at Dewey's tinfoil snake and hoped this was going to be a late night for her.

Dewey hooked up the alligator clips to the screws attached to the electronic box where the Cable Vision wire normally attached to the television. "That should do it," he said.

"So now what?"

"Now we turn on the TV and enjoy havin' all the stations folks get with satellite dishes without payin' a cent. All it cost us was the price of four rolls of aluminum foil."

"It didn't cost us nothin'," I reminded him. "We *stole* the foil from our moms, remember?"

"Even better," he said, rubbing his hands together. He pulled the button on the television that turned the set on. For a minute the screen stayed dark, then it slowly grew into a picture of white static.

"Works well," I said sarcastically. I snuck another glance out the window. The weather had cleared up considerably from this morning. It had been four days since we'd gotten back from Disney World, and every day since we'd returned had been full of pouring rain, including the beginning of this one. This afternoon, though, the sun had finally broken through the clouds and cleaned up the sky.

Dewey changed the channel to more static. "Somethin's wrong. We didn't hook somethin' up properly."

"You know what's wrong?" I asked. "You're tryin' to get satellite TV with aluminum foil."

"Wait, this *has* to work. I had it all figured out." He started rapidly switching channels. Then he came to a channel that was clear as Mount Bell on a brisk autumn morning, as my mother would say. "Look!" he said, nearly screaming it. "It works! Look how clear it is!"

I had to admit it was clear.

"Told you it would work!" He went around the dial the entire way and found three more channels we could get. All tremendously clear. This seemed to satisfy him immensely.

"So you're happy with your invention?" I asked.

"I'll say."

I looked at him and blinked. "I'm a little confused."

"About what?"

"Who exactly you'll be marketin' this to."

"What do you mean?"

"I mean, is this for folk who can't afford Cable Vision but happen to have a surplus of aluminum foil and one or two favorite channels they simply cannot live without?" I once again looked at the foil running along the edge of the floor everywhere. "Or will you try and make it some sort of home décor product? Not to mention the fact that you can't really charge more than the price of four rolls of aluminum foil for it or people will just go out and buy their own and set everythin' up for themselves."

Dewey frowned, perplexed by my complex questions. "It's a start, okay? I have many inventions. I've already filled half a notebook,". he said. "You may have been wastin' time in Disney World with blue and red knights, but at least *I* was doing somethin' productive."

Nodding, I said, "Okay. Now, do you mind if we try to get all this put away and see if we can make the television work properly again 'fore my mom gets home from work?"

Dewey glared at me. "You just don't know genius when you see it."

"You're probably right. I don't. I've never really been much of a noticer of brilliance."

He unhooked the alligator clips. I began to roll up the two hundred feet of foil.

Just then my sister, Carry, came into the living

room. She'd been out with some friends all day and I hadn't even heard her come home. "Abe?" she asked quietly. I looked up into her blue eyes. Her blond curls swayed on either side of her face. "What the hell are you two doin'?" she asked.

"Preparin' ourselves for the future," I said. "It's comin'. And it's full of aluminum foil."

"And other inventions!" Dewey said. "Wanna see my notebook?"

"Mom's gonna kill you," Carry said.

"I know," I said.

CHAPTER 2

Leah Teal pulled her squad car into the driveway of the home of Sylvie Carson. She was attending because of a call Sylvie made to the station saying something about somebody illegally trespassing on her property. Leah wasn't entirely sure of the report that was taken because she hadn't taken it. Her partner, Officer Christopher Jackson, had. Like most times when Sylvie Carson called, Officer Jackson laughed after hanging up the phone.

"Guess who that was . . . *again*," he had said.

It bothered Leah when Sylvie was made fun of, especially when it was by Chris. She had a pretty good hunch as to why it irked her so much, too.

"You know," she had told Chris, "it wasn't so long ago that I can remember folks makin' all sorts of a ruckus 'bout you bein' hired by the department."

"Yeah, well, those folks were wrong. They just like to hate people," Chris said. "Especially black people. This is different. The woman is nuts. She calls the station every week."

"This *isn't* much different, Chris. Sylvie can't help

the way she is no more than you can help the color you is."

"What's wrong with the color I am?"

"That's not what I meant and you know it." Leah looked back at Police Chief Ethan Montgomery's office for a little backup but his door was closed. She could see through the partially opened blinds hanging down over the window in his door that the chief was sitting back in his chair with his hands behind his head watching the television that hung from the ceiling in the corner of the room. The chief loved to watch his sports.

Chris wouldn't let things go. "Leah, most people get better over time. But Sylvie's gotten worse, far as I can tell. Her calls are coming in at an all-time high." That was likely true. Leah had at least noticed them more, and she was the one who usually ended up attending to them.

"And every single one turns out to be some sort of false alarm," Chris said. "I don't know why you even bother showin' up. I stopped takin' her seriously a long time ago."

"Because it's our job to show up, Chris. Because for every hundred or so false alarms, there might actually be one real emergency and it's for *that* real emergency I attend to the ninety-nine others. Besides, what else do I have to do? We live in a town of barely two thousand people; it's not like our phone's ringin' off the desk."

"I'd rather do the crossword than deal with Sylvie," he said. Leah couldn't believe how heartless he was being. She was about to tell him that when he started talking again. "I'm sorry," he said, "but I've just reached the end of my wits with her. I think it's on account of the baby. I think she must be all hormonal or somethin'."

Okay, Leah knew then it was time to end her conversation with Officer Christopher Jackson, or she would say something she definitely would regret.

Grabbing her pistol from her desk, she headed for the door. "Well, I'm gonna go see what she needs. At least one of us is gonna represent this department."

Chris laughed behind her. "Have fun."

It was the part about the baby that had almost pushed Leah over the edge. Even now, sitting in her car in front of Sylvie's house, thinking about that baby kept Leah worked up to a degree that wasn't healthy for nobody.

Generally, Leah tried not to think about Sylvie's baby, especially when she was off shift. It was the sort of thing that would lodge itself into her head and wouldn't get unstuck for hours while she lay in bed trying to fall asleep. To make matters worse, she couldn't even refer to it as anything but "The Baby" because Sylvie Carson hadn't given it a name yet. It had been three months now, and the girl still called her daughter "The Baby." Whenever Leah asked her why she hadn't named her, Sylvie told her, "It's so much responsibil ity. I get too overwhelmed thinkin' that whatever I come up with is gonna be with this girl for the rest of her life. It's a huge decision that's gonna affect everything. Nothin' I think of is good enough. Not for my daughter. Not for her whole life."

Leah couldn't argue with her. It was pointless telling Sylvie that anything was better than "The Baby." So Leah just let it lie as best she could. But her brain wouldn't let go of it quite so easily. It hung on to things like the baby not having a name and how *that* might affect the rest of her life. Or what effect having a mother who could barely manage to keep herself together an entire day might have.

Some babies come into the world with better chances than others right from the start. This one seemed to come in with a pretty bad poker hand, at least in Leah's eyes, which was probably one of the big reasons Leah felt compelled to take Sylvie's calls seriously.

Leah also suspected she had a soft spot for Sylvie because deep down she felt they weren't so different. If fate had changed up some of the pitches Leah had been thrown, her life might have turned out very similar to Sylvie's. In some ways it had.

They were both single mothers. Sylvie had The Baby and Leah had two children: a fifteen-year-old daughter named Carry, and a twelve-year-old boy named Abe.

Both Leah and Sylvie had lost the fathers to their children unexpectedly. Sylvie's was named Orwin Thomas and he had been barely an adult when Sylvie got pregnant. He just up and disappeared one night without even leaving so much as a note. There was no indication the day before that anything was wrong. He took Sylvie's car, a few dollars cash they'd kept in a jar, and some clothing. He left her three months along in a pregnancy she then had to face all alone.

Leah's husband, Billy, coming home from work after pulling an overnight shift, had accidentally run his car—headlights first—into an oncoming car while passing an eighteen-wheeler. Abe had only been two. Those had been very hard times for Leah. She didn't like to think about them, even now.

Neither Leah nor Sylvie had living parents. Sylvie's had died tragically when she was in her teens; her mother was murdered and her pa took his own life shortly thereafter. Leah had lost her parents when they were older; her ma from a stroke a year after Leah had lost her husband, and her pa to cancer three years later.

But that was where the similarities ended, because at least Leah could cope with life. Sylvie was a different story. Sure, she had emotional problems (yet another reason for Leah being upset at Chris. Although, comparing her disorder to him being black would probably not be a good idea on Leah's part). Possibly it was post-traumatic stress disorder brought on from what happened when Sylvie was a kid. She'd actually seen her baby brother get murdered just a few feet away from her. It happened long before Leah became detective, back when she was only fourteen. But Leah's father had been on the force then, and he had handled the case, so Leah knew a lot about it.

After Leah's husband, Billy, died, there were times Leah didn't think she would make it. And she hadn't had to deal with any of the psychological trauma Sylvie faced. Leah tried not to forget that. No matter what it looked like from the outside, this girl was rising above herself— or at least trying to—and that was something to be applauded, not laughed at.

Leah couldn't imagine what her own life would've been like had she been in the same shoes Sylvie was during her childhood. Leah tried to picture what it would be like watching her own uncle, Hank, get shot to death right in front of her when, not ten minutes earlier, she had been ready to enjoy a happy supper with her family.

She shivered. It was so horrific, she couldn't even think about it.

Yet it was something Sylvie had to live with every single day of her life. And everyone seemed so surprised the girl was a little messed up. Something like that had to do strange things to your mind. It had to haunt you in unimaginable ways.

Sylvie was a lost soul trying to navigate in a world she always seemed to be trying to catch up with.

Leah got out of her squad car and headed for the few wooden steps that rose to the landing in front of Sylvie's front door.

Sylvie's house was small and old. It would be considered a shotgun shack if it weren't for the hallway and bedroom someone had added on some time ago. Shotgun shacks were normally fewer than twelve feet wide with no more than three to five rooms, all arranged one behind the other.

The outside had once been painted white, but most of the paint was flaking off the siding, leaving the bare wood showing underneath. The picture window that looked out of the living room beside the front door had the drapes pulled shut, but Leah could see the yellow light of a lamp through the crack between them. Leah had been inside enough times to know that was the only light in that room. At times like this, after the sun was down, that light cast everything inside with an amber glow that threw long, eerie shadows.

It certainly didn't help the atmosphere any.

Leah stepped up and knocked on the wooden door. Like the siding, the paint on the door was also starting to peel. "Sylvie?" she called out. "Sylvie, it's Detective Teal. Alvin Police."

It didn't take long before she heard the chain slide and the dead bolt shoot. Like always, Leah waited while Sylvie opened the door a few inches and made sure Leah was who she said she was. Leah didn't really mind this behavior. She would rather see somebody overly protective than the other way around, although Sylvie's protectiveness crossed the line well into paranoia.

"Hi," Sylvie said. Her dirty blond hair hung straight down over her eyes. For a brief moment, those eyes caught the moon, and Leah saw its reflection in their speckled blue pools.

Sylvie Carson looked and dressed like a homeless person. She'd gotten worse since Orwin took off. It was funny, because Leah could tell if the girl dressed in nice clothes and wore proper makeup she could be really pretty. Maybe she looked this way intentionally. Like a victim.

Yet the baby seemed clean enough. That had been a huge worry of Leah's when Sylvie first brought her home from the hospital. Leah really hadn't wanted to involve the state with the child's care, but part of her suspected she would eventually have to step in given the way Sylvie was.

So Leah had kept a close eye on the baby for the past three months. Sylvie had given her many opportunities to do so with all her calls. Every time Sylvie called into the station, Leah just chalked it up as another chance to check on the welfare of the baby.

Leah heard Sylvie slide the chain again. Then the door opened completely. "Thanks for comin' out," Sylvie said.

"Not a problem," Leah said stepping inside. "Glad to see you're okay."

Sylvie immediately locked the door again behind Leah. "Yeah," she mumbled. She was always very quiet when she talked. Quiet, pensive, and uncertain. It was very much like dealing with a child.

Which, Leah assumed, Sylvie probably still was. Chronologically, she wasn't much older than a teenager. What had she turned on her last birthday? Twenty-two? And hadn't Leah read somewhere that when something traumatic happens in childhood the person emotionally stays at whatever age they were at when the event took place?

Leah was pretty sure wherever she had read that fact they'd gotten it right because Sylvie had been five when she lost her brother and, in many ways, Sylvie still seemed like a five-year-old trapped in a twenty-two-year-old girl's body.

Surprisingly, given her appearance, Sylvie's home always had that just-tidied-up-in-a-rush look when Leah showed up. That might be because she just had tidied it after calling the station—Leah had no way of knowing. But at least she kept it fairly neat. Each of these little things—the clean house, the clean baby, and other little changes—gave Leah some hope that Sylvie might have it together enough to actually be a proper mother. God knew she appeared to love the child enough. If love was all you needed (like that Beatles song said) then Sylvie was like a billionaire.

Unfortunately, Leah didn't think John Lennon had taken everything into account when he wrote that song. He'd probably never met anyone like Sylvie Carson.

"So what's the problem?" Leah asked.

"Someone's been in the yard," Sylvie said.

Leah sighed. This wasn't a surprise. The girl always thought someone was in her yard, or spying on her, or something.

"Place looks nice," Leah said, for now tabling the "someone's been in the yard" discussion.

"Thanks."

"Baby okay?"

"Yeah, she's fine. A bit colicky, I reckon."

"That'll go away," Leah said.

"I think so," Sylvie said.

"You okay? You look pale," Leah said.

"I'm fine."

"So," Leah asked, "what exactly makes you think someone's been trespassing on your property? Who's been where?"

"The yard," Sylvie said. "Someone's been in the backyard." She was wearing an old oversized LSU Tigers T-shirt that hung untucked over gray sweatpants. Her hands trembled as she wrung them together while speaking. Leah could tell she was scared. She was hoping her little conversation diversion might settle Sylvie down.

Leah knew enough about Sylvie and her calls to know this would undoubtedly turn out to be another false alarm.

The living room had a dark hardwood floor that creaked when you walked across it. The drapes in the window were missing some hooks, and that made them hang awkwardly from the inside. They were once white, but now they looked a more pale washed-out yellow than anything else. Dark stains covered one.

Tattered magazines were stacked on the oval glass coffee table in the room's center. An old TV with wood panel trim sat on some plastic crates on one side of the table. Two paintings of clowns hung crookedly on the chestnut-paneled wall behind the TV.

"Been cleanin', I see," Leah said.

"I like it clean for The Baby."

"That's good. Babies need things clean. You should clean yourself up, too."

"What do you mean?"

Leah pointed to the oversized LSU shirt with the holes ripped in it. "Don't you have any clothes of your own? Orwin's stuff's gettin' a mite old."

"These are comfortable. Besides, my money goes to The Baby."

The Baby. It made Leah cringe every time Sylvie said it.

A small white cat came in and brushed up against Leah's leg, purring.

"Snowflake," Sylvie said. "Get outta here. Leave Officer Teal alone."

"Oh, she's all right," Leah said, bending down and lifting up the cat. She'd come here enough times that she knew the animal well. It was an indoor/outdoor cat that had surprised Leah by lasting as long as it had. Sylvie had gotten the cat as a kitten after Orwin left her. Normally, cats allowed to go outdoors in these parts became prey to other animals pretty quickly.

There were two small unmatched sofas in the room: one was green and threadbare, the other was taupe, with silver duct tape covering up tears in the upholstery. The only light in the room—a black metal floor lamp—stood beside the sofa. Its bulb shined a circular pattern on the white textured ceiling.

"You know, this place would look a lot better if you had more light," Leah said.

"I only have one lamp."

"I'll see if I can dig up somethin' for you."

"That would be nice."

"This one makes the room too dark."

"I don't mind it," Sylvie said.

The baby was asleep on a small blanket on the green sofa. She was wearing pink pajamas that appeared to be as clean as she was. So clean, they didn't even look like they'd ever been washed. The baby's brown skin shone in contrast to those pajamas. She'd inherited that skin color from her daddy.

Leah walked over with Snowflake in her arms and looked down on her. She appeared healthy. Leah hoped to God she was doing the right thing leaving this baby with this girl. "New PJs?" she asked Sylvie.

"Salvation Army," Sylvie said.

The living room looked into the kitchen. The kitchen lights were off, making it appear creepy by the light of this single lamp with the yellowish bulb. An old kitchen table with a brown Formica top stood in the darkness with three chairs around it in various states of disrepair. Behind it, the kitchen window allowed a view into the backyard, but from where she stood, Leah could only make out shadows. Living here alone with just a baby and this creepy lamp, it was no wonder Sylvie was seeing things in the backyard. Even if it *was* clean, this house was old and ghostly. It felt off, somehow.

Leah rubbed the cat under its neck, listening to it purr louder. She wondered how Sylvie ever managed to give *it* a name. She just hoped her daughter didn't end up with a name like Snowflake. But then, she figured even Snowflake would be better than growing up with no name at all. "What makes you think someone's been in your backyard?"

"Things have been moved," Sylvie said. "An' there's footprints."

Leah sighed. This was obviously turning out to be

another false alarm. She wanted to take Sylvie's mind off the immediate problem. Deciding to try to put it somewhere else, she asked a different question: "Found a name for your daughter yet?"

A pause followed. Then, "Not yet."

"You gotta name her soon, Sylvie. It's not good for a baby not to have a name."

Another pause. "I know. I will."

They stood there in silence a minute or two, then Leah said, "Why don't you show me what's been moved?"

She followed Sylvie through the kitchen to the back door, noticing the dishes in the sink had been recently washed but not dried. Sylvie didn't turn on any lights, but Leah could tell the house was cleaner than ever. Every time she came to Sylvie's there appeared to be some improvement in some way. The only thing that didn't seem to improve were the number of calls into the station.

A shotgun stood beside the back door, propped up against the wall. Leah knew the answer to the question she was about to ask before even asking it.

"That thing loaded?"

"You betcha. No point in keepin' an unloaded shotgun around, now, is there?" Sylvie said.

"You do realize how dangerous it is, right?"

"You guys tell me that every time you come in here and every time I tell you the same thing. You won't take me seriously, so that shotgun's the only recourse I have. I ain't livin' with my baby and bein' unable to defend myself. Not when someone's after me."

Leah let out a big breath. There was no point in arguing with her. Not while she was like this.

Sylvie fumbled with the dead bolt on the back door until she finally opened it.

"You got a light out here?" Leah asked.

"Burned out a few weeks ago."

"Should replace it."

"I will," Sylvie said. "Haven't had time."

Leah pulled out her pocket flashlight. She wasn't in uniform because she didn't wear one, but she had a pack snapped around her waist containing small items she commonly used. Her major gear was in her car, packed in her "go bag."

"You see that you do. Not safe having no light back here," Leah said, coming down the steps that led to the backyard. Sylvie followed behind her in shoes that had holes bigger than golf balls. "Those the only shoes you have, girl?" Leah asked.

"Yeah."

"Get some new shoes, too."

"Can't afford new shoes. The Baby takes all my money."

Once again, Leah felt something pull inside her. She liked this girl. Deep inside, she was rooting for her to win a war she never should have been involved in to begin with. A war that enlisted her without any permission.

What Sylvie had improved upon inside the house was more than compensated for by the state of the backyard. It looked like it hadn't seen any attention for a long time. Car engine parts littered the long grass and wildflowers that fought to choke each other back from existence. It had rained the past few days. That morning there were spotty showers, but the sky had started to completely clear just as the sun began to set. Still, everything had that wet smell to it. Even though it was a bright night (now that Leah's eyes had adjusted to being outside and seeing by the stars and moon), it still *felt* wet. Rainwater pooled in everything around her. There were jars, stacks of old newspapers, tires, even an old, broken kitchen sink. The yard was maybe a quarter acre before the surrounding forest choked it in, yet somehow it held a treasure trove of junk so well hidden that, until now, Leah hadn't even realized Sylvie had so much crap out here.

She followed as Sylvie walked slowly over to some small flowerpots that stood on top of a wooden box laid on its side against the back of the house. "Here," she said, gesturing to the pots. "These."

"The flowerpots?" Leah asked. She had pulled out a notepad and had her pen poised over it, ready to start a report.

"Yeah."

"What about them?" Leah asked.

"They was moved," Sylvie said. "They used to be inside the box. Now they're on top."

"When were they inside?"

"Yesterday."

"How do you know?" Leah wondered what kind of person notices something like clay flowerpots. She never would. She doubted many other people would, either.

"I saw 'em," Sylvie said.

"How can you remember somethin' like that?"

"I just do. I noticed 'em."

"I'm sure they were where they are now and you just reckon you saw 'em inside," Leah said, trying to placate the girl.

"No," Sylvie said. Leah heard the frustration in her voice. She'd heard it many times before. "They were *inside.* I'm *sure.* Somebody moved 'em last night. Or during the day today."

"Why would somebody move your flowerpots?" This was the rational question that Sylvie Carson's mind seemed incapable of asking itself.

"I don't know."

"What else was moved?" Leah asked.

Sylvie hesitated. "Nothin'. Just the pots."

Now it was Leah's turn to pause. "That's it?" She realized she hadn't written anything down and was probably making the girl feel bad. She quickly wrote on her pad: *Flowerpots moved. From inside to top of wooden box.* "You say you have footprints?" Leah asked, glancing up.

"In the vegetable garden."

"Show me."

Sylvie led her to a patch of dirt that could only be a vegetable garden by mere designation. If it ever had been such a thing, many years had passed since then. Now it was a patch of ground with spotty grass and weeds that had grown in not quite as dense as the rest of the yard. Some of it was bare of any growth. Those areas were a gray color, and Leah suspected the ground was clay there. The clay looked moist and soft on account of all the rain.

Sylvie brought Leah's attention to one of these patches of clay. "Here. There's one here," she said. She moved over about two feet, straining to see in the night's light. "And here."

Leah shined her flashlight on the spots. Sure enough, the imprints in the clay could've very well been footprints. They might also just have been natural indentations made by the weather. They were pretty formless. Any detail they had—*if* they ever had any— had been washed away by the rain. "They don't necessarily look like footprints to me," Leah said. "I can't make out any details."

"They were detailed earlier," Sylvie said. "I *saw* them. They *were* footprints."

"Maybe you made them?" Leah asked.

Sylvie looked at her. "They're this big," she said, holding her hands almost a foot apart. "I'm a seven. They ain't mine."

"They don't look like anythin' to me," Leah said.

"Not anymore. But they did."

"I believe you."

"No, you don't."

No, I don't, Leah thought. "Okay," she said. "Let's say they *are* footprints. So somebody came into your backyard and moved your pots up to the top of your box and left footprints. So what?"

"I don't like strangers near my home. I have a baby."

Good girl. Too bad her worries were so misplaced. "I understand that," Leah said. "But I don't reckon this would be the kind of person you'd have to worry much 'bout, do you?"

"I would be worried 'bout anyone comin' into my yard," Sylvie said.

Leah thought about this. She didn't know what to say to the girl. All she could really do was tell her the truth. "I'm sorry, Sylvie. There ain't nothin' I can do with what you showed me. I'm afraid I need more to go on than some pots that may or may not have been moved and some spots in the clay that might possibly be footprints."

"They *was* footprints," Sylvie said. Leah could tell she was almost angry now, she was getting so frustrated.

"Okay, they was footprints. Listen, Sylvie. Think about this: Say they still was *perfect* footprints. And say the pots were obviously moved. Even then, *what would you expect me to do?*"

"Figure out who moved 'em?" Sylvie replied, forming it more like a question than an answer.

"And do what then?" Leah asked. "Nobody's really broken any laws now, have they? *Maybe* trespassin'. But it ain't like I'm 'bout to arrest someone for movin' a few pots."

Sylvie took a deep breath. Leah could tell the girl was shaky. "So what're you sayin'?" Sylvie asked, her voice quivering. "I'm supposed to just stay here with my baby while people come into my backyard just as merrily as they please?"

Leah held up her hand. "I can tell you're upset and worried. How about this?" Everything in Leah's head was telling her not to do what she was about to do, but she didn't listen. She already knew she was going to do it. It was the only way she could come up with of getting out of here and still making Sylvie happy in the process. "I'll give you my home number. You have any problems, you can call me. *Any* time, day or night." The quarter moon rose in the night sky like a tipped grin. "Try the station first, of course. If I'm not there, try me at home. How does that sound?"

Sylvie thought this over. "Okay, I suppose. I guess it might help if somethin' else happens. You're the only one who ever comes right away anymore."

Ouch. That last one stung. Leah immediately tried to cover with an excuse. "Things get really busy sometimes, Sylvie," she said. But as soon as it came out, she realized both of them knew it was a lie.

They went back inside and Leah wrote her home phone number on a blank page of her report pad. Ripping out the page, she handed it to Sylvie, regretting the action the moment she felt the paper leave her fingertips. "Remember," she said. "This is only for emergencies, and *only* after tryin' the station first. Deal?"

"Deal," Sylvie said. She seemed a lot better. Being inside probably took the edge off. Leah couldn't imagine what it was like to be as paranoid as Sylvie, but being paranoid like that *and* being outside at night had to be even worse.

"Thanks for comin' out," Sylvie mumbled.

"You don't have to thank me," Leah said. "It's my duty to come out. It's my job. Just like your job's to look after your daughter. You just do me a big ol' favor, okay? Find her a name nice and quick?"

"I'm tryin'," Sylvie said. "I really am tryin' hard."

"Try a little harder. I don't think it matters as much as you go on about it matterin'."

"Wish I thought same as you," Sylvie said.

Leah walked to the front door. "Just take care of yourself, all right? And look after your girl." She unlocked the door, opened it, and stepped out onto the porch. "Don't forget to lock up behind me."

Leah walked down the stairs, hearing the door shut and the dead bolt shoot in her wake. She thought she probably didn't need to add that last bit. She doubted locking up her doors was something Sylvie Carson ever forgot to do.

*In Michael Hiebert's haunting and powerful novel,
a long-ago tragedy echoes through small-town
Alabama as one woman tries to track down a
serial killer.*

Detective Leah Teal is privy to most of the secrets
in her hometown of Alvin, but there are always surprises to be had. Like the day she agrees to take her
daughter, Caroline, to see a psychic for a reading. The
psychic homes in on Leah instead, hinting at a string of
gruesome killings and insisting that she intervene to
prevent more deaths.

When you go looking for trouble, you never know
how much you'll find. Sure enough, the psychic's
scant clues lead Leah to a cold case from six years ago,
when a young woman was found shot to death, her
eyelids sewn shut. As Leah digs deeper into old files, a
second unsolved case surfaces with the same grisly
pattern. While her shrewd young son, Abe, observes
from the sidelines, Leah races to prevent another horrific murder, unaware of just how deep the roots of evil
can go.

Taut, suspenseful, and rich in Southern atmosphere,
A Thorn Among the Lilies is a mesmerizing novel of
loss and vengeance, and the lengths some will go to
out of loyalty and love.

Please read on for an exciting sneak peek of Michael Hiebert's third Alvin, Alabama, novel

A THORN AMONG THE LILIES

now on sale wherever print and e-books are sold!

PROLOGUE

Alvin, Alabama—1976

The moon hangs in the sky above Alvin like a sickle surrounded by a field of stars. It's a pretty night, but it's cold, being barely two months since Christmas. Susan Lee Robertson is on her way home from the five-and-dime after buying a quart of milk for her baby, who is at home with her twelve-year-old son. The milk sits on the passenger seat beside her.

Rain had been pouring all day, but it finally let up and a westerly wind quickly blew out all the clouds. But the dampness is still in the air, making the storefronts on either side of her look slick, like oil paintings. She hits a pothole and the car bounces in a splash of rainwater, nearly hydroplaning into the oncoming lane. She's driving east up Main Street when she comes to the intersection of Sweetwater Drive. It's a one-way intersection, with no stop signs for Main Street, so Susan Lee continues through with the streetlights reflecting brightly from the hood of her car.

That may explain why, when it happens, she never sees it coming.

A blue Buick with out-of-state plates screams through the stop sign on Sweetwater Drive from Susan Lee's left. The driver, Anna Marsh, is coming back early from a bachelorette party for one of her friends after having a fight with the maid of honor. The party was at the Rabbit Room, a place normally reserved for male patrons and female strippers who take off their tops for ten-dollar bills. But, somehow, the fourteen girls in the wedding party managed to come up with enough money and a good enough argument to convince the owner of the Rabbit Room, Gus Snow, into letting them have a girls-only night with male strippers. And, of course, cocktails. Lots of cocktails.

Anna Marsh never did well when it came to lots of cocktails.

She doesn't hesitate at the stop sign. Without touching her brakes, she T-bones Susan Lee's silver Honda, hitting it near the rear of the car, causing it to spin, and caving in the driver's side, breaking both of Susan Lee's arms—one when the door collides with it, the other when it's slammed against the console. The top of her spinal column is partially severed on impact. The windshield of the Honda explodes in a shower of glass as Susan Lee Robertson's body (which was not secured by a seatbelt) gets tossed through it in a sideways motion. The glass rains into her eyes, blinding her for life.

She lands headfirst on the asphalt in front of her car after bouncing off the hood and is still lying there unconscious when the authorities show up. "I reckon she's lucky to be alive," one of the EMTs says to another.

"I don't know if you'd call this lucky, Jerrod." They try to ascertain where her head is bleeding from. A pool of blood has formed beneath it, with tiny rivers that run along the road.

Carefully, they lift her onto a gurney and place her in the back of an ambulance. She's taken to Providence Hospital in Mobile, where she'll remain in a coma on life support.

With Susan Lee still alive, Anna Marsh is arrested for first-offense DWI. Her blood alcohol level is measured at just over 0.12. Her license is revoked.

Despite her Buick looking like an accordion, Anna's wounds are superficial. She actually gets out of the car and can walk. She doesn't look any worse than if she'd fallen down a few stairs.

Authorities take a slurred statement from her. Turns out she lives in Clarksdale, Mississippi, and, along with her other thirteen friends, came down to Alvin specifically for the bachelorette party. Her friends had arranged a limo back to their hotel, but after her fight with the maid of honor, Anna decided to drive herself home.

Probably not the best decision she ever made.

Twelve years later, when doctors take Susan Lee off life support and pronounce her dead, a jury at a circuit court changes Anna Marsh's sentence, giving her five years for reckless vehicular manslaughter, the maximum sentence in Alabama. Her appeal is turned down.

But before that, for twelve years of her life, Susan

Lee Robertson lies in that hospital bed unconscious while the world continues to go round without her.

Twelve long years.

For her, it's just a blink.

But for those who love her, it's an eternity. . . .

CHAPTER 1

Almost Thirteen Years Later

It was a clear winter day when the Christmas parade wound its way down Alvin's Main Street. Which, of course, meant it was cold. Dewey said it smelled like snow, but I told him he was crazy. First off, it ain't never snowed in Alvin far as I know, and second, it wasn't *that* cold. I guessed it to be probably in the midforties somewhere. Still, I was glad I had my heavy jacket on. I wasn't used to this sort of weather.

We were all standing together as close as we could, which was extremely strange for my sister, Carry. Normally, Carry liked to be as far away from everyone else as she could get, but I guess huddling to keep warm took precedence over trying to look cool. Other than me, Dewey, and Carry, there was my uncle Henry, who had come down to spend the holidays with us.

Christmas was barely two weeks away, and boy you could sure feel the excitement in the air. I loved Christmas. It was the best day of the year as far as I was rightly concerned. My mother always played Elvis songs at

Christmastime and he had this one that was called something like "If Every Day Was Christmas." I found myself thinking that same question all the time. Of course, then it probably wouldn't be so special. Which sounded just like something my mother would say.

More and more, I found myself saying stuff that sounded like it should be coming out of her mouth instead of mine.

Carry was extra lucky. She not only got Christmas to celebrate, but four days later, she got her birthday, too. If she had been born just four days earlier, she'd have the same birthday as baby Jesus. I'm glad she didn't. That would be just too weird.

"Here they come!" Uncle Henry said. "Can you see all right, Abe?" he asked me.

"I certainly can!" I said.

Down the street, the float my mother was on turned the corner and came into view. There was a tall riser up front where Hubert James Robertson, the mayor of Alvin, stood waving to people on both sides of the street. Beside him, on much lower risers, stood my mother on his left and Officer Chris Jackson on his right. Both my mother and Chris worked for the Alvin Police Department. Chris was just a regular officer, but my mother was a detective, which meant she didn't have to drive around in a special car or wear a special uniform. She could go out looking any way she wanted. Although, sometimes, she worked as a normal officer, too. They were the only two police officers in Alvin other than Police Chief Ethan Montgomery, who ran things at the station.

"Where's Chief Montgomery?" I asked, blinking into

the sun as I looked up at Uncle Henry. A cold breeze hit my pant legs, sending a chill up my body.

Uncle Henry shielded his eyes with his hand, almost looking like he was saluting someone. "I don't know. You'd reckon he'd be on there, too."

There were all sorts of floats. The one my mother was on didn't seem to "be" anything in particular, but the one coming up behind it was a pirate ship advertising the Alvin First National Bank. It was big and it blocked out most of the stores on the other side of the street. It had a huge Union Jack flag that flapped and snapped in the winter wind.

"Isn't that a weird float for a bank?" I asked.

"What do you mean?" Dewey asked back.

"I mean, didn't pirates *steal* money? It's like they're sayin' they're gonna steal your money."

"You think too much, Abe," Uncle Henry said.

"Maybe they're sayin' that they'll steal money *for* you and put it into your account," Dewey offered.

"Maybe it's *just* a friggin' pirate ship," Carry said.

She could be very unsociable at times.

Someone in a giant kangaroo suit came bounding down the side of the road and stopped right in front of us, waving.

I waved back, but the kangaroo didn't move on. It just kept waving. I felt very awkward and uncomfortable, waving from the sidewalk with the kangaroo two feet from me, waving from the street. Finally, the kangaroo reached up and took off its giant head. It was Police Chief Montgomery. "You guys all havin' fun?"

"Um, yeah. It's dandy," Dewey said.

"It's okay," I said.

"My feet are killin' me," Carry whined. "How much longer is this thing anyway?"

"They're all having a terrific time," Uncle Henry said, swatting the back of Carry's head.

Chief Montgomery leaned in, and whispered to Carry, "At least you don't have to hop around in a stupid kangaroo suit. My legs feel like Jell-O. I can't *wait* until this is over. I reckon there's only three or four more floats until the big guy comes round and finishes it."

"The big guy?" Dewey asked.

"You know," Chief Montgomery said. "Mr. C? Ho ho ho? St. Nick?"

"Santa Claus!" A huge smile beamed from Dewey's face.

Oh my God, he didn't really still believe in Santa, did he? Me and Dewey were practically exactly the same age. Our birthdays were within days of each other, which meant he would be thirteen in March. Someone had to put an end to this.

"Dewey," I said, "you do know there is no real Santa, right?"

I got instant glares from three people. Even Carry joined into the Glare Group.

"What?" I asked. "He's almost thirteen, for cryin' out loud. Do you want him to go into the workforce believin' in the tooth fairy?"

"Wait," Dewey said, sounding dejected. "There's no Santa *and* no tooth fairy?"

"Dewey, you have no baby teeth left. Why do you even care 'bout the tooth fairy?"

"She was nice to me. She gave me money."

"He's got a point, ass face," Carry said. Uncle Henry swatted the back of her head again.

"Language," he said. To me, he didn't sound too much like he meant it.

"Are you serious about Santa?" Dewey asked.

I took a deep breath and let it go, looking at all the heads shaking behind Dewey's back. I smiled. It was a terribly faked smile. "No, Dewey, I'm just pullin' your leg. Of course there's a Santa Claus. Who else would be eatin' those carrots and drinkin' that milk you put out?"

His face immediately transformed. The wonder was back. It sort of peeved me off because he was living in a world much more spectacular than the one I was.

"And just so you know," he said, "I *am* aware there is no Easter bunny."

I squinted at him. "Why do you reckon there's no Easter bunny, yet you believe in Santa?"

"Duh. Why the heck would rabbits be givin' out eggs? It makes absolutely no sense."

"He's got a point," Uncle Henry said.

Everyone fell silent and I realized the Existence of Santa Claus and Other Miscellaneous Childhood Lies discussion had come to an end. The silence was finally broken by Uncle Henry asking Carry: "So, what does my little sugarplum want for her birthday this year?"

Carry smiled. "It's super cool."

"What is it?"

"I want you and my mom"—she hesitated and examined me and Dewey—"and I guess you two little rug rats too if you want, to come with me to a psychic while I get my fortune told."

"What a neat idea," Uncle Henry said. "But if you want me there, you're gonna have to do it earlier than your birthday. I'm only stayin' until the mornin' after Christmas and then I have to go."

"Okay, I'll talk to Mom. Maybe we can book an appointment this week. I reckon it'll be so cool."

"Just remember, sugarplum, a lot of those so-called psychics are frauds. They only tell you what you wanna hear. Or they're gypsies. Gypsies give me the willies."

"I'm not gonna *tell* her what I wanna hear. I'm not gonna answer any questions. I wanna see what she can figure out without me sayin' a word."

"Well, that sure should be interestin' to watch."

"Maybe I'll find out that one day I'll be rich," Carry said.

"Or that you'll die an early death in a house fire before you're twenty," Dewey said.

We all looked at him. "What?" he asked.

"Oh, nothin'," I said. "There's just somethin' wrong with you, is all."

CHAPTER 2

Me and Dewey were playing tag in the backyard. Tag was one of those games we didn't play for very long, on account of there being just the two of us and it getting a mite boring. You really need more than two people to play tag properly. Mainly, it was just fun being outside this close to Christmas. Me and my mother had spent the last weekend hanging lights up around the eaves of the house. Now it looked really Christmassy. I just couldn't wait for Christmas to come.

One game we used to play a lot of I would call "balancing rocks on sticks." It consisted of taking a stick and a rock and trying to see how long you could go with the rock on the end of the stick before it fell off. Now this was more of a sport for two people. In fact, you could just as easily do it with one person. It was the perfect multiplayer game.

Truth be told, there just wasn't much to do outside in the afternoon in winter in Alvin. Tag or otherwise. We were too used to the heat to stay outside too long in the cold, and some days it would rain something fierce and it felt like God was throwing ice at you. My backyard wasn't the most fun place on the planet to hang out on those days. Sometimes we'd just run around to stay warm.

Even the trees looked like they hated it outside. We had two cherry trees in the backyard and neither had any leaves left. All the leaves had fallen off and died. I was starting to feel like them leaves, as Dewey touched me, and yelled, "You're It!"

I decided I couldn't be It for one more round. "Let's stop playin'," I said.

"How come, Abe?" Dewey asked.

"Well, for one, I'm outta breath. For two, it's too damn cold out here. I'm dyin', Dewey."

"What's for three?"

"Um . . ." I knew for three had to be the clincher. "For three, I think we can probably go inside and get my mom to make us some hot cocoa."

"That sounds great!"

Dewey never gave up a chance for free food, no matter what it was. It was his weakness, the way Superman couldn't go near kryptonite. Everyone has a weakness, I think, and Dewey's was rustling up free food. We could be having the time of our lives and I could stop, and tell him, "Hey, old Newt Parker just called and invited us over for raccoon, wanna go?" And Dewey would be on his bike in a flash, ready to make the trip.

Newt Parker was no longer with the living souls of this world, but when he was here, many folk thought he ate barbecued roadkill. Myself, I have no convictions either way as to whether or not the rumors were true or false. I do know this, though. I had enough belief that the rumors *could* be true that I would never go for a barbecue at Newt Parker's house. Dewey, on the other hand, would go in a flash, if for no other reason than to be able to tell people he ate barbecued road-killed raccoon with Newt Parker. That's just how Dewey was.

So, compared to the dead raccoon, my offer of hot cocoa was a quick way to get me out of the stark cold of the backyard and into the warmth of the house.

We got inside and pulled off our boots. It took Dewey at least twice as long as me to get his off his feet on account of I think he outgrew his last year or something. Do twelve-year-old feet even still grow? I had no idea. Maybe his ma just bought them too small. Dewey's ma wasn't the sharpest crayon in the box. Of course, I never told that to Dewey.

My own mother was in the kitchen on the phone. Carry kneeled on a chair beside her, anxiously watching while my mother made some phone calls. I figured out pretty quick what they were doing—they were trying to book a psychic to see Carry for her birthday present. By the sounds of things, they weren't having much luck.

"No," my mother said, "it needs to be *between* now and Christmas. Sometime this week would be best . . . okay, thank you for your time." She hung up and looked at Carry. "That's eight I've called. They're all not working through the holidays."

Carry frowned. "Stupid psychics. Don't they know that's when they'd get their most business?"

"Maybe it's just as well," my mother said.

"Don't give up now!" Carry said. "There's still some you haven't tried."

"I know, and I will, I just don't want you to get your hopes up too high."

"If they're all psychic and stuff," Dewey said, "why

do you have to call them? Shouldn't they just know you're comin'?"

I looked at Dewey. "You're an idiot."

My mother said, "I reckon he has a very good point."

Carry didn't hear the exchange at all. She had her head in the phone book. "Try this one. Madame Crystalle—True Psychic Medium from Persia. One hundred percent satisfaction or your money returned in full."

"Wow," my mother said, "that's going out on a limb. And she's not a gypsy if she's from Persia. I'm a little leery of gypsies. Okay, what's the number?"

Carry told her as my mother dialed. "Hello, I'd like to book an appointment with Madame Crystalle. . . . Oh, that's *you*. Well, hi. My name's Leah and I'm the detective here in Alvin, and my daughter, Caroline, would like to see you and get her fortune read for her birthday. . . . It would have to be sometime this week. I know, it's sort of last minute." My mother always told everyone she was the detective here. I think she thought it brought her some kind of respect or something that she wouldn't get otherwise.

She stopped talking, held the phone away, and said to Carry, "She's gone to get her schedule."

Placing the handset back to her mouth, she said, "Yes, I'm still here . . . *tomorrow*? Yes, tomorrow works *fine*. What time? Two o'clock. Perfect. Oh, and is it okay to bring along her family to watch? Okay, that's great. Thank you."

My mother hung up and smiled at Carry. "You're goin' tomorrow at two!"

Carry beamed back. "This is goin' to be so awesome! Thank you, Mother!"

"What if she tells you somethin' bad?" Dewey asked.

"Why are you being so negative?" my mother asked back.

"Because *most* things are bad. Read a newspaper or watch the news. You never see happy stuff."

"I'm sure Carry's stuff will all be nice and happy."

"Yeah, but what if it isn't? What if she says, 'Your mother's gonna get shot next Wednesday while on duty'?"

"Dewey!" my mother snapped. Even I looked at him like this was out of line.

"I'm just sayin' she could, so you should be prepared for somethin' like that."

"I reckon maybe it's time for you to go home," my mother told him.

"Actually," I said, "we was hopin' for some hot cocoa."

My mother took another look at Dewey and exhaled slowly. "All right, but no more talk about 'bad stuff,' you hear?"

"Yes, ma'am," Dewey said.

He fell quiet. I just looked at him, and whispered, "You're an idiot."

CHAPTER 3

The psychic's shop turned out to be a very small building that me and Dewey had ridden by on our bikes many times and had not noticed. The shop couldn't have been more than ten feet tall with a sign in the window that read:

Madame Crystalle
True **Psychic Medium**

100% satisfaction
Or your money returned in full.

The pink blinds behind the sign were pulled closed, so you couldn't see inside. A large shrub hid most of one side of the building. The rest of the building was painted black, which was obviously the reason me and Dewey never saw it. You don't normally look for small black buildings while out on bike rides.

The only really strange thing on the outside of the place was this statue right beside the door. It stood between the sidewalk and the steps leading up to the door, facing down toward the hustle and bustle of town. It was a frog standing on his hind legs. It stared wall-eyed down Main Street at all the other shops. In its hands it held a top hat, and its mouth was wide open with a bright red tongue. It seemed so out of place it took a minute for my brain to even figure out what I was looking at. Me and Dewey must've missed it because it was set back a bit, and you had to look right at the building to see it.

"Why is there a frog standin' here starin' off down the street?" I asked my mother. "It looks kind of creepy."

"I don't rightly know, Abe, but I think maybe we should all go inside before we freeze to death," my mother said.

"Reminds me of that frog from that cartoon," Dewey said. "The one that will only dance and sing for one guy. Only this one wouldn't fit in a shoebox."

"I agree with Abe for once," Carry said. "It's really creepy. No wonder she was available for a readin'. She probably scares off most customers with this frog."

"Now, don't go writin' her off just because of some crazy statue outside her shop," Uncle Henry said. "Look at her sign. It says, '*True* Psychic Medium.' Not only that, she'll refund your money if you ain't satisfied. I'd say that's pretty darn good. I also agree with your mom. We should go inside before we freeze."

"I guess," my sister said.

Uncle Henry looked up at the roof; then his eyes fell to the door. "So what do we do? Just knock?"

"I dunno," my mother said. "Maybe try the door."

Of course, before anyone could say another word, Dewey's hand was on that doorknob. He turned it and the door opened. A bell on the top of the door rang out, announcing our arrival.

We shuffled into a small room that was more like a landing for the top of a narrow stairway. A beaded curtain hung at the entrance to the stairway. The small room we found ourselves in smelled funny, and the walls and ceiling were all colored red, matching near on exactly the tongue of the frog statue outside. The floor was white with repeating red diamonds. Nobody seemed to hear the bell that rang because we stood there, all crammed together on that small landing for a good five minutes and nobody came to see us.

"What's that smell?" I asked.

"Incense," my mother said.

"What's that?"

"It's supposed to have mystical powers, I reckon," Uncle Henry said. He sneezed. "I think I might be allergic to it."

"It has mystical stink," Dewey said.

"What do we do now?" my mother asked.

"Hello?" Uncle Henry called out. "Anybody home?"

From downstairs, behind the beaded curtain, a heavily accented woman's voice called up. "Come downstairs!"

We pushed our way through the curtain. The beads were all glass and very beautiful. Green, red, blue, yellow, with the light reflecting inside of them. They made a loud swishing that sounded almost like water as we went through them. The stairway wound down in two tight circles. I was behind Uncle Henry. It was too narrow to go any way but single file.

About halfway down, Uncle Henry bumped his head. At that exact moment, from the bottom of the stairs, in a much quieter and lower voice than she had used before, we heard the woman say, "Be careful of head. If you are tall, those stairs are like plague."

"You'd think, bein' psychic and all, she'd have told me that *before* I hit my head," Uncle Henry whispered before letting go with a big sneeze.

"I heard that," the woman replied.

When we made it to the bottom, there was another beaded curtain to go through that exactly matched the one at the top. Again, it sounded like a waterfall as we all pushed through it and came to our final destination. I felt my eyes grow as big as paper plates. We had descended into the weirdest room I'd ever seen in my entire life.

Everything was a deep golden yellow. The room was maybe twice the size of the small landing we managed to squeeze onto at the top of the stairs. On one side were rows of shelves holding candles of all different types. Every one was lit, and that was the only light in the room, so it cast an eerie, flickering glow on the yellow walls, yellow curtains (which hung on some walls and were obviously just for show as we were underground), and yellow tablecloth that covered the round table on the other side of the room. The cloth came right down to the floor, which was a deep pile carpet, also in golden yellow.

On the other side of the table sat who I assumed to be Madame Crystalle. I had no idea how she got in to sit on that chair. From where I stood, it looked like she would have to spend the rest of her life seated there, as there was no way in or out.

She wore a leather headband with gemstones set along it, and had long strands of beads in her curly, deep auburn hair. It hung down past her shoulders. Her lips were very red, and her eyes were very blue and they sparkled in the candlelight. I immediately liked her because of her smile. It was one of the warmest, friendliest, and reddest smiles I'd ever seen.

The first thing she did was look straight at Carry. "You must be Caroline," she said, and extended her hand without standing. I didn't think it was possible for her to stand from where she sat.

"I am," Carry said happily.

"I understand it's your birthday," Madame Crystalle said.

"Well, not for another week or so, but we wanted my uncle to come along and he's leavin' the mornin' after Christmas."

"Ah! Early birthday present. So nice!"

"You talk funny," Dewey said.

"Shut up!" I snapped in a whisper to him.

But Madame Crystalle just laughed. "I am from Persia. Everyone talk like this in Persia."

"And I bet she speaks better English than you speak Persian," Carry said to Dewey. Uncle Henry sneezed again.

"I always thought Persians were cats," Dewey said.

Once again, I told Dewey to shut up, but Madame Crystalle laughed very loudly at what he said. "We are people, too. Oh, and also carpet. Or, how you say? Rug. Persian rug."

"How come you ain't got no crystal ball?" Dewey asked.

I wished he'd stop asking questions.

"Oh, crystal balls don't work," Madame Crystalle said. "They're all just hocus-pocus, fluff stuff. You either real medium or you're not. If real, you don't need crystal ball to tell you anything."

"Oh," Dewey said.

"I'm Leah," my mother said, extending her hand with a smile. She did it quickly, before Dewey could say anything else.

Smiling, Madame Crystalle went to shake my mother's hand, but as soon as their hands locked Madame Crystalle's face changed immediately.

"What's goin' on?" Dewey asked.

"Please," Madame Crystalle said. "Sit in chair." Her face was very serious as she gestured to the chair across the table from her.

"No, this is for Caroline," my mother said. "I'm just here to watch."

"There will be no charge. There are things you must know. Sit. Now. Before I lose them."

Reluctantly, my mother sat in the chair. I could tell Carry felt a little put out just by the expression on her face.

"You . . . you work in justice, no?"

"Yes, I told you that on the phone. I'm the detective for the Alvin Police Department." I figured my mother had just caught the psychic in a trap. She was using information she gained ahead of time from the phone call my mother made to set up Carry's appointment.

Madame Crystalle closed her eyes and held both my mother's hands. "I see something almost indescribable. It is someone . . . a sort of, how you say? Maniac. A tailor. Deprives those of their sight. Very dangerous."

"Who are you talkin' 'bout?" my mother asked. I could tell she had grown a bit anxious.

"Just listen, before it goes away," Madame Crystalle said. "I see a body in darkness, waiting. I see writing. Writing on the body."

"What does the writing say?" my mother asked, but Madame Crystalle shushed her.

"I can't see enough to read it, just to know it's there. But remember the number seventy-eight. It is important. Remember the maniac tailor. Knowing this can save many lives over the coming times. I . . . I see a name on a sign. . . . 'Welcome to . . . to . . . Gray . . .'" She paused again. "'Gray . . . Gray . . .'" Then she stopped.

She let go of my mother's hands. "Sorry, it's gone."

"What *was* it?" my mother asked, her voice shaky.

"Did it not mean something to you?"

"No, can you give me some more information?"

Madame Crystalle shook her head. "No, I can't tell you what it was I just saw. I don't remember details, the visions come like that. I just knew I had message and it was for you. If not useful now, I am sure you will find useful soon. It was a very powerful message the way it came through."

"That freaked me out a little," I said.

"Me too," Dewey said.

Uncle Henry sneezed.

"You still up to doin' yours?" Uncle Henry asked Carry.

"Yeah," Carry said as though he just asked the stupidest question ever. "Mine better not be in code like Mom's was, though. I want to actually understand it."

"I will try to do better for you," Madame Crystalle said. "Please, take seat."

My mother got out of the chair and let Carry take

her place. I noticed my mother was shaking, especially her hands. I think she was more freaked out than anyone. It was pretty spooky.

Madame Crystalle took a deck of cards from somewhere beside her and handed them across the table to Carry. She had them with the backs up and the backs were pretty neat. They were black with a silver ring painted on the center. Inside the ring was a red dragon curled up with its wings hanging down over the bottom of the ring. The deck looked thicker than a normal deck of cards.

"Shuffle these," Madame Crystalle said. "Use overhand shuffle, though. I don't want my cards bent."

Carry did as she was told. "When do I stop?" she asked.

"Go for as long as feels good to you. You are imprinting your future onto the cards."

Carry shuffled some more, then came to a stop. She looked like she was about to set down the deck, then she started shuffling again for another minute or so. "I just felt compelled to," she said.

Madame Crystalle smiled. "This is good. It means you go with your instincts."

Finally, Carry actually did stop. "Okay, what do I do now?"

"Hold the deck in your left hand and make three piles of cards on the table from left to right."

Carry did and then Madame Crystalle leaned over and picked up the piles from left to right with *her* left hand. I couldn't figure out what was so important about everything being done using lefts.

She laid out seven cards in all and in the end they formed a T shape. First she laid out five cards in a straight row and then two cards beneath the center card in the row. Some were upside down from me and others weren't. I wondered if that mattered. And boy, if I thought the backs of the cards were neat, the fronts were even better.

Each one was different. The first looked like an old scraggly tree with a green gem tangled in its root. It read "Ace of Pentacles" on the bottom.

The second was the Five of Cups and showed a dwarf drinking something out of a bottle with his back against a tree and five cups in the grass around him. The dwarf looked drunk to me.

The third one was The Lovers and showed two dragons looking like they were about to kiss. That one sort of disturbed me. Dragons don't kiss. They go and burn down castles and collect treasure.

The fourth one was the Four of Cups and showed a lady with very long ponytails standing at a table where four little lizards were playing with four golden cups. Two of the cups were on their side, the other two were standing.

The fifth one (which was the last one along the top row) was the Queen of Wands and showed an older lady with a beautiful dress made from purple and gold silk. She was seated on a tall wooden throne with a blue dragon sleeping at her feet.

The remaining two came down from The Lovers card. The first one was the Knight of Wands, which showed a younger-looking man riding a dragon in the moonlight. This one was pretty awesome. I would love to ride a dragon. Especially at night.

The final card, at the very bottom of the *T,* was the Two of Cups, and it showed a young man and woman holding hands in a garden with a huge moon over their heads and the face of a dragon inside the moon. It almost looked like they were getting married or something.

"What do they mean?" Carry asked, anxiously, just as Uncle Henry sneezed for what seemed like the hundredth time.

"Well, let's see," Madame Crystalle said. "I see you are smart in school. This is good. I also see you know it. This, not so good. You would have more friendships if you didn't always act so sarcastic."

Carry's face reddened. She hated getting lectured the best of times. Now she was being lectured by a psychic whom she got as a birthday present.

Madame Crystalle noticed Carry's reaction and quickly covered. "It's okay, though, you have good heart. See these cup cards? Cups represent love and compassion. You have many. So your heart is in right place. But . . ."

"But what?" Carry asked.

"You get very lonely at times," Madame Crystalle said.

"No, I don't," Carry said back snarkily.

"You cover it with your sarcasm or your quick wit. But you wish you had more friends. You also long for a boyfriend."

We all sort of giggled at that and Carry's face went completely purple. This was turning out to be the best birthday present ever. I started thinking for my birthday I'd get Carry a psychic reading.

"Well, I have good news for you," Madame Crystalle said. "I see a boy in the immediate future. Someone more than just a friend."

"He won't be nineteen and drivin' a red Pontiac Firebird, will he?" my mother asked, referring to a boy we once caught with Carry in the backseat of a car. "Actually, he'd be twenty now."

"No, but he will be older than you, Caroline. And he'll probably have dark hair. Brown, black, maybe a dark red. And don't worry about your mother. See this card here?" She tapped the Queen of Wands. "This is your mother and she's sitting right beside one of your cup cards. Which means she will be approving of your love choices from now on. So this new boy for sure your mother will be accepting of him. But, I see at first you won't trust her to be, and you will try to hide your relationship. Rest assured this is unneeded. Your mother will not try and sabotage anything."

There was a little more after that, but that was the main part. That was the part that made Carry happiest (and most embarrassed). I thought it must be weird, living her life now, just waiting for this boy to drop into it who is going to become her new boyfriend.

By the time we left Madame Crystalle, I noticed a change in every one of us. Carry was in deep thought, probably about this new boy. My mother was in deep thought, probably about the stuff she was told that made absolutely no sense to anyone. Uncle Henry had changed because he found out he was allergic to incense. I was quietly cursing myself because I forgot to ask Madame Crystalle about the frog standing outside her shop, and Dewey had changed because he found out that, along with rugs and cats, there were also Persian people.

CHAPTER 4

That night, Leah lay in bed unable to sleep. Her encounter with the psychic kept rolling around in her mind. What happened earlier had affected her more than she had thought. She didn't really believe in psychics or the ability to "see the future" at all; in fact, she normally referred to it as "hocus pocus gobblody gook." But her ad hoc session with Madame Crystalle had been so intense, Leah couldn't help but be touched by it.

The problem was, the woman didn't make any sense. Leah was a logical person, and there was no logic in what she'd been told. It was just a bunch of sketchy details without any definition. And to top it off, Leah kept going back to the fact that she had *told* Madame Crystalle on the phone she was a detective. That part made it a little too convenient for Leah's liking.

Leah remembered every word the psychic told her. She'd gone over the words at least fifty times in her head, and there was nothing there she could do anything with. None of it made any sense. Some of it was downright ridiculous and funny. A maniac tailor who deprives people of their sight. Now *there's* an image that's really hard to conjure up in your imagination. Something about finding a body in darkness with writing on it. The psychic had been unable to say anything about the writing at all.

Yet, writing on a body found in darkness is pretty specific. They aren't just things you pull out of your sleeves. So this was where Leah was torn into possibly believing the woman and attempting to follow up on the clues. But really, what clues did she have? She didn't even have a name or place for a victim. Or any kind of context to put this into.

It was the last piece of evidence Madame Crystalle had given Leah that made Leah consider trying to follow the sparse path of clues; it was the one thing that was tangible and possible to get something out of. The words on the sign: WELCOME TO GRAY . . .

It was a partial on a road sign. *That* should be traceable.

This road sign was something Leah might be able to find. But so what if she did? She still had no idea what it meant.

Did she even *want* to know what it meant? And sweet Jesus, if Police Chief Ethan Montgomery ever found out she was hunting around on a case with the sparse evidence she had been given from a psychic, he'd have a heyday with it.

It would probably be the day before Leah had to start looking for a new job.

"I guess you ain't goin' to get much sleep tonight," she said to herself, deciding her best course of action at this point was to get up and go fix herself a mug of warm milk.

Sliding her feet into her slippers, she stood from her bed and slowly padded her way down the hardwood floors into the kitchen. Opening the fridge, she pulled out a carton of milk. She closed the fridge door and immediately her pulse went up twenty notches and she nearly jumped right out of her slippers. Hank had moved beside the opened door while she was peering in the fridge.

"God, Hank, you tryin' to give me a coronary?"

"Sorry. I guess I'm a little sneaky in my old age. I just heard you walkin' round and thought I'd come check on you, make certain you were all right."

"Oh," she said, almost in a sigh. "I'm okay. It's just that psychic has me in a bit of a tizzy."

"I can imagine. The woman was pretty intense. *I* was almost left in a tizzy, and it wasn't even me she was talkin' to!"

Leah pulled a pot from one of the cupboards and put it on the stove. She turned on the burner and poured in some milk. "Would you like some warm milk, too?" she asked Hank.

"Hmm. Actually, that sounds like it might just hit the spot. Thank you."

Leah poured more milk into the pot and returned the milk carton to the fridge. Then she came back and started stirring the milk with a spoon as it simmered on the burner. "So," she asked, "seriously. Why *are* you up?"

"Oh, you know me," he said. "I don't sleep at the best of times. And your sofa is comfortable and all, but it ain't no bed in no five-star hotel room." He laughed.

"I'm sorry," Leah said. "I wish we had somewhere else to put you."

Hank raised his hand. "No, no, I'm not really complainin', I'm just bein' funny. I don't mind the sofa at all. So, about that psychic lady—you gonna act on anythin' she said?"

"Well, that's just it. Even if I wanted to do somethin' based on what she told me, she didn't actually *say* anythin' I could possibly use to do anythin'.'"

"Well, she told you folk are in danger. She told you someone is blindin' them and that he's actin' like some maniac tailor, which could mean lots of disgustin' things when I think it over."

Leah set two mugs on the counter, took the pot of milk off the burner, and carefully tipped it to fill them with the now-warm milk. "Is that what *you* heard?" she asked Hank. "Because that's not what *I* heard. I just heard a bunch of half-baked facts all rolled together." She handed one of the mugs to Hank.

"Thank you," he said. "That's because you chose not to try and form the bits and pieces of information she gave you into somethin' real. You're too analytical. Sometimes you need to fill in the blanks yourself so that you can create—or at least finish—the story. Your story might not always be the right one—fact is, most of the time it probably isn't—but it gives you a place to start. And as you go you can change your story as circumstances change and you gather more facts."

Leah took a sip of her warm milk. It felt good going down her throat. "Ethan would kill me if he knew I was even considerin' doin' this."

"Yeah, well, Ethan owes you a lot. He knows that. Hell, half this town knows that. Take chances, Leah. It's the only way in life to push yourself to your full potential, and if we don't all reach our full potential, what's the point in being here?" He took a sip of his milk. "This is really good milk, by the way."

"It's just milk warmed up in a pot, Hank."

"Still really good."

"Thanks."

A silence followed while Leah thought about what the psychic had told her. "So, say I *do* try and follow this up, Hank. Where the hell do I start? The only thing she gave that's even slightly possible to research is a partial on a road sign."

"Then that's where you start. The road sign. Then at least you'll know what town she's talkin' 'bout."

Every bone in Leah's body was telling her not to do this, telling her that following the scattered advice given to her from a Main Street psychic was a dumb idea. And yet, she knew, deep down in the pit of her gut, that was exactly what she was going to do. So she may as well stop fighting it and just give in and get it over with.

"What made you so smart, anyway?" she asked Hank.

"Watchin' you grow up," he replied.

"We both know what I'm gonna do," she said.

"Yep, you've decided already," Hank said.

Leah sighed. "I guess I have. Sometimes I hate my gut instincts."

"Your gut instincts are what make you good at your job."

Turned out, this time, she didn't have to listen to any instincts.

A case from the past sparks a nightmare for Detective Leah Teal in Michael Hiebert's masterful new novel of suspense.

Fifteen years ago, a serial killer tagged by the media as The Stickman spread terror throughout Alabama and became Alvin police officer Joe Fowler's obsession. After six months and at least fifteen victims, Harry Stork was identified as the Stickman and Fowler shot him dead. The killings stopped. For a while.

Now, more bodies are turning up, each staked through the chest with a stick-figure drawing in the killer's signature style. Detective Leah Teal—Joe Fowler's daughter and Alvin's sole detective— receives a letter before each victim is found, just like her late father did. The only people who knew about the letters were the cops on the task force back then—and the killer himself. Did Joe shoot the wrong man, or was one of the detectives he handpicked involved all along? As a single mother, Leah tries to balance an increasingly disturbing case and a new relationship with caring for her children— bright, perceptive Abe, and teenaged Caroline, who's in the first flush of young love. But with each menacing communication, each gruesome discovery, Leah realizes just how personal, and how devastating, the truth may be.

Weaving lyrical prose and emotional richness into a taut, gripping mystery, Michael Hiebert creates a fascinating novel of life, love, and death in a small Southern town.

Please read on for an exciting sneak peek of Michael Hiebert's fourth Alvin, Alabama, novel

STICKS AND STONES

coming in July 2016 wherever print and e-books are sold!

PROLOGUE

Alvin, Alabama, 1974

The Stickman.

Harry Stork.

A year and a half of Detective Joe Fowler's life.

Joe Fowler; one of the two main officers working the Alvin Police Department, and the only detective. The other cop is a tall, lanky man with a bad comb-over whose name is Strident. Officer Peter Strident. Strident has the eyes of an arctic wolf—that crisp morning sky blue—and when he looks at you, it feels like he sees right *through* you. Nobody interrogates a suspect like Strident.

What Fowler lacks in his eyes, he makes up for in gumption.

A year ago February, the first evidence that Harry Stork would eventually come onto Detective Fowler's radar appeared when Stork's first victim turned up beneath the tracks at Finley's Crossing. A black male, mid-thirties, turned out to be one Waylon Ferris. Ferris's body was found shirtless. His hands and feet hog-tied behind him, putting him in an almost reverse-fetal position. A thirty-eight-caliber bullet hole entering the back of the skull, a big exit hole in the front.

Even more horrific, a wooden stave was hammered through Ferris's chest, staking him into the ground. On a piece of paper affixed to the stave, a drawing of a stickman made in black permanent marker.

Lack of blood and brain matter at the crime scene and evidence from the ligature marks on his wrists and ankles suggested Ferris was shot somewhere else, somewhere he had spent a day, maybe two, before his killer put the bullet through his brain.

For the press release, Fowler held back the stake and the paper attached to it.

Waylon Ferris was victim number one.

A succession of killings followed, all inside or circling the small town of Alvin, each with the same MO: shirtless victims inversely hog-tied with a .38 Special-caliber slug entering the back of the skull. Victims ranged in age from mid-twenties to early forties, men and women, black and white. Each one staked to the ground with the picture of a stick figure. The female stick figures had circles for breasts, hair rising to tips on either side of the head.

Every killing brought more cops into the mix. Fowler created a task force and managed to continue holding back the staked paper with the stickmen from the press. Until the information leaked out after victim six. Someone on the task force talked. Someone obviously needed cash.

Almost immediately, the killer was tagged the Stickman by the media. Fowler hated the name. Thought it trivialized everything, almost turning it into a game.

The case was long and arduous. Too many victims. Too many pieces of paper with bloody stickmen.

Nine in total, that is, *if* Fowler knows about all of them.

Nine bodies, almost a year and a half away from his daughter—Leah—and his wife, Josephine. Because Fowler is *like* that. Even when he's home, if he's on a case, he's *still* on the case. He lets them get to him. They pick away at his bones, eating him up until he solves them. They take their toll on his family, especially on his daughter, Leah. He worries about her and how she's affected by his stress. It's the part of the police game he hates most.

Harry Stork.

The Stickman.

It took Fowler too long to figure out they were the same man. When he did, Stork disappeared.

That was almost a month ago.

But tonight, Fowler and four other officers surround an abandoned shotgun shack with Stork inside. He'll be taken either alive or dead. It's all up to him now, how he plays it.

The dilapidated shack is set back in the woods, flanked by tall oaks, their boughs heavy with Spanish moss. Fowler's positioned at the shack's rear door. Fog and a light mist cover the ground, making the dense forest ghostlike. If not for the band of stars and the silvery gold of the moon overhead, Joe Fowler wouldn't even be able to see his own hands.

The rest of the officers are broken into two teams of two, waiting at the shack's front for Fowler's instructions. Team A will batter down the door, Team B will rush in and clear the front room. Team A will move on to clear the rest of the place.

Joe Fowler is Team C, protecting the only other exit, other than a window. Stork won't have time for windows.

Pushing his fingers through his short, graying hair, Fowler feels sweat pop onto his forehead. He brings the blow horn to his lips. "Come out, Harry!" he yells into it. "You're surrounded. Come out or we're coming in! And if we come in, it could go bad." He rubs his chin, feeling three days' worth of stubble. He wonders if maybe Stork wants it to go bad, wants to go out in a blaze of glory.

A fitting end to the Stickman? Maybe.

From the windows, the occasional flashlight beam dances erratically into the night, the only indication Stork's still alive. He silently moves from room to room.

Fowler counts to five. Stork stays quiet. Stays inside.

"All right," Fowler says. He tosses the blow horn onto the loamy ground, lifts his walkie-talkie. "Team A, go! Team B, ready! Team C is ready!"

Dropping into a crouch, Fowler pulls his weapon, readying himself in case Stork's stupid enough to come out shooting.

There's a *boom!* as Fowler hears the front door go down. "Front clear!" Someone shouts.

"He's running!" Someone else.

It all happens in a blur. The back door bursts open, and Harry Stork appears, silhouetted by the flashlights from the cops in the hall behind him. Fowler sees the gun in Stork's hand, tightens his grip on his own weapon—a snub-nosed Colt Cobra revolver—and readjusts his crouch, balancing his weight on the balls of his feet.

"Drop your weapon!" Fowler screams. "Drop your weapon or I will shoot!"

Stork hesitates while his eyes adjust to the darkness. He must've dropped his flashlight in the scramble. He sweeps his gun blindly in front of him. Fowler sees the barrel tremble. "Don't kill me!" Stork yells, panicked. "I was set up! I'm a fuckin' patsy!"

"Then drop it, Harry!" Fowler calls out. He notices a slight shake in his own hand. Arthritis. Doc gave him the news six months ago. He readjusts his grip and the shake goes away, replaced by a tingling pain shooting up his right arm. Fowler knows too well what it means: He's getting too old for this game.

He pushes the thought away, focuses on Stork. Everything becomes a tunnel around the man. Stork hasn't dropped his weapon. "Drop your gun!" Fowler shouts again.

But Stork doesn't. Instead, no longer blinded by the night, Stork levels the barrel straight at Fowler. There's little choice left. In that split second, Fowler reacts on instinct, pulling off a .38 Special round destined straight for Harry Stork's heart.

Fowler wanted to hit the man's gun arm, but overcompensated, too afraid he might miss. Too afraid Stork wouldn't. Fowler's shot clips the edge of Stork's lower left ventricle, the kind of shot there's no coming back from.

The gun barrel goes limp in Stork's hand before

falling and rattling on the broken wooden porch at Stork's feet. Stork falls right behind it.

And that's how it happened the night the Stickman went down and Joe Fowler gave his life back to his wife, Josephine, and his daughter, Leah. The daughter who would one day follow in her pa's footsteps.

CHAPTER 1

Fifteen Years Later

Summer came to Alabama the way it always did, like a twister out of the east. The heat from the early morning sun pounded down on the red maple and black gum trees out along Cottonwood Lane. Officer Leah Teal drove by these trees every day on her way to work, but this was the first day she could remember in a long time it being so hot at only half past seven.

Everything was alive in vivid colors. Alvin looked like a picture book filled with images of white clusters of berries bursting on the mayhaw, and yellow, green, and orange flowers popping out of the tulip trees, late bloomers. Even with her window rolled down, the air lay in the car like a dead animal, making the heat even more intolerable. As she came to her turn, the smell of sweet bay magnolias trying their best to bloom wafted inside. Drifts of cottonwood fluff fell like snow onto the brown hood of her Bonneville as she turned down the hill.

As she drove, Leah hummed a tune, unsure of what

it was. She was in good spirits lately—ever since Christmastime, really, because of a man she was rapidly falling for: a detective out of Birmingham whom she'd met on her last big case, a case that started with a psychic—of all things—and ended with a serial killer.

Things were never dull for long around Alvin.

The detective's name was Dan Truitt and he was different from any man Leah had ever met. She hadn't dated a lot of men in her life. In fact, Dan was the first in over a dozen years since her husband, Billy, died in an automobile accident.

For too long she had let that accident spin her life out of her control. Now she felt like she was finally taking her life back. And Dan Truitt was helping her do it. No, more than that, he was making her *want* to do it. She was starting to admit to herself she was falling in love.

Pulling her sedan to a stop at the curb outside the Alvin Police Station, Leah exited the vehicle and was immediately overwhelmed again by the melting, stagnant heat. Honeybees buzzed around the red buds on the sweetshrubs planted in front of the station's windows.

She picked up the *Alvin Examiner* from in front of the station door on her way inside. The station was locked, which meant she'd beaten Officer Chris Jackson to work. Officer Jackson was the only other cop at the Alvin Police Station apart from the chief, Ethan Montgomery. Jackson was also black, which caused quite a stir in this little community when he first came on the force, but that quickly faded. Now he was respected as much as Leah or Ethan.

After putting on a pot of coffee, Leah took the

newspaper she had tucked beneath her arm, pulled the elastic off it, and unrolled it.

She read the front page and her happy demeanor immediately changed.

The headline read: *15 Years Later, Stickman Strikes Again*.

The photograph beneath the headline could've been a lot more gruesome than it was. It was taken some distance from the crime scene, which left out a lot of the details described in the article. It didn't matter; Leah knew immediately what the actual scene would've looked like. The victim, unnamed in the paper, would've been shirtless with her ankles and wrists bound together behind her back. Her body would be staked to the ground, through the chest, and attached to that stake would be a piece of paper with a stickwoman drawn on it. But that's not what would've killed her. A gunshot wound to the back of the skull would've done that job. Leah didn't have to see it all in a picture; she could imagine it pretty well. She'd lived it.

Scanning the photo, Leah made out strangler fig and cypress trees. The dirt looked soft. She guessed the body was found near water. Indeed, the article confirmed it had turned up on the bank of Leeland Swamp, an area surrounded by forest just outside of the ranch lands in the northwestern corner of Alvin.

And then the rest of the train caught up with her thoughts and she realized what this really meant. It made her breath catch and her heart tumble into her stomach.

She had lived the case vicariously through her pa, Joe Fowler, fifteen years ago when he spent a year and a half hunting down a serial killer. But—

Her pulse quickened.

Heat rose to her face.

This, all because there was one thing Leah knew with absolute dead fact: *But . . . what I'm looking at, it's . . . it's impossible.*

Her pa killed Harry Stork, the man who earned the nickname "Stickman" in papers from one side of Alabama to another. Shot him through the heart. The *Birmingham News* had called it "The Shot Heard 'Round the World." It made the front page. Suddenly everyone knew about Alvin, a town with a population of just over six thousand people almost nobody in Alabama had ever heard of.

She glanced up to the newspaper's date, hoping for some bizarre reason to find the paperboy had accidentally delivered a paper from 1974, but today's date stared back at her under the black script headlining the *Alvin Examiner*. She hadn't *really* expected to see anything else.

But how . . . ? The more she thought of it, the more impossible it was.

The door opened and she jumped. It was Chris. He took one look at her sitting on the edge of her desk, paper in one hand, forgotten coffee mug steaming in the other, and closed the door quietly behind him. "How you doing?" he asked in his low-timbered voice. Chris spoke slowly, and with near on perfect enunciation. It made him sound as though he was a man who chose his words carefully and said them with reverence. "I see you got the coffee started." He smiled, wiping his brow with his uniform sleeve. "Man, is it hot."

Leah said nothing back, and he realized she was reading the paper.

"Oh," he said, with a big sigh. His smile faded quickly as he plunked into his chair. "So you know." He ran his dark fingers through his cropped black hair. Sweat, even at this early hour, popped over his hand. He looked like he wished he would've called in sick.

Leah snapped the front page of the paper toward him. "This can't be the Stickman," she said. "The Stickman was Harry Stork and my pa *killed* Harry Stork fifteen years ago."

"Yeah, I know," Chris said, "but he shows every sign of having come back to life."

Leah bit her lower lip. It couldn't be Harry Stork. She remembered her pa on that case like it was yesterday. He would come home physically exhausted most nights, but mentally he stayed on the job twenty-four/seven. His brain never stopped trying to solve it. It took him near on a year and a half to finally do it, and, near the end of it all, Leah and her ma both thought he would be needing intense therapy. It all tied up because of a lucky break, an anonymous tip called in to the station—although he would never use the word *lucky*. Leah could hear him in her mind. "No," he'd say, "lucky would've been catching him 'fore anybody had to die. This ain't luck, Leah, after all this time, this is God throwing down justice." Back then, he had told her she was too young to understand, but one day it would all make sense.

He lived long enough to get her on the force after he left, but not long enough to find out exactly how much sense his words would one day make.

She was more like her pa than she ever cared to admit, but Police Chief Ethan Montgomery constantly reminded her. Like her pa, she took full responsibility for everything that happened during any of her cases. Any blood spilled was spilled on her own hands. She took everything personally, same way he had. And, like him, it wore on her. She wondered how much of the stress contributed to the cancer that finally took him.

Leah's son, Abe, had been six when his grandpa died. Leah always consoled herself with the fact that he at least got to know his grandpa those half-dozen years. Not like Abe's own pa, Leah's husband, Billy, who died in an early morning head-on collision that took him out of not only her life, but Abe's, and her daughter, Caroline's, life, too. Billy left them all far too early. Leah doubted, if not for the shoe box full of photos she had given him, that her little Abe even re-membered what his pa looked like. He was only two when Billy passed.

Now Abe was thirteen and Caroline turned sixteen this past Christmas, and Leah wondered how different things would be for them if they hadn't lost their pa twelve years ago—if Billy hadn't decided to pass that eighteen-wheeler in front of him.

But there was no point in thinking about it; some mistakes you just can't come back from. Billy's deci-sion to pass that truck that fatal morning was one of those mistakes.

She still missed Billy and her pa, but her pa was dif-ferent. Somehow, she still felt him with her some days. She even found herself talking to him during those times when she could badly use his sage advice. Of course, he never answered, but it still usually helped to ask the questions.

Ethan Montgomery had hired Leah's pa and he'd also agreed to bring Leah on when her pa suggested it. And after all this time, he was still working at the station, although every year he seemed to come in later and later. These days, he rarely arrived before eleven. Leah expected he would just keep being later until there was no time left in the day and that would be when he retired. Until then, he spent most of his time behind a ridiculously large desk in a squeaky chair watching the Crimson Tide stop the Auburn Tigers from making any yardage.

Because of the connection her pa had to Ethan, Leah knew she was treated differently than Chris. She was made "detective" not just to walk in her pa's footsteps, but also to allow Ethan to pay her a higher wage. She and her two kids needed all the help they could get. This was something Ethan and her pa arranged without her even knowing, but now it was pretty much common knowledge. At least Chris didn't seem to hold any animosity toward her because of it. She wondered sometimes, though. Especially on those days when Chris sat at his desk doing nothing but crossword puzzles his entire shift. Even if the phone rang, there were days he'd wait for her to take the call.

She didn't mind so much. Chris was more of a desk cop anyway. That's how he was cut. According to Ethan, Leah was different. Chris did have some special talents, though, like his uncanny ability to unearth the details of juvenile records.

"I see your mind moving," Chris said to her. His

regulation boots were up on his desk and the coffee he'd fetched for himself was sitting beside his hat. Leaning back in his chair, he put his arms behind his head. "What I don't see are the details moving around. Care to let me in?" He spoke tentatively, almost like he was scared.

Leah looked back at the paper. "This is impossible."

Chris just shrugged.

"It's a copycat. It's gotta be. But why would someone copycat a case they had to dredge up from fifteen years—"

Chris cut her off. "I know what you're thinking, but it's not a copycat. It can't be."

"Yes, it can, Chris. Remember, the holdback about the stakes with the drawings was leaked. That's how Harry Stork *became* the Stickman."

"I know," he said. "But the staked stickman page wasn't the only holdback. There was another. A *big* one. And it wasn't leaked."

A thought suddenly came to Leah, one that probably should've come long before now. "Wait a minute. Why am I just reading about this now? Which police department was on the scene last night? Last time I checked, Leeland Swamp was in *Alvin*."

"Yeah," Chris stumbled. "That . . . I . . . we . . ." He glanced at the door to Ethan Montgomery's office. It was mainly glass, like the walls, but brown blinds hung down that Leah couldn't remember ever seeing open. She could only imagine how much dust was collecting inside them. Of course, now the door would be locked. Leah glanced at the white clock hanging in front of her desk on the wall between the door and the window. It was twenty past eight. They wouldn't see Ethan for another two or three hours.

"What time did you get the call?" Leah asked. She remembered Chris was still at his desk when she left. She doubted he would have stayed much longer than fifteen more minutes, and she had gotten home just after five.

"What call?"

"Whoever found the body. I'm guessing it must've been around five?"

Chris scratched the back of his head. "Ethan called me at home," he said.

Leah tried to process this. "Ethan was still here when it came in? That's"—*a miracle*—"unusual."

"Yeah, um, the body hadn't turned up yet."

Narrowing her eyes, Leah asked, "What do you mean? Wait, if this holdback you're talking about was so secret, how come you know about it?"

"Ethan told me about it yesterday. What matters is, it wasn't a copycat kill. It's more than that. Ethan was pretty clear."

Leah felt the heat rise in her skin. A trickle of sweat ran down the back of her blouse, tracing a line from the bottom of her bra strap, along her vertebrae, and right into her brown pants.

"Sure is hot out there," Chris said, looking out the window.

Leah snapped the paper at him. "What aren't you telling me? What do you mean 'the body hadn't turned up yet'? What's this super-secret holdback and why did Ethan tell *you*?"

Chris took a deep breath. "Leah, it was a long night.

We searched that swamp for three hours before finding the body."

"What are you talking about?" The hair rose on the back of her neck. "I wasn't called in on any search last night."

"That's on account of we didn't know how you'd react to it. With what happened with your pa and the Stickman fifteen years ago and all . . ."

Leah's stomach roiled. Anger swooped in like a hungry vulture. She did her best to hold it back, but heard the edge it put on her words when she spoke. "If you hadn't found a body, how would you know . . . ? Wait, I am missing something here. What made you even know to *look* for a body? What aren't you telling me?"

Chris said nothing, just shifted uncomfortably in his seat.

"Someone had to call someone," Leah said. "I don't . . ." No matter how much she tried to make sense of things, nothing worked.

Chris let out a big sigh. "Man, it's hot."

Leah's anger swelled. "I am getting mighty pissed off about talking about the goddamn weather, Chris. If there's something you're not tellin' me, I'd best be making your mouth start going sooner rather than later." Both Chris and Ethan knew Leah had a temper. Neither of them ever wanted to push the envelope and find out how bad it really was.

When she looked back at Chris, he had seemed to take a sudden interest in the floor.

"Okay, first things first," she said. "Tell me about the stuff."

"What stuff?"

"The super-secret stuff that actually *was* held back from the press throughout the Stickman murders."

Chris sighed again and took a big drink of coffee. He was running out of stall tactics. "Well, for every victim, this station—well, your pa—was given a letter."

Leah cocked her head. "Letter? How was it given? Who gave it?"

Chris shrugged. "Apparently it came from the Stickman. It would be left in an envelope with no postmark or address, simply your pa's name written across the front. Inside there was always a single piece of paper folded three times. It had a drawing of a stickman, a time, and a location."

"A time and location of the killing?"

"Yeah."

"Sounds weird. Why didn't my pa just show up and arrest the Stickman then?"

"The locations were general. Like the one last night simply said *Leeland Swamp, 8:30 P.M.* That's a large area to search in two and a half hours. Not counting travel time. And we had to assume it could also mean somewhere in the surrounding forest."

"So the time in the letter designates when the body will be dumped at the secondary crime scene?"

"According to Ethan it's more like the maximum time in a range. So, when the letter comes in they knew they had from whenever it was opened until the time it said before the body was staked."

Leah thought this over. "If the staked drawings were leaked, this letter thing could easily have been, too."

Chris held up his palm. "I know what you're thinking, but listen. Not every cop on the task force knew about the letters. In fact, Ethan said other than him and your pa, there were a half-dozen or so other detectives in the loop, each handpicked by Joe. After the first leak, he wasn't about to take any chances."

"And forensics said all the letters were written by the same person?" Leah asked.

"All except the last one. They had a weird slant to the left."

"And what was different with the last one?"

"The last one was the one that came the night your pa shot Stork. Mobile said the handwriting didn't match the rest. It could be the same person, but if so, he wanted it to seem like someone else."

"The night my pa shot Stork? There was no victim that night."

Chris put his feet back up on his desk. "No, the letter was for Stork. It had the address of the shotgun shack. The actual address. There was no time. Harry was holed up there. He was there when your pa and Strident arrived with the other officers. And there was one more difference."

"What was that?"

"The letter had the initials *H.S.* written on it."

"Harry Stork?"

Chris nodded. "One would gather, yes."

"I thought Stork's whereabouts came from an anonymous call?"

With a shake of his head, Chris said, "That's the story your pa made up. He didn't want to release the holdout."

"Why not, if Stork was dead? The Stickman case was solved."

Chris shrugged. "That, I don't know. I asked Ethan that exact question and he didn't seem to know, either. He just said your pa asked the other four cops to keep the letters secret. Said your pa always said the case felt 'unfinished.'"

Leah considered this. He did always go back to the case. Even years later, she remembered him bringing home Stickman files and staying up late some nights poring over them. She hated those nights. "No wonder my pa got so wrapped up in that case. I always thought he seemed to take it particularly personal. Now I understand. It *was* personal. He was getting letters addressed directly to him."

Chris nodded. "Can't get much more personal than that. Plus, Joe was the one being quoted in the papers and being interviewed on the news. He was the face of the Stickman task force."

It was Leah's turn to sigh as her eyes went to the clock. "I don't suppose we're goin' to see Ethan anytime soon. You'd think he'd want to tell me all this himself," she said, trying to keep her anger and frustration out of her voice. Truth was, she also felt a bit betrayed by her pa not confiding in her about the letters all those years.

"So," Leah said, "the letter came last night after I left?"

"It came after I left, too," Chris said. "Ethan found it on his way out jammed halfway under the door. He called me right after I got home. Said he almost didn't open it. Figured it was probably another thank-you card from the Ladies Auxiliary for your helping out with their Mother's Day parade."

Leah gave her coffee mug a half turn where it stood

on her desk. "Mother's Day was at least a month and a half ago. Besides, this one didn't come to me. It came to you and Ethan. Or . . . ? Who was it addressed to?"

Chris took a deep breath and blew it out slowly. Sweat was dotting his forehead. She didn't bother following his gaze when it shifted to the window.

"Well, you know . . . that doesn't really matter." Chris stood from his chair, walked over to the coffeemaker, and poured two new mugs full. To one he added three teaspoons of sugar and some cream. He left the other black and handed it to Leah, nodding to her half-filled one. "I think that's probably getting cold," he said and sat back down.

Without saying thanks, Leah took the mug. She stood there silently, holding it and slowly shaking her head.

"What?" Chris asked.

Her emotions rose to the surface. "The letter wasn't goddamn addressed to you *or* Ethan, was it? Christ, no wonder he's not here yet. Chickenshit."

Chris scratched the back of his head again. "It was just like all the other times," he said. "The information was delivered to us. The police."

"Last time it all came to my pa. Exactly *who* was this new letter addressed to?"

Chris didn't answer. He sat in his chair and ran his fingers once more through his hair.

"Who was it addressed to, Chris?" Leah said, louder.

"You," Chris said, almost too quiet to hear.

"Who? Say again?"

He swung his chair toward her. "You. Okay? The letter came addressed to *Leah Fowler*, so obviously whoever is behind this doesn't know you were married."

"Or he wants to drive home a point," Leah said in a clipped tone before falling silent. When she spoke again, it was quiet and pensive. "Otherwise, did Ethan say it was exactly like the other ones?"

"Yes. Exactly." Chris took a swig of coffee and turned back toward the window. Leah was pretty sure *he* couldn't wait for Ethan to get in to the office, either.

"And you didn't call me in?" she asked. "You and Ethan decided to just handle this alone like a couple of cowboys?"

"We thought you might freak out," Chris said. "You have in the past."

"You could have *used* me," Leah said, growing louder again. "You needed as many cops as you could get. I should have been called, goddammit!"

"Well, Ethan said not to."

"Well, Ethan and I are goin' to have some discussion when he gets in." She looked at the clock again. That big black minute hand was inching its way closer and closer to twelve. "That is, *if* he ever gets in."

Chris took a big, calming breath. "Don't you find it hot today?"

"Show me the letter," Leah said, trying to remain calm. "Surely you thought to make a copy of it."

"Of course, but it will only make things worse."

"Show me the goddamn letter!"

"All right." Chris reached into a file folder on his desk and pulled out a piece of paper. Leah could tell it was a photocopy because it had no fold creases.

"Mobile has the original?"

"Yeah. Their forensic experts are goin' to see what they can get off it. Maybe a fingerprint—I don't know. There won't be nothin' on it. We all know that. This guy's smart." He stopped mid-sentence and corrected himself. "*Was* smart."

"Yes, *was*, because this guy is *not* the Stickman, Chris! Are you not hearing me? The Stickman was Harry Stork and Harry Stork is dead. The dead don't come back."

"Well, this time, maybe one did," Chris said.

The time and place on the paper was 8:30 P.M. Lee-land Swamp. The stick-figure drawing had breasts and hair. It was female.

"What time did you get to the swamp?" Leah asked.

"Around ten after six."

"So you had under two and a half hours to try to save this woman's life." She looked once again at the photo on the front page of the *Examiner*, her brain automatically filling in the missing details. A hideous sight. "Does she have a name? Our victim? Or do you just want me to keep referring to her as 'she'?"

Chris wiped his forehead with his right hand. He was starting to sweat in his uniform, even though Leah hadn't noticed an increase in temperature. "Abilene Williams. Married with two kids. She went missing around eight-forty-five after dropping her son off at school."

"So one of you at least went to her house and told her husband what happened?" It actually surprised Leah that they didn't leave that fun bit to her.

"Of course. Here." He handed the rest of the file folder to Leah. She flipped through it quickly. Copies of photos and sketches made at the scene. Reports.

"It's all in here. Her husband was pretty frantic when we got to their house."

"That surprises you?" Leah knew what it was like to lose a spouse. Frantic didn't even come close to describing it. "Two and a half hours isn't nearly enough time to search that swampland, especially not for two people," she snapped. "You would've had a lot better chance with me helping. I should've been called."

"In retrospect, I agree."

"In retrospect, you and Ethan are assholes. What you two did last night is wrong on so many levels. The letter came to me, I should've been called *then*. And if not, once you opened it and you saw what it was, there should've been no question."

"I didn't open it, Ethan did."

Leah bit her tongue. "I know."

"We don't always make good decisions, Leah. We aren't perfect."

She let out a fake laugh. "No, you definitely aren't goddamn perfect. Don't worry, I know you wasn't the one making the orders. It's Montgomery who's goin' to get a piece of me. *If* he ever comes in."

Chris smiled. "He's probably 'fraid to."

"Don't smile. There ain't nothin' funny. A woman is dead, possibly because of dumb decisions made by this department."

Chris sipped his coffee. "Sure is hot outside," he said absently.

Leah just slinked down in her chair. "I should've been goddamn called."